THE HIDING DOOR

IN SARAH'S CLOSET

T.R. SCHAAP

This book is for my wife, Janie, who has tolerated my writing habits and pushed me to get back in there. My mother, Jeanette, who, by example, planted the seeds to be a writer; and my lovely children who, at a young age, inspired me to tell them a story about the little door in the back of their closet. Sweethearts, I finally finished it.

Acknowledgments

The first version of *The Hiding Door* was published back in 2020. In this version, I have changed the cover design, self-edited quite a few mistakes, and put back a chapter that was left out of the original. It is Chapter 4 and is called, Little Sammy. When I first published this book, that chapter didn't seem to help the story, but after so much time has passed, I realized it was important to me, and the completeness of the story.

I would like to acknowledge a few people who read the original version for me. I can't begin to tell you how much I appreciate their willingness to tell me the truth. Of course, my wife Janie was the first to read the book all the way through, and then on vacation with our good friends, Linda and Dennis Batie, she got Linda to read my story. Janie and Linda, both retired teachers, encouraged me to keep writing.

Besides the readers in my immediate family, I give honorable mention to other dear friends who took up the challenge: Margorie Koenig, Lori Rorabaugh, and Sazja Fletcher. Thank you.

I was happy to be able to get my book edited by Kristen Hamilton, of Kristen Corrects, Inc. Thank you, Kristen. Kristen was patient with this new author and gracefully put up with my constant questions.

Thanks to Crystal Burton at Kingsman Editing Services for doing a great job formatting my manuscript, again.

Thank you to Sharon Larson at Larson Sound who did the Audiobook for *The Hiding Door* and is also doing the Audio for *A Plan To Kill*.

My last note of acknowledgment goes to Mrs. Peggy Holcomb. I originally asked her to do a painting for my cover and she did a great job. The problem was that I chose a different cover design, by Driven Digital Services. For this second edition, I've decided to go with the original plan and use Peggy's painting. It truly represents my first vision of what the cover should look like.

CONTENTS

CHAPTER 1

Trouble

Joplin, Missouri, 1927

By the time the cool, overcast morning slipped away, midtown church bells had tolled twelve o'clock, and a smothering blanket of warm humidity had rolled in over this small Missouri mining town. Large oak trees reached quietly over the street to become a convenient roost for cackling blackbirds near the city's one avenue of elegant Victorian homes.

A few blocks away, a small boy pushed open a screen door, jumped on his bicycle, and pedaled off. The delicate sound of a coal-black Model T rattled by, and a woman's distant voice threatened her child to get home now, or there would be hell to pay. He was not the only kid in trouble.

Streetwise thirteen-year-old Julian Daniels was left alone most of the time. He knew how to keep himself busy. Ragged pants, a stained undershirt worn too long between washings, bare feet, and brown hair blended with fine Missouri dust. In his mind, Julian owned Joplin. It was his to roam.

Mom worked nights and slept days. Too much freedom in a small town can be fun and dangerous. It was a place small enough that you knew everyone by their first name. If someone used your last name, you were probably going to have a bad day.

When it was convenient, Julian attended school. When it wasn't convenient, he learned by watching when and how to work the streets, smells told him what was cooking at each house, and doors left unlocked. He was good at it most of the time, but not always. Today, Julian was going to have a *last-name* day.

Julian Daniels knew where it went wrong, and it wasn't his aim; Lord knows, that was perfect. His throw was clean, curving gracefully across the blue sky. The landing was the problem.

Julian's pitch of a rotten apple floated through the humid air as if being held back by second thoughts until it smashed into the face of Shorty Dean—shoving him and a tin box he was carrying flat onto the ground, knocking hell loose in the process.

"Oh, crap!" Julian spun around and ran, his body racing to keep up with his mind's lightning-fast realization of what had just happened.

Shorty had two sons still living with him. Pug, the youngest at seventeen, was walking next to Shorty when he got hit and bent over to help him. Older brother Lenny spotted Julian running away and waved his arms at Pug. Lenny had been looking for a reason to beat this little street kid to death—now he had one.

"Come on!" Lenny shouted. In seconds, Pug and Lenny tried keeping up with three baying hounds with the scent locked on Julian.

Julian could hear the dogs and knew the Dean boys were running fast to catch up. Julian figured it would only be a matter of seconds before death would be summoning; *Come, my stupid son—this way.*

The Dean boys already had a reputation for killing small animals of any sort, and all too soon, his small bones would be added to the collection scattered in the woods near their house. Julian's muscles screamed for more energy *right now*. He needed to run faster than any small animal.

In the alley behind the Victorian homes, Julian ran as fast as he could, startling the blackbirds into unwilling flight. Bitching and cawing, they flew away, threatening to come back.

Gritty streams of sweat dripped down his face and neck, soaking his stained undershirt. Just before dodging into the backyard of a large home, Julian swung his head around to see if death had caught up with him. He jumped up on the familiar wooden porch and pulled the screen door so wide open it slapped hard on the side of the house, then disappeared into darkness before the door had a chance to swing back.

His sweat-soaked shirt made it feel extra cool inside the darkened hallway leading to the forbidden foyer at the front of the house. He pulled back on thick burgundy-colored curtains next to the front door and peered out of a parlor window, far enough back so he would not be seen. He glanced nervously up and down the street to make sure no one had followed.

Julian's heavy breathing barely slowed when his ear was jerked from behind. He yelped as he looked into the eyes of Miss Fannie Lee Blakely, madam of the house.

"You little ninny bastard," Fannie roared with a

grinding voice. "What the hell are you up to now? I told you to *never* come up here!"

"I ain't done nothing," Julian cried to Fannie, squirming under the painful grip on his ear. Julian squealed as Fannie jerked his ear again. As she pulled him closer, her caustic breath blew angrily on Julian's face; he struggled to keep from hacking up his meager breakfast. The wild commotion roused several house girls from the back parlor, sitting down for their usual afternoon tea and gossip session, to see who was getting the what-for. Fannie raised her tightened fist to club Julian at the slightest hint of deceit.

"I know you done something because you don't do nothin' 'cept get in trouble. Out with it, you little turd, what have you done?"

Julian tried to think of a story Fannie would believe, but with his rising ear pain, he could only think of one option—come clean.

"I ain't done nothing, except piss off Shorty." Julian winced as Fannie dropped his ear from her vice grip. She cocked her head forward as a chicken readies to peck, narrowed her eyes, and let out an audible grunt of disbelief.

"Hmph. The Deans? Didn't you already make them mad? What in hell did you do now?" Fannie reached for Julian's ear again. He jumped back. Julian rubbed his ear and thought so hard his brows furrowed.

"I . . . Well, you see, I kind of borrowed a couple apples from the market. So, when I was walking back over here, you know, to make sure my chores were all done and so . . ." Julian paused after the small white lie, straightened out his undershirt, and pushed back his shaggy brown hair with his fingers.

"Yeah, yeah, get on with it!" Fannie pushed.

"So, as I was walking past the Dean's place, I noticed Shorty trying to carry a box to the house—you know, like a small chest or something. Anyway, one of them apples was bad, so I threw it away, right? I just tossed it." Julian looked over to Fannie with a smart-aleck grin as if he had planned everything so carefully. "Well, actually I tried to aim it at one of the boys—you know Lenny and Pug—but I guess I'm not a good aim, and I'll be damned if it didn't hit Shorty in the bucket, knocked him flat on the ground. Lenny and Pug spotted me, so off I run. Of course, I can move faster than those two lame buzzards, so I got away." Julian felt satisfied, a big smile plastered across his face. He figured this situation was handled.

"Well, I'll be damned," Fannie said. After hearing Julian explain what he'd done to Shorty, she laughed out loud, and, to Julian's relief, a grin bloomed over her face. "You know, for a little smart-ass, you may have really pissed those boys off good this time. Don't that beat all."

Julian's smile faded.

Fannie shook her head and started to turn away, then made a quick U-turn and came down close to Julian's face.

"But next time," she warned, pointing her index finger at Julian's nose, "they'll just kill you . . . and they'll never find your body in that old mine they work in, either—*if'n* there's a body to be found, that is." Fannie turned back toward the kitchen, clutched a torn dish towel. Julian heard Fannie talk to herself as she walked away. "I'll be damned, Shorty lyin' there. Don't that beat all."

Julian sighed and let his muscles relax. He thought to himself, *Maybe the rest of the afternoon will be quiet.* Suddenly, Julian heard heavy boots step onto the front stoop, then pounding on the front door. Both Julian and Fannie froze. Fannie spun around; her eyes connected instantly to Julian's. They both knew this was not normal. It was too early for evening business, and then, most patrons just walked in. Julian witnessed the devil's fire ignite in her eyes. He felt his inner soul shrink away.

"You get to the back of the house, now!" Fannie said, her friendly demeanor gone in a heartbeat. Julian turned and ran, but he didn't go to the back of the house. He darted behind another set of curtains that separated the foyer from the bar area. He watched as Fannie looked around to see if anyone was in the room with her. Julian figured the girls had already gone up to their rooms, and he could hear Joey, the bartender, probably stocking booze in the back room. Fannie smoothed out her apron over her long-faded plaid dress and turned to open the heavy front door. She didn't act surprised to see Lenny and Pug, who both appeared to have been running hard.

"Hello, boys. Is there something I can help you with?"

"Sorry to disturb you, Miss Fannie, ma'am, we just need to"—Lenny interrupted himself and spit a brown slurry off to the side, wiping his face with his bare arm—"have a little conversation with your little man, Julian, if you don't mind, that is?"

"Well, I do mind. I've sent him away for the rest of the day. Now, if there is nothin' else, I've got work to do, so you boys run along." Fannie appeared to be done talking and got ready to shut the front door.

Lenny gave Pug a quick look. Julian couldn't see Pug's reaction, but it must have given Lenny the advice of hesitation. It would be a horrible death if Pug and Lenny picked a fight with Fannie. He was sure, though, that no matter how much they wanted him, they would not get past this pissed-off, old black woman.

"No, ma'am, not really." Lenny turned to leave. He hesitated and turned back around, a crooked smile on his face. "Well, yes, ma'am, there is one more thing. Just tell your little man Julian that I have something for him. Just to come by when he got a chance. Good day, ma'am."

Keeping at least one unblinking eye on Fannie, Lenny backed away a couple of steps, drew another wad of something up in his throat, spit it out in the bushes near the porch, then spun around and walked down the steps to meet up with his brother Pug, already in the yard. Under her breath, Fannie mumbled, "Idiot bastards."

As the boys walked away, Lenny playfully threw a punch at Pug's shoulder and Pug returned it. The two laughed out loud, being as cocky and noisy as they could. Fannie slapped her dish towel on the door jamb, shook her head, and slammed the door shut. With the noise of the door shutting, Julian disappeared upstairs before she could see him.

Downstairs, Fannie made her way through the foyer, whisked past the bar, and stomped up the grand stair-case toward the ladies' rooms, creating a familiar rumble moving toward Julian. He knew that sound. Then, dead still.

He knew what she was doing; it had happened before. One flight down, Fannie had detoured to Millie's room. He could hear raised voices and arguing. Fannie was picking up reinforcements. He had to do something—the battle would soon be at his door.

"Lord God Almighty! Get your ass up! Your good-for-nothin' son has done it again!" Fannie stomped over to the bed, slapped both hands on Millie's hips, and rolled her over. Millie's brown hair flew across her face as she raised a hand over her squinting eyes and into the face of Miss Fannie hovering over her.

Julian cautiously tiptoed, like a nervous black cat, watching the floor as he stepped around well-known boards that creaked, up close to his mom's partially open bedroom door and peered in. It didn't take long before Julian felt the tension boiling between Fannie and Millie.

"Get up, damn it! Get your lazy butt up and help me with that brat ah yours." Millie's stunned appearance made her seem like she had been hit with a club, slowly moved from the bed, her voice raspy from a long night smoking cigarettes.

"What's he done now?" she asked, pulling her hair back and looking around for her smokes.

"He's got them Dean boys riled up again. This time, they come to the house looking for him. I should let them have him, for all you care!"

"Well, what the hell do you want me to do about it?" Millie reached for her lighter and lit up a cigarette. A thin wisp of smoke blew from her mouth up into the room. Fannie became furious.

"Do about it? *Do* about it? I want you to get up there and beat your son's sorry ass and tell him to quit stirring up trouble with the Deans. He's gonna get himself killed, for one thing, and for another, this crap ain't good for my business . . . It gotta stop, *today!*"

"Okay, okay, I'll go up and see what I . . ."

As Millie waved Fannie off, the women heard a feeble knock at the door. Fannie pulled the door open—Julian stood in the doorway. Both Fannie and Millie were dumb-struck. Fannie put her hands on her hips, ready to speak, but to her surprise, Millie began first.

"Tell me, son, do you go out every day and *look* for trouble?" She blew smoke up in the air over his head and glanced at the back of her hand as if she were telling time, then leaned over to put her half-smoked cigarette in a nearby ashtray. Julian assumed she did that to get a clean hit with the back of her hand across his face. Charging his reflexes, Julian stepped back and hung his head before answering.

"No, ma'am, not really. I guess, ah, bad luck jus' seems to find me, I don't know." Julian acted like he didn't have a clue and shrugged. He knew how to play his mom. *Just relax and let her run her mouth for a few minutes. She'll get tired of the confrontation and quit.*

"Well, first of all, you'd better apologize to Fannie and then back up to your room for the rest of the night. You're getting too old to spank, so you'll just stay up there for the next couple of days and think about what you've been doing."

"Yes, ma'am." Fannie, who wanted to see pain inflict-ed, threw up her hands and turned around to leave. Julian thought he had to defend himself.

"Miss Fannie, I'm sorry, I ain't trying to get in trouble." Julian kept his eyes down, toward the floor. Fannie turned around and walked back a couple of steps to face him.

"Look at me. Look at me! You already in trouble, *real*, bad trouble—somewhere inside that thick skull of yours, you're a *good* kid, you really are. You just need to realize that you're going to get hurt messing around with them Dean boys. I don't doubt for a second that they gonna hunt you down and either kill you or beat you so bad, you're gonna wish you were dead. For them to come to this house looking for you? Well, that tells me you're not safe, anywhere!" Fannie's eyes looked fearful; Julian could see she was anxious. Millie stood and shook her head in token agreement as Fannie took over being the mother. Puffing on another cigarette, Millie reached over to the bedpost and pulled a robe off to put on over her nightgown.

"I understand, really I do," Julian agreed humbly. At the same moment, he wondered, *Fannie got no kids, why does she care?*

"Help me understand better. Just *why* did you throw that apple at Shorty?"

"I wasn't aiming at Shorty; I wasn't trying to hit anyone. I just threw it," he whined back to Fannie. "I wished I'dah hit Lenny—he's the one that hurt me the most, that night at the Pick—and I swore to myself I'd get even." Julian hung his head back down, rocking himself on his heels. Then, Fannie issued another warning.

"Well, you stirred up more than you can chew and spit out this time. God have mercy on your soul, boy!"

"Yes, ma'am."

Fannie shot a glance at Millie. "Your days are numbered, too, girlie! You'd better clean up. I can drag in better stock just walking down the street, and I wouldn't have to deal with your whiney crap and this troublemaker son of yours."

Millie hesitated, then glared at her delinquent son. "Julian, you go on and get back up to your room and except for your chores, you stay there," Millie said. "From now on, you do not—hear me!—you do not come into the guest areas at all. Period!"

"Yes, ma'am." He turned around and walked away. Julian knew his mom was fuming inside, but why didn't she say anything? *What if Fannie throws us out, then what?* At the turn of the stairs, Julian hesitated and crouched down to listen.

Again, Millie conceded.

"I'm sorry, you're right. I have to do better, and I will." She got up and walked past Fannie and into the hallway toward the bathroom down the hall. For a few seconds, Fannie didn't move, just stared at the floor, shaking her head before turning to go back downstairs.

Julian could hear doors opening down the hallway. Two of the other house girls, Lupe and Jean, quietly came out and scurried down the hall—to get the latest news about Millie, Julian assumed.

A few days earlier, Julian confessed to Fannie about the feud he had with the Dean boys, ever since Lenny and Pug pushed him around at the Miner's Pick Saloon a couple of months ago, for peeking in the door.

Lenny, at eighteen the oldest son of Charles "Shorty" Dean, was an agitator, mentor, and provocateur to his younger brother Pug. Since neither of them could legally get in the saloons, it was their Saturday night entertainment to hang out with some work buddies, smoke Lucky

Strikes, heckle street girls, drink "finisher" wrapped in brown paper, and just shoot the bull, while Dad was inside drinking for his health.

Prohibition had slowed down open sales of alcohol, but a drink could be found pretty much anywhere any place. It was obvious to almost everyone that Prohibition was ignored, especially in small mining towns. Local police turned a blind eye and life went on as usual with only an occasional large bust of an organized group just to show the feds that something was being done.

That particular evening, Julian had been hanging out in the same area as the Deans along Main Street. His best lookout spot was a dark area in front of an adjoining building, next to the Pick, where he could lean back and casually observe patrons coming and going out of several different saloons.

With all the street smarts a thirteen-year-old could possess, Julian had become skillful at blending into groups of stragglers, dodging through alleyways, slipping into recessed doors, and crouching behind beat-up trash cans, waiting for the right moment. Occasionally, he would sneak a peek inside one of the smoke-filled halls to get a feel for anyone getting ready to leave. He knew he had to practice how not to look at someone, but still know every move they make. Julian studied the club doors to keep an eye out for his mark.

Julian's favorite chump staggered out with a young lady, preferably tipsy, clutching his arm laughing out loud, full of love and booze, quick to slap or jab her lover if he glanced at another woman's teasing smile as if she cared. Just a regular guy in a stained shirt, work boots, a whiff of body odor, and smelling of liquor. A second-shift crew leader type of guy.

If Julian recognized him as one of the higher-up mine managers, he would steer clear; he knew better. He was looking for a sucker—with money, anxious to show off—a guy who told people he was really in charge of the whole plant—now *he* was going somewhere. Julian's deep well of opportunity would never run dry, especially in this busy mining town, full of anxious miners coming and going from one job to the next.

After midnight, the time to hit grew late, and anyone coming out of a club was fair game. Once they stepped on the sidewalk, Julian would run up in his ragged clothes, acting worried, upset, pockets inside out, with an emergency—a need for immediate cash—and whimper, "Baby sister, no milk, Mama's sick!" The hook, just like catching fish.

Now what decent, God-fearing, benevolent gentleman could turn down a desperate child, especially in front of his new girlfriend? A few lucky times, the lady would unwittingly help him out and encourage the sucker to give fifty cents, or maybe even a dollar. Julian suspected it was because she was probably living through tough times herself.

Julian perked up as he recognized a gal from one of the other brothels in town. He knew she would help work the chump to give him a little more.

"Ahh, sweetie, look, poor boy!" she pleaded, looking back at her brave soldier. Begrudgingly muttering cuss words in vain, the gentleman reached into well-traveled pockets for small change, then to his wallet to pull out a dollar bill, which was instantly grabbed by Julian. A polite "Thanks" and he was gone, two out of the three involved were satisfied with the exchange.

Julian heard Lenny Dean yell something down the street, then saw Lenny throw down a half-finished cigarette and stomp it out with his foot.

"It ain't right. He keeps getting away with that trick." Lenny grabbed the finisher from Pug, swallowed a quick drink, and handed it back to his brother. Pug and Lenny had seen the ruse pulled on several unsuspecting dupes in the last couple of weekends; one of Julian's school friends told him about it. Some of Lenny and Pug's work buddies had been suckered by Julian and they wanted everyone to know.

Julian hated to move from his spot—it was the right time of night. One more look in the saloon door, and he'd be done.

Pug came up from behind Julian and shoved him into the saloon, pushing him spread-eagle on the beer, spit, and cigarette butt-covered floor. People in the bar started yelling as Julian got up and tried to run out of the saloon. Someone threw a bottle.

Outside, Pug and Lenny were ready for him. Lenny grabbed Julian as he ran out the door and landed a punch on the side of Julian's face, forcing him to the sidewalk, scraping elbows and hands. Pug kicked Julian's thighs and poured finisher over Julian's head. Julian managed to get up and run off, but not before getting his pockets ripped open and emptied.

It took a week for Julian to show his face, but this time he moved his scam around the block and down the street, being careful to stay away from the Deans' hangout. The beating he got from the Dean brothers burned deep into Julian's mind, and he vowed to himself to pay back the Deans someday for that beating. Until that time, he had to lick his wounds and keep shut about it. He had other business to tend to.

Julian climbed up to the small loft in the attic he used for a bedroom—and now sanctuary—lay on his back, and took a deep breath, but it was little comfort to know the Dean boys were gone. He knew he was going to eventually deal with it somewhere down the road.

* * * *

On the outside, the Sunset brothel appeared to be any other large Victorian-style home built in Joplin by wealthy mine owners, bankers, and businessmen. Rich deposits of zinc and lead underground brought in a landslide of mining activity; instant wealth followed soon after with the building of stately homes befitting their owner's new social standing.

New mining jobs also brought in a flood of young adrenaline-charged men willing to work and play hard, followed instantly by gambling halls, brothels, and bars offering to help satisfy their instinctive pursuits.

Over the last ten years, many of the upstanding members of the community had been selling and moving out to build new homes in the more rural Webb City area, north of Joplin, taking their innocent children and protected wives away from the flirtatious "cat houses" and tempting gambling establishments in midtown, allowing more less-than-desirable establishments to move in.

The Sunset was a handsome two-story red-brick mansion with a large porch across the front and down one side. Inside the home—a large elegant foyer, a parlor with a bar, and a beautiful dark wood grand staircase leading to rooms upstairs. In the back of the house—a large kitchen and pantry. Out back—a discreet shaded area for tying up a horse or parking a carriage or Model T.

The home was placed conveniently within walking distance of the county and city government offices and just a couple blocks behind most of the gambling halls, saloons, and restaurants lining Main Street. Its discrete location was also helpful in avoiding attention from the feds, especially during the time of Prohibition. Before Fannie bought it, it had been a bank president's home with plenty of room for a wife and six children. After some cheap but effective remodeling, it provided a roomy place to entertain gentlemen.

Most local people either didn't know about it or chose to ignore it. Husbands certainly would not bring up the subject, and wives would rather no one discuss it in any shape or form; it didn't fit in with tasteful dinner conversation. Those who knew called it the Sunset, though no signs were posted to advertise the products offered inside. An eight-bedroom house of prostitution—illegal, but in good standing with local authorities, thanks to Fannie's timely donations. Miss Fannie Jo Blakely is a forty-six-year-old black woman and madam. Most people in town would have a hard time accepting that a black woman could own a brothel and run a successful business, that is unless they had a confrontation with Fannie. That would probably be their first lesson with a strong-minded black woman.

Regular customers and the ladies who worked there knew it was *her* house. With a firm hand, she made sure everything stayed in working order: the food was ordered on time, the laundry got changed, the wine stayed corked and the girls fresh.

Upstairs, the once-elegant and grand bedrooms had been divided up into smaller rooms, just large enough for one dresser with a pitcher, a porcelain bowl for washing, a steel frame double bed, and a post to hang a hat, trousers, and drawers. Down the hall, conveniently located for all, one small bathroom stuffed with a large tub and a variety of racks and hooks for towels and robes—all the amenities a fine lady would need.

Downstairs, dark furniture covered in thick velvet richly adorned the Sunset's reception area. Erotic Baroque- and Renaissance-period paintings of reclining or fainting nudes hung on the walls to encourage thoughts of passion with her clients. In the front of the house, layers of white lace and dark crimson damask draped over large windows and soaked up smoke, alcohol, perfume, and languid parlor conversations.

The house was a thriving business. The reputation of the Sunset had become well-established over the years, and Fannie could always count on her regulars dropping in. Fannie loved to welcome them back and, after a few drinks at the bar, a few dirty jokes, and a kiss for herself, handed them over to their preferred lady for the night.

Chapter 2

Friendly Church

A few days after her run-in with Fannie, Millie Daniels sat alone on the back door steps in her house robe, smoking a cigarette. She figured it must be before six in the morning; the neighbor's back porch light was still on. She knew old Mrs. Thurman always turned it off by six. Within a few minutes, after she sat down, the sun peeked over the horizon to the east—a promising sign. Mack, her latest steady customer, had left some time ago. She had offered him breakfast, but he didn't care to be around people. As a hopeless, lonely feeling washed through her body, she took a comforting pull from her cigarette.

Warm streams of sunlight filtered through the trees, yet Millie shivered when a cool nip of air chilled her legs. She blew out a puff of smoke that billowed around her stringy hair. Staring vacantly at the cold, damp earth below, she felt like crying.

"Damn it!" Millie bit her lip and mashed the last stub of her cigarette into the wooden step, pulled up her robe, and leaned back against a post. Looking up at the pale morning sky, she desperately wanted to think positive thoughts, but they kept getting slapped back by her nagging conscience.

After more than ten years off and on with Fannie, she was fed up. In another month, her little boy would be fourteen, and she knew it would only get harder to stay here. When he was a small child, the other girls always helped out, and Millie managed well enough. They seemed to like having a cute little boy around the house to mother or tease; it was easy enough to keep him occupied in a room separate from the adult activities. As Julian grew older, the cuteness turned into curiosity, attitude, and anger.

At age sixteen, Millie Ruth Martin had run away from her parents' home in Knoxville, Tennessee, hitching rides going west with just enough money to get to Kansas City. She couldn't live with her sexually abusive father and lazy, uncaring mother for another day. Her older brother, Harry, left a year earlier and had become a successful alcoholic in Kansas City, so when she left home, she knew she'd have a place to go—probably in a local tavern—but at least it was something.

Millie's intuition had been accurate. Her brother's home wasn't more than a hall closet. His instructions were short and sweet: She could have *that* corner. Two days after she arrived in Kansas City, she fell effortlessly into bed with a local part-time carpenter, John Daniels. By the time she gave birth and named the baby Julian, John was long-gone with another woman, leaving the young mother and child alone and desperate. These were times when child support meant your family will take care of you.

On the chaotic streets of Kansas City, Millie eventually found a kind woman willing to take her and the small child in—in the warehouse district. The woman, an attractive middle-aged black lady, recognized a familiar sight: a young gal struggling to raise her baby. This was the first time Fannie and Millie met. For Millie, finding Fannie provided stability.

Soon after she turned twenty-seven, Millie left the business to live with a man she hoped would be a father figure to Julian, now eleven. Her break came when a gentleman named Henry Hoag showed up for her favors. Henry, in his early thirties, homely and alone, easily fell in love with Millie the second he set eyes on her. By his third visit with Millie, he began asking her to consider leaving the brothel to live with him. She had been approached numerous times before, but his efforts seemed sincere compared to others.

Two weeks later, alone in the apartment that they had rented together, Millie sat at her kitchen table. She had pushed away her stained cup of cold coffee and buried her head in one hand, twisting and wrenching her hair with the other, tears streaming down her face. Henry had proved quickly that he had no idea of what children Julian's age required for attention or how quickly their anger could escalate when shoved into a corner. With no investment other than time, he had simply gone out for a midmorning smoke and never returned. Rent was due soon, and she had no way to pay it. She and Julian were facing a pending eviction.

Millie and Julian went out looking for him, but by dusk, she knew he had gone for good. The next morning, Millie woke up to the sound of a choir singing "When the Roll is Called up Yonder" echoing through the empty streets, reaching their tiny apartment. Millie decided she had to do something. She cleaned herself up, put on her best dress, woke Julian, and got him dressed. Together they walked toward the singing. With no job, no money, and no hope, she knew enough about churches to realize she could probably get help.

On their way to the church, Millie talked to Julian about why she wanted to do this. She knew he did not understand the emotional issues or why she got in this mess, but she knew he understood the smell of food. Across the street from the church, Millie tossed her cigarette, stepped on it, and turned to Julian.

"Son, I need you to be on your best behavior, okay?"

Julian seemed distracted by the activity around the church. He had never seen so many people dressed up this early in the morning.

"Sure, Mom. Are we gonna stay long? Because I'd like to go down to—"

"I don't know," Millie interrupted. "Depends. Long as it takes, I suppose." She looked in her purse and pulled out a handkerchief before snapping it shut.

Over the top of the two large front doors, a painted wooden sign read in bold letters: THE LORD'S SOUTHERN CHRISTIAN BIBLE CHURCH OF KANSAS CITY, and below, the church motto: BELOVED, IF GOD SO LOVED US, WE OUGHT ALSO TO LOVE ONE ANOTHER – 1 JOHN 4:11. Millie and Julian crossed the street and walked to the front door where a smiling gentleman greeted them with a small flyer listing the order of service.

When he opened the door, the music seemed to envelop them. Curious faces smiles, and warm hands reached out to greet them. Walking down the church aisle, Millie noticed a group of people up on the stage. The music director said a few words of praise for the Ladies'

Auxiliary, then with his right foot, stomped out a quick four-count and a small makeshift group of musicians—a piano player, a banjo player, and several enthusiastic tambourine players—plowed headlong into "Standing on the Promises," stirring up the thrilled audience into hand-clapping, shouting, and singing in every available key and octave.

Millie was relieved to find an obscure location near the back of the church, behind several women wearing large-brimmed hats. Until she understood what was going to happen, she was content to observe things from a distance. *Let's just see how this goes, a little at a time.*

* * * *

At the end of the service, several prominent church ladies from the auxiliary greeted Millie and Julian. One lady, Helen Castle, standing behind the other ladies, waited patiently for her chance to visit, in private, with Millie and Julian. When the others walked away, Helen moved closer.

"My dear, I'm Helen Castle—and please, just call me Helen. I'm one of those stuffy ladies in the church auxiliary."

"Very nice to meet you, Helen," Millie said, shaking her hand. "My name is Millie Daniels, and this is my son, Julian."

Helen turned to face young Julian. She gave him a slight smile, something Da Vinci would have modeled for the *Mona Lisa*, seized both his hands, and looked Julian directly in the eye.

Julian wasn't sure what to do—no one had ever taken his hands in this fashion, not counting the sheriff, especially an older lady wearing fancy lace gloves.

"Mr. Julian Daniels?" She spoke as if administering an oath of office. Julian had a feeling it was going to be a bad day. He tried to swallow but couldn't.

"Yes, ma'am?"

A big grin appeared on Helen's face.

"Are you taking good care of your mother?"

"Ah, I hope so, ma'am." Julian glanced over to Millie for reassurance. Her expression was anxious. He took that to mean, *Don't mess this up, kid.*

"Thank you, son. Just keep doing that and you'll be fine." Helen turned back to Millie, edged up closer, and whispered, "Millie, we are so pleased that you and your beautiful son have joined us today."

As Helen talked, Millie studied her. Her teeth were clean, and her clothes gave off a wonderful fragrance. She wondered what it would be like to smell that fine. She had perfume, but this aroma smelled of a woman with culture. She wanted to lean up against that smell for the rest of the afternoon.

"Thank you, ma'am; this is a very nice church," Millie said. "Everyone has been exceptionally pleasant and friendly to my son and me. We will come back and look forward to hearing the Lord's message, I'm sure."

"That's the best attitude—sounds like you already know how to take everything." Helen gave Millie a sly grin. "With a grain of salt, honey. Grain—of—salt," she said deliberately.

After Helen walked away, Millie noticed her hands—

they were shaking. She felt nervous and wondered if she was acting properly. She wasn't sure if it was from being anxious or because she hadn't eaten in the last twelve hours.

* * * *

Elaine Haskins, Ruth Nagel, and Gloria Williams, three ladies Millie had visited with earlier, walked over to Helen and hugged her.

"Excuse us, Millie, is there any chance that you and your son could join us downstairs for dinner?" Ruth asked sweetly. Julian's ears perked up. He looked directly at his mother, ready to provide his opinion, just in case she might have any doubts about his answer. She glanced at him. His answer came quickly without a prompt.

"Sure, Mom, it's okay with me."

Millie turned her eyes back to Ruth and answered politely, "I suppose we can—I just feel bad that we weren't prepared for this. I'm afraid we didn't bring a dish, being new to the area and all." Julian stared at his mother like she was crazy.

"Oh, wonderful, just wonderful," Ruth replied. "Not to worry, don't even think about it. Please, come down with us, and we'll find you a table." Julian beamed at the prospect of a full meal.

As they reached the bottom of the stairs, Julian could see most of the church congregation had already assembled and were preparing to give grace before food was served. Julian's stomach reacted immediately to the overwhelming sight and smell of food, growling so loud that the pastor had to speak up. Julian didn't hear a word spoken—all he could focus on were tables covered with so much food, he felt like his eyes would pop out of his face.

A large turkey, cooked to a golden brown, much of it already sliced up. Sweet potatoes covered in melted marshmallows. Mashed potatoes, gravy, candied sweet potatoes, jellied cranberries, homemade dinner rolls, a big bowl of homemade butter, sliced ham, green beans, several fruit salads, fruit gelatin dishes, iced tea, and lemonade.

When Julian saw the dessert table, he felt faint. Enough chocolate cake to *kill* him. Pies and more pies. Cookies, brownies, and so many other treats he couldn't even name. Had he died and gone to Heaven? Within a few minutes of seeing all this food, he realized that he might just have to become a minister. He wondered, *Do they get this every Sunday?*

* * * *

At the end of the prayer led by the pastor, Millie was sure she heard Julian say the loudest "Amen." Then she lost sight of him. Once the dinner was underway, Helen, Ruth, and Gloria grabbed Millie and pulled her over to the tables with all the food. Millie tried not to overload her plate, but the ladies got extra plates so she would be able to have a little something of each dish—most importantly, those they prepared.

As the ladies sat down, Millie noticed Julian over next to some other boys near his age, choking down as much turkey as he could. Then she took her first bite. The flavors and tastes were overwhelming. Gloria, sitting next to Millie, brought the subject up first.

"Millie, sweetheart, where do you live?"

Millie had a feeling they were aware she was in trouble. They could probably tell that Julian's clothes were at least one size too small and looked like they hadn't been cleaned for some time. They could see Millie's clothes hung on her. These ladies were, after all, the Ladies Auxiliary of the church, and one of their faithful duties was to look after the poor and indigent in the neighborhood. This young lady and her son walked right into their midst.

Millie answered, her head down, "Just down a few blocks and over on 9th Avenue." The ladies didn't push her. The area was well-known. Millie knew she would eventually have to give answers. Without thinking about it, her nervousness began to show, as she rubbed her hands and pushed her hair behind her ears several times.

Once dinner was over, Millie thought she and Julian could just excuse themselves to leave. Yet, in a moment that seemed right to leave, Elaine Haskins walked over and asked Millie to come upstairs for a short visit. She offered Julian the opportunity to stay in the basement and help with clean-up.

At the top of the stairs, Elaine ushered Millie into a room just off to one side of the church lobby, where they sat down on a few chairs near the church secretary's desk.

"Millie, sweetheart, you must be going through some hard times. Do you have a home?"

Millie hesitated—she wanted more time to think of

an answer when a tear fell off her cheek, answering the question.

"This is so hard," she sobbed. Elaine reached over to the desk for a tissue and handed it to Millie.

"I know, sweetheart, I've been there too."

"You have?"

"Yes, it's been quite a few years now, when I was barely into my twenties. I was in the same circumstance. Maybe some of the reasons were different, but I was homeless and hungry. I had no place to turn, no family here, no one. The ladies here at the church took me in. That's why I'm talking to you today. I wanted to, because of my experience."

"That's nice of you, to care enough." Millie wiped her eyes and bowed her head. "I have an apartment, but only for a few more days. We'll have to be out by next Thursday." She added, "My last place of employ didn't work out, and I need to find something new." She didn't want to say that she worked at the brothel, or that she left because a client had convinced her to.

Millie's heart was collapsing inside. She was afraid of letting all of her anger and hurt out in the open. Millie didn't want to explain everything about her past, too embarrassed to divulge how many awful things she'd been part of. She didn't feel worthy to even be inside the building, let alone stay for a visit and have dinner. Yet, the ladies treated her wonderfully. She felt like she was in a dream and didn't want it to end.

Elaine asked if it would be okay for them to bring over some food and extra clothes later in the afternoon.

"Millie, how about if I ask the pastor to contact your

landlord about doing something for you, so you can stay on a while longer, okay?"

"Yeah, that would be nice." Millie rubbed her nose with another tissue and smiled at Elaine.

* * * *

In the late afternoon, the food and extra clothes Elaine had promised were delivered by two teenage girls and one boy. In the next few days, as time permitted, Millie visited with Elaine and Helen and watched how they sat, spoke to each other, showed compassion, expressed kindness, and shared.

By Thursday, the church helped with rent money and Millie was out looking for work in the mornings, while Julian attended school nearby. She spent a few afternoons talking with the church pastor, Mr. Scott, agonizing over her feelings in each meeting.

Afterward, she thought she felt uplifted and encouraged—sure, her new life would begin with her next walk out the chapel door. In the late evening, however, she had misgivings, and insecurities about fitting in, and not feeling like she was a true part of this life.

Then, too, she had longings for companionship, friends, a smoke, a drink, and a wild night on the town, which nagged at her relentlessly. Her bored inner voice hinted at trouble, doubts, and issues—this apartment is too small, let's go get a drink, he's asleep anyway. She wanted out—out to have fun.

In a few more days, Millie felt emotionally and

physically wrung out. Her friends at the church knew something was wrong. Several of the ladies took turns trying to counsel her. Her most satisfying conversations were with her closest friend there, Elaine. Millie poured out her heart to Elaine often, intimate heart-wringing conversations that, when finished, seemed to solve the matter once and for all.

Millie still carried doubts around until the next meeting at a Wednesday evening service. The pastor gave an invitation to those who wanted to give their life to the Lord, as he always did in this part of the service. To Elaine's surprise, Millie squeezed her hand and got up. She began crying as she walked up to the steps of the stage and went down on her knees to openly confess her sins—spilling out the last few pieces of her past life, praying that it would forever wrench her soul clean of emotional and painful experiences.

Maybe she didn't lay her heart down; maybe she held back some vestige of her past she couldn't let go of. What-ever it was, after a few more weeks, Millie felt a growing frustration in her heart, not only in her attempts to keep up with the church auxiliary ladies but with her desires and feelings, like she wasn't good enough for this.

One by one, those ever-present weaknesses wedged into her life—always easy, just a short break—a cigarette or two, just one drink, just this one time. The easy way eventually led her to where she felt most at home: lying on her back in a rowdy mining town in southern Missouri, and back in the business.

CHAPTER 3
The Blakely Blossom

The early afternoons at the Sunset were always quiet—
it was nap time. Fannie sat alone in her room with her
door closed. She stared into a large cabinet with the doors
open wide, shelves full of books and clutter . . . except for
one bare spot. Fannie blinked, her eyes fixed on an empty
space where a coin box used to sit. A tin box full of gold
coins.

Tears rolled down her cheeks, remembering what had
been taken from her—a thief swindled her life savings
away from her future. She kicked the cabinet door with her
foot, slamming it against the frame. Years of saving and
sacrifice, collecting gifts from customers, to be taken away
by that son-of-a-bitch, bastard, good-for-nothing crook,
Charles Dean. She knew it was him who took it. She just
knew it. Why did she trust, why?

It was just six months ago when Shorty, on a dare,
came to visit. He arrived with two of his mine buddies,
there to make sure he fulfilled his mission.

The chosen chaperones, Little Ricky and Junior,
seized Shorty and soon gushed into the Sunset, stumbling
and cussing, each one trying to out-yell the other. Shorty's
redneck companions were tall, thin, and each missing at
least one tooth. Even in this part of the country, they were
odd.

The noise level at the Sunset ramped up a few notches and the whole house knew they had arrived. The intrepid romantics walked straight to the bar, a safe haven for any real man planning his next intelligent move, in a search for true love. The hollering continued until Fannie signaled several gals to cozy up close on each side of the boys, give a teasing preview, and engage the gents in playful sex talk.

Paying no attention to small details, like missing teeth, the Sunset ladies didn't disappoint, and after a few drinks—and a few gallons of pure Southern hospitality—the rednecks were escorted to their rooms.

That is, except for Shorty. He wasn't escorted anywhere. Charles "Shorty" Dean, a short, fat fifty-some-thing man with an unpleasant reputation, chewed tobacco and had a mean temper. His scruffy whiskers and bourbon breath only intensified the repulsive odor coming off his body and clothes. Fannie knew as soon as she saw him that it would be the ultimate test of her hospitality and, for a moment, seriously thought about sending him away. Her own house rules specifically stated that *"a man must have a sense of decorum as to character and hygiene."*

Fannie cautiously walked up to the bar, next to Shorty. Jean and Millie escaped into the front parlor holding their noses.

"Well, hello there, Mr. Dean, how are you this fine evening?"

Shorty turned his head, eyes half closed, looked up at the well-dressed black lady staring at him, and spoke slowly.

"Hello? ah, yes." Shorty thought it would be proper to say more, but strong alcohol and the look on Fannie's face left him blank.

"Mr. Dean, I must inform you that we have a dress and hygiene code that we try to maintain for the benefit of our guests and ladies. You seem to have misplaced that information somewhere between the decision to come here and now," Fannie spelled out for him in a firm business voice.

Shorty gave her a smirk like she was eating rotten apples.

"Miss Fannie, I believe? I am not only dressed appropi, appropp . . ."

"Appropriately, Mr. Dean," Fannie spoke for him and folded her arms.

"Yes, that's the word I'm speaking for. Anyway, Miss Annie," he announced, pointing at her with a bent finger. "I am good for this and I will be jus' fine." He turned back to the bartender, Joey, and produced a wobbling head smile, apparently thinking he had won something. Joey took one step back and continued rubbing a clean shot glass with his bar towel. He knew what was coming. If pushed, Fannie's backhand swing was as good as a Remington shotgun blast, any day.

"Mr. Dean, I know you're okay. This is about your hygiene, not your ability to pay," Fannie explained.

"Miss Fannie, would you like to have a drink with me?"

"No, Mr. Dean, I have a much better deal for you." She motioned for Bernice, one of her live-in girls, a tall Indian woman, to come over and give her a hand.

"Hey, now this is what I call service," Shorty praised as they each took an arm and escorted him to a large bathroom just down the hall from the bar. Shorty was too drunk to realize what was about to happen, and even if he did, too drunk to put up much of a fight, especially with the two women escorting him.

"Mr. Dean, instead of making you go home and clean up, we're going to do it here. There will be an extra charge for this service, just so you know," Fannie warned as Bernice shoved him into the bathroom. Bernice turned on the water in the tub and Fannie proceeded to undress Shorty.

"Well, now this will be fun." He helped unbutton his shirt. As the clothes flew off, Fannie threw them out the door as fast as she could.

"Aren't you ladies going to get in with me?"

"Not just yet, Mr. Dean," said Bernice. "You go ahead and relax, we'll be with you shortly." Bernice giggled as she looked at Shorty slowly lowering his chubby, hairy body into the hot, foamy water. A loud "Ahh" echoed in the bathroom. Bernice whispered to Fannie that it probably was the sound of all the little critters dying as Shorty drowned them in scalding water.

Crowning the special ceremony, Bernice took a stiff brush and a bar of lye soap to his back. As Shorty relaxed, he leaned his head on the back of the tub and, in a few moments, was out like an Edison light bulb. Goodnight, sweet prince.

* * * *

Fannie let him soak for a while then went in and pulled the rubber plug. As the warm, soapy water, drained out,

Fannie filled a bucket of scalding *cold* water. She walked over to the tub and poured the water on Shorty.

"Ahhyeoo!" Shorty yelled like a wild jungle ape. The surprise baptism launched his body straight up and out of the tub, leaving him shaking and his teeth chattering. Fannie threw him a large towel.

"Here's a clean set of trousers and a shirt. Put them on while your other clothes are soaking in the back. I'll meet you at the bar and we'll discuss your bill."

Shorty felt like he'd been beaten and dragged through purgatory backward. He finished putting on the borrowed pants and fumed. *Well, hasn't this just been a real fine evening?* Shorty found himself in an awkward time when a guy wants to stay drunk, but he knows he's headed to sober.

Angrier with each passing second, he prepared himself to go out to the bar and give Fannie some of his attitude. As he reached for the door's porcelain doorknob, he heard Fannie coming down the hall. He jumped back, expecting her to walk in. She didn't. He paused. *What's she up to?* Shorty went back to the door, bent over, carefully turned the knob, and peeked through the small open space.

Across the hall into what must be Fannie's office, he could see her moving around, putting something in a tin box on a shelf. Suddenly, he noticed a small gold coin. *There must be hundreds of them in that box*, he thought. He closed the door and stood for a moment, pondering. His criminal mind cheerfully trampled over any vague inkling of conscience and thought, *Maybe I should rethink how I'm gonna handle this.*

A knock at the door snapped him out of his thoughts.

"Mr. Dean? You okay in there?"

Shorty grabbed the doorknob and opened the door, a big grin across his face.

"Well, I sure am, Miss Fannie. And I'm lookin' for you." His sweet voice surprised Fannie. She expected an angry, pissed-off customer, that she was willing to sacrifice and send off to her competitors.

"Well, you found me baby cakes," said Fannie. "Now, why don't we go up to the bar and get you all squared up? Your sidekicks are raring to go back to the Miner's Pick for another round of Old Maid."

"Let 'em go, I'm gonna stay here," Shorty said. Shorty threw his hands up, waving them off like they were two bothersome children. Shorty looked over at Fannie and grinned. "Let's go have a drink."

Fannie flashed her eyes back to Shorty with suspicion—something was up. She knew Shorty's reputation and couldn't quite figure out why he had turned into a loveable cupcake.

While Joey was mixing his drink, Shorty walked to the front and told his two buddies to go ahead without him, then walked back to the bar.

"Pretty lady, would you let me buy you a drink, now?" Shorty asked, trying his best to be romantic.

"Well, Mr. Dean, you certainly may," Fannie answered. She looked over to the bartender and held up two fingers. "Joey, one for Mr. Dean here, too." Joey jumped into action mixing her favorite drink, the Blakely Blossom. A double-dark bourbon with a jigger each of scotch and tequila, embellished with a maraschino cherry floating on top. As the two shot glasses full of dark liquid slid in front of them, Fannie grabbed one and put it in front of Shorty.

"Mr. Dean?" Fannie stared Shorty in the eye. "Did you enjoy your bath and refreshing cool rinse?" She laughed as another round of drinks slid in front of them. Shorty shook his head indifferently, staring down at the bar top.

"That, Miss Fannie, was a surprise, like nothing I have ever experienced before and, I might add, will be worth remembering even if I didn't get what I came for." Shorty deliberately emphasized each word. He smiled and pulled a drink to his lips.

"I'm sorry about that, Mr. Dean. How can I make it up to you?" Fannie looked down at her drink when she spoke. She didn't want it getting around that her parlor didn't satisfy all guests, in some fashion or another. Fannie also knew that it wasn't always the handsome man that needed her brothel's product. Shorty's answer was predictable—a mischievous smile and raised eyebrows. After another round, Fannie walked him upstairs to her private room.

* * * *

Within a few days, the relationship between Shorty and Fannie became the first order of gossip in the house. Jean, Millie, Bernice, and Lupe gathered in the early afternoons to drink coffee and gab on and on about the improbable love affair between Fannie and Mr. Dean.

Two months after it began, it stopped, dead cold. The girls of the house knew the exact second the affair was over. Fannie's screaming could be heard a block away.

They all rushed to her room to see what the matter was. The tin box was missing.

At first, Fannie didn't want to believe that it was Shorty. But, as she interrogated each girl one by one, she came to realize she had trusted the wrong man and let him have too much freedom in the house.

She couldn't call the police because, technically, her business wasn't legal. Despite each having a favorite girl at the Sunset, Fannie knew at least two high-ranking officers at the police department would demand their share to keep things quiet and let the business stay open, even if they were to find the coins. And then there was the revenuers, the IRS. She knew if the police didn't keep it all for themselves, they would just make a quick call to the feds. How would that be explained? It was just her loss, her devastating loss.

* * * *

A week after the incident with the Dean brothers, Julian was still exiled to his room, except for school and chores. On Wednesday night, cool rainy weather seemed to keep customers away from the Sunset. Julian heard footsteps coming up the second flight of stairs. He quickly put away his coins and paper money he'd been counting. Fannie knocked at the door once and then entered. The room was lit with one lonely forty-watt light bulb dangling from the bare wood ceiling, and the walls unfinished with two-by-four studs.

Julian had managed to find several thrown-out pieces

of furniture, including a nightstand that he used for a desk, a broken chair, and several wooden fruit boxes he kept to store his clothes. His bed was a flat, stained mattress in one corner of the room with a pile of blankets scattered over it.

"Hello, Julian."

"Hey, Miss Fannie," Julian answered, as he got up from his mattress.

"No, no, sit down, you're okay. May I visit with you for a minute?"

Julian pulled up a small wooden chair for Fannie. "Sure, what's up?" he asked, backing away. For Julian, these little visits usually hadn't been pleasant experiences for him. He'd learned to be cautious around Fannie.

"Sit down, Julian, please, sit down."

Julian sat down cross-legged on his tattered flat bed.

"I've been trying to remember something, something you said a couple of weeks ago, after you and the Dean boys had your little altercation, do you remember that?"

"Yes, ma'am, sure do."

"I thought you had mentioned something about a small chest, something that Shorty was carrying before you threw the apple at him?"

"Yes, ma'am. The chest, is that what you're wanting to know about?"

"Yes. You see, I owned a small metal box—it was made of tin, actually. Well, it came up missing about the time Mr. Dean decided he was no longer going to visit us here at the Sunset."

"Yes, ma'am, I remember that. I mean, I don't remember why he didn't come by anymore, but I remember the box, ma'am."

"Julian, do you remember any more about that day? Could you tell where Shorty was taking that chest, or was it open or did it seem heavy?"

"Oh, hard to tell ma'am, probably was heavy. He struggled a bit to move it, I could tell that. Seemed to me that one of the boys acted like they were gonna help him carry it and he must have told them no because it was like he shooed them away. I can't say for sure, that's just the way it looked to me."

"Thanks, Julian, you've been very helpful. In fact, you can be off your detention as of tonight," Fannie said, in what seemed to Julian a rare moment of kindness.

"Thanks."

"You're welcome, have a good night, then." Fannie turned to go out the door, but, Julian had one more question.

"Miss Fannie, ah, do you think that Shorty took your tin chest?"

"Julian, if you were old enough, I'm sure you'd be in the gambling halls over on Main Street betting on all sorts of games. There's one bet that I think you could win for sure, the bet that old Shorty had something to do with the stealing of my tin box." Fannie let the deep thought sink into Julian's brain; for a second, her eyes glared intensely. "And someday . . . I'll get it back." With that, she pulled the door shut.

Julian didn't move. He listened in silence to the diminishing sound of footsteps as they marked her path to the main floor and went silent.

Julian wondered about all the events that had taken

place in just the last couple of months. Everyone was thrilled for Fannie that she had found someone to be with, then the awful betrayal by Shorty. It proved to everyone at the Sunset that his terrible reputation could be believed, although none of them ever thought otherwise.

Soon after Fannie left his room, Julian opened his attic door and slipped gingerly down the steps to the kitchen for a bite to eat. Fannie always had something good to eat somewhere in the kitchen or tucked away on one of the shelves in the pantry.

Inside the pantry, the aroma of spices and fresh bread was spellbinding. A large wooden table sat in the middle for rolling dough or mixing cereals. In the kitchen, a large wood stove took space on the west wall, a table and chairs stood near the back door with a window looking out the back, and a large chopping block sat in the middle of the room near the new electric ice box. To Julian, this was a hungry night owl's paradise.

He barely made a sound as he walked through the upstairs hallway down the grand staircase and into the kitchen. When he pushed through the large kitchen doorway, a silhouette of someone's head appeared.

"Ayy! Hmph." His yell was muffled as a small hand slapped over his mouth and an arm wrapped around his waist, pulling him close. A woman's small-framed body pushed Julian against the wall. He felt panic and then a surprise of sensual warmth. It was hard for him to process all his feelings and sensations in such a few short seconds. He struggled, then relaxed.

"Julian, shh, it's me. It's me, Jean!" she whispered and held him against the wall. Julian squinted until his eyes adjusted to the darker room and he saw Jean's face.

"Jean! What are you doing? God, you scared the bejesus out of me!"

"I came to get something to eat, probably like you, eh?"

"Yeah, I was starving."

Jean seemed to gaze deep into Julian's eyes. She loosened her grip on Julian and stepped back. Julian felt a sudden loneliness, a cold void as she pulled her warm, soft body away from his. Inside his body, new feelings emerged. He instinctively knew what they were.

"It's a good thing it's dark in here, I only have my undergarments on," Jean teased, waving her finger at him. "Your mother would be very upset with me if she knew we were here like this." She touched his arm before turning around to walk away.

"Yeah." He took a deep sigh, watching her move. "I wouldn't want that to happen."

"Maybe there's something to eat in the pantry. Have you looked?" Jean gestured for Julian to come with her into the pantry. It was darker in there, but she had already tipped Julian off that she didn't want the light on, so he didn't try.

"Besides, I don't think my mom cares what I do." Julian scoffed. "I think it's only Fannie who would have a heart attack if she caught me with you."

"Oh, your mom gets plenty mad when us girls sit around and gossip. Some of them tell her that they are going to have you." She got closer and stared at Julian, making a clawed hand with her fingers. "She tells them she'll scratch their eyes out if they do." Jean turned to look around for a snack. "And you're right about Fannie, but she would probably kill both of us."

"Yeah? Who says that?" Julian asked.

"Oh, you wanna know, huh?" Jean teased.

"Yeah!"

"Well, for one, Lupe, she's said stuff like that."

Julian felt embarrassed—he'd never had anyone talk about him that way. "Oh well, I guess Mom will have to keep an eye on her, huh?"

"If Millie knew everything, she'd be upset."

"Yeah, that'll be the day my mom gets that excited. She'll never know anyway," Julian whispered. He strained his eyes to look around the shelves for something to snack on.

"Oh, someone will tell her," Jean claimed. "Do you see anything in here worth munching on?"

Julian located a large bread box and opened the lid. "Here's a loaf of bread. Let's take it out to the kitchen so we can see to slice it. I wonder if there's any meat we can cut to make a sandwich."

"I don't know, I'll look in the ice box." With Julian following behind, Jean walked out of the pantry to Fannie's new electric refrigerator and pulled on the handle. As soon as Jean opened the refrigerator door, the bright light inside came on and the outline of Jean's body was exposed through the thin nightgown she had on. Julian's eyebrows raised and in a moment of shy embarrassment, he thought he should turn his head away, but didn't. A surprised Jean turned around to face Julian and started laughing at her accidental exposure. She quickly closed the refrigerator door and, after a few seconds, walked back over to Julian, who was smiling.

Jean poked Julian in the ribs.

"Okay, smarty pants. This time, you open the ice box and look for some meat. I'll cut the bread."

"I guess that'll work, although I thought things were going just fine."

"Yeah, I'll just bet you enjoyed that."

Julian reluctantly went to the ice box, opened it and found some turkey meat wrapped up in heavy brown paper, and brought it back to the large chopping block to slice it.

After making a couple of turkey sandwiches, they shuffled to the small kitchen table and ate and talked in the dark. Julian told Jean of the strange visit he'd had earlier that night with Fannie and how she'd asked him about a tin chest that Shorty Dean had stolen from her. Jean knew what happened and told Julian that the reason Fannie had been so upset over the last few weeks was that she had been duped by Shorty.

"So," Jean asked, "did she tell you what was inside that chest?"

"No, I just supposed it was some important papers, old rings or, you know, family stuff. I couldn't imagine why he wanted it."

"It's full of gold coins! Twenty-dollar gold pieces and other valuable coins she's collected over the years. Her entire savings!"

"No! You're kidding!"

"No, real gold and a whole bunch of it!"

"Shh, we'd better keep it down, someone's going to hear," Julian warned.

"They're all up on the next floor anyway, unless they're coming down to eat, too. They probably can't hear us, I hope." Jean got up and walked into the hallway that led up to the bar and the social area to see if anyone was around. Julian felt relaxed, enjoying this quiet time with Jean. They had never really talked before—at least, not personally like this, not like they were close friends.

When Jean walked back into the kitchen, past the pantry door, he admired her small figure and long blond hair. Julian was hoping she could find another reason to pin him against the wall one more time. For now, he just wanted to continue their private conversation; it made him feel more like an adult. When Jean walked past him and sat down at the table, Julian leaned over to pose a question.

"So, you're telling me that Shorty took Fannie's life savings?"

"Yep," Jean replied, picking up her sandwich for another bite.

"It must have been dang heavy, then. When I saw Shorty carrying that chest, it appeared that it might have been full of something." Julian tried hard to remember more details, now that he knew what it contained. "So, how is she going to get it back, did she say?"

"Naw, she's been awful sad about it and sometimes, she'll mumble something like, 'I'll kill that bastard, if I ever get my hands on him,' you know, stuff like that."

"Wow!" Julian thought for a few moments. "I can't imagine how you'd get past those Dean boys, but it sure would be nice to have a bunch of gold, huh?"

"Oh yeah, I could retire and go on a long trip. I would

build my mom and dad a home. It would be wonderful," Jean said.

"I don't know what I'd do. But, for sure, I'd get out of this place. I'd like to buy my mom her own place, too, so she wouldn't have to do this, you know." Julian secretly wondered what he would do with that much gold. To be able to go out and buy something, without worrying about the cost, would be a dream. Surely it would solve all his problems.

"Yeah, you know she's upstairs with Mack, don't you?" Jean asked. Julian thought Jean was trying to make him jealous.

"No!" Julian got up from his chair and walked over to the chopping block. "Damn, I don't like that jerk." He turned around to Jean. "He's an ass, I don't know what she sees in him."

"Oh, I know what she sees in him: a way out of here. And I'm sure Mack's looking for someone to mother him—his little toy—to keep his drawers folded, you know. If it helps at all, none of us like him either. He's a creep." Jean picked up the silverware and put it in the sink, and together they made their way out of the kitchen and up the grand staircase.

"I just don't like what's going on," Julian confided.

At Jean's door, Julian stopped for a moment to say goodnight. As he was about to speak, she leaned over and kissed him on the lips.

"Goodnight," she whispered. When her door closed, Julian stood in the hallway, unable to move. Eventually, he turned toward the attic and swaggered upstairs for the night.

At the same time, Millie's door opened, and Mack quietly slipped down the hallway. A thin cloud of blue cigarette smoke curled up over his head as he vanished down the stairs.

Chapter 4
Little Sammy

The next Wednesday morning, three days after the Dean boys had visited to invite Julian out for a little 'apple bobbing', Fannie, unable to sleep, had gotten up early to do laundry and a few small chores.

Mid-morning, she heard raised voices from a few of the ladies coming from the kitchen. Curious, Fannie nonchalantly walked from the laundry room through the kitchen past Millie, Jean, Bernice, and Cee Cee who were sitting at the large table drinking coffee, stirring their morning gossip. As she walked out toward the foyer, Fannie fussed with a dish towel and acted disinterested.

Every once in a while, Fannie would pop in to refill her coffee, add a couple of lumps of sugar and, depending on the quality of the conversation, either roll her eyes at their despicable language or give an audible huh, followed by a loud clank of her spoon, soon after. Some of the ladies were using '*damn*' and '*hell*' as if Emily Post had declared them '*proper for daily use at home or in public events.*'

"No one has any class anymore," Fannie mumbled loud enough for them to hear her as she cleaned out the drawers in the foyer buffet.

After a few minutes of moving clutter around, her eyes fixed on something, in the way-back part of the drawer she was cleaning. Under a pile of useless papers, trinkets, and broken thread spools she spotted something that caught her breath and made the boisterous voices from the kitchen fade into an echo from some far-off dream.

Fannie's head lowered as she let out a sigh of held-back emotions and memories that flushed into her heart. It was then, she remembered why it was put back so far. *'I should have put it away in my room, if'n I had any damned sense!'* she murmured to herself.

A small piece of wood, roughly whittled to look like a horse. She stared at it, unable to stop the tears rolling down her cheeks, remembering a little boy, who was never far away from her heart. Fannie's thoughts rushed into the past.

Just after noon, on a Saturday in August 1907, the rain had moved on, the rest of the day turned hot and muggy in the thick bush and tree-lined farmland near Charlotte, North Carolina. The tall grass was still full of moisture, as the young mother walked barefoot with her son Sammy out to the corral behind the neighbor's house. She had finally given in to Sammy's whining and begging. She was on her way to go over and ask the neighbor, Mr. Jenkins if it would be okay for her son to ride one of his horses.

Whenever Sammy would see Mr. Jenkins out working with the horses, Sammy would run lickity-split out the back-screen door to go see what he was doing. Sammy, was fond of one particular horse, covered with beautiful roan-colored hair, of red and brown.

"Mr. Jenkins calls him, Gidyup, Mom, that's funny, huh?" Sammy laughed at himself.

"He is a pretty horse, son, that's for sure." Fannie

complimented. She was nervous about his interest, in horses. Sammy was pretty small for his age and this horse, Gidyup seemed so tall, especially as he ambled up close to the fence, sticking his large muzzle up to Fannie's hand and blowing hard, spraying a fine mist from his nostrils.

"Oh!" Fannie jumped back, wiping her hand on her apron, both she and Sammy started laughing. Mr. Jenkins came out when he saw Fannie and her son at the corral.

"Gotta watch those sneezes!" Mr. Jenkins yelled as he walked across the yard to the corral.

"Mr. Jenkins!" yelled an excited Sammy. "Mom said it would be okay, if I rode your horse, right mom?" Sammy looked back to his mom for reassurance. Mr. Jenkins walked up to Fannie and took his hat off.

"Good day to you, Ma'am."

"Good day, Mr. Jenkins, is Mrs. Jenkins doing alright?"

"Yes, a little better, Ma'am, however, still not a hundred percent."

"You give her my best, won't you?"

"Yes, Ma'am, I certainly will, she'll appreciate your concern. And, Bill, he's working down at Beggar's corner?"

"Yes, sir. He's hopin' to get on full, maybe he'll get somethin' today."

"I'm sure he'll do fine. The Mrs. and me, we pray for him, too."

"Thank you, Mr. Jenkins, polite of you to say."

Sammy was getting impatient with the fancy nice talk and tugged at Fannie's skirt and apron.

"Mom, tell him it's okay!"

"Well, Mr. Jenkins, would it be too much trouble, I

mean, is it alright if my boy Sammy rode your horse?"

"Oh, sure Miss Blakely, Ol' Gidyup, he's a pretty calm horse. Sammy will do fine. I'll quick get a saddle on him and we'll lead him out to the field."

"Thank you so much, Mr. Jenkins. Sammy, you can go on with Mr. Jenkins and make sure you help him, but don't get in the way now, ya hear?"

Sammy had already run off with Mr. Jenkins before Fannie could finish her sentence. After a little while, Mr. Jenkins and Sammy walked 'Gidyup' out to the field and towards Fannie.

"Now, Sammy," instructed Mr. Jenkins, "Climb up on that fence and we'll get you going that way." Sammy eagerly got up on the cedar wood fence and with Mr. Jenkins' help, cautiously slid into the saddle. Sammy's eyes grew big as he realized the immense size of the horse. It scared him. Maybe he wasn't so sure about doing this, after all.

Fannie could tell he was frightened; his eyes gave away his true feelings. Fannie felt the urge to stop him right there, but hesitated, 'This is what he's been wanting to do,' she reminded herself.

With so much noise disturbing his peaceful afternoon, Gidyup acted jumpy, nervously jockeying back and forth then, seemed to settle down.

"Whoa, boy, whoa," calmed Mr. Jenkins, while patting Gidyup on the neck. "There ya go. Now son, Stay calm, just hold on to the reins and let him do all the work. All you have to do is say giddy-up, and he'll start. Don't have to do nothin' else, just let him do it, okay?"

"Okay, Mr. Jenkins," replied Sammy, with an uneasy voice. "Giddy-up" The large horse slowly turned and walked toward the center of the field.

"See, that's the way, son!" Said Mr. Jenkins approvingly.

About thirty yards out, Sammy turned in the saddle to look back at his mom and grinned, then threw up his left hand to wave and yelled back to her.

"Hi, Mommy!"

A relaxed Gidyup, immediately spooked, reared up with a jerk and leaped into a full gallop, throwing the small boy violently back to the ground.

Fannie instantly ran around to an open gate, screaming his name. From a distance, she thought she saw his hand come up, maybe Sammy was getting up? When she reached him, she threw herself down beside him and put her right hand under his head. She felt the wetness of blood on the back of his head and the cruel, sharp rock below it. Slightly opening his eyes, he looked up at her. His lips whispered "Mom" and with a faint smile, he stopped breathing.

Her body shook and trembled; burning a hard look up to the heavens, she cried out with a scream that echoed down the valley.

The sorrow and heartbreak of losing a child would never go away. It's been more than twenty years, but he is with her still; he will be forever. Little Samuel Louis Blakely will always be nine years old.

Fannie quietly cradled the little carving in her fingers and lifted it to her chest, letting her tears fall. In a few seconds, she slowly turned and opened the door to her office. A new place was found to put the little horse.

CHAPTER 5
Dog Food

1928

Julian pulled another blanket over his head to block out the light of the morning sun, which beamed through the small gable window of his attic room. Half awake, drifting in and out of sleep and semi-conscious thoughts, a loud knock at the door startled him. He knew it had to be someone he didn't want to see.

For a moment, he thought it might be a dream and he fell back asleep until his mother walked in and plopped alongside him on his mattress. Millie shook the pile of clothes and blankets, covering the thin mattress, hoping something under the mound would move.

"Julian, sweetheart?" She could see two bare legs at one end and one arm lying limp out the side, so she knew she was patting in the right place. She shook it again. The pile moved slightly, and it made a sound.

"Mmahh."

Millie pushed at it one more time.

"Julian, come on, honey, I need to visit with you a little bit." The pile reacted again with agitated jerking. The first to budge were legs that pushed back and forth like a steam locomotive starting up.

"What did I do this time?" Julian's voice was muffled

by layers of blankets and pillows.

"You didn't do anything—at least not that I know of. I just wanted to visit with you a little bit. I've decided something and I want to discuss it with you."

"What?" Julian's voice was hoarse.

"Well, I've decided that it's time we leave the Sunset."

Julian rolled over, exposing his face and messy brown hair. He looked up at his mom, surprised.

"Leave? The Sunset? You and me, leave?"

"Well, we might have some help. Someone else might want to leave with us, too," she said, looking away as she answered.

"Mack, right? That new guy who's been coming by, right?" Julian said.

"Yes, honey, Mack. He's a good man, sweetie, not the usual kind of guy that would come into a place like this. I mean, he works steady, he's got an automobile, he's responsible, he knows how to fix things around the house, he's not a terrible person."

"Okay, okay, I get the idea." Julian was tired of hearing about it. "To me, he's like every other bum that walks into this place. He's not special. I don't know this guy and you've only seen him a couple of times, right? So, how do we know for sure he's okay?"

"Yes, it's been just a few times, but we've talked so much. I feel like I know him so well. Besides, Julian, I need to get on with my life. I can't do this much longer; this is a young woman's business, not for women getting older like me."

"Jeez Mom, you're not that old." Julian sat upright and the blankets pooled around his waist. He searched his bare room. "Where would we go?"

"Oh, I don't know, maybe up north, or maybe west of here—lots of growth, you know. We've heard of lots of people going to Detroit to work in the car factories, some people heading out west, like to Wyoming to work the oil fields, to California to work the fruit fields or factories out there."

"It might be nice to get out of here, I've pretty much run out of friends around this old town, anyway." Julian plopped himself over on his back and thought, *It would be one way to get away from Shorty's boys.*

"That's the way to look at it." Millie perked up. "Now, I need to go get some washing done. You need to clean up in here and then get your chores done for Fannie, okay? Then off to school. You can't be late anymore, promise?" Millie picked herself up and walked to the attic door.

"Yeah, I'll get up. So, when are you going to decide?"

"I'll know in the next day or two, but we'll talk about it some, again—oh, and sweetie, let's not say anything just yet, okay?"

"Sure." Julian was, after all, his mother's son, and at the end of the day, he was still going to be loyal to her. She was all he had, for now.

After the door closed, Julian rolled back over for a few minutes, stretched, got up, and kicked his blankets and pillow into the corner. After some breakfast downstairs, he found the after-school chore list Fannie had written up for him to do, cleaned up, and took off for school. He hadn't been outside much since the incident with the Deans, so this morning's walk to school felt refreshing; it put him in a good mood.

Looking around town reminded Julian what his mother said about leaving, so maybe their days in this old town were over. That sounded good to him.

* * * *

After school, as he was walking back to the Sunset, he began to daydream about Fannie's box of missing gold coins. *When Mom and I take off, if we had that money, we'd be able to buy a house way out in the country, maybe an automobile.* Julian tripped on a tree root that had grown into the dirt path and he fell, barely catching himself before he rolled into some thistles alongside the trail.

"Damn!" he yelled. Julian brushed his pants off and looked around to see if anyone noticed his clumsy fall. In the distance, he could see the steam from one of the mills that crushed ore from the mines. *Shorty and the boys are still working*, he thought. He brushed his pants off and walked a little farther, this time keeping his eyes on the path for more roots. Then it hit him. *Why not just mosey on over to Shorty's place and just get that box? Their door ain't locked—I can just walk in and take it, as long as it's before they get home.* That would be just the ticket to have himself a big pile of gold coins.

Julian's imagination roiled on as he tried to convince himself. After a few more blocks, he started to talk himself out of it. *It's probably too heavy and for sure Shorty's hidden it where I wouldn't be able to find it. Besides, if they did catch me, they'd kill me on the spot.* Julian nodded in agreement with himself. *Mom and I'll be fine, just us two. We don't need that dumb gold.*

* * * *

A few days later, in the early evening, as he was walking along the dusty alley behind the Sunset, Julian noticed an automobile parked in the back lot. Julian wrenched his face—that was Mack's jalopy. He bristled. *Damn it.* He sprinted the rest of the way to the house then jumped up on the porch and gently pulled open the screen door with the wooden thread spindle used for a doorknob.

He walked through the kitchen, peered around for anyone who might see him, then dashed up the stairs and down the hallway to the ladies' rooms. He had to be careful. He walked up to a spot on the wall outside his mom's room, knelt, and glanced both ways before putting his ear up against the wallpaper. His instincts told him that with Mack coming by so much, something was up—and he wanted to know what it was.

"But what will I do with Julian?" whispered Millie to Mack, the part-time railroad worker and full-time customer of Millie's. Arnold "Mack" McKenzie wasn't the kind of guy you paid much attention to if you were to pass him on the street; he kept to himself. Only those who worked on his rail gang were acquainted with him, but none of them knew him. In his world—if you didn't smoke, drink, and cuss like him— he probably wouldn't have anything to do with you.

"Give the little troublemaker to Fannie. She tries to be his mother anyway," Mack growled.

"Mack! Don't talk like that, he might hear you!" scolded Millie.

Through the paper-thin walls and the cheap wallpaper, Julian listened and picked up another piece of the puzzle that would be his future. He held his breath and strained to hear the sounds too low or muffled to make out. The coil springs in Millie's small wrought iron bed squeaked as she moved; Mack's cough turned into hacking, making the private conversation almost inaudible. It didn't matter. Julian had heard enough to figure out what was going on. He knew all too well his mother's nature and what this meant to him.

Inside the room, Mack and Millie's conversation continued.

"Hell, he's old enough, let him go," Mack said. "Just tell him to hit the road and make his own God damned way! That's what I had to do; besides, it'll make a man out of him. The kid has to learn for himself!" Mack flicked his cigarette ashes on the floor and took another deep draw. Millie looked at Mack with disgust.

"No! I couldn't do that, my poor baby!" Millie was angry with Mack. Mack heaved up like he was going to laugh, but instead, began another round of coughing.

"Honey, I want you to come with me," Mack said, after catching his breath. "But bringing that little bastard isn't gonna work. I want to travel light, so make up your mind. I'm leaving Friday morning." Mack pulled his arm from under Millie. Millie gave Mack a dirty look.

In a comforting gesture, Mack rubbed his hand over her thigh a few times and patted her, but his large scratchy hands didn't provide comfort to Millie's pale smooth skin. Mack rolled over—with a grunt and another hacking cough—lifted himself out of bed and slipped on his pants. He pulled a Lucky Strike out of his shirt pocket, lit it, and looked down at Millie, waiting for his answer. Millie stared up at Mack, her eyes doubtful and hurt.

"All right, I'll speak to Fannie." She threw the blankets off, briefly exposing herself, to lean over and grab her nightgown. Mack took one last swig of bourbon from a stubby glass on the dresser and belched. Millie got up and stepped into her slippers.

"I'll come by Friday morning, around ten."

"That'll be fine." Millie tightened the nightgown around her body. Mack walked over, leaned down, and kissed her on the side of her face. Without saying another word, he turned around and left the room. The smell of his cigarettes, bourbon, and sweat lingered in the air.

Crouched down along the wall away from Millie's door, Julian was hidden, so Mack didn't see him when he left, but Fannie did. *Whack!* A large flat hand slapped the back of Julian's head, rolling him over in pain.

"What do you think you're doing, little hellion!"

"I wasn't doing nothing," replied Julian, rubbing his head, tears in his eyes. Fannie grabbed him up by the back of his shirt collar and pulled him close.

"So, am I supposed to think you were leaning down there kissing the wall? I saw you doing nothing. Now, get back upstairs or you'll know what doing nothing is when I get done with you!"

Millie could hear Julian in trouble again and Fannie getting all worked up. She quickly put on her house robe and ran out into the hallway. As she opened her bedroom door, Julian brushed past Millie with a hurt look. Fannie stepped around the corner with her hands on her hips.

Julian hesitated in the shadows. He had to hear. If

this was the night, it would all change for him.

"What are you planning now? You know he was listening in on you," Fannie yelled.

"I'm leaving. Mack wants me to go up north with him, to Detroit, so he can work in the automobile plant—you know, get married, start making a living."

"And just what would you do while he's making a living?" She took a step closer to Millie's face. "You wouldn't know how to be a proper wife if it slapped you in the face! You know it ain't gonna be any good up there. You'll just end up in the same place! You've tried this before!"

"For all I know, you may be right, but look at me. I'm almost thirty. I've got to decide what I'm going to do. All I ask of you is that you keep an eye on Julian for a while—you know, until we get settled and all," said Millie. "I'll come back and get him as soon as I can."

Julian, hearing this, quietly ran back up to his small attic room and threw himself on the pile of blankets and clothes. Tears of anger rolled down his face. He grabbed a small porcelain cup and hurled it against the wall, breaking it into bits. He knew that Fannie was just one more brothel madam that treated him like she was his wicked stepmother, and his mother was going to abandon him. He hated both of them.

* * * *

The next afternoon, Millie pulled Julian into the back parlor room and closed the door. He knew what she wanted to tell him.

"Julian, I . . . ahh . . ." Millie hesitated and began to cry. Julian came out with it.

"You're taking off, aren't you?"

"Yes, honey."

"So, what am I going to do?"

"Mack has asked me to go with him to Detroit. He wants to work in the new automobile plant up there. And he thought you might do better on your own—you know, now that you're old enough and all."

"So, what am I supposed to do for money? Where am I gonna live?" Julian knew it wasn't about money; it was about losing his mother. He hated her at times, but he wasn't ready to lose her. This time, he knew he was going to be left behind.

"Juli, you're old enough to go out and work now. You can find a job just about anywhere. I'll leave you some money, so you can get by for a while."

"Yeah, right, work in the mill or selling magazines. I'll make about a dollar a day if that much." He looked down at his feet in despair. He knew he couldn't stop his mother once she had decided what she wanted to do.

"Well, it's settled then." Millie stood up and began to walk out of the room, thinking Julian felt okay with it. "Mack's going to pick me up in the morning. You can stay here at the Sunset until you decide to go to work and get your own place. Fannie likes having you around to help with the chores, you know, and the girls are all fond of you. They like having you around because you help them with stuff and—"

"I don't want to be their maid service, I want to get out of here, with you!"

"Maybe we can send for you, once we get settled in. Would that be okay?"

"Yeah, sure," said Julian, resigned, knowing that he would probably never hear from his mom again.

"That sounds real good," said Millie. "I know you'll do just fine, Julian." It was done. Millie left the room. Julian felt betrayed and alone, again.

* * * *

The Friday morning air was humid. Mack loaded Millie's stuff into the back of his black Model T, his armpits stained with sweat. Julian had reluctantly come down from his room to see them off. Millie had roused him earlier and prepared breakfast for him and Mack down in the house kitchen. The two angry men in her life came in and sat at the small utility table in silence, as Millie fried up more bacon. For Julian, it was all he could do to be in the same room with Mack and he knew exactly how Mack felt about him. Julian didn't feel any need to hold back. If Mack started up, he was ready.

"What you going to be doing then, Julian?" asked Mack, shoving more bacon into his mouth. On the table was an overflowing ashtray and a lit cigarette, the smoke streaming up in gray layers over the table.

"What do you care?" replied Julian. Mack snapped a look at Julian, and Julian felt his blood run cold. Millie turned around from tending the next batch of eggs, ready to intervene.

"Listen, little buddy. Don't be giving me the smart

mouth or I'll slap you from here to the middle of next week."

Mack dropped his fork, picked up his cigarette, and leaned back. Julian sat with his head down, brooding. He could feel his blood pumping through his veins, his blood pressure soaring. He wanted to jump up and hit Mack as hard as he could. Julian knew he was no match; Mack probably had experience with this situation.

"Boys, just stop it. This isn't going to make it any easier," pleaded Millie. Julian looked up across at Mack. He knew it would probably get him another beating, but it didn't matter now. He had to say it.

"It would be easier if Mack would just go back to the hole he crawled out of."

Mack pointed his fork at Julian and glared down his nose at him, ready to get up.

"I'm warning you, boy, you'd better shut up."

Millie quickly wiped her hands off and came over to Julian. She leaned down and put her arms around Julian to hug him.

"Julian honey, please. Stop it. It's not going to change anything." Julian shook her off, turned in his chair, gave her one last stare, and left the kitchen. Mack resumed eating and didn't say another word. Millie leaned against the kitchen counter and put her face in the dish towel to hide her eyes.

Twenty minutes later, Mack and Millie were outside ready to go. On the porch, Fannie, Jean, and Lupe were watching and had already said their goodbyes. With a shawl around herself to keep warm, Millie walked over to Julian for one more hug before getting into the open-top car. Julian brushed off her kiss and hung his head; he didn't want to see them leave. Mack motioned for Millie to get in. She turned back to Julian—he stared up at her one more time.

"You always told me I was the most important person in your life."

"Honey, you are, you still are, but I've got to have someone. I need someone to live my life with." Her self-defense went unheard.

"Someday you'll wish I was around," said Julian. "Then you'll want me to be there." Julian pulled away from Millie and walked up to the back porch of the Sunset.

Reluctantly giving up, Millie turned around and got into Mack's car. Her life had been this, a family tree of bad choices, each one causing more grief and making a down payment on the next mistake to follow. Millie was unable to see beyond her need to have someone to rely on. This gruff, anti-social loner seemed to fit the bill.

Mack jerked the shifter into gear and, with a pop and a honk, backed out of the driveway and drove off, leaving a cloud of dust, smoke, and the fading noise of his car. Millie didn't turn back. Julian stood there for a moment. He felt stunned. He wanted to scream.

Julian looked around to see if anyone was watching, but he was alone. In a few seconds, he heard the unmistakable sound of Fannie stomping toward him. The screen door flew open.

"Get your butt back in here and get your chores done, quit your moping around, now! I haven't got all day. Get upstairs and gather up the laundry!"

Julian ran back into the house and started picking up

the sheets from the previous night, occasionally wiping tears from his eyes. Outside each room were piles of sheets the ladies had left to be picked up in the morning for laundry. Up and down the hall he moved, gathering each set and running them down to the basement to be laundered. With each sheet, Julian thought to himself how badly he wanted to get out of this stupid place—he wanted a different life than this.

It suddenly occurred to him that he did know a way to get out of town. He stopped in his tracks as he remembered the chest at Shorty's house. Now he was ready to go get it. Whatever it took, he had to do it—this was his ticket out of town.

* * * *

Monday after school, the determined barefoot boy took off toward the Dean's place. Before long, he was standing next to a large oak tree a few hundred feet away from their house, watching to see if there was any activity in the yard. Julian knew the doors would be unlocked—the Deans didn't have to lock up; they had dogs and guns. *Probably took the dogs to work with him, that's what he usually does*, Julian told himself.

The white clapboard house was set back from the gravel road about eighty feet and on the slope of a hill. On the left side of the house, a dirt lane led back to a large open gravel parking area and several outbuildings and sheds. Large trees shaded parts of the house. The porch area was open except for four posts holding up the roof.

The house looked quiet, and more importantly, nothing moved or barked. Julian walked slowly, trying not to make any sound, staying in the dust and avoiding the gravel. Once safely at the steps, he tiptoed across the front porch and opened the screen door. He twisted the knob on the front door and walked inside.

Right away, the stench of three bachelors almost forced him to turn back. His life in an environment of heavy perfumes and dreamy aromas of fresh cooking hadn't prepared him for this. The stench of body odor, dirty feet—and maybe someone didn't flush the toilet for a couple of days—could forever destroy his senses. *They aren't bringing women in here, that's for sure.* He wondered to himself if this might be the real reason Fannie broke up with Shorty.

There was hardly room to walk so Julian knew that finding Fannie's precious tin box in this mess would be near impossible. As Julian tumbled his way toward what he was hoping would be Shorty's bedroom, he stubbed his toe on a rifle lying on the floor and let out a loud cry.

Julian jumped up and rushed into the first room he could find. Lucky for him, it turned out to be Shorty's room, the only bedroom on the main floor. He opened drawers, moved boots, and casually tossed clothes, guns, and hats to clear his way. *That stupid box is not that small. It has to be somewhere in this pile of crap.*

"Ah ha!" Julian found the tin box just under the far side of the bed covered up with a blanket. He looked it over and found a hole where a small key was needed to unlock it.

"Dang, I don't have time to find the stupid key," he

muttered. Julian picked it up with a grunt and returned to the front door and pushed it open, absentmindedly letting the screen door slam behind him as he started across the front porch to the steps.

In a split second, he heard a sound that gave him a cold shiver—it might as well have been death tapping him on the shoulder, only it was worse. A tap on the shoulder from the dark angel would be a peaceful moment compared to the raging killers running toward him in the form of two big, ugly, hungry, man-eating dogs at dinnertime. Amazingly, in the same instant, Julian remembered every word of the Lord's Prayer. "Our Father, who art in Heaven, hallowed be thy name. Thy kingdom come, thy will be done . . ."

With no time to run off the steps, especially carrying a heavy tin box, he instinctively moved back toward the front door and froze. His eyes bulged as two fierce barking canines ran right up to him, inches from taking their first bite of Julian Daniels.

He was prepared for his life to flash before his eyes. *Will anyone really know what happened to me?* The authorities would find fresh bone fragments and a small and empty tin chest, that's all. *Maybe not even that—Shorty would most likely hide the gold again and throw what's left of his bones out in the yard for the dogs to play with.* Then, sadly, no one would ever know what happened.

The dogs' barking was aggressive and angry, backing up and then jumping toward him as if they were going to leap into his face.

Julian noticed that if he just looked up and not directly into their eyes, the intensity of their attack let up slightly. He stood as still as he could and closed his eyes, his thoughts of dying a gruesome death, of becoming dog food, eased into acceptance of the inevitable. His body relaxed. After a moment, he wondered why they hadn't eaten him. *Are these dogs going to save me for later? Maybe they just want to see me crap my pants.*

After a few seconds, he began to block out the constant barking of the dogs. He stared out beyond Shorty's driveway thinking that if a chance came up to run, he wanted to know what obstacles would be in his way. It certainly would be sad to have a chance to run, only to trip on another root, then be mauled. A gravel driveway, ditch, trees. *If they do back off, I'll have to run real damn fast.*

Then, he heard another sound coming from the back-yard—it was a truck. The dogs quit barking and turned their heads to listen. Shorty had just pulled in.

The dogs bolted from the front porch around to the side of the house, to warn their master.

Julian took off running, carrying the heavy tin chest with both hands, hoping with his life that the dogs would be distracted long enough for him to make a clean getaway. He was wrong—again.

He had barely reached the end of Shorty's dirt drive-way when he heard the dogs running toward him and even more intense barking.

Julian had taken off from Shorty's house in the oppo-site direction from home and was headed straight for a wooded area with a creek running through it. If nothing else, he assumed, the dogs would have to fight their way through the brush to get to him—but he didn't realize this was their true specialty, hunting the elusive prey, stupid prey—barefoot prey that liked to run and hide in bushes. Julian struggled through the brush, while the dogs gained on him. He bolted sideways and ran back to the side of the road so he could run faster.

Just before they were about to nip his heels, a small black Model T puttered past Julian. He tossed the chest in the back and then jumped in himself, the dogs trailing behind but starting to slow. Julian kept his head down, lying flat on the bed of the truck. The driver, a gray-haired woman, didn't turn back. The truck kept a steady speed down the road.

Another mile down, the small pickup pulled up to a feed store and stopped. The driver, apparently still unaware of the weight difference in the back, got out of her truck and walked into the store. Julian, thanking God for the twelve-thousandth time, sat up and picked up the tin box.

The walk home was just like being in church, waiting for the potluck to begin. He just knew it was going to be good.

CHAPTER 6
Time to Go

The next afternoon, Julian kept to himself in his attic room, so he could prepare to leave. He knew his life wasn't worth a plug nickel in Joplin any longer and was surprised the Dean boys hadn't come for him already.

Late last night, when it was dark and still, he went out behind the Sunset and buried his stolen treasure. He would be traveling by foot and knew it would be impossible to carry the box with him.

It was mid-morning by the time Julian got up. Urgent to get down to the shared hallway bathroom, he desperately hoped no one else would be around. When he finished and was coming out to go back upstairs, a door opened down the hall.

"Julian." Julian spun around and, in the shadows, he could see Lupe standing in her doorway.

"Can you come here for a minute?" she asked. Julian looked over at Lupe and grinned. She had been teasing him lately, pinching his sides whenever they passed in the hallways. He had been warned to stay away from the girls, but he didn't care anymore. Who was there to care?

"You know, I'll get in trouble if I get near you."

"I'm not gonna hurt you. Anyway, your mama's gone now, ain't nobody gonna bother us. Just come over here and see me for a minute."

"Lupe, I got a new mama, Miss Fannie. She's pretty sure *she's* my new mama and she'll beat both our butts to mashed potatoes if she catches me here with you," Julian said. He looked away from Lupe, but he couldn't deny that he felt attracted to her. He didn't know what it was, but he felt a warm, anxious feeling when she talked to him.

"But I want to be your friend, Julian." Lupe worked her way up close to Julian and gave him a long kiss, bringing a rush of warm blood throughout his body. He fought for a small moment until his warm, taffy-like muscles gave way. When she finished, she smiled and wiggled away to her room.

It took Julian a few seconds to recover before hurrying back to his room. After he closed the door, he let out a deep sigh and realized that was exciting but close. He had already been in enough trouble so far and certainly didn't need any more attention on himself.

* * * *

Saturday morning is the time to be quiet. The ladies had worked through a long night and they would be sleeping in late this morning. Julian knew it would be extra chores and possibly a beating if he woke anyone up. Today was special, so if he moved around at all, it had to be like a prowling cat, every step planned before the next.

For now, though, he lay still on the flat mattress up in his loft, thinking about Jean, Lupe, and his new feelings toward girls. He wondered about his encounter with Lupe.

For Julian, who desperately wanted to be loved, it was an agonizing choice. He had to keep telling himself that it didn't matter. He had to go ahead with his plans—he had already decided—he knew what he had to do.

As he lay on his rumpled bed, Julian thought of the heavy tin box he had buried in the backyard. He had convinced himself that it would be too much to carry with him; besides, someone would probably rob him, anyway. He was sure it would be safer here until he could come back when he was better prepared to put it somewhere safe. Still, it was tempting—the thought that so much money was just sitting there waiting for him to pluck out a few coins.

But, it wasn't his. He couldn't answer the *Why not just give it back to Fannie and leave with a clear conscience?* question. He still held on to the dream of a quick remedy to his problems. Except, now the person he needed the remedy for had abandoned him. He didn't need to fix anything, except his own leaving.

Julian rolled over and got up on his hands and knees, carefully loosened a board on the wall with his fingers, and pried it open. He pulled it out, just a few inches, then reached in and pulled out a red Sir Walter Raleigh tobacco tin. He pulled the top off, turned it over, and dumped out the contents on his mattress, spreading out the coin and paper money to count it. With the five dollars his mom left him, $3.35 in change, and twenty $1 bills he saved doing various chores, asking drunk guys for milk money, and digging through customers' pockets and robes, he had a total of $28.35. With this much traveling money, he could get to the coast, he thought. He was set—almost.

He pulled on his best worn-out pair of jeans. Over his undershirt, he ceremoniously put on a long-sleeve cotton shirt, something he couldn't remember doing except on those rare visits to church. The sleeves didn't quite fall to his wrists, but he knew he would roll them up anyway. It was exciting to him—he was doing something. He leaned over and pulled out a pair of worn brown hand-me-down shoes and tied them tight. For a young boy used to running around barefoot with barely a stitch on, this amount of heavy clothing made him feel awkward and stiff. Now, just one more thing to do.

Julian neatly folded up the money he saved and stuffed half of it in one shoe and half in the other. He grabbed his beat-up fedora hat, a prized possession left behind by a traveling salesman, and a small duffel bag stuffed with a few clothes, and carried it over to the door.

He glanced around one more time to make sure he had cleaned everything out. Funny, the room looked weak and empty, too small to hold his dreams back. He smiled and allowed himself a moment, for the future he imagined here was now beginning. He turned and stepped out of his attic room, careful not to make the boards creak.

Julian walked down the well-worn steps and into the main upstairs hallway covered with a shabby carpet runner, a barely visible Persian motif. In the dark evenings, it appeared almost elegant, in the morning shadows, tattered and dog-eared.

Julian crept down the hallway. Then, he noticed one more hurdle: getting past Miss Fannie's room. Julian held his breath as he walked by her doorway. Thank God it was closed. He delicately lifted the screen door to keep it from squeaking and pushed it open.

The sun was just beginning to throw beams of light across the horizon; a warm breeze ruffled his shirt. He felt alive; the fresh air smelled like a new adventure. His plan—his future—was beginning: head north to Kansas City and from there, catch a train west.

Julian walked down the dirt alley for a short way, then turned around to have one last look at the Sunset brothel. He pulled his hat down tight, threw his duffel bag over his shoulder, and without notice, slipped away from his small southern Missouri town, sure that no one would ever miss him.

Dust from the dirt road swirled around his brown shoes as he made his way out to the main highway. He leaned down, picked up a rock, and heaved it into a nearby pond still shrouded in a morning mist. A dark-haired skinny kid, damn sure he wouldn't ever again be teased or slapped by another madam or get pushed around by drunk customers. Most of all, he wanted to start clean. So far, things were looking really good.

* * * *

After two days, four blisters, and a bad case of alone, Julian's last ride dropped him off on the outskirts of Kansas City, Missouri, and he stood wondering if it mattered which direction he walked. Along the way, he had managed to hop rides with several farm wagons, a talkative farmer with chickens, and one jerky, exciting ride in a new automobile. He slept one night at a farmer's house and one night in a wheat field. His last ride, a trucker hauling ears of corn to a local cannery, told Julian this was where he had to get off.

As the trucker drove away, Julian threw his arm up to wave goodbye and thanks, looking forward to seeing what kind of city Kansas City had become, since he last saw it with his mother. Julian didn't have time to reminisce—he had to keep moving. He turned and walked west, toward the train station. Julian's next stop: Cheyenne, Wyoming.

CHAPTER 7

Dixie's Diner

It had been two full days of travel in the well-used passenger train before the porter announced the next stop would be Cheyenne, Wyoming. Curled up on a leather bench, Julian tried to get a little sleep before reaching his destination, but between the side-to-side rocking of the railcar, the endless clatter of rails, stops with no one boarding, and his nightmares, he felt wrung out.

Rumors had been going around between passengers that this rail service was going to be discontinued. New roads were being built; more people were driving themselves west, loaded down in old Model Ts and remodeled delivery trucks to carry lifetime possessions cross-country.

Hearing the voice of the porter yelling out the imminent arrival of their destination, Julian lifted himself to stare out the window. He remembered leaving Kansas City, its trees and greenery so thick that he was unable to look past the rail right-of-way. This landscape stretched out before him was an endless plain, with few trees or green bushes in sight, just the colors of tan and blue meeting at some distant point on the horizon.

Now and then, he saw a lonely farmhouse, or someone scratching the earth's surface, asking for a hand. It did not look like they were going to get an answer. He wondered if there would be a town to arrive in. He put his face against the window looking west, hoping to see something ahead that would encourage him. Nothing—just small hills of rock, sand, and dirt. On the other side of the railcar, he could see a few travelers on the highway, both coming and going, each one with their reason. Julian hoped he had made the right choice.

As Julian stepped down off the Union Pacific passenger train in Cheyenne, he was sore, stiff, and hungry. With hunger gnawing at his insides, it was time to find food.

Walking through the station, Julian was awed at the magnificent structure that seemed so out of place in this windy, wide-open country.

He limped through the cavernous marble-floored train station and out into the bright sunshine of this hard-looking town, which, at a glance, seemed to him like the end of the line. The mountains to the west were so far away, high, and seemed impenetrable. When he turned back east to look up the street, he was even less impressed. He thought, *Is this why they call it the plains, 'cause it's so plain?*

Swirls of dust blew down the main road, shocking Julian with a cool breeze against his tired body. Shivering, he quickly learned that sunshine felt warm and, in this country, the shade was very cold. After walking for a while, his stiff muscles loosened up and he felt better.

The cool, dry air had a clean flavor all its own until he got a whiff of something being fried down the street, recharging him from his hunger pangs and reminding him that he was hungrier than a range buffalo. Down on the left side of the road, he could see a sign: DIXIE'S DINER.

That'll have to do, his stomach told him.

As Julian walked in, a young couple with a baby was just leaving. Julian held the door open with one hand and put his duffel bag on his other shoulder. The wind blew his brown hair down over his eyes. As he let go of the door, he brushed his hair back so he could see where he was headed. Inside, two older men sat in one of the corner booths, one of them nimbly rolling a small cigarette with his fingers, the other sipping black coffee from a stained china cup. Far on the other side, in the back corner, he saw an empty booth and quickly walked over to it. The heavy smell of fried food, cooking spices, and freshly brewed coffee reminded him of home.

He closed his eyes and let his tense shoulders relax, settling into the booth. When he opened his eyes, someone was standing beside him, tapping a pencil on a pad.

"Where you goin', kid?" asked the waitress, whose nametag read DIXIE. Her wire-rimmed glasses, anchored by a gold chain, defied gravity, barely clinging to the end of her pointed nose.

"Not sure yet," Julian answered. "Just west, to find work."

"There are jobs all over the place, if you don't mind working for free, ha!" she said, sweeping the room for the audience's reaction.

Julian stared up at her like she was senseless. "Yeah . . . well, I need to make some money, so I can eat." Julian didn't mean to be rude to the lady, he just wanted dinner.

"A lot of these ranches up here will feed you and give you five dollars a month spending money for a clean shirt if that's the kind of work you want. Anyway, you gonna order something?" Dixie licked the end of her short worn-out pencil and put it down on her order pad, ready to write.

"I'll take some pancakes, ma'am, and some juice."

"Ah, you got money?" She hesitated and raised one eyebrow.

"Yeah." He wondered to himself, *Why would she ask that?*

"Coming right up, then. Monte, grub!" she yelled. "Give me a set of flaps for the young gentleman here!" She glanced back at Julian and told him that he might want to go in and wash up, so he could find his mouth to put food in it.

Julian got up and walked to the other side of the restaurant to the bathroom. Once he looked in the mirror, he knew why she asked. He didn't look like he could pay for someone's free advice, let alone food.

He washed his face, hands, and arms in the bathroom sink. Staring in the mirror, Julian hadn't realized how much he had grown in the last few months. His pants didn't seem to cover as much of his legs as they used to. No wonder his feet hurt.

Julian wiped up and went back out to his booth. Dixie stopped in her tracks; she couldn't believe what she was seeing. Julian could feel his face getting warmer; it seemed everyone in the place was staring at him. She walked up with his juice and coffee and inspected Julian's face.

"Well, now, don't you look a lot better, son. I win my bet with the cook; I told Monte you *were* human. I'll go get your cakes." She turned and walked over to the kitchen window to pick up Julian's order. When she came back, she slid the plate over in front of Julian and leaned over.

"Listen, kid, if you need some help or a place to stay, you let me know, okay? My name's Dixie. Maybe you could wash dishes for me."

"Thanks, ma'am, I'm okay for now. I need to keep moving."

"Suit yourself, young man. Thanks for coming in."

When Julian finished, he grabbed his bag and left seventy-five cents for the meal and a ten-cent tip for Dixie.

The breeze coming at him from the west felt stronger than when he walked over to Dixie's. Julian pulled his hat down in front of his face as far as he could. After walking a few minutes, he stopped and grabbed a flannel shirt out of his bag and threw it on over his light cotton shirt. He knew that he had been lucky up until now, catching rides up from Joplin to Kansas City, but from Cheyenne West, it appeared that the road was going to be rougher and probably with fewer rides. He was sure he couldn't afford the train any farther west unless he found a job and saved some money.

As he walked into town, he could see quite a few homes north of Main Street, but farther north, it looked like more prairie. He wondered if it might be best to take Dixie up on her offer, stay in this town a while and save up some money. He could learn how to wash dishes.

South of the railroad tracks was a collection of shacks and a few barns, so he turned north from Main Street, hoping to find a park or someone's yard to rest in.

North of Main Street, where all the businesses huddled together, he walked up a road passing several big homes, a school, and a small corner market. Stopping, he could see that the homes became more spread out over the countryside.

This seemed so foreign to Julian. In the south, whether you were in town or the country, there were always so many trees and bushes that sometimes you couldn't see the home next to yours. Here, there was nothing to hide what you did or what you saw.

As Julian passed a large home on a corner lot with a front yard sloping down to a barrow pit, he found a spot in the sun, far enough away from the house so he couldn't be seen. Julian threw down his duffel bag and pulled out another shirt to put around his shoulders. Sitting down on the cold brown grass and weeds, he hugged his legs and curled over, putting his head against his knees.

Julian had barely closed his eyes when he heard someone scuff their shoe in gravel. The sound moved toward him.

"What the hell are you doing on our place?" yelled a young voice standing a few feet away.

Julian opened his eyes, put his hands up to shield them from the sun, and glanced in the direction of the voice to see the silhouettes of three boys. Just as he turned to get up, one of them pushed him over and another kicked him deep in his side.

"Ahh, God!" Julian yelled. He rolled to one side and looked up to see several boys. One of the kids lunged forward and hit Julian in the face, then a hard kick landed on his shins, breaking the skin. Julian propped up on his elbows, rolled over on his side, and yelled back. "Stop it, I didn't do nothin'!"

Just then a woman's voice yelled out. "Jeremiah! Robert! Freddy! You boys stop that!" A young woman came rushing up the side of the road, toward the boys. The boys spun around and froze. Julian saw the menacing glare she gave them. Maybe they had seen this look before.

"We were just trying to get this kid off Pasky's place!" one of the boys yelled out in vain. He began backing away. The lady had a mad look in her eye and walked right up to his face.

"You let John worry about his own yard. This boy is none of your concern. Leave him alone!" she scolded. The first boy turned and ran, followed by another. One boy was left facing the woman.

"Sorry, Miss Tanner," he said, his voice apologetic.

"Freddy Perkins, I'm surprised that you, of all people, would be involved in something like this, really! Help me get him up."

Miss Tanner and Freddy helped Julian to his feet. It was all Julian could do to stand up. After being beaten up, his body was stiff and sore.

"Miss Tanner, I was just tagging along with Jeremiah and Robert and they started picking on this kid," said Freddy.

"Well, you get along and see that you don't tag along with those two again, and I'll be talking to your mother about your behavior."

Freddy turned and walked in the opposite direction from where the other boys went.

Julian leaned down to pick up his travel bag, and when he turned back to face his rescuer, she reached over to brush Julian's shirt off. He jerked back in reaction to a hand coming at him.

"It's okay, son, I'm not going to hurt you." With warm

fingers, she delicately brushed away his long scraggly hair
and turned his cold, bruised face side to side, looking him
over with a perceptive eye. Even with her precise care, he
winced in pain as bruises were touched.

"So, what's your name, son, where do you live?" she
asked.

"My name is Julian, ma'am, Julian Daniels, I'm from
Missouri," Julian replied, wiping the tears from his eyes.
The pain from getting kicked and hit was unbearable, and
he felt sick. Miss Tanner gripped his arms to hold him
steady. Julian shivered and felt as if his knees were going
to give out on him.

"Do you have a place or family here in Cheyenne?"

"No, ma'am. I'm by myself, traveling through," he
said.

"Well, you're not traveling anywhere right now." She
examined his skinny frame, bruises, and ragged clothes
and shook her head in disgust. "Julian, my name is Catherine Tanner, I'm one of the teachers here at the grammar
school. You're going to come with me, and we'll get you
mended up, all right?"

"Yes, ma'am. Thank you for helping me."

"You're welcome, son. Anyway, from the way you
look, you wouldn't get to the edge of town, let alone over
any mountain passes. We'll get you mended up a bit before
you think about going any farther." Catherine pulled her
scarf around her face, grabbed one of Julian's arms to
guide him, and turned into the wind for the short walk to
her house.

* * * *

The two-story, white clapboard house featured a covered porch held up by four white posts. The front door held a thick beveled glass window, framed with a white lace curtain that hid the view into the front living room. Catherine bought the house from her parents after she completed graduate school in Denver and got hired to teach in the Cheyenne schools.

Catherine was excited that other homes were finally being built in the neighborhood. The town had been plotted well out into the countryside, but the roads were paved only in the main parts of town.

Catherine's father, Jim, had planted several pine trees over the few years he and his wife Anna lived there, but with the short growing season, they had only grown a few feet, feeble protection against the fierce wind and snow storms that blew through this country. Given enough time, Catherine was sure they would help and knew her house was built solid. It had become her private sanctuary, a comfortable refuge against man, beast, and weather.

When they arrived, Catherine pushed open the front door and helped Julian hobble inside and over to a sofa. Julian lay down, his muscles still aching, mumbling that it felt so good to relax on something soft.

"Let me get some wet towels. I'll be right back, you just lie still," she commanded to Julian with a stern finger. By the time Catherine came back, Julian had fallen asleep. Instead of waking him, she just took his shoes off and covered him up. *Poor kid*, she thought to herself, *who knows what he's been through.*

Later in the afternoon, she noticed her homeless boarder waking up. Catherine got busy preparing a bath and laid out towels and a bar of soap.

* * * *

When Julian opened his eyes, he was confused, until he heard a voice come from the back of the room. He leaned forward to get up, but the pain in his sides quickly put him back down.

"How are you feeling?" asked Catherine, watching him from a rocking chair a few feet away. He moved slightly to look.

"Oh, I'll be okay, I guess, just need to patch up a little."

"If you want, you can clean yourself up in the tub. I put some towels out for you. Are you hungry?"

Julian could smell something cooking and his hunger pangs were already grumbling. Catherine got up and walked into the kitchen.

"Thank you, yes ma'am, I sure am."

"Well, you get cleaned up and then we'll get you fed. Throw your clothes out in the hallway and I'll get them washed for you," Catherine called from the kitchen. As soon as she mentioned clothes, Julian thought of the money he'd stashed in his shoes.

"Miss, are my shoes here somewhere?" Julian asked politely.

"Yes, over by the table, and don't worry, your money's safe in your shoes, or what's left of them. And I'm pretty sure your toes are getting too big for your shoes," Catherine quipped. "I'll pick up a newer pair for you from the church along with some larger clothes, as soon as I get a chance to walk over there."

"Thank you, ma'am." Without saying another word, Julian went into the bathroom and in a few minutes, threw a ragged heap of ornery-smelling clothes out in the hallway. After draining out the dirty tub water and wiping down the ring around the inside, Julian put on the clothes neatly folded on the toilet lid and walked out to the dining room where Catherine had already put a large scoop of fried potatoes on his plate. As Julian worked on his meal, Catherine asked him about where he came from. Once Julian finished telling his story, she was amazed he had made it this far.

"Look at the bruises all over your body, Julian. You're just a kid. A few bruises, cuts, and scrapes are part of life, but you're a mess. You're still young enough and you'll mend okay, in time. But, if you're planning to go farther west, you'd better know what kind of country is ahead of you. You might think about staying around here for a little while until you're strong enough to travel again. It just gets tougher the farther west you go."

Julian thought for a while, then glanced up at Catherine. "Yes, ma'am. I'm feeling beat up right now, that's for sure."

"Well, I don't normally take in strays, but, you can stay here for a couple of days, so you can heal up. I'll ask at the church to see if anyone needs a young man to help around the farm or ranch."

"Thanks so much for the help, ma'am. I'll stay out

of the way and be going as soon as I can," he answered. Julian wanted to heal up quickly; he felt awkward in this situation with Catherine. Being helpless wasn't something he was used to.

"Julian, since you're not a student, you can call me Catherine."

"Yes, Catherine." Julian hesitated for a second. "So, you're a teacher, here in this town?"

"Yes, Julian. I teach several grades. Fourth and fifth. This is my second year."

"You seem, ah . . . you seem too pretty to be a teacher." Julian, curious how a woman—especially a beautiful woman like Catherine—got into an important job like teaching, felt embarrassed to ask.

"Well," Catherine said, "thank you, Julian. That was a nice compliment, I think." She smiled back at Julian across the table.

"I, I just had never seen a woman teacher, it just seems different to me." Julian kept eating between questions. "All of my teachers have been men."

"Yes, that has been the normal routine, up until a few years ago. I'd like to think in a few years, it will be normal to see women teaching. More and more, I meet young ladies who are thinking about becoming teachers. But, even so, it could take a few years before it will be common. Julian, did you attend school down in Missouri?"

"Yes, ma'am—I mean Catherine. I wasn't a good student, though. My mom didn't care what I did, as long as I stayed out of her way."

"Well, if you stay around here for very long, you should get back into school. You need to get your high school diploma, if nothing else. Surely you'll need that if you want to have any kind of career."

"Yeah, I will. Just depends on where I end up, I guess."

Catherine could tell Julian was worn out, physically and mentally. "Why don't you just go lie down and take it easy for a while? We'll see how things turn out, okay? I've got a spare bedroom upstairs, so let's put your stuff up there for now."

Finished with lunch and up in his temporary room, it didn't take Julian long to be fast asleep again. A full belly, clean clothes, real sheets on a real bed—it all seemed too good to be true. Someone was being nice to him. He had to be dreaming.

CHAPTER 8
Third Showing

In July 1928, Miss Catherine Marie Tanner had just turned twenty-five years old and had her own classroom with nineteen students; eight boys and eleven girls. Catherine, raised by Christian missionaries, was miraculously able to get past elementary and high school and into higher education without getting married. She credited her scrawny bird-like legs, thick glasses, and fervent reading habits.

The rules of the school district were very specific about teachers' outside activities and she was resolute to follow every one of them. To be seen with a man outside of the school environment was taboo—no dating—and in public, always present yourself with dignity and humility. Although not specifically stated in the teachers' contract, female teachers were expected to stay single. So far, she had been able to fulfill that contract. Her daily uniform consisted of gray ankle-length dresses—pants of any type were never allowed—and her blouses always covered up to the neck: plain, certainly nothing with color. This was normal, so the restrictions didn't bother her; in fact, she felt honored and proud to have the position.

The Reverend Jim and Anna Tanner, Catherine's parents, had been missionaries in India for three years before Anna got pregnant. In 1903, Catherine was born, so with the start of their family, they decided it would be best to come back to the States and settle down to raise their children in a stable environment. Eventually, Jim and Anna moved to the windy, plains town of Cheyenne, Wyoming to be near Anna's mother, Emma. Jim supplemented his earnings as a pastor by doing carpentry and painting work. The Tanners fortunately found a house close to Emma's home, and not too far from a church where he was to become the pastor.

The house was originally built by an Army sergeant who was stationed nearby at Fort Russell military post. When he got reassigned, the house became available just in time for the Tanner family to purchase, in 1906. Catherine was three years old at the time. Four years after Catherine was born, Anna gave birth to their second child, a son, James, in 1907.

Tragedy struck in 1911 when Catherine was eight years old. Her four-year-old brother Jimmy disappeared one Saturday afternoon. He just didn't come back from playing. Several members of the Tanner family came from far away to help search, along with most of the residents in the small city, to no avail. Though they were comforted and surrounded by their belief in God and family, Catherine's mom and dad were inconsolable. Little James was never found.

In 1920, after allowing Catherine to complete her basic schooling, seventeen-year-old Catherine was sent to preparatory school in Denver and her parents left to go back to the mission fields in India. For the time being, the house was rented out to an older couple who, fortunately, kept it in good condition.

On occasion, on orders from her parents, Catherine would take a bus trip up to Cheyenne to visit the house and check on her grandmother Emma.

Visiting the house in Cheyenne reminded her of James and, over the years, she never lost hope that she would someday find her brother. On one of her visits, she was shocked to find her parents' old house empty. Inquiring further, she had learned that the old gentleman and his wife had just left, without telling anyone. No one around knew them well enough to say for sure, but their clothes were gone and the house was clean. The house on Cribbon Street was back in her hands, and it needed someone to take care of it.

In India, Jim and Anna were fully engaged and dedicated to their missionary work, constantly in demand to organize congregations and build meeting halls. It didn't look like they would be coming back anytime soon. Even though they were sponsored by several churches, money was always tight. So, it was disturbing for Anna and Jim to read the news from Catherine about the renters abandoning the house. How would they pay the taxes? Keep the house up? Surely, it was providence as they read further in Catherine's letter that she had decided to move back up to Cheyenne and commute back to Denver as needed to finish her classes. Anna was thrilled that Catherine would be able to stay in the house and help keep an eye on her grandma Emma.

Within the year, Catherine had applied to the Cheyenne School District and, after several months of nervous anticipation, she received a letter of acceptance. She believed completely that the notoriety and popularity of the state's new governor, Nellie Tayloe Ross, America's first elected woman governor, had something to do with it. She was living in a new age of women's equality.

Sadly, a year later, just five days after her twenty-second birthday, Catherine received news that her dad had been killed in a train accident in India. Her mom, Anna, would be returning home in a couple of months after the replacement missionaries had arrived.

On her return, Catherine insisted that her mother move in with her, but Anna had already arranged to live with her mother, Emma, in her house, just a quarter mile from Catherine's. It was a good decision—a year later Catherine's grandmother passed away, with her daughter Anna and Catherine at her bedside. Anna decided to stay at her mom's house.

With her mother nearby, Catherine visited often and developed a close-knit group of girlfriends, attended the local Christian church where her dad had been a pastor, and worked diligently every night to keep up with grading papers and preparing the students' curriculum for the next day. Her weekends were filled with work on the house and garden. She felt comfortable and happy; her life was orderly and manageable.

* * * *

Julian spent most of Sunday lying down or with his feet in a big tub soaking in Epson salts. Catherine had seen the bottoms of his feet and declared them a disaster zone. She walked down to her church in the afternoon and picked up some boys' clothes and shoes that looked like Julian's size, did some sewing on his ragged clothes, and prepared her lessons for school.

Monday morning brought with it cold, gusty winds from the west, making the house feel like a freight train was passing by just outside the windows.

The loud wind woke Julian, frightening him at first. Julian heard a sound coming from downstairs, so he got up, put on pants and a shirt Catherine had left at the foot of his bed, and slowly made his way down to the kitchen. Whatever she was cooking smelled wonderful.

Catherine could hear him limping toward her, and without turning around she spoke. "Good morning, young man, are you feeling okay?"

"Yes, I'm feeling better, long as I don't bump any bruises."

"I'll bet they really hurt. If you can, you might want to rewrap some of those wrappings. I'll be off in a few minutes to my classroom, so if you'll sit down, I'll fill your plate."

Julian looked in amazement as his plate received a pile of fried potatoes, bacon, and eggs. He certainly didn't get this kind of treatment back home. He was used to self-serve meals.

"Now, I can't do this every morning, but I think we need to fatten you up a little bit," Catherine said. "You're pretty thin for a boy your age."

"Please, ma'am—ah, Catherine—that's plenty." Julian accepted another spoonful of potatoes and began eating. "I'll work on your yard today, ma'am—uh, I mean, Catherine—and clean up around the shed."

"Don't worry about that, just light duty, you don't need any more bruises."

"Yes, ma'am . . . Catherine." Catherine put on her coat and told Julian to read a book if he got bored. She would be back in the late afternoon after school was out. Wearing lace-up black shoes, an ankle-length dark gray dress, and a starched white blouse, her large overcoat and scarves flowing behind her, she grabbed up a large pile of papers and books, gave Julian one last smile, and flowed out the back door.

The screen door slammed against the frame and quickly the house became very still. Julian sat for a few minutes and thought about where he was. It amazed him to think that he was here in some stranger's house, in some strange town, eating her food and she just left him alone. Back in Joplin, he would have quickly gathered up what he could and made his way off down the alleys. Here, of course, he didn't know where the alleys led to.

He finished his breakfast and then hobbled into the living room to lie down, his belly bulging from the plateful of food he had just devoured. He made his way over to the large stuffed sofa, threw a couple of small pillows to one end, and plopped himself down.

After a while, he thought, *You know, this is nice, this must be the good life everyone talks about.* Julian let his thoughts drift while his eyes panned over Catherine's furniture and belongings. *This is a great place, for a teacher.*

As Julian daydreamed, the colors in the draperies reminded him of the Sunset. He began to think about Maria, his friend from school, and Lupe, the girl from the Sunset. In a few minutes, with a full stomach and love on his mind, he drifted into sleep.

What Julian wasn't counting on were the nightmares from his past life at the Sunset and verbal scolding from Fannie. He woke up from his restless sleep with a jolt, hitting the rug-covered floor hard, and bumping his bruises.

"Damn," Julian said. He gingerly crawled back up onto the sofa, took a deep breath, and decided to lie on the bed in the upstairs bedroom Catherine wanted him to use. He stopped at a bookshelf and found some titles that looked interesting. After he pulled them out, he slowly made his way up to the bedroom. Crawling onto the bed, he tried to read for a while but fell back asleep.

Later in the afternoon, his boredom reached its peak. He got up and wandered around the house again. On the upstairs landing, he glanced casually into each of the other rooms to see what Catherine had that might be interesting to him. The room next to the one he was using, at the front of the house, was used to store boxes, books, papers, and several pieces of old furniture. Julian walked to the back of the house and into a bedroom that he thought certainly must be Catherine's. The room was plush and full of memorabilia.

A large fluffy quilt lay over the bed. Small pillows, dark curtains, and pictures of her family on the nightstand. Catherine's room was the biggest of the three bedrooms and contained some unusual pieces of furniture. What stood out to Julian was the dark wood bed frame, which appeared too large for the room and featured several strange carvings on the tall headboard.

Julian walked closer to see the picture on the

nightstand when something on the tall dresser caught his eye. It was an ornate chest. He figured it must have been at least ten inches wide and six or seven inches tall, covered with carvings. To Julian, it looked oriental, with Chinese-like figures carved around the outside with a small lock on the hasp. *Hmm . . . This chest must have something valuable in it, to be locked up like this.* He lifted it. It seemed heavy for its size.

Let's have a look inside, he thought. Julian opened the nightstand drawer and searched for a key. Nothing. He went through some of the dresser drawers and still, found no key. Eventually, he wandered into the other rooms, searching for something to help him get it open. He knew his room didn't have any keys, so he walked again into the spare room next to his and looked into boxes, to see what he could find.

He decided to open the two doors to the clothes closet and pushed aside clothes and a few boxes, then he noticed a small door on the back wall of the closet. *That's strange*, he thought. It seemed to be maybe two and a half feet square. *I wonder what that's for?* He got down on his knees to examine the door.

The door had a small crystal knob on one side. He pulled on it, but at first, it didn't budge, so he tugged harder and it squeaked open. A rush of cool air brushed past his face and, as he peered inside, it was pitch black. Not a speck of light or reflection. He sat back on his butt, glaring at the black space. *Can't see a damned thing,* he thought. Julian glanced around the room, leaned back, and picked up a small box lying next to a stack of larger boxes. He took careful aim and threw the box into the black space.

To his surprise, he heard the sound of the box hitting and sliding on the floor. Just like any box, but he couldn't see it anymore. It was just gone. Again, he sat for a few seconds, trying to figure out what this was. Julian wondered, *If I put something in here when I'm ready to go, I'll know where it is. I'll take off in the morning after she leaves for school. She won't miss it, in that short of time.*

He got up and walked back into Catherine's room. He stood for a while and looked at the chest on top of her dresser. *It's got to be full of valuable stuff, just like Fannie's.* His mind wrestled with promises made, the wrong thing to do, and what he should do. *I told Mom if I had money, I'd come and save her—what about the gold coins at Fannie's? Will it still be there?* With no point of reference to consequences, he grabbed Catherine's carved box from the top of her dresser and took it to the smaller bedroom at the front of the house.

With the small door to the black space wide open, he thought it would be easy to just drop it in and shut the door. As he gently sank onto his sore knee, he lifted the chest and leaned into the darkness, to shove the box in. The chest was heavier than he had imagined, especially when he tried to put it toward the back, into the dark area, where it couldn't be seen.

He sat it down and then lifted it one more time to get it farther back in, this time putting his full weight on the sore knee—and the pain shot through his body, making him jerk forward into the dark space. His face fell hard on the box and he let out a yell as he crashed on the chest, hitting the floor and rolling over on his side. He pushed against the floor to lift himself, enough to turn around and leave, bumping the edge of the door on the inside, near the jamb, and it swung shut.

The darkness was absolute and frightening. Julian quickly slugged the little door open with his fist, letting fresh light stream inside. He pushed the chest out of his way and fell out onto the wood floor, breathing hard. Julian stood up, brushed off his borrowed pants, and let out a big sigh before he stopped cold in his tracks.

Something didn't seem right. He looked around. A minute ago, this room was full of boxes, and stacks of old papers, and the smell was different. It took him a few seconds to register his thoughts.

"Weird," he whispered. He thought maybe he had come out on a different side of the house. He cautiously walked out of the bedroom and onto the landing area of the stairway. Julian turned around and was sure he was in the right room, but now the whole upstairs seemed different. The house was empty. *What is happening? This is weird*, he thought.

Julian rushed into Catherine's room and looked around. Nothing—a bare, empty room. He turned and ran downstairs. Catherine's furniture was gone. His pulse rate increased, fear poured over him, and for a moment, he wondered if he had brain damage from his beatings.

A noise he wasn't familiar with distracted him, coming from outside the house. Julian hunkered down until the noise went away. He limped slightly as he walked over to the front window and stared out: a green lawn, cement sidewalk, and a paved street lined with large shade trees. His mouth fell open; he was trying to take it all in as he compared the lush green vision in front of him to the dry, dirt-covered yard that used to be there.

A sleek blue automobile drove by. Startled, he jumped back from the window, then quickly looked again. He stared down the street and saw more, many more of those funny-looking vehicles. *What in the good Lord's name are those? Automobiles? Spaceships?* Maybe he'd been taken to Mars. *What are those things?*

He stepped back from the window and peered toward the back of the house. Julian felt himself begin to shake; he knew he was breathing hard and tried to calm himself down. But he was curious—maybe he did have brain damage. "This can't be happening," he murmured.

He glanced out the window by the front door again, but this time he didn't see any moving vehicles, so he opened the door and cautiously stepped outside. He spied a rolled-up newspaper in the corner of the lawn, so he ran over and picked it up, then sprinted back up on the porch and into the house. Julian unwrapped the paper and read the date. Friday, July 14, 2000. *No way . . . oh, good Lord Almighty, what have I done!* Julian's head spun with wild thoughts. He was sure that he was in a dream.

Julian spent a few more minutes wandering through the house and looking again and again at the paper to make sure he didn't misread it. In the kitchen, he found a small card and a ballpoint pen lying on the counter. The name Samantha Bingham was printed across the middle of the card. WILD WEST REALITY—CHEYENNE, WYOMING, it read. He sighed. *At least I'm still in Cheyenne.*

The kitchen had completely changed from what he knew at Catherine's. The cabinets were new, white and the counters were covered with some kind of smooth rock, maybe marble. The lighting was nice, bright in the right places, and there was a counter between the kitchen and dining room with comfy stools. Julian sat in one for a few minutes and turned around and around.

Julian picked up the pen and, after a few minutes, realized that this thin black cylinder object did something. As he held it in his hand, he inadvertently clicked on the end of it and the small ball point popped out. He put it against the paper next to it and a scribbled line of ink appeared.

"Wow!" Thinking quickly, he did some crude arithmetic on the back of the card. *So, if this is 2000, that's seventy-two years gone by. Damn, this is too much to believe.* It was at this moment that Julian wondered if he had come on to something. *If I am really in this time, huh* . . . His mind rolled through possibilities. He tucked the business card into his pants pocket and turned to go upstairs.

Julian ran through his options: He knew for sure that Shorty, Pug, and Lenny were going to kill him. Now, Catherine would probably want to kill him, too. *But, if I'm here, they'll never find me!* Then he remembered his money and clothes back at Catherine's.

As Julian ran back upstairs, he wondered about the chest. *Damn, if Catherine notices that it's missing, I'll be a dead man. I've got to get my stuff, come back here, and make a clean getaway.* He knew he would have to hurry before she got home from school. Then it hit him—would he be able to go back? What if this was a one-way ticket?

In a few seconds, before returning to his time, Julian hid the box in the empty master bedroom and was back at the closet door and climbing inside. Julian thought, *If she catches me, I'll just play dumb. I don't know nothing about no box, yeah*. The plan was perfect, flawless. He closed the closet door behind him.

Sitting inside the pitch-black space, the anxious feeling returned. Julian prayed to himself, *I hope this works.* He opened the small door slowly so he wouldn't make a noise and peered out to see if he was in the right place. To his relief, he was back at Catherine's. Julian climbed out and shut the small door. He pushed the small boxes back where they were, in front of the door, and closed the bedroom door.

Julian hobbled down the stairs to get his things by the sofa when he heard the back door opening. *Damn it!* His heart sank—Catherine was home. Julian quickly sat on the sofa, his heart beating fast.

Catherine walked into the kitchen and dropped her books and papers on the counter. She took off her long overcoat, laid it over a chair next to the table, and peered into the living room.

"Well, how's our patient doing?" she asked Julian with a smile.

"Oh, I'm doing better, I think. Still sore, though," he replied.

"I'll just bet you are. Did you change those bandages, like I told you?"

"Ah, well, not really. I didn't think they needed it."

Catherine walked closer to where Julian was sitting and could see a little blood on part of his sock, below his dungarees.

"Well," she said, as she folded her arms, "you might want to rethink that plan." She glanced down at his leg, indicating with her nod that there was something to see.

Julian looked down and saw the blood.

"Whoa, well, ah. What do you know? But it didn't bother me, must have just happened, because—" Catherine stopped him before he could finish.

"Why don't you just march into the washroom next to the kitchen right now and change those out? I'll be back down in a few minutes to check on you." Julian had heard that tone of voice before; hearing it again now was starting to upset his stomach. As Catherine walked out of the living room, she gave Julian one last parting shot.

"You know, I deal with rascals like you every day," she said, pointing her index finger at Julian, a slight smile on her face, "so I'm gonna be pretty keen on making you get done what you need to get done, understand?"

Julian nodded, but his whole body screamed *Run!* He knew that in a few minutes, she would be using his full name. His stomach began to spin, and his instincts begged him to crawl under a rock for protection. He understood now why the tough kids had obeyed so well when she showed up to break up the beating they were giving him.

＊ ＊ ＊ ＊

Upstairs, Catherine walked into her bedroom and shut the door. At her dresser, she opened one of the drawers to take out a different blouse to wear. She glanced up at the pictures sitting on the top of the dresser and continued looking through the clothes. Finding one, she backed up and sat on the edge of the bed. She took off her thick black lace-up shoes and rubbed her feet.

Then, Catherine heard a woman's intuition bell ring. She looked back up to the top of her dresser. Something was different. Something was gone? Catherine stared a little longer, then it hit her—her Chinese gift box was gone. The carved box was given to her when she was a little girl; a missionary friend of her parents had given it to her. *Where is it? It's gone!* a voice inside her head yelled. Catherine quickly searched the room. Maybe she had moved it and had forgotten where she'd put it. She looked under the bed, in the closet, in a corner, in the spare rooms, in the hall closet—no, it was gone. *If I didn't forget where I put it, If I didn't move it, who would have?*

Catherine didn't want to think about it. She didn't want to believe that the person she was trying to help might have betrayed her, might have stolen something from her. Anger built up inside. She was mad at herself for letting this happen—how could she have been so stupid to allow this, why hadn't she put her guard up sooner, why did she let some stranger in the house?

Catherine went back to her bedroom and sat on the edge of her bed for a moment. She was so upset, she could spit. She hurriedly tucked her blouse in and put on a pair of house slippers. She prepared herself for the worst and marched downstairs to confront Julian. Her demeanor immediately became the stern disciplinarian she sometimes had to be.

* * * *

Julian was right—it didn't take long for the gates of hell to break open. As instructed, he had gone into the washroom to clean up his leg wound. When he heard stomping feet coming his way, as it happened so many times at Fannie's, it was almost too much for him to handle. He thought to himself, *Lord, just take me now.* In a matter of seconds, Catherine was at the washroom door.

"Julian! Where's my wooden box? Julian!" Catherine demanded, her angry eyes filled with hurt. "What did you do with my wooden hope chest?" Julian turned around. His brilliant plan started to crack.

"I don't know, what? What are you talking about?" He looked up at her with a perplexed expression, his best acting so far. Like a herd of charging dinosaurs, *Play dumb, play dumb* kept pounding through his mind.

"I have a small wooden keepsake box in my bedroom; it had important papers in it," she explained carefully. "It is of no use to anyone but me. Now . . . it's missing from my room. You were the only one in the house, so you must know where it is!"

Julian was still holding out, somehow believing he could handle this, acting like he didn't have a clue.

"I can't believe you would do this. I've been kind to you, Julian, and now you do this to me! Where is that chest? It has very valuable papers in it, nothing you would ever want or know what to do with." Catherine got up close to Julian, tears in her eyes, and stared him in the face. "*Give it back*, Julian."

Julian's heart was tearing itself apart. He knew he was wrong, and he was tired of being wrong, tired of being on the beating end of a stick.

"I don't know what you're talking about, really, I

don't," Julian offered bravely.

Catherine was distraught. Julian squirmed at her every word; he knew this was bad, but he couldn't confess now, it had gone too far and he knew she wouldn't believe his fantastic story about a magic door. *A small closet door that takes you to the future? Insane.*

Then with a calm, steady voice, Catherine gave Julian the ultimate slap in the face.

"Julian, I can't trust you in my house any longer, I want you to leave . . . now! Get your stuff and get out. Please do not come back, unless you're going to tell me where that chest is."

"Where am I going to stay? How am I going to eat?" he pleaded, hoping to stir up some small portion of softness in her heart.

"Well, I guess you should have thought of that sooner, Mr. Daniels. Now pack up and leave!"

With that, Julian got up and went to the upstairs bedroom—with Catherine close behind—to pack up his clothes. Without saying another word, he rolled his clothes into a small bag and made his way downstairs to the front door. He wondered how he was going to get that chest out now.

As the front door shut hard behind him, he could hear her making sure it was closed tight and the deadbolt firmly in place. Above him, a clap of thunder ripped through the valley and rain began to pelt the trees around him.

He knew that, unlike everyone else in this town, she would probably start locking doors. To Julian, however, the chest was not that important. It was the closet door.

As he walked away from Catherine's house, he openly

cussed at himself for being so stupid. Yet still nagging in the back of his mind, he couldn't stop wondering about what happened inside that small door.

Chapter 9

First Look

Cheyenne, Wyoming, 2000

"Wake up. Sarah! Wake up."

Twelve-year-old Sarah Roberts didn't want to wake up. Her father, Michael, rolled her over and brushed her bushy blond hair from her face.

"Babe, are you ready to get up?" he said. "Come on, Sarah, it's time to get moving. Little sister has already beaten you to the table."

Mike knew she didn't want to get up, sure that her spot was warm, cozy, and private. She would probably be content to just let this day happen without her.

"Sarah, come on, baby. Get your little hiney moving, let's go!"

Mike, trying to keep the girls on schedule, grabbed her up into his arms. Sarah screamed and laughed as he nudged his scratchy beard into her neck, dragging blankets, kid, and frizzy hair to the breakfast table.

"Here you go, honey. Do you want peanut butter on your toast? How about you, Gracie?"

"Yuck, Dad! Just jelly," eight-year-old Gracie replied.

"Do we have any juice?" asked Sarah.

"Sarah, the juice is on the table, duh!" said Gracie, getting up to walk out of the kitchen.

"Sarah, isn't today the day for the cheerleader tryouts?" asked Mike.

"Yep, and Dad, Jennifer's mom will be there," Sarah said. "Jennifer told her mom about you, so she'll be looking for you, huh, huh . . . huh, huh." Sarah motioned a dance move. "And you need to take me, too, so don't forget about that."

"That's right, how could I forget?" He sat down at the table with his morning coffee, watching Sarah eat her toast.

"You know, she's really cute and she's nice—to me, anyway. Of course, Jennifer doesn't think so. Her mom's always telling her not to do stuff. You know how parents are." Sarah smiled as she looked up at her dad.

"You mean, she's trying to discipline her child?"

"Yeah, I guess, but seems too strict to me."

"That's because you have a pushover for a dad."

"Sarah's been writing in my diary again. Tell her to stop it!" Gracie whined.

"I did not!" Sarah yelled.

"Sarah, you'd better not," Mike warned. "You guys nced to leave each other's stuff alone."

"I didn't touch her stupid book. Anyway, she's into my stuff all the time, too!" Sarah replied and caught herself admitting to the crime. "Oops."

"See!" Gracie said. "I told you she was—"

Gracie was interrupted by a knock at the back door. Mike walked over, opened the door, and Sarah's best friend Sophia, rushed in. She threw her school backpack across the floor, plopped herself in a chair, and scooted up next to Sarah. She shook her wild red hair away from the table and looked directly at Sarah with a grin. Then she smiled up at Mike.

"Good morning, Sophia." Mike tipped his coffee to Sophia.

"Hi, Mr. Roberts." She leaned forward close to Sarah and began quizzing her.

"Sophia?" Mike asked. "Do you want some juice?"

"No thanks, Mr. Roberts."

It was obvious to Mike that the two girls had more important things to discuss. While the girls went to their room to get ready, Mike got up and began cleaning up the breakfast dishes. He was glad to see the girls in a good mood and silently enjoyed the gossip and noisy house.

"Gracie, honey, do you have your stuff ready for school? Girls, do you want to ride with us?"

In a few minutes, Mike's silver SUV pulled away from the suburban home in the rolling hills outside of Cheyenne, Wyoming, full of girl talk and morning radio news.

* * * *

After dropping off the girls at school, Mike made his way through the morning rush hour. At thirty-two, Michael Gordon Roberts didn't have to work hard at keeping in shape. In addition to keeping up with the schedules of his two young daughters and working, he went to the gym at least three times during the week and jogged occasionally with a couple of friends.

The girls always seemed to have school projects, athletic competitions, or music lessons to go to. To make Mike's life more interesting, the ladies at the power company kept trying to play Cupid and match him up with some of their friends. He appreciated the thought, although, so far, none of the ladies had been the choice he would have made.

Mike wasn't thinking at all about finding someone. The importance of time had slipped away for him. Three years since Elizabeth passed away and all he thought about was missing her and taking care of the girls. If he did think of dating, he knew that he would never be able to find anyone like Elizabeth, especially someone the girls would also love.

In the first couple years after her death, he would find himself picking up something of hers or smelling a piece of clothing she once wore or holding close one of her necklaces or, the most potent memory tease of all, passing by someone who wore the same perfume as she did. That would always put him in a quiet, somber mood.

Anyone who worked closely with Mike could tell he had been emotionally destroyed after losing Elizabeth—and he knew it, too. Lately, he'd been trying to open up more —attending social functions for the company and even handling grocery shopping by himself, without Sarah or Gracie along to help.

Mike and Elizabeth had purchased a spacious home in the countryside five years ago and their first year in the house was wonderful. Liz kept busy buying furniture, putting in the yard, landscaping, and decorating the house; she was so happy. Then, breast cancer. It was discovered too late and by the end of the second year, she was gone.

Since then, he hadn't had any real ambition to keep

the house up. It took more effort than he could muster to mow the lawn, trim, and clean up the flower beds that she had so carefully designed and planted. She was no longer there to be proud of him, and it just became another chore. Even though some of the neighbors chipped in to help during the early days, while he spent his time at the hospital, they'd since moved on and the yard quickly started to resemble so much of the prairie surrounding the city. The neighbors that once helped were now grumbling about its appearance. He was thinking it was time to find something a little more manageable, and maybe just to make a change.

On his way to the office, a road construction barricade caused Mike to make a detour to a side street he rarely drove on. As he watched for the right road to turn on, Mike noticed an old house with a *For Sale* sign in the front yard. He knew the area well, but didn't remember seeing this house or, if he had, never paid attention to it. He pulled over and jotted down the realtor's name and number. Parked in front of the house, Mike stepped out of his car and searched the area for a minute. He wondered if this could be the kind of home that would do him and his daughters some good. It appeared to be a pleasant enough neighborhood.

Mike worked as a field operations manager for the local power company. As soon as he arrived at the office, he began preparing for a meeting coming up at noon. While working on his presentation, he stopped and thought about the house he saw this morning. He reached into his shirt pocket and pulled out a piece of paper with the realtor's number and decided to call.

The real estate office receptionist told Mike that the agent working on this house was no longer with the agency. One of the other agents could help and, without asking, put him through to Samantha Bingham. He couldn't believe it, was it Samantha? Mike and Samantha had gone to school together but didn't date. Mike remembered how boy-crazy Samantha was over Chuck Bonner, all-star athlete, and all-around cool guy, or so he thought.

"Hello, Samantha Bingham, how can I help you?" she chirped.

"Samantha! What are you doing?" Mike asked.

"Doing fine."

"I thought you and Chuck moved to Denver?"

Samantha hesitated for a second.

"Who is this?"

"Mike Roberts."

"Mike? Mike Roberts?" Samantha yelled, "Oh, Mike, it's so good to hear from you. God! Mike, how are you?"

"Yep, it's me. Doing good—you know, just work, work, work."

"Well, it's funny you should ask first about me and Chuck."

"I thought that would get your attention."

"Yes, it did. Let me see, me and Chuck. You know, Mike, we would probably be in Denver together right now if old Chucky baby hadn't decided that it was time to be Don Juan with several ladies at the plant."

"I'm stunned. I thought you two had such a great thing going. When did that happen?"

"Since Chuck left?" answered Samantha.

"Yeah, you know, since you two split up, did you get

divorced?" Mike asked.

"Yes, we did," she answered. "I couldn't take his fooling around, I'm just funny about that kind of stuff, but Mike, what about you? Are you and the girls okay?"

"That's why I'm calling. I think it's time to get looking for a new place and, well, maybe energize myself a little bit, and put some of the past behind us. It's time I moved on. If not for me, at least for the girls' sake, you know?"

"I'm sure we can find something," she replied. "Give me till this afternoon to gather up some addresses."

"Well, when you take a look, there is only one home, in particular, I'd like to see. I saw it this morning on the way to work. It's the house you've got listed at 4892 Cribbon Street."

"Oh Mike, I love that house, the inside is wonderful. This will be fun; I can't wait to show it to you. When do you want to see it?"

"How about four-thirty this afternoon? I've got meetings before that."

"Sounds great, honey, I'll get it set up. Shall we just meet at the house then?"

"Yep, that'll work great."

"Okay, sweetie, I'll be there."

* * * *

Mike arrived five minutes late, and Samantha was waiting for him. As Mike got out of the car, Samantha walked up and gave him a hug and a kiss on the cheek. Leading him up the sidewalk to the front door, Samantha explained that the house had been on the market quite a while, but it had only been shown once or twice.

Mike thought the house looked large from the outside, but he was curious if the inside would be big enough. It had a wide front porch area with four large pillars that seemed to be holding up the bedrooms on the second floor.

"What are you looking for? A home that you can fix up?" asked Samantha, proudly wearing a bright yellow *Realtor of the Month* button from her agency.

"I'm not sure," Mike replied. "This house is in a nice area, but it sure needs a lot of work. The paint is chipping over there," he said, pointing to the weathered slat siding.

"Okay! Okay." Samantha grabbed him by the arm. "You're starting much too soon on the price negotiation part of this. Come inside and see if you can find something that will make you want to buy this house."

Samantha inserted a key into the dark wood front door and turned the brass knob. Mike felt a slight breath of air as the door opened. Right away, he noticed the air inside had a wood polish smell to it and, once Samantha closed the door, it became very quiet. Street sounds disappeared almost as if they never existed. Samantha explained that the carpets were new and they still had all the original wood trim around the doors. Mike was impressed, slowly moving through the good-size front living room. Samantha walked ahead of Mike to familiarize herself and then came back to bring him along.

"This house has four bedrooms and a study, which would be great for a computer or game room, and don't you just love all the dark woodwork around the doors?"

Without waiting for an answer, she continued, "Originally, the only bathroom was on the main floor, but the last owner had it remodeled, added two bathrooms upstairs, and remodeled the kitchen. All the electrical and plumbing have been updated to the current code, which I'm sure you, being the electrical kind of guy, can appreciate. The garage was added six years ago and has a loft that would be quite suitable for making it into an apartment if you wanted to. It is available for immediate move-in, just in case you wanted to know," she said to Mike, rubbing her hand on his arm.

"Now, did I say I was going to buy it?" Mike quipped, a grin on his face. She playfully grabbed him by the arm and pulled him toward the kitchen. Samantha walked into the kitchen first to show Mike something, but she stopped.

"What's the matter, Samantha?"

"I'm just confused, I guess. I left a business card in here yesterday when I checked the house out to make sure it was ready to show, and now it's gone."

"Maybe someone else came in and showed it?"

"No way, I'm the only one with a key."

"Wow, I don't know, maybe ghosts?" Mike joked as he continued looking at the cabinets. Samantha kept looking around, in drawers and on the kitchen floor.

"Very funny, I don't think so."

"Well, I'm sure it's around somewhere, it'll show up. Or is that your last one?"

"Oh, hell no, I got boxes of these buggers, you want more?" She laughed and tugged at Mike to move on to the next room.

Samantha continued to chatter about different things

she liked in the house, like the cupboard space, and tried to steer him to the best features of the house, but he didn't hear a word she was saying. Mike was mystified by the woodwork around the windows and doors.

The dark wood trim was worn and had several noticeable nicks—but those types of marks and scratches meant character to him. Even though the house had been empty for a while, it was immaculate. Mike thought to himself, *Why hasn't this house sold? Maybe there's some secret about this place that I should know. This house is so old, what past could be buried in these old plaster walls?*

"Come on, Mike, let's go have a look upstairs. I think you'll love this part of the tour."

The staircase, built wide enough for the two of them to walk side by side, was made of dark mahogany wood and the steps were covered with thick tapestry carpet. The solid handrails felt smooth and cool on Mike's hand.

At the top of the stairs, the landing space was wide and roomy so Mike could easily turn around and see each bedroom doorway. Mike walked into one of the two front bedrooms, situated with a small bathroom between them. As he searched the room, he noticed a small white door in the back of one of the closets, which shared the wall with the small bathroom. *Plumbing access door*, he thought to himself. Mike knew that was a common way of accessing plumbing pipes in homes that didn't originally have plumbing installed. "Pretty normal," he muttered to himself. Mike stood for a second staring at the door and thought that for a small plumbing access door, it sure had a fancy glass knob on it. Satisfied, Mike made his way out to the hallway where he could hear Samantha opening closet doors.

"Samantha," asked Mike, "do you know when this hall bathroom was added to the house?"

"Oh, yeah, I wondered about that, too," Samantha replied. "I looked it up in the building records this morning, and it's not too clear, but our building inspector downtown figured it was in the early 1920s. That's when most of the older homes in this area started putting in bathrooms. I guess the cold, brutal Wyoming winters were a pretty good motivator to make that change."

"I was curious because I noticed that plumbing access door in one of the bedroom closets, which kind of tells me it was an add-on from the original structure."

"That's probably true," Samantha agreed. "I've heard that this home was once owned by a schoolteacher and before that a missionary couple from Iowa. I couldn't tell you if it was either one of those people that put that in."

"Interesting," Mike responded. But his mind had moved on; he was still concentrating on the wood frames around the doors and how well the rest of the home was put together.

"Mike, dear! Come here and look at this!" yelled Samantha. Her voice was muffled even though she wasn't very far away. Mike walked into the master bedroom and turned to see Samantha kneeling over a small trunk along the wall. She looked at him with surprised eyes.

"Can you believe this?"

"What is it?" asked Mike, leaning down.

"I don't know, but I can't budge this clasp," replied Samantha, who seemed delighted with her find.

"You act like this is the first time you've seen this."

"It is. I was just here yesterday, when I left my business

card, and this trunk wasn't here, I swear!"

"Maybe the current owners dropped it off to store it for a while?" asked Mike, now intrigued with the ornate wooden box.

"I don't think so," Samantha said. "The old man who's selling this house said I would have the only key. I don't know much about the house except for that and he did tell me, in the few minutes we got to visit, that a young teacher once owned this house."

"Wow, that's interesting. I wonder what happened to her?"

"Don't know, moved on, got married, new school . . . lots of reasons. He never told me."

Mike stopped and looked at Samantha directly—now, he was curious—he didn't want to buy a house that had some bad voodoo connected to it.

"Well, there must be some good reason. Did she die? Was she murdered?"

"Oh, no, no, no! Nothing like that." Samantha shook her head. Mike gave her a serious look. "Mike, I'm not supposed to give you the seller's name, you know. Some people want to remain anonymous."

"Samantha, I'm not trying to pry, I just wanted to know if something bad happened here."

"I know, Mike, and I can tell you, nothing bad happened." Mike tried to read the face Samantha was making. "Okay, here's the deal. The former owner said that the house was given to his family when the young teacher left. He didn't say why she left, she just left. Then, after several years, his family grew, so he bought the larger house across the street. He kept this house as a rental. Just had it remodeled late last year, he put a ton of money into it, and now that it's finished, has put it on the market. His name is Fred Perkins, still lives over there. He's a nice guy, a widower. If you met him, you'd want to be his neighbor," Samantha said, grinning up at Mike.

"Sounds like a pretty decent guy, huh?"

"Yes, actually, he's a real sweetheart."

"I just didn't want to get into a house that had, well, you know, bad karma . . ."

"I understand, Mike, and I would be the same way. I promise. No one has died here or becomes a ghost— nothing icky like that." She waved off any further descriptions.

"Well, so maybe this mysterious chest is his?"

"I don't think so; he's already cleaned everything out. Besides, when he had it remodeled, it was completely gutted out and all new carpet . . . Cabinets, stonework, bathroom fixtures, and tile were replaced."

"But, the woodwork—it's beautiful, it looks original like it has some scars, some nicks, and bruises in it."

"Yes, that's original. Fred didn't want that changed. Anyway, that chest wasn't here, so I suppose that if you buy this place, this happy little surprise could be yours. Unless, of course, that person I'm going to show it to later on today decides to go for it . . ." Samantha was starting to sound like a used car salesman.

"Yeah, right," said Mike. "Now who's playing the game? You said this house hasn't been shown that much."

"Well maybe just a little, but believe me, once people hear about this trunk, they will want to take a second look at this place. You can have a house smell like fresh-baked bread, but put an ornate chest in it and boom, it's sold." She snapped her fingers and smirked. "Besides, you have to admit this is a damn cute house, and the remodeling job . . . well, you know that was expensive."

Now, Mike was starting to feel the pressure. He didn't want to admit to Samantha how connected he felt to the house; he knew he had found something that felt warm and comfortable. Samantha stood up and began to walk toward the door.

"So, do you want to see more stuff?"

"No, that's okay. I like it, though. How soon did you say a person could move in? That is if they wanted to buy the place."

"Now!" Samantha smiled. "I mean, it's empty. Just have to bring your stuff in."

"So, how much money down do they need?" Mike asked, showing off a wide grin.

"I'm pretty sure the owner will be very lenient on that issue. He's been pretty anxious lately about getting it sold. I didn't hear anything over the last few weeks and then yesterday, Fred called me up, out of the blue, and tells me he would be very liberal on the terms—for the right family, that is. Very strange to say the least, hmm? Then you show up. Spooky."

"Well, I still have to sell my house—you know, so you can list that one, too, if you want to. Or, I could get Roberta Tilden to put a sign up if you don't," Mike teased.

"Now, don't start with that, mister. I already have a sign on it." Samantha laughed. "I already put it up this morning, seconds after you left your house."

"Jeez, that's what I call service." Mike laughed at

Samantha's quick wit.

"Well, when you get a chance, between the rest of the day and tomorrow, come down to the office so we can sign papers and get the necessary appraisals arranged."

"Sounds like we have a deal then, huh?" asked Mike.

"Let's go get you qualified, Mr. Money Bags." She noodled him in his side and grinned. "This'll work out just fine. We'll have you moved into this beautiful house in no time," she added, pointing to her shiny yellow realtor's button.

* * * *

A few nights later, Mike and a couple of enlisted friends, including Samantha from the real estate office and John Kelley from the power company where Mike worked, arrived to help Mike and the girls move. Some of them were in the old house packing up stuff while the bigger guys started moving the larger appliances and furniture.

Sarah and Gracie had already picked out their respective bedrooms and Mike could hear their excited chatter upstairs. Then, he heard them call for him to come up. Mike bounded up the stairs and into the large back bedroom. He knew exactly what they were yelling about—the ornate wooden chest.

"Look what we found, Dad!" Sarah yelled.

"Isn't it beautiful?" Gracie said.

"Yes, it's very nice, but you didn't find it, it was already found. Samantha and I found it when I saw the house a few days ago."

"Oh," sighed Gracie, "I thought we'd found treasure."

"Well, for all I know, it could be. I wasn't able to get it open. I don't have the key and I didn't want to damage it. So, until I can get a locksmith in here, I'll just put it out of the way." Mike lifted the chest and put it on the floor inside the master bedroom closet. "Now, did you ladies figure out who gets which room?" Mike asked. The girls took a firm grasp on Mike's hands and dragged him back across the hall so they could each show him their chosen rooms.

Later in the afternoon, Mike noticed that John Kelley had taken quite an interest in Mike's new house. Mike had seen him a few times just standing still in the living room looking out into space. Mike wondered what John was thinking about, but never got a chance to quiz him about it.

CHAPTER 10
Cooking Lesson

Several hours after being thrown out of Catherine's house, the sting of her anger still festered inside Julian's belly. When he thought about it, he felt sick, because he had hurt the lady who was trying to help him. His mom told him once, *Don't bite the hand that feeds you.*

Now, with the practical lesson behind him, he could only cuss at himself. It hurt when Millie and Mack left for Detroit, but this felt worse. He owned this mess. More than anything, he wanted to go back and apologize, but he knew it wouldn't turn out well. He walked past Catherine's house several times but couldn't build up enough nerve to go up to the door.

His only salvation that first cold and homeless night was Dixie's Diner. *Might as well see if that job is still available,* he thought. He was down to his last few dollars and the wages of sin couldn't support him.

Lucky for Julian, Dixie welcomed him back and started him out washing dishes. She also had some space in the storage area behind the restaurant where he could set up a cot and bunk down. Julian also found unexpected entertainment from Dixie's head cook, Monte.

Monte seemed to throw more food around than he got on the plate, but somehow, he managed to keep up with the orders. The customers loved his food, the atmosphere of the diner and, of course, everyone loved Dixie.

After a couple of weeks, his confidence grew stronger. He started taking more chances walking closer to Catherine's house, getting to know the neighborhood and the locals. He decided that Saturday morning after the breakfast dishes were done, he was going up to Catherine's to apologize. But a few hours into the morning rush, he noticed that the dishes seemed to be piling up faster than he could wash. *What's going on out there?*

Julian walked around the end of the sink and looked ahead to the back of the grill where Monte was slopping the food around. Monte stopped just long enough to turn his apron around to the cleaner side, which to Julian didn't make sense—it seemed to him that the apron was dirty on *both* sides. Monte gave him a big grin, his short, stubby unlit cigar precariously hung out of his mouth, stuck on his lower lip.

"Wanna cook?" Monte, a short, plump black man, yelled back to Julian. If Monte jumped up and whacked it like a tennis player, he still barely had enough height to move the tickets down to the done side.

"Yeah, right, I'm sure Dixie would be thrilled with that, eh?" Julian replied.

"Oh, get your butt up here, ya little whiner." Monte motioned with his greasy spatula and lifted the wet cigar away from his lips. "Come on!" Monte yelled in his raspy voice.

Julian laughed to himself; listening to Monte made him want to clear his throat.

Monte pointed his spatula at Julian. "It's her diner,

but it's my grill!"

Julian grinned and stuffed his wet dish towel into his belt and went forward.

"Now, here, you use this spatula." Monte handed Julian a small-handled metal spatula and then warned Julian, "But, never, never put your grubby little hands on mine. You do, and I'll kick yo' ass." Then, Monte gave Julian a big grin, exposing several missing teeth—missing, most likely, Julian figured, from fighting with someone who tried to take his precious spatula.

"Now, see them tickets?"

"Yeah."

"Them's what you look at when Dixie yells 'Grub.' Okay?"

"Oh, I almost forgot, uh . . . Can you read?" Monte asked. His chubby, whiskered face wrinkled with the question.

"Uh, yeah, I did finish the fourth grade, jeez."

"Oh, well, okay then, you must be smarter than me, huh? You look up at them tickets and they'll tell you what the guy orders out front, got it?"

Julian looked up at the tickets and was immediately confused with the hieroglyphics laid out before him:

2-2, burned pig. Joe
4 flaps, joe n' juice
6, flaps, joe

"Uh, okay . . . and what does that mean?" Julian asked.

Monte looked up at the ticket and shook his head. "Now, if that ain't the easiest order, I don't know what is.

Look, ding-dong, it's two Cowboy breakfasts, the Number 2 on the menu, which is hash browns, bacon, two eggs, and toast. Now, what the hell is so hard about that?"

"Well, criminy! How was I supposed to know that?" Julian yelled back.

"You gotta think. You know, use that fourth-grade educated cement block on top of your neck," Monte said, then under his breath he mumbled, "Dumbass . . ."

"Okay," replied Julian, trying to get back to the lesson. "What's the burned pig thing?"

"They want their bacon well done . . . crispy." Monte threw up his hands and looked up toward the opening in the wall toward the dining room and yelled to Dixie, "Dixie, come in here and beat some sense into this kid for me, will ya?"

From the dining room, Dixie yelled back to Monte, "Take another bite of chew and calm down!"

"Okay, so flaps is pancakes, right?" asked Julian, glaring at the second line.

"You got it, little brother. Maybe you did graduate from the fourth grade. Now, let's get to makin'. Here, you do it."

"What do we do first?"

"You got to think about what's gonna take the longest to grill," Monte instructed. "You know, like a slice ah ham will take a little while or you gonna put some bread on the grill to toast it. Now, we have most of the stuff made up already, you know, like the bacon over here in the pan?"

"Oh, yeah, I remember you cooking that earlier today."

"Right, and remember you mixed up them eggs for

me this morning, in the cooler over there? Excuse me." Monte leaned past Julian and spit into a small bucket that sat beside the grill. "Now, look." Monte wiped his mouth off with a wet dish towel and pointed to the tickets over his head. "Up there, there's another order we need to get done, so now you do it. Take your paddle and dip into that bucket of butter on the edge of the grill and slop some down here."

Julian nervously dipped his spatula into the bucket of melted butter and let it float peacefully over the grill. Monte shook his head.

"No, no, no, damn it, you gotta go fast, nothing dainty about this job, throw it in there and slide it across the grill then grab two ah them eggs and break 'em open like this, then grab some bacon and a pile them hash browns and get 'em all cooking."

"Okay, okay." Julian tried to move quicker, growing more nervous. Julian knew his jerky methodical movements were driving Monte crazy.

"Boy, you're making me nervous. Don't make so many unnecessary moves, I'm getting tired of watching you. Smooth, son, work smooth." Monte motioned with his hands his usual careless style. "Did you see that? Huh, yeah. That's what I mean. Now, look at them hash browns—they're all dry. Slop some more butter on them, then they'll have some taste. Now grab the salt and pepper shaker and start at one end and smoothly . . ." Monte grabbed the shaker away from Julian and showed him how to work fast. "You know, son, I know this is the first time and all, but you might as well get used to working fast, 'cause when you get a crowd ah people out there, they don't show you no mercy, you gotta be Mr. Lightning back here, okay?"

"I know, I'll get it." Both of them worked together for another hour and Monte shared with Julian more tricks, the magic of putting together a great breakfast.

After his shift, Julian decided it was warm enough outside to walk up to Catherine's house and see if she was home. It was dark by the time he arrived at her house and Julian could see one small light on. He slowly walked up to the house, up the steps, reached to grab the front door handle, and stopped, his heart beating fast.

He couldn't do it.

He turned around with his head down and walked back to the center of town, back to his cot behind Dixie's café.

CHAPTER 11
Mysterious Neighbor

Even at eighty-five, Fred's large calloused fingers were still nimble enough to slip a metal button through the well-trained hole in the shoulder strap of his overalls. He picked up his sweat-stained cap on the kitchen table, rested it on his bald spot, took one last swig of cold coffee, and pushed the oiled screen door wide open. The smell of a neighbor's breakfast wafted through his yard and mixed nicely with the fresh cool morning air.

He limped out to the garage and admired his healthy flowers growing between the sidewalk and the lap-sided building. He was on a mission—there was something stored in a box high up on a shelf that he needed to get down. He opened up the garage door for more light, then grabbed his old seven-foot wooden ladder leaning against the side of the shed, and walked inside humming an old tune from his early days.

He had been listening to Billie Holiday singing "I'll Be Seeing You" on his record player; it reminded him of Margaret. She'd been gone almost five years, now. Since then, he'd learned to become independent. Not his choice—if he had his way, he would depend on her forever. They were a perfect match. Now that she was gone, it was a daily struggle to keep his spirits up. This mission had helped remind him he still had a purpose in life.

They had been married sixty-one years by the time she passed from heart disease. Together, they had two daughters, Melissa and Linda, and a son, Dennis. Both daughters lived in the Denver area and visited now and then. Dennis, his only son, was killed in Vietnam. Fred kept a memorial to Denny along with pictures of Margaret and their daughters on his bedroom dresser.

Ever the proud veteran, Fred served in the Navy during WWII out in the Pacific and attended meetings once a month with some of the guys that were still around, down at the VA hall. Unfortunately, those days, he was more likely to see them at the VA hospital, in Denver. His only other social activity was over at Community Christian Church, a couple blocks east of his house. Otherwise, he read, studied his table puzzle, scratched his head, and tinkered around the house and yard all day, looking for something that needed repair.

His favorite chore was lifting the canvas on his perfectly maintained 1929 Chrysler Imperial, a car he'd kept in the garage all these years and only taken out when asked to ride it in parades. He used it for his daughters' weddings and graduations, but most importantly, for several romantic evening summer rides with Margaret to get her favorite ice cream.

Today was a special day. He had a promise to keep, something he'd been looking forward to for a long time.

Fred gingerly stepped up the wobbly old ladder and reached for a box high above him on a shelf. He strained to grab the cardboard flap, which was curled and torn over time. When Fred grabbed the cardboard flap, dust brushed off and into his face. He instinctively closed his eyes, his hand slipped loose from the box flap, and his right arm flew backward. It seemed to pull him out into space and down to the floor. He knew it was going to hurt. A sudden thump and pain on the back of his head—and all went silent.

It was wonderful and warm, reliving memories of things long forgotten, now real and fresh. He could almost touch, almost talk, gliding through his thoughts without being tethered. The sensation of pain was slow in coming, but it did, and when he woke up, he was looking up toward the roof of his garage. He knew he was hurt badly; he had sharp pains in his back and arm. He couldn't remember what happened, but his view of the rafters told him something wasn't right. He thought he might have been laying here for several hours, but he wasn't sure.

The sound of footsteps on gravel broke Fred's thoughts. Opening his eyes slightly, he could barely make out the image of a man coming toward him. He motioned with his finger for the man to come.

"Hey, buddy, you okay?" It was the power company's meter reader.

"Please, can you get someone to help me?" Fred spoke in a weak, raspy voice. The young man came closer and knelt beside him.

"You bet, old timer, we'll get you some help." The man, dressed in the local power company uniform, grabbed his company radio and asked someone to have an ambulance sent to Fred's address. "Sir, what's your name?"

"Fred, Fred Perkins."

"Help is on the way, Fred, I'm gonna see if I can

get in touch with your neighbor Mike and have him come over, too. Just lie still, I'll be right back." The man jumped up and walked just outside of the garage door and pulled out his radio. "Mike, this is John Kelley, you copy? Mike?"

"Hello, John, it's me, go ahead."

"Hey Mike, I'm at your neighbor's house, across the street. Looks like he's had a bad accident inside his garage. Are you in the area?"

"Oh, good grief. Yeah, I'll run right over there, John, I'm not too far away."

"I called dispatch and had them call 911, so they're on the way. I just wanted to let you know, you might want to go over and be with him until the ambulance arrives."

"Thanks, John, I appreciate that."

Fred slowly rolled over to his side and tried to lift his arm. Shooting pain ran through his arm and body. His arm didn't go anywhere—it must have been broken. Fred painfully slumped back down, knowing he couldn't move anymore. In a few moments, he heard someone running toward him.

"Whoa, partner, just lay still where you are," John cautioned as he walked back into the garage. "Your neighbor Mike will be along in just a few minutes. Can I get you anything?"

"No, I'm fine, I'll just lie here and enjoy the view," Fred said matter-of-factly, not meaning to make a joke of it, although John laughed.

"Okay, suit yourself, I think that's Mike coming up the street now." Mike's truck pulled up fast, and in a few seconds, he was in Fred's garage. "Hey, John. Thanks again for helping out here."

"No problem, Mike. If you've got this, I'll go on with my route."

"Sure, go ahead. I'll visit with you later, huh?" Mike knelt beside Fred and looked him over to see if there was any immediate medical trauma he needed to take care of. In the distance, the ambulance's siren grew closer.

CHAPTER 12
A Rush of Cool Air

It seemed like a long weekend—unpacking more boxes, a trip to Grandma's house, and getting the homework done. Monday morning came with yawns and tired faces. Mike zipped the girls off to school, and then himself off to work. In the afternoon, Sarah and Gracie came home after school one at a time and plopped onto their beds, worn out from their exhausting day at school. Still, when the phone rang, it was a mad race to be the first to answer it. This time, Gracie won by a nose.

"Daddy! Yeah, we're okay—no, Sarah!" Gracie barked, as Sarah tried to grab the phone away.

"Let me talk," Sarah said. Gracie ignored Sarah.

"Oh, I don't know, there's not much to do," Gracie replied. "But I'm tired of opening boxes." Gracie rolled her eyes. "Okay, here's Sarah."

"Dad, I have a new teacher, Miss Palgan." Sarah was excited to tell her dad about her new teacher. After being alone for two years, Sarah thought it would be nice if her dad went out and had some fun. "Yes, Dad!" Sarah said with a teasing voice. "She's single."

Mike laughed at Sarah's attempts to match him up with her teacher; he was embarrassed, but not interested. "Well, isn't that something? Did you find all that out in just a few minutes today? Well, maybe sometime in the future we'll have a parent-teacher conference and I'll meet your new teacher, eh?"

"Yeah, sounds like a good plan," Sarah said, satisfied with her matchmaking skills.

"I'll be home in a little bit. You guys be sure to lock the front door and call me here at the office if you need me, okay?"

"Dad, we'll be all right. And, I'll be sure to drop your name to Miss Palgan again," said Sarah, emphasizing her teacher's name, "just so she won't forget."

Sarah ran up to her room to find eight-year-old Gracie playing in her closet. "What are you doing in my room?" she whined.

"I'm playing people! You've got all the stuff in here, and besides, Dad told me to clean up my room, this way it won't look messed up," Gracie replied, sitting cross-legged. She turned back to concentrate on the small group of characters in front of her. Her brown curly hair tumbled down over her face, and her body bent over with only her two spindly legs giving a hint there could be a little girl somewhere in that pile of toys.

Sarah couldn't argue with her logic. This is something the two sisters allowed themselves to enjoy together, something their mom Elizabeth used to sit with them and play, too. Sarah sat down and joined her sister. Anyone walking into the room would have a hard time spotting the two girls jabbering to each other as they pretended the real lives of these little plastic figures.

As Sarah was moving one of her people, she looked up and over Gracie's right shoulder and noticed wood framing on the back wall of the closet. It seemed to be a door.

"Gracie, look at that door!"

"So? What's it for?"

"I don't know, let me over there, so I can see."

Gracie pulled the group of her people out of the way and Sarah leaned over toward the door.

"You'd better not do that, Sarah, Dad's gonna get mad."

"No, he won't, I'm not going to do anything, I'm just going to check this out, it's probably just nothing." As Sarah climbed over Gracie, she grabbed at the round crystal knob and pulled. Nothing. "It's stuck, I need a screwdriver."

"Sarah, you're going to get in trouble!"

"Oh, quit fussing, let me try this." She couldn't get it to open. Sarah ran down to the kitchen and got one of her dad's screwdrivers from the junk drawer and ran back upstairs to her bedroom, fell on her knees, and jammed the screwdriver into the thin space between the door and the frame. It took the twelve-year-old one good shove to pry it loose.

It popped open enough for Sarah to get her hand on it and pull it open. Gracie leaned over behind her, with her hand on Sarah's back. Sarah pulled slowly. As the small door creaked open— cool air rushed past—they stared into black darkness.

"What do you see?" asked Gracie.

"Just darkness. Go get me Dad's flashlight, so I can see what's in here." Gracie sped off downstairs and was back within a minute. Sarah switched the light on and pointed it into the small opening.

"Can you see anything?"

"Not really, but it doesn't look scary," Sarah lied and swallowed hard. She put the flashlight down and got closer to the opening. "I'm gonna reach my hand in and see how far it goes."

"It looks scary to me, Sarah, you'd better not," Gracie warned.

As Sarah leaned over to put her hand in, she fell forward to one side and into the dark space. Gracie upset that Sarah ignored her, impulsively pushed the small door shut. "That'll show her," Gracie said to herself.

But what seemed like a perfect opportunity to give her sister a little payback left Gracie feeling scared. It seemed odd that she didn't hear any screaming from inside the door. Gracie was sure her furious, screaming sister would be tumbling out of the dark space at any moment—but it was only quiet. After a few more moments, Gracie decided to open the door herself. She pulled on the crystal knob and could only see a dark, empty space.

"Sarah! Sarah? Sarah, you come out, right now!" Gracie poked her head in the doorway to see if she could spot Sarah hiding against the side of a wall, but she could only see blackness. "Sarah?" she whispered.

Gracie got up and walked around the room, keeping a close eye on the small open door. Tears began to fill her eyes as she circled and paced, wondering what her next move would be. Little did she know, Sarah could come back, if she would only close the door.

* * * *

Sarah let out a weak yell as she landed on her side, on the solid floor surrounded by darkness. Angry at her sister, she immediately pushed back on the door, expecting to fall out in front of Gracie and start yelling at her. When it opened, she peered out to the room and stopped halfway between the darkness and the drab, box-filled room.

"Gracie?"

Dead silence.

A collection of strange boxes, papers, and a small table told Sarah this was a different house. Sarah finished climbing out of the dark space and stood up. She began to feel anxious when she realized she wasn't home. *This is all wrong. What's going on? Where is Gracie?*

The more she looked around, the more scared she became. Her eyes filled with tears—*But wait.* As she turned in circles, she felt like the room was familiar. It sure seemed like it could be her room, but where did all this stuff come from? Sarah called out again.

"Gracie? Gracie?"

Silence.

She looked around for anything familiar. She went out of the room and into the hallway and then into the larger bedroom toward the back of the house. Her heart pounded. In the large bedroom, the clothes in the closet were certainly not her dad's. They appeared like they belonged to a woman, but they didn't seem like clothes someone would wear these days. Boots, shoes, and slippers. Prints on shoes? Whatever. As Sarah looked further,

she found long gray skirts, white blouses, gray wool sweat-
ers, and long dark wool coats. *Good grief, this girl needs a closet
makeover.*

Sarah walked over to the bed—a huge pile of quilts
and blankets so inviting, she wanted to jump on it and
fall asleep. Over on the dresser, she noticed an old picture
on the nightstand, a black and white picture of someone's
family. Behind it, a picture of a young lady, in one of those
long gray dresses and a group of Indian children. *This must
be the lady who lives here. She's pretty, except for that hairdo.* Next
to that, a perfume bottle with a rubber atomizer attached.
She picked it up and squeezed, spraying a sweet bouquet
of scent—right in her face.

"Caaghh!" She coughed and rubbed her nose. "Jeez,
now I'm gonna smell like somebody's grandma!"

Curious, she walked out to the stairway landing and
was preparing to run downstairs to look at the rest of the
house when she smelled something that she hadn't noticed
when she first came through the closet door: a wonderful
combination of spices. *It must be coming from the kitchen. Is
someone living in this house?*

Suddenly, she heard the back door open and close.
She turned and ran for the closet she came from. Sarah
pulled the clothes apart and grabbed the knob on the small
door—it opened, making a small squeak. The thumping
sound of someone walking up the stairs was getting closer;
she managed to quickly fall into the darkness once more.

As soon as she was inside, she turned around and
pushed the small door to open it. It wouldn't budge. She
pushed at it again. It wouldn't open. In total darkness,
she started to panic as she felt around the frame of the

small door to see if she had the right area. Confused and panicky, she kicked at it again and again.

* * * *

Gracie sat cross-legged with her face resting on her hands, sobbing, staring at the open door in the back of her sister's closet. Then she heard a commotion—was it her dad coming home? She got up quickly and closed the small door; she needed to clean up before he got there.

In that same instant, the door swung back open and slammed into the wall on the other side. Sarah climbed out.

"Well, finally, it opens up," she gasped. Gracie jumped up to hug her big sister.

"Sarah! Where were you? Where did you go? I called and called for you, but you didn't answer me! Where did you go, Sarah?" Gracie sobbed. Sarah gave her another hug.

"You little brat, I should beat your butt. Did you hold that door so it wouldn't open?"

"No, I just left it open and closed it just now, I didn't know what to do!"

"Well, it must have worked when you closed it because I kicked and kicked on it and it wouldn't open." Sarah got up and walked toward the bathroom.

"Where did you go? I was so scared!"

Sarah turned the bathroom light on. "I don't know, Gracie. I don't know where I went, but if I told you what happened, you'd think I was crazy."

"You're crazy anyway for doing that, what happened?" Gracie demanded.

"Not now, later, I've got to go potty, then we've got to get this cleaned up before Dad gets home."

CHAPTER 13
Neighbor Comes Calling

Settling into the new house was a fun time for Mike and the girls. They spent a lot of time trying out places where furniture could go, how to get the groceries down from the tall cabinets in the kitchen, and decorating each room. It was easy in their last house: Elizabeth made all the decorating decisions and she had plenty of ideas, yet in this house, Mike was on his own with two young aspiring interior home decorators—and to his surprise, he thought they did quite well.

For the most part, Mike was pleased that the girls were able to find a simple and fun diversion. Mike eventually took some time to set up his garage workbench. After his tools were in place, his next task was to bring out that mysterious chest from his closet and see if he could get it open.

After setting it down on the bench, he took a few minutes to admire the intricate woodwork and solid hasp that held its contents privately inside. The lock was a very old mechanism, yet it seemed brand new—not a trace of rust or wear whatsoever. It wasn't something you'd normally see on a piece that looked like it could be an antique. He delicately poked at it with several sizes of screwdriver, and a piece of wire, and even tried some of the keys he had saved in a junk drawer, to no avail.

In the house, Gracie was in the kitchen opening a box of macaroni and cheese, a treat for her dad and the only meal she knew how to prepare, but she was proud of it, and Mike knew he had to always compliment the cook. He'd accepted it as part of the job.

Sarah was just opening her homework on the dining room table. They were both surprised when a couple of loud knocks hit the front door. Both girls wondered who it could be; they didn't know anyone in this neighborhood. Sarah and Gracie raced to the door and opened it up. Standing in front of them was an old gray-haired, whiskered man, his right arm in a sling.

"Hello, little ladies, is your dad home?" Fred said, smiling.

"Yeah, I'll get him, okay?" said Sarah, as she turned and ran to get her dad.

"Dad! Dad!" Sarah yelled out from the back of the house. "It's for you. Some old guy at the front door!"

"I'll be right there, honey!" Mike knew his project could wait; he didn't want to have anything happen to this beautiful little box, so he covered it up with some towels. The tools remained on the workbench where he found them.

At the front door, Gracie stood guard, holding the door, and stared up at Fred with a sheepish grin.

"And, your name is Gracie?" asked Fred, leaning down to get a closer look.

"Yes," she said shyly. Mike walked up to the door, with Sarah behind him, and put his hand out to Fred. Gracie wondered how he knew her name. She noticed his eyes watered.

"Well, hello neighbor! Are you feeling better?" said Mike. He carefully shook Fred's left hand.

"Yes, I am, thanks to you," replied Fred. Mike motioned for Fred to come into their house.

"Please, come in and sit down, would you like something to drink?" asked Mike.

"Oh, no thanks, I shouldn't stay long." Fred set his cane against the side of the couch. "I just came over to introduce myself formally and to say thanks for the help the other day. My name is Fred Perkins."

"Fred, good to meet you, I'm Mike Roberts and these lovely young ladies are my daughters, Sarah and Gracie." The two girls giggled at their dad's compliment.

"Are you getting all settled into the house okay?" Fred asked politely.

"Yeah, I think we've turned the corner on most of the unpacking. We still have a few boxes, here and there. Mostly incidentals, nothing important."

"Glad to hear that." As they settled in their chairs, Fred fidgeted nervously. He took a few seconds to look around at the walls and new furniture.

"Well," began Mike, "Samantha, our real estate agent, tells me that you once owned this house, is that true?"

"Yes, for a few years anyway. You know, I love this house, it has a lot of history for me . . . Yep, probably have a lot more before it gets too old to live in." Fred reminisced, "I've only lived around here for the last eighty-five years, so I've picked up a little knowledge about these homes. This one, besides being a home for my family for quite a few years, has been a particularly nice home and a couple of fine people have lived here." Mike and the girls nodded politely. Fred took a deep breath and sighed. "But, enough of my old memories. I'd better get on with my mission, here. I want to say thanks for coming to my aid the other day. That nice young man was in the right place at the right time, I'd say. I'd probably still be lyin' there if you and he hadn't helped."

"Well, the thanks should go to John Kelley, on our service crew. He had our office call 911. If he hadn't come along, well . . . you're right, who knows how long you would've been there."

"Please, let him know that I'm grateful for his help. He needs to know what a lifesaver he was." Fred got up to leave, and Sarah handed him his cane. He looked at Sarah intensely for a moment then leaned over to her.

"Thank you, sweetie." Then Fred whispered close to her ear, "Honey, please be careful in this house, okay?"

"Sure, Mr. Perkins."

Mike had gotten up to open the front door and didn't notice Fred's comment to Sarah. He turned around to help Fred out the door. "Fred, if you don't mind me asking, what were you trying to do, when you fell?"

"Oh, I had some old papers I was trying to get down, some pictures and old stuff from when I was a kid, just reminiscing, you know. Well, I'd better get moving on. It was great to meet you, Mike, and your beautiful daughters, and if you need anything, please don't hesitate to come over."

Fred put his cane on the floor and walked to the large front door, waved goodbye, and slowly made his way down the steps and across the street to his home. Sarah and Gracie watched from their living room window then ran back into the dining room to finish their gourmet macaroni and cheese dinner.

"He seems like a nice old guy, huh Dad?" asked Gracie.

"He sure does," Mike said. "I hope we get to know him better."

"Maybe he could come over for dinner sometime," said Sarah.

"Yeah, that'd be great, I'll bet he's got some interesting stories to tell. Nice of you to ask, Sarah," Mike replied, his mouth full of macaroni. "And, I must say, this macaroni is just the best I've ever had in my entire life, wouldn't you say, girls?" Gracie nodded in agreement.

* * * *

Later in the evening, Sarah sat doing her schoolwork and biting her nails. She looked over at her dad and wondered if she should tell him what happened earlier in the day. Gracie kept giving her nasty, worried looks. Finally, she came over next to Sarah, sat down, and grabbed a throw pillow.

"Are you going to tell Daddy?" she whispered.

"I don't know." Sarah slowly turned the pages of a book she wasn't reading. "If I do, then what? Is he going to want to see it—and what if he doesn't come out? What if something awful happens?"

"You're going to have to say something because we just can't leave it there and forget it."

"I know, but I don't know when."

"Sarah, what was behind the door? You never told me."

"You gotta promise never to tell anyone, okay?"

"Okay." Gracie shrugged, because a promise only lasts as long as your memory, in her book.

"When I went through the door, I came out in a different time, like back a hundred years ago!" Sarah said, trying to tell Gracie how excited she was without making too much noise.

"Awh, right," Gracie said. "Liar, that's impossible."

"It may be impossible, but that's what I saw. Old clothes, old furniture. It was the same house, but with someone else's stuff in it, some lady's clothes. Before I could look around anymore, I heard someone come in the house, so I took off back into the closet."

"Whoa, that's too much. You're makin' this up, aren't you?"

The phone rang and Mike called out for Sarah.

"Sarah, it's Sophia!"

"I'll take it in here, Daddy!" Sarah turned to Gracie. "We'll talk later."

Sarah picked up the phone and left Gracie to ponder what happened behind that door. Gracie shut her book and went up to her room to read.

As she walked into her room, she went over to her window that looked out over the front lawn and street. Across the street, she could see Fred's house. In his front window, it appeared that Fred was staring back at their house. Gracie quickly stepped back and shivered. *Why is he watching our house?*

Downstairs, Mike tapped away at his computer keyboard, writing business reports due the next morning, oblivious to anything else going on. Gracie ran downstairs and found Sarah, still on the phone.

"Sarah," she said in a strained whisper. "Sarah!"

"Just a minute, Sophia, my bratty sister is bugging me. What!?"

"Go look out the front window, at Fred's house, can you see him?"

"See what?"

"That neighbor, Fred, he's staring at our house."

"So, what?" Sarah turned back to her phone conversation "Okay, Sophia, sorry, it was nothing."

With that rejection, Gracie turned around and went back to her room, vigilant to keep away from her window.

* * * *

By Friday, Sarah couldn't get out of her mind what she experienced going into that small door in her closet. All week it had been bothering her. For several nights, she even dreamt about it. *Why did it happen to me? Maybe it never happened. Maybe this kind of thing happens now and then; maybe dreams happen while you are wide awake, too.* But curiosity won, and she knew she would have to go there again.

After school, when she got home, she found Gracie upstairs in her room.

"Gracie?"

"What."

"Hey, I need you to help me for just a few minutes."

"With what?"

"I'm going to climb through that little closet door again. I have to see what's in there, so I need you to keep watch for me, all right?" she asked.

"No, Sarah, you can't go! Dad will kill you, he'll be so mad!"

"Nothing's going to happen and maybe I can bring something back, so Dad will believe me. That's all I want to do, to get something to show Dad," Sarah reasoned. Gracie began to tear up and tried to talk Sarah out of it.

"Sarah, I don't want to lose you, too! I don't want you to go away."

Sarah stood still for a second, realizing what her sister was saying. She walked over to hug Gracie. "Gracie, I'm going to be right back, I promise. I'm just going to pick up something, I promise." Sarah reassured her, "Just give me five or ten minutes."

Gracie couldn't stand to watch; she ran out of the room and around the corner to her room and slammed the door shut. Sarah stood there, watching her run off. She turned around and looked at the small door behind her clothes. She was determined to get answers.

Sarah reached down and pulled her clothes aside, got down on one knee, and reached for the crystal knob on the door. She put her small fingers along the crack of the opening and pulled hard. The door creaked open, and Sarah felt a slight wisp of air pass by. It was dark, but she felt that she would be okay.

Slowly, she put one hand in then the other, and leaned in, putting one leg in and then the other. She pulled the small door shut behind her and pushed it open, just as fast.

Once again, as she came out, the same papers, boxes, and furniture were stacked on the floor. Sarah remembered the wonderful smell of spices—a smell like Thanksgiving, warm and inviting. *Yummy,* she thought to herself.

* * * *

After Gracie heard Sarah close the little door, she ran back into Sarah's room, to wait for her. Gracie bit her lip, hating the thought that Sarah was doing this again. *Just wait till she comes out!*

It was taking too long. She felt nervous. Sarah said it would just be a few minutes. Gracie grew more anxious, but this time, she left the door alone and waited.

* * * *

Sarah moved quickly from the front bedroom onto the upstairs landing. Except for the furniture and carpets, she realized that this house was the same as hers. Sarah tiptoed down the staircase covered in a tapestry carpet, and over to the front window, where she pulled the large, heavy curtain back and looked outside.

Her eyes grew wide open in disbelief.

There were only two other homes across the street and a large field. A Model T car sputtered by. She thought maybe there was a parade in town, but then she noticed that another car down the street looked the same. When she opened up the front door, it didn't make its familiar squeak. Outside, there were only a few small trees, and a couple walking across the road were wearing clothes that were out of date.

Just up the street, Sarah picked up some movement. Behind a lilac bush, a scruffy-looking boy stared at her, about fourteen years old. She stepped back, not liking the looks of him, and noticed a newspaper on the front step. She picked it up and took it back inside with her. Safe inside, she peeked through the curtains again; he was still staring in her direction, though she could barely see him.

Then she glanced at the top of the paper, the date was Tuesday, March 21 . . . 1928! *Oh, my God!* she thought. *1928? This is crazy, it just doesn't make sense.* She put the paper down near the front door. She knew that this was her house, but it was another time.

CHAPTER 14
Hog-Tied

On Friday afternoon, Dixie told Julian he might as well take the rest of the afternoon off, it had been a slow day. Julian wondered, now that it was spring if it might be warm enough to walk back up to Catherine's house and check around. This time, he was determined to know more about that closet. This time, he was going to get in; he carried a small screwdriver with him.

He threw on a jacket and left out the back door of Dixie's. In a little while, he was on the street near Catherine's house. Before trying to enter the house, he stood just down the street, behind a small bush, and watched.

To Julian's surprise, a young blond-haired girl stood on the front porch looking back at him. He'd never seen her before. Julian wondered, *Did Catherine move?* Maybe this girl was a relative or neighbor, or maybe she was snooping around Catherine's house. He knew she had seen him when she quickly went back into the house. *I'll bet she's not supposed to be there,* he thought. He hesitated another minute, then moved toward the house. He nonchalantly walked up to the back door and shoved the screwdriver into the doorjamb; it opened easily. Julian pushed the door open and walked in. As quietly as possible, he gently closed the door and waited against the wall to see if he could hear any sound. His heart raced.

* * * *

At that same moment, Sarah stood near the large front room window and heard a noise from the back door. She recognized the sound and turned quickly, looking back through the house. She froze but didn't see or hear anything. *Maybe it was just the wind.* She began walking toward the stairway. If someone did come in the back door, she would need to be gone.

At the stairway, she took each step as carefully as she could, being sure not to make a noise. At the top of the landing, she moved faster into the front bedroom.

* * * *

Julian heard a sound, confused at where it came from. He started moving, tiptoeing as fast as possible through the house, looking around and quickly making his way to the front of the house, then over to the stairway to look upstairs.

He caught just a brief glimpse of a girl's leg as it disappeared past the stairway railing. He quickly raced up the steps, taking two or three at a time, trying not to make noise, but that didn't matter now.

In the doorway of the bedroom, he saw the girl getting down on her knees to open the closet. He jumped into the room and made a terrible noise to scare her.

"Hey!"

The girl turned and screamed even louder, scaring him. Julian ran over and grabbed the girl's arm, spinning her around, throwing her spread-eagle out on the carpeted floor. He jumped on top of her and pinned her down with his knees, grabbed both of her hands, and held them down, with his.

"Who the hell are you?" he demanded. She tried to wrestle free but couldn't. Terrified, her breathing was hard. She began to cry.

"Get off me, you're hurting me!"

Julian's strength overpowered her; he tightened his grip on her and searched for something to tie her up with.

"Shut up! Quit crying. What the hell are you doing here?"

"I'm just looking around," she cried. "You're hurting me, let me go!"

"No way, you're not going to mess this up for me! I have to get through that closet door!" Julian reached over to the closet and picked up a belt and several boots. "Don't move!" He pulled shoelaces out of a pair of shoes nearby and made a makeshift set of cuffs around the girl's wrists.

"Ouch! You're hurting my wrist!" she cried. Julian put the belt around her ankles so she couldn't run. He dragged her to Catherine's bedroom and shoved her into the back of the closet. Taking another pair of laces, he wrapped them around her hands and tied them off, then took a scarf from one of the coats, tied it around her face, and forced it into her mouth, to keep her quiet.

"That should keep you here for a while. I hope you didn't have to pee."

The girl's wide, teary eyes glared back at him. Julian

turned fast around, shut the closet door, ran over to the front bedroom and into the small closet door, and was gone.

* * * *

After a few minutes of waiting and squirming, Gracie couldn't wait any longer. Missing sister or not, she had to pee. She jumped up and ran across the stairway landing in the bathroom. Even at eight years old, she knew that if anything was going to happen, it would happen while she was gone to the bathroom.

* * * *

After leaving the girl tied up in the closet, Julian opened the small door hoping to go forward to the strange and vacant house he found before. Now, as he peered into the room, he was startled to see furniture, pictures, and stuffed animals. Someone had moved in.

The once-empty room he had found was now filled with girls' clothes, a bed full of stuffed animals, and a poster of a girl singing. He didn't have time to stop and think about it. He had to move, right now.

Someone knew he was here, and it was just a matter of time before they would come looking for him. Even though he didn't know her name, the girl he tied up meant someone else knew about the closet door.

First, he had to find Catherine's hope chest and make his getaway. He crawled out of the closet, got up, and carefully walked into the hallway and into the other bedroom to search for the chest. He noticed a light on in the bathroom and heard someone inside. Any moment, he could be caught, again.

He dodged into the master bedroom and looked for the chest—in the closet, under the bed, next to the dresser. *Damn, it isn't here.* He walked over to the bathroom door, where the light was still on. He ran across the upstairs landing and down the stairway.

At that moment, the bathroom door opened. Gracie came out and walked back into Sarah's bedroom to keep her vigil by the closet door.

Julian continued his search. He wasn't going to let this get away.

After looking in every room, he reluctantly gave in. He figured that someone must have moved it where he would never find it. *Damn, all this wasted time on that dumb box. I'll probably get caught and beat up just trying to leave this stupid town.* Julian walked through the kitchen, unlocked the back door, and ran around the back side of the house to make his getaway.

* * * *

At five-thirty, Mike arrived home from work, parked his car in the driveway on the side of the house, and walked up to the back door. To his surprise, the back door wasn't latched shut. Concerned, he pulled it open, walked in, and immediately called out for the girls.

"Sarah? Gracie?"

No answer.

He rushed through the kitchen and yelled again, yet still no answer. Mike hurried up the stairs to the girls' bedrooms and found Gracie fast asleep on the floor in Sarah's room, in front of her closet. He knelt beside her and woke her up.

"Gracie, Gracie, sweetheart, wake up, honey, wake up," he whispered gently to her. When she opened her eyes, she seemed confused.

"Sarah? Daddy? Is Sarah here? Where's Sarah?"

"I don't know, honey, I haven't seen Sarah. Did she go over to Sophia's?"

"Daddy, something else has happened and if she hasn't come back yet, something's wrong." Gracie got up on her knees. "She went through the closet—she did it one other time, but this time, she didn't come back!"

"What do you mean, gone through the closet?" Mike asked.

"Through the hiding door," Gracie cried, "the little door there, see?" She pointed to the little door at the back of Sarah's closet.

Mike quickly figured it out in his head. The doorway appeared to be maybe two and a half to three feet tall by two feet wide.

"But that's just an access door for the plumbing!"

"I don't know what it is, Daddy, I just know that when Sarah went through there, she went to a different time, she told me." Gracie said, "Sarah said it was like a long time ago."

Mike studied Gracie's face and then back at the small door, wondering if his precious little Gracie had gone over the edge, mentally. "Let me understand, honey. Sarah went through that little door and hasn't come back?"

"Yes, Daddy, she's in there!"

Mike took a deep breath and let it out slowly, trying not to anticipate the worst.

"Then, let's have a look, honey." Mike leaned over to the door and pulled on the crystal knob to open it. He felt the same rush of cool air and the same deep darkness Sarah had seen. Mike shivered. He was startled to see no plumbing or cobwebs.

"Oh, my God," he whispered to himself. "Sarah!" Mike yelled out. "Sarah, are you in here? Sarah!" His heart sank.

"No, Dad, you have to go inside and shut the door. As soon as you get inside, then you open it back up and you'll find her," Gracie cried.

Mike, down on his knees, looked back at Gracie. "Honey, this isn't some kind of joke, is it?"

"No Daddy, I promise, she's in there somewhere!" Gracie's tears told him she was telling the truth.

"All right, honey, I'll go in. I'll find her. You wait here."

"Wait? That's all I've been doing, Daddy!" Gracie said.

It was all he could do to get his large frame through the small opening—not a pleasant task for someone with borderline claustrophobia—but he managed. Once inside, a quick sense of fear fell over him as he positioned himself around to open the little door back up—what if it didn't open? He gave it a shove and right away he could see the soft afternoon light pierced through the opening.

* * * *

Catherine put her key in the front door and unlocked it, opened the solid wood door, stepped inside, and turned around to close it, making sure it latched. As she walked through the front room, she dropped her books on the dining room table, on her way into the kitchen to brew herself a cup of tea. Once the tea was on, she pulled her starched white blouse up out of her waist belt and let out a tired sigh of relief that her long week was over. Sitting down at the dining room table, she lifted her long skirt to untie her shoes, removed the hairpins from the bun in her hair, and scratched her head. She picked up a paper from one of her students and started to read it.

There was a loud bump. Catherine froze, not moving a muscle, listening.

Then, another bump.

This wasn't a normal sound. She sensed something. She knew she heard a knock or a thump, like someone hitting a wall. She immediately thought about Julian, fearing he might have come back.

Catherine got up from her dining room chair, ran back into the kitchen, and grabbed a knife from one of the drawers. She cautiously walked through the dining room and into the living room, pausing to see if she could hear another sound. *Did I just hear a man's voice?*

* * * *

Mike pushed open the door and with some effort, pried himself out of the cramped space, mumbling about the small opening. He crawled out on his knees and looked around before getting up. A bedroom with a couple of stacks of boxes and a table. The house smelled different than the room he had just left.

He got himself up and stepped over to the front window to look out and inadvertently kicked a small box on the floor.

* * * *

Catherine carefully crept up the stairway and to the landing. She heard the sound of something being hit and immediately knew it had to be Julian, probably back in the spare bedroom searching for more stuff. In the corner of her eye, she noticed movement in the front bedroom. Catherine jerked to a stop and looked in disbelief as a stranger stood in the middle of the bedroom, turning to face her.

"Who are you!?" she yelled, thrusting her knife out in front of her body, startling the man. The look of terror on Catherine's face made him step back.

"Holy cow!" he yelled. Surprised, he threw his hands up in the air. "I'm not going to hurt you!"

"I said, who are you?" Catherine demanded, waving the knife in a menacing motion. "What is this?" she demanded. "What's going on, why are you in my house?"

He kept his hands up, fearing an attack from a scared woman with a knife. "My name is Mike, Mike Roberts, and I'm not dangerous, I think my little girl is somewhere in your house."

"Uh-huh, sure, right . . . and how did you get into my house? Why would your little girl be here?"

"I know this sounds crazy, but I came through that little access door inside that closet. The little door—right there, to be exact." Mike pointed to the small closet door behind the clothes.

"You're crazy. You're a fool if you think I'm going to believe that! How could you come through there? It's for the plumbing!"

"My daughter, Sarah, came through this little door here in the back of your closet, which I thought was a plumbing access door. Well, at least it is in my house, but for some reason, it . . . ah . . . well . . . it . . . ah . . ." Mike stammered, hunting for the right words to explain his situation.

"Now I do feel like a fool. It seems that it, or whatever's behind that small door, changes the time you're in. For me, it's the year 2000. And for you, it's like seventy or eighty years earlier, something like that. Anyway, that's how my daughter, Gracie, explained it to me."

Catherine looked back at Mike, not buying his explanation.

"Mister Roberts—or whoever you are—you, you are out of your mind. It's 1928, and you expect me to believe this? And, if your daughter is here, where is she?" Catherine continued to hold up her knife.

"I don't know, that's why I came through, so I could find her," pleaded Mike.

"Just don't move for a minute," Catherine said, trying to understand what this Mike person was saying. "Let me take this in, because this all sounds like a fairy tale to me."

"It would to me, too, miss, I assure you. I would certainly have serious reservations, as well. In fact," Mike reasoned sincerely, "when my younger daughter Gracie told me that my daughter Sarah had come through that small closet door, it was . . . unbelievable, to say the least. But now, it appears that I have traveled back in time, and from what you tell me, to 1928. So, her story must hold some truth." Mike shook his head in disbelief. "So, if we can, please, I need to find my daughter. Please."

Mike's plea seemed genuine. Catherine lowered her knife. Her muscles relaxed, and she took a deep breath.

"Okay, but don't try anything funny. I'm going to keep this knife handy." Catherine stepped aside so Mike could start looking around. "Go ahead." She motioned with her hands. She kept a distance, not letting her guard down entirely, just yet.

"Thank you," Mike replied. He lowered his hands and began walking into the other room. "If your house is like mine, there is another bedroom right next to this one, right?"

Catherine stared at Mike like he was nuts. He grinned.

"Yes, there is a spare bedroom and, in the back, my room." Catherine stood back to let Mike pass. "I still don't know if I can trust you," Catherine warned.

Mike hesitated and then slowly walked into the hallway, turning to go into the next bedroom. Mike looked around in the spare bedroom that was once Catherine's childhood bedroom. It still contained her small single bed and was decorated for a small girl.

"This is very cute," he complimented, after finding nothing.

"My bedroom is here, in the back," said Catherine, pointing to the bedroom toward the back of the house. "You said her name is Sarah?"

"Yes, Sarah," Mike told her. "Sarah! Sarah!" Mike yelled out. "Sarah, are you here?" Both Mike and Catherine stood still, to hear.

Just then, they heard a knocking sound, like the sound Catherine had heard earlier. They walked toward the sound into Catherine's master bedroom and opened the closet doors. There, rolled and tied up on the floor, was bushy blond-haired Sarah struggling to get free.

"Oh, my God!" Catherine yelled. Mike dropped to his knees and began untying Sarah and took the scarf off her face.

"Honey, are you okay? What happened?"

"Just untie me quick, Dad, I have to go to the bathroom." In moments, she was running to the bathroom. Mike glanced over at Catherine. She gave him an apologetic look.

"Well, Mr. Roberts. I guess I owe you an apology."

"No, no, please, it's all right." Mike waved her off. "I would have done the same thing if you suddenly appeared in my house—or maybe I wouldn't have." Catherine turned back to Mike.

"Mr. Roberts, maybe you can explain now, what is—"

"Please, you can call me, Mike." Mike extended his hand to Catherine.

"And I'm Catherine Tanner." She shook his hand. Both were able to smile at each other now. He had a friendly face; she realized that now, maybe the danger had passed.

Mike tried to explain what he knew about the closet, so far.

"Catherine, this is hard for me to believe, too. I had just gotten home from work and my daughter Gracie—my youngest daughter, not this one, I also have an eight-year-old—she told me this horrifying story of Sarah being lost behind this small closet door and, of course, I . . . I'm wondering what I should do and if could I even believe her story. I mean, what could I do?"

Sarah ran back into the room and hugged her dad.

"Are you better now, sweetie?" Mike asked.

"Yes, I had to go so bad," Sarah replied. Catherine watched as the girl interacted with her dad. He seemed to be a good father figure. Mike turned to Catherine.

"Sarah, this is Miss Catherine Tanner. She lives here, in this house."

"Hi, Catherine."

"It sounds like you've been through a lot honey, can I hug you? I hope you're okay?"

"Yeah, I'm okay." Sarah smiled.

"Sweetheart," Catherine began, "maybe you could do a better job of explaining what's going on; your dad seems to be confused. Can you tell us what happened? How did you get here?"

"Gracie and I, my little sister, are always playing games in the closet. We sit under the clothes. The house is new to us, so I was just curious, you know, what was behind this small door in the back of my closet. Anyway, when I opened it, I fell in. When I opened the door back up and crawled out, I ended up in your house." Sarah looked over at her dad, shrugging. "Anyway, I looked around and found old-style clothing and—oh, sorry Catherine."

Catherine smiled back at Sarah.

"It's okay, honey, it sounds like it was very confusing for you."

"Yeah, because I didn't know what to think of it. I mean, this is all so weird. So, when I came through this time, some guy attacked me—a young guy, maybe my age or a year or two older . . ." Catherine stood up straight and gasped.

"Oh, my God! Julian, it's Julian, it has to be, he's come back." Her mind racing, she quickly glanced around the room trying to think how this could be.

"Who's Julian?" Sarah asked.

"He's a young boy that I took in after he'd been beaten up by some of my students down the street. I was just trying to help him out, but he took something from me, so I kicked him out. It's been several months—I thought he might have left town. But it sounds like he's back and he's able to get in here. Honey, I'm sorry that you had to get in the middle of—"

Sarah stopped Catherine.

"Wait a minute! Dad, we need to get back. If that was him, he's gone back through the closet, to our house. Gracie is there!"

"I just came through," Mike said. "Gracie was fine."

"Julian still went through that closet—he told me he was—so he might still be around, and Gracie is there alone!"

"Maybe that's why the back door was unlatched," Mike said. "We better not risk it. Come on, honey, let's move!" Mike turned to Catherine as he started walking toward the front bedroom. "My daughter, Gracie, is in the house alone!"

"I'm so sorry about this, maybe he didn't see her?" Catherine said, offering a small ray of hope as she followed Mike and Sarah into the bedroom.

"I can't take that chance; I have to make sure," Mike said impatiently.

Catherine wanted to help and rubbed her hands in frustration. Mike leaned down under the clothes in the closet and began to open the small door. Sarah's eyes lit up with an idea.

"Dad!" Sarah said. "What about Catherine? Let's have her come with us!"

Mike stopped in his tracks and stood up. He knew Sarah might be right, but wondered, for a quick second, if this might be too big of a challenge for Catherine to undertake. He looked over to her, standing next to Sarah.

"Oh, no, no, no." Catherine waved her hands. "I'm not getting in there."

"Catherine, she's right," Mike said. "I didn't stop to think about it, but it would be excellent to have you come with us. You know what Julian looks like!" Mike pleaded.

"Oh no, there's no way I'm crawling into that awful place, through those pipes and the filth and spiders, no way!"

"Well, I need to get back to see if Gracie is okay!" Mike said anxiously.

"Then you go right ahead, don't let me stop you," Catherine said.

"The problem is, I don't know what Julian looks like."

"Sarah does, don't you honey?" Catherine asked.

"Ah, not really—I mean, I kind of remember a little about him. But I was too scared. He scared me out of my wits, tied me up, and dragged me over to the closet. I was fighting him. I don't think I could recognize him."

"It's all right, Sarah. This whole deal is a surprise and a shock to each of us. Time travel is too much, I know. Catherine, I'm sorry for intruding into your home," Mike said apologetically. "Come on, Sarah, we'd better get back!"

Mike and Sarah both got on their knees at the small door and prepared to climb inside.

"Sarah, I'll go first. I need to make sure Gracie is okay. I don't think there's enough room for both of us, so you get in right behind me, okay?"

"Okay, Dad."

Catherine stood with her arms folded over her chest, tapping her foot. Mike shut the door and was gone. With the door shut, Catherine asked Sarah something.

"Sarah, would you mind waiting for a few minutes with me?"

"No, is something wrong?" Sarah asked.

"No, I just need to clean up before I do this. Look at me, I'm such a mess."

"No, you're not," Sarah said. "You're a beautiful woman. Even messed up you look good."

"Thank you, honey, but I need to fix my hair and get some shoes on. You know, a woman shouldn't go out unless she's properly dressed—has the right shoes on and has her hair combed, isn't that right, Sarah?"

"Well, yeah, I guess," Sarah answered, shrugging. "At least shoes."

Together, they walked back into Catherine's bedroom,

where she picked up a large brush from her dresser and began combing out her long blond hair. Catherine pulled her hair back and quickly put a large clasp in the back of her hair to hold it firmly.

"Now, Sarah, what do you think is right for this dress, the black shoes?" Catherine lifted her long dress modestly enough to show her matronly large-heeled black shoes. "Or, just a minute . . . these black shoes?" She revealed to Sarah another pair of black shoes exactly like the first pair.

Sarah recognized Catherine's sense of humor and played along. "Hmm, I think the first ones."

They both broke out in laughter. Catherine tucked in her white blouse and grabbed a sweater from her closet then announced to Sarah she was ready to go. They rushed over to the closet and, in a few minutes, all was quiet.

Chapter 15
A Different Ride

When Mike opened the door, he found Gracie sitting cross-legged on a small pillow in the middle of the room, waiting impatiently, her head resting on cupped hands. Bored to tears.

"Daddy! Where's Sarah?" Mike climbed out of the doorway and embraced Gracie.

"Honey, Sarah's fine, she's right behind me. Are you okay?"

"Yeah, I'm just so tired of waiting for everybody." Gracie pouted. Mike hugged her again, thrilled to have her safe in his arms.

"Honey, did you see anyone come through the closet door, besides us?"

"Nope, it's just been me, sitting here, all alone. Why?"

Mike didn't answer. He was already running to the other rooms, searching in closets and checking behind doors. Mike sprinted down the stairs to look around with Gracie dutifully following along, when suddenly, they heard a commotion in one of the upstairs bedrooms. They ran back up the stairs in time to see Sarah and Catherine just standing up, after coming through the small closet door. Sarah smiled at her dad and privately nodded at him to look at Catherine's hair, now put up so she would not get it tangled in cobwebs.

"Catherine, I can't believe it. You decided to come?" Mike asked, his pulse jumping at the sight of her.

"I just couldn't stand by and wait to find out what was going on," Catherine said. "I have to know if it was Julian causing all this trouble." Catherine paused. "That, and before I visit someone's house, I think it's only proper to fix my hair and put shoes on." She grinned at Mike, then turned and winked at Sarah. Gracie watched wide-eyed, holding tight to her dad's waist.

"Well, I'm just glad you came. This is a bizarre event, for all of us." Mike turned to Gracie. "Gracie, this is Miss Catherine Tanner, she is the lady who lives in the house where Sarah's been going. Catherine, this is my youngest daughter, Gracie."

"Hello, Gracie, nice to meet you, I'm glad to see you're safe."

"I wasn't doing anything, just sittin' here waiting for you guys," she said. Mike could see she felt left out, so he got down on his knees to talk to Gracie.

"Honey, thank you for being the brave soldier and watching the door for us, but as I mentioned earlier, we think someone else came through this closet door. Whether you know it or not, you might have been in some danger. A boy named Julian came through this closet earlier, and now we need to find him."

Gracie looked at Sarah with big surprised eyes and put her hand over her mouth. Catherine came over next to Gracie and Sarah.

"Are you girls all right? Sounds like you both have been through a lot."

"Yeah," said Sarah. "It was scary, though, tied up in your closet. I didn't know what would happen." Mike hugged Sarah. Catherine looked up at Mike, a supportive smile on her face.

"The real question, Catherine, is are *you* okay?" Mike asked.

"I guess I'm all right, I just don't know what to make of all this. My head is spinning, and you say it is what year?"

"If you can wrap your head around this, it's the year 2000. We just completed 1999."

"No, that can't be," she said incredulously. "That's too much to think about." She shook her head and changed the subject. "Okay, so we're here, how do we find Julian?"

"I suppose we need to figure out where Julian might have gone to. Catherine, since you know Julian better than we do, what do you think? Do you have an idea what he was intending to do?"

"I don't have any idea. He must have found the door, too, and used it to get away."

"Well, we know he's on foot, so he can't get very far. Maybe we should get in the car and just start driving around to look for him."

"Oh, you have a buggy or one of those fancy touring autos?" said Catherine. "If so, I'll need to get a scarf for the wind." Sarah and Gracie laughed.

"Ah, no. Catherine, our car, or automobile, is enclosed. You know, covered up, so the wind is not a problem." He grinned sheepishly. He wasn't sure if he was handling this right, but he sensed Catherine was in store for quite a cultural shock.

"That's good." Catherine tidied herself up. "Because I don't like to smell all those fumes and smoke, you know, from those nasty engines." Then she looked at Mike with a dubious expression. "You're going to tell me you don't have noisy engines either?"

"Nope," Mike answered happily. "We're going to ride in something quiet and clean—it will have a very smooth ride, I promise."

"This is going to be fun, Catherine," Sarah said. "I think there have been a lot of changes in seventy-two years."

"Girls, I think this may be a fun adventure for Catherine, but we can't show her everything all at once. We'll show her around later, but for now, we need to find Julian and get him back to 1928," Mike said. "Let's go get in the SUV." He glanced at Catherine and smiled.

As they left Sarah's bedroom and out onto the upstairs landing, Catherine gasped at the changes compared to her house.

"Oh, my gosh! This is my house?"

"We've done a few things to it since you saw it last," Mike explained.

"You mean, five minutes ago in 1928?"

Mike smiled. He wondered to himself how Catherine must feel. *Her mind must be reeling from all this change.*

As they walked down the stairway, he walked beside Catherine and explained a few of the changes that were made when the house was remodeled. Sarah and Gracie followed behind, looking at each other and making eyes. The girls took Catherine's hands and pulled her in to look at the living room. She stood in the middle of the room for a minute, confused.

"Some of these things don't seem to be furniture. Do they do something?"

"Yeah, we have several games and of course, our television, over here." Sarah walked toward the TV. "I'll bet this all seems pretty weird to you, doesn't it?"

Catherine looked over to Sarah and nodded with a helpless expression in her eyes. "I feel like someone who just woke up from a hundred years of sleep."

Sarah picked up the remote and pushed a button. "Are you ready for this?" she asked.

"I don't know, do I need to take cover?" replied Catherine. The screen quickly came up with pictures of the local news. Catherine covered her face in amazement.

Sarah tried to explain how they watch live programs from around the world, cartoons, cooking programs, and movies. Sarah and Gracie then pulled her into the kitchen to a small cubby area that they had turned into a home office.

"Catherine, look at this." Sarah explained, "This is a computer."

"It has a black area. Is it a TV, as you call it?"

"Oh, the screen? No, well, I guess in a way it's like a TV. Pictures do come up on it, but it's more for doing homework and Dad does his work on it. I'll show you more later."

Catherine turned around to look into the kitchen and couldn't believe her eyes.

"Is this my kitchen? Oh my gosh, it's . . . It's beautiful!" She walked over to the granite counters. Mike walked into the kitchen to help move everyone out of the car. He smiled as she felt the cool smooth surface with her hands.

"And the lights, the cabinets, it's just unbelievable how you've made it look. Now, my place will seem so drab and old."

"I'm sure for your time, it's very nice," Mike said.

"I can't even imagine having all of this stuff, and Lord knows how I would ever figure out how to use it. This is all so complicated, I don't know, I think I'm gonna faint."

"Well, the car is ready, let's get moving." Even though Mike was enjoying Catherine's discovery of the kitchen's new appearance, at least for this time, he was worried that it would become too much for her. *Possibly, she's a stronger woman which I'm giving her credit for. I'll let her discover it as it comes and see how she deals with it.* His mind turned back to current events. They needed to find Julian.

"All right then. Ladies, after you." Mike motioned to the back door.

"I'm hungry, are we going to eat tonight?" Gracie said.

"Oh, good grief," replied Mike, "I completely forgot about getting the girls some dinner. I'm sure everyone's hungry. Catherine, are you hungry?"

"You cook, too?"

"Yes, but probably not tonight. We'll search for Julian for a while, then go get something at a restaurant."

"Go get dinner?" Catherine asked. "Am I going to be out of place in my dress?"

"Actually, it looks nice, I like it," Mike said, pointing at Catherine's long skirt. He meant it. She was beautiful.

"But I'm going to look pretty old-fashioned, aren't I?"

"It's okay," Sarah piped in. "We'll do some fashion

makeovers later." Catherine laughed and hugged Sarah.

"Thanks, sweetie."

On the way out to Mike's SUV, he escorted Catherine toward her side of the car and hurried ahead to open the door and show her the seat she would sit in. As Catherine approached Mike's SUV, her eyes looked surprised; she stopped and stared at the car.

"This is an automobile?" She reached out to touch it.

"Yes," Mike answered. Catherine glanced over to Mike with a questioning look. Mike stood by her door and offered her a seat in the front. He took her hand and she awkwardly climbed up into the gray leather seat. Once she sat down, she slid toward the back and snuggled comfortably into the soft padding; a smile radiated across her face. She turned around to see how the girls were doing.

"Oh, this feels so wonderful!" she said. "What kind of material is this?"

"Leather, it's just been dyed this color," Mike told Catherine. He reached over her and pulled out the seatbelt and gingerly wrapped it around her waist. She breathed in his aftershave.

"What's this for?" Catherine asked.

"Safety, just in case we have to stop suddenly."

"Am I going to get killed in this thing?"

"Well, we'll make every effort not to."

Sarah rolled her eyes and Gracie couldn't stop giggling in the backseat as they buckled themselves in.

"Every state has passed laws that require you to buckle in every time you're in a car . . . ah, automobile," he corrected himself.

"It's okay, Mr. Roberts, you can call it a car," Catherine jabbed at him.

Mike felt he had been patronizing her. Once he got himself buckled in, he turned to Catherine to explain. "Listen, I'm so sorry about all of this. Especially for all the new things you're being bombarded with. It must be mind-numbing, trying to take all this in. I guess the girls and I need to just go slow and let it sink in."

"Michael it's okay," Catherine said. "Yes, it is a lot—I'm in a daze with all this, and it's just so very incredible to all of us, even the girls. But, don't worry about me; I'll just take in what I can and the rest of it will just have to be picked up later, I hope."

"Thanks, Catherine."

Mike started the car and slowly backed out of the driveway and into the street. Mike was looking over at Catherine and smiling when, at that moment, his eyes caught something in the bushes along the side of his house. Mike strained to look. Catherine quickly turned her head and saw it, too. He pulled the car over to the curb and jumped out.

At first, it was a tentative walk, but as he moved closer, he broke into a run—he was looking at a body. Catherine too, furiously tried to unbuckle her belt and climb out of the car. She took off after Mike but stopped short of the body lying on the ground. Sarah and Gracie got out and ran up beside Catherine. As Mike reached the body, he realized it was his neighbor Fred, half covered by the shrubs against his house.

"It's Fred," Mike yelled out. Catherine and the girls ran up to Mike.

"Fred? Fred who?" Catherine asked.

"Oh, Fred Perkins, our neighbor across the street."

Catherine's face paled; she cupped her hand to her mouth and got down on her knees to see if she could help.

"Catherine, he doesn't look so good. He's breathing. I'm going to try and roll him over," Mike said as he carefully lifted Fred's shoulder to bring him over.

"Oh, my God," Mike said under his breath. "He's cut the side of his head. He's not bleeding anymore, but it's a nasty gash." Catherine leaned over close so she could see how bad it was.

"Do you want a towel for the blood?"

"Yes, maybe we can use that to make him more comfortable." Catherine turned around to look at the girls, standing a few feet away.

"Gracie, honey, can you run and get me a towel, quick, please?"

"Here's the house keys, Gracie!" Mike threw them to her. As soon as she picked them up off the ground she ran into the house. Mike looked over to Catherine with a somber expression in his eyes.

"I think we'd better get some professional help here. I'm going to call for an ambulance." He pulled out his cell phone and dialed 911. After giving them his address information, he handed the phone to Catherine and attended to Fred. Catherine gave the phone a skeptical look and handed it back to Sarah.

Gracie ran back from the house and gave the towels to Catherine. Mike helped Catherine gently put the towels around Fred's neck and head. Fred moved slightly and moaned.

"Hang in there, partner, we're getting you some help."

Catherine looked at Mike with a scared expression—he could tell she was worried sick.

"What do you think?" she asked.

"I can't imagine what he was doing over here. He's hurt pretty bad. He'd either fallen or had been hit with something pretty hard. I just wonder if this was the work of our little buddy, Julian?"

"Oh, God, I hope not. I don't want to think he's capable of this. But he's angry with me and he's scared, and I just don't know what he would do."

"I wish those guys would hurry up," Sarah said. Both she and Gracie were huddled together. Without moving him anymore, Mike looked Fred over to see if he had any other injuries.

"Fred, can you hear me?" Fred moved slightly but didn't answer. Mike looked up at Catherine, his eyes filled with concern. In the distance, the sound of sirens moved closer.

A police cruiser arrived first. The officer ran up next to Mike, his flashlight out and shining down on Fred. As the officer began asking Mike questions, a medical EMT unit pulled up, followed by another police cruiser. As the EMTs gently took over care of Fred, Mike stood up next to Catherine. A policeman walked over to Mike, handed him a contact card, told him to call his number if he could provide any further information, and prodded Mike again about what happened.

"We had come out of the house and were just taking off when I noticed something lying beside the house. I stopped and jumped out of the car and ran over. The closer I got, I realized it was Fred. We didn't see anyone running." Mike rubbed his forehead. He was still sick about what happened to Fred. Mike couldn't believe it—why Fred?

"Officer," Catherine spoke. "Officer, we have our suspicions. I mean, we don't know anything for sure, but you might keep an eye out for a young kid, maybe fourteen or fifteen, I'm not sure of his age."

"You think this kid could have done this?"

"I don't know if he had anything to do with this, but it's a possibility," Mike offered. Shivering from the cold air, Sarah and Gracie moved over next to Catherine and Mike.

"Who is this kid? Do you know his name?"

"Julian, sir, Julian Daniels," Catherine answered. "But I don't think he meant to hurt Fred, it must have been some kind of accident. This just doesn't seem right."

The policeman wrote down notes and promised to let him know if they found anyone. Mike gave him his cell number and asked him to call if they came up with anything.

"What's going to happen to Fred?" asked Sarah.

"I don't know, honey. We'll go to the hospital later and see how he's doing. We're pretty much the only family he has right now. And, speaking of that, I'd better call his daughters in Denver and let them know what's happened."

"I'm just sick about this," Catherine said.

"Where would Julian have gone?" Sarah asked.

"I could tell you if we were back in 1928," Catherine said. "Because there weren't many places to hide out."

"Catherine, did Julian say anything at all that might tell us where he was headed?"

"He mentioned once that he wanted to go west, but

that was so long ago. I just don't remember anything that might help. He may have changed his mind since then. I'm just not sure what he was planning."

"Okay. If you want to climb in the car with the girls to stay warm, I'll run over to Fred's house to get his daughters' phone numbers. Then maybe we can look around a little bit before we get something to eat. I'll bet you're hungry, too, huh?" Mike asked Catherine.

"Yes, my dinner plans were interrupted by an intruder," Catherine quipped.

Mike smiled back at Catherine. *At least,* he thought, *she's got a sense of humor about all of this.*

"I'm okay, Dad, I snacked a little after school," Sarah admitted. Catherine looked over to Mike as she got in the front passenger seat. Sarah and Gracie climbed into the back seat and buckled in, again. Mike started the car and was about to turn back to Fred's house when Catherine spoke up.

"What will you do with Julian, if we find him?" Catherine asked.

"That's a good question. I don't have a real plan."

"I know what I'd like to do to him!" Sarah wisecracked. Catherine turned and smiled at Sarah.

"I guess we would just have to hold him for the police if we're able to," Mike replied. Catherine didn't answer; she was staring out the passenger side window. "Catherine, what are you thinking?" He had a feeling she was pondering something. Catherine kept glancing toward the house where they found Fred; her fingers tapped on the center console nervously. She turned back to Mike. He saw a devious look in her eye.

"Wait," Catherine said. "There's something very important I need to do; maybe it will help. I've got to go back through the closet, but I'll be right back. If you want, Mike, you go ahead over to Fred's. I'll be back soon."

"Catherine, are you sure about this? Is this something that has to be done, now?" Mike asked, worried that she might try something risky or go home and never come back.

"Don't worry." She patted him on the hand. "I'll be right back, I promise. Maybe it would help if I took Gracie along with me?"

Gracie's eyes lit up at the mention of being included in something so exciting. She unbuckled her seatbelt and jumped up, leaning over the center console. "Dad, can I? I'll be okay with Catherine!"

Mike caved easily, finding that he easily trusted this schoolteacher from 1928. "Sure, that'll be all right, I guess. But hurry!"

"She'll be okay, I promise, Mr. Roberts," Catherine reassured him. "This is nothing dangerous, just an errand I need to take care of." She smiled at Mike. Gracie crawled past Sarah and opened the door. Catherine fidgeted with her seatbelt until Mike delicately reached across the center console to push the release button.

"Okay guys, we'll go grab a bite to eat after you get back," Mike promised. "Gracie, when you get back in our house, call my cell number and we'll come back to pick you two up."

Catherine and Gracie grinned at each other and waved goodbye to Sarah and Mike, as they took off for the upstairs closet.

* * * *

Upstairs at the small closet door, Catherine looked at Gracie.

"Well, sweetheart, looks like you and I will have our own little adventure, are you ready?"

Gracie beamed up at Catherine. "Let's go!"

Catherine yanked on the small closet door. Gracie effortlessly scrambled through the small opening, turned around, and held out a hand to help Catherine. After bending down to fit through the opening, Catherine gathered up her long dress behind her. In a few seconds, they were gone.

CHAPTER 16

Hit and Run

Within the hour, Sarah and Mike had already returned. Upstairs, in the house, the little closet door creaked open, and out spilled Catherine and Gracie onto the bedroom floor, giggling. Sarah heard them and ran up to the bedroom to see Catherine tugging on a black belt around Gracie's waist. Both were dressed in long gray dresses trimmed with black thread and white blouses.

"Hey! I want one too!" Sarah asked. "Does everyone back there wear long dresses?"

"Well, not everyone. If you're a teacher, you are required to wear a long dress, and it's usually black. Ladies in my time wouldn't dare be caught in anything else. They would certainly not wear trousers, like a man, I'm certain of that."

"Wow, that explains a lot."

"You see, honey," teased Catherine, "I am a modern, fashionable woman—of my time anyway." Catherine playfully primped her hair in front of a mirror on the dresser, Sarah and Gracie giggling behind her. Gracie was thrilled with herself; she couldn't stop grinning and twirling around in her new long dress and black lace-up boots. Catherine explained to Sarah that Gracie was wearing a dress that she once wore when she was Gracie's age.

"You know, Catherine," Sarah said, smiling, "I think this style is coming back in. You may be ahead of the curve, girl."

"I'm sorry. Curve?"

"I think she's giving you a compliment, Catherine," Mike said, as he walked into the room, relieved to see Catherine and Gracie. "Good to have you back. Did everything go all right?"

"Yes, it went just fine," Catherine answered, smiling at Mike.

"Still," said Sarah, staring at Catherine's outfit with a critical view, "I'm thinking we should go to the mall tomorrow and pick up a few things for Catherine."

"Well, I'm not sure if we need to go that far," said Catherine. "After all, I still have to go back home—I have a teaching career, mind you. Anyway, I couldn't afford to live the way you do, that's for sure."

"Sarah, Catherine's right, she does have a home to go to—and remember, we brought her here from a different time, as strange as that may be. It's not like we can just keep her here with us." Mike caught Catherine's eye. "Can we?"

Catherine looked at Mike with a Mona Lisa smile.

"Okay, so is anyone hungry yet?" Mike said, changing the conversation. "I promised that we'd go get something to eat, are you ready to go?"

"I'd love to prepare something, but I'm not sure if I would know how to work with your new appliances," Catherine offered.

"Don't worry about it, we'll get in the car and go get something. It'll be faster to do it that way." On the way out to the car, Mike asked Gracie how her adventure went. "Well, Gracie, did you two have fun?"

"It was so cool, Dad. Catherine has tons of teacher clothes and she has these old shoes they are so cool and she has some hats!"

Catherine interrupted, fearing Gracie would spill too many beans about her dressing habits, real or imagined.

"Yes, we got some things done, didn't we sweetheart? And I left a note for my mom. She likes to check in on me every so often, so I didn't want her to worry about what I was up to. I think it was fun for Gracie to see how my house looked, and especially the kind of modern conveniences I have." Catherine laughed. "I think she'll appreciate how convenient your appliances are compared to what they were in 1928, right Gracie?" Gracie energetically nodded her head.

"Dad, it would be fun to live like that. Did you know that she has to put wood in the stove and get a fire going to get it hot?"

"Is that right? I don't know, Gracie, just imagine how nice our kitchen must seem to Catherine. Would you like to build a fire every time you wanted to make mac and cheese? Huh?" Mike said, laughing.

"No!" Gracie replied. Sarah and Catherine both rolled their eyes at each other.

* * * *

Mike had planned to continue looking for Julian, but after dinner, as they were walking out to the car, he asked

Catherine about going up to see Fred. She agreed and said as cold as it was, Julian wasn't going to get far; he still may be fairly close by.

At the hospital, Mike, Catherine, and the girls walked up to the information counter and asked for Fred Perkins' room. Catherine seemed confused by all the electronics, blinking red lights, alarms, computers, and television monitors everywhere she looked. At the nurse's station, they were directed to Fred's room, halfway down the hall on the right.

It was quiet as they walked in; Fred's eyes were closed and a large white strip of gauze was wrapped around his head, an IV in his arm and several monitors pinged away. They walked up to Fred's bedside, and to Mike's surprise, Catherine sat in the chair next to Fred and was the first to speak.

"Fredrick?" she said. "Fredrick, sweetheart, it's Catherine Tanner, I'm here with Mike and the girls." Mike was completely at a loss for words. He looked back to the girls, and they too were wondering what Catherine was doing. She gently rubbed her hands over Fred's.

"Miss Tanner," he said, his weak, raspy voice barely audible. Fred turned slowly to face Catherine. "Is that you?"

"Yes Freddy, it's me," she said.

"Am I in Heaven?"

"No, not yet, you're still with us," Catherine spoke softly.

"It's been a long time, but I was there, Miss Tanner, I was waiting . . . for him, like you asked." Fred's weak voice cracked as he struggled to answer.

"Freddy, you don't have to explain. We're just worried about you right now, dear, we just want you to be all right. I know you were there, sweetheart." As she patted his rough large hands, tears rolled down her face. "Thank you for being there, Freddy. You just rest for now and we'll wait until you have enough strength to visit." After a few moments, Catherine turned around to Mike, who had moved up closer next to her.

"Catherine, ah," asked Mike in a whisper, "do you know Fred?"

"Yes, Mike. Back in 1928, Fred was . . . well, *is*, one of my students."

Mike was flabbergasted. "Oh, good grief."

"Mike, when I went back just a little bit ago, with Gracie, I went over to Fred's house and talked to him. His mom and dad live just a few blocks away from my house. I told him that in the year 2000, if he was around then, at this particular time in the afternoon, to keep an eye out for Julian, he might be coming out of this house. I also told him to be careful not to get injured, but I see now that didn't work too well. I wasn't sure how this time change thing would work—I wanted to stop Julian. My plan didn't work too well, I feel terrible."

"I'm sure I would have done the same if I were in your shoes." Mike wondered to himself if the small door could function that way—so many years apart. Manipulating time, events, and what effect it would have on everything else, he just didn't understand how that would work.

"You might have, but I feel so guilty. Fred's injured and we have no idea where Julian is," Catherine said.

Sarah and Gracie had walked over to the other side

of Fred's bed to visit with him. Fred looked over at them and smiled. Gracie seemed to have put aside any misgivings about their spying neighbor.

"Mr. Fred, are you feeling better?" asked Gracie.

"Yes, I am feeling better, sweetheart. I have a little headache, though," Fred replied weakly.

The duty nurse came in and checked Fred's pulse and temperature, then adjusted his IV.

"Nurse, who's the doctor treating Fred?" asked Mike.

"That is Dr. Patterson, he's just down the hall right now, if you want to talk to him. Are you family?"

"No, we're Fred's neighbors; we were the ones who found him earlier this evening."

"Well, you probably saved his life, he got a pretty nasty gash on the back of his head."

"I've called Fred's daughters about what happened and they're planning to come up from Denver right away. I imagine they'll be here first thing in the morning," Mike told the nurse. He decided to go down the hall and speak with the attending doctor and let Catherine and the girls visit with Fred.

Mike caught up with Dr. Patterson at the nurse's station. The doctor explained that they would be keeping Fred at least until Sunday afternoon, depending on how well he responded to his treatments in the next couple of days.

"You know, Mr. Roberts, I don't think Fred's been in to see a doctor for quite some time, so we're going to take advantage of that and run a few tests on him."

"I'm glad to hear that. Although we are just his neighbors, he's like a grandpa to the kids and we don't want anything to happen to him," Mike said in a low voice.

"We'll be back in tomorrow to check on him and take him home when he's released."

"That will be fine. You know, at his age, he'll mend quickly. He'll be all right."

"Here's my card," Mike offered. "It's got my home number and cell number in case you need to reach us." Mike went back into Fred's room—the girls were talking with Catherine about her students and especially Fred and what kind of a student he was—gathering ammunition, Mike suspected. He walked over next to them at Fred's bedside and close to Catherine's ear.

"We should probably go," Mike whispered to Catherine. "The doctor's giving him something to help him sleep. He said they might release Fred sometime Sunday afternoon, depending on how he does. They're also going to run some extra tests while they have him." Catherine nodded in agreement, turned around to say goodnight to Fred, and kissed him on his cheek. Mike, right behind Catherine, told Fred they would be back sometime tomorrow and check on him. Fred smiled a weak smile and then drifted off into sleep.

* * * *

On the way home, Mike presented Catherine with a surprise offer. The two girls were giggling about something in the back seat and Catherine seemed quite comfy and warm in the SUV's soft leather seats.

"Catherine, which house would you like to stay in tonight?"

"Oh, ah, I hadn't even thought about it, I guess I was just daydreaming. I suppose I should sleep in my bed; wouldn't that be the proper thing to do?" Her look was serious as she waited for his answer.

"Oh, yes, that is certainly the proper thing to do. But . . . we have that spare bedroom downstairs and I know the girls would be wild with excitement if you would stay over. They would just love it, and of course, I would be wild with excitement, too!" he joked. "I think it's also practical. That way, I can fix you a first-class breakfast and then we can go up and visit Fred, later in the morning. You know, we still need to find Julian," he reasoned, looking over at her with a big smile.

"Yes, I suppose that's true," she answered. "But, even though we're in the year 2000, I still have to think about propriety and appearances. You know, I'm a Christian woman, I have to protect my reputation."

"Yes, Miss Tanner, I understand. We'll respect whatever you want to do. On the other hand, it would be pleasant to have you stay. You'd have your room, and the girls can share, so you'll have all the privacy you want," Mike promised, trying to allay Catherine's anxiety.

"Well, then Mr. Roberts, that's a nice invitation, but I really can't. I do need to get back to my place. I will, however, come back in the morning and we can continue our search for Julian and check on Freddy."

"I understand. I'm sure we'll be just as excited if you would join us in the morning for breakfast, around nine?"

"I will do that," Catherine answered with a smile. Mike was impressed how graciously Catherine had walked through that issue—and pleased with himself that he had asked, and let it go, without making a fuss.

* * * *

On the drive away from the hospital, through the busy city streets, and then into dark, quiet residential areas, Catherine couldn't recognize any part of her small western town. Wouldn't it be fun to share this with her close friends back at school?

That reminds me—of school, I need to finish my reports. She reminded herself that Monday was only a couple of days away, she needed to get serious and get back to her responsibilities at school, her students, and friends.

* * * *

Julian figured he had now committed the crime that would get him the electric chair. He took Catherine's treasured box—he had helped to injure that old man, and worse yet, left him for dead. After leaving Catherine's house, he ran toward the center of an unfamiliar town and looked around for a place to hide out until morning. What started as a warm afternoon was quickly turning into a cold, windy night.

The only thing he knew in this part of town used to be Dixie's Diner and wondered if the restaurant could still be around. He figured Dixie was certainly gone and Monte had smoked his last cigar, but at least it was a place he knew and might be able to sit in a warm booth for a while.

After walking for several blocks, he came up to the

area that he was sure was the location of Dixie's place. Instead, he found an insurance office, a payday loan store, and Garcia's Mexican Restaurant. Nothing that looked like the old Dixie's.

He sat down on the sidewalk facing south and could see in the distance the trucks running east and west on the freeway. He knew he was making it too easy on the police, if they were searching for him, sitting against a building on a major street running through town. The more he looked at the trucks he realized that he might as well go out to the truck stop and try to get a ride. He stood up and peered around.

On the side of a building just down the street was an advertisement with a picture of a mother giving her son cough syrup. Julian turned away; he didn't want to see happy family pictures, they meant nothing to him. Feeling more alone than he had ever been, the thought of going home became a vacant idea. Julian turned east and walked.

East of town, a couple of miles out, a large truck stop stood just off the freeway. As he walked into the truck stop's café, the size of the room with dozens of people moving around overtook his expectations. *This is probably what put Dixie out of business*, he thought. Julian found a table on the far side of the room and slid across the seat. He opened the menu and looked for a few seconds before folding and slapping it hard on the table. *A bowl of soup, $4.50?* He sat back. Julian still had fifteen dollars in the good part of his shoe, but every item on the menu was between five and ten dollars.

A waitress came up.

"What's up, kid? With your folks?"

"Uh, they're out in the truck," he lied. "I wanted to eat, but, uh, I guess I'd better just wait till they get in here. Do you have any crackers?"

She grabbed some out of her pocket and tossed them down at him. "So, you don't want anything?"

"No, I'll get something later. Thanks for the crackers, though."

Feeling small and worthless, Julian slipped out of the faux wood seats, head down, and walked out of the restaurant toward the big trucks lined up getting fuel. He parked himself on one side of the station, trying to get out of the way, and started to eat his crackers. The crackers only made his stomach growl more.

Julian's light shirt was no protection from the cool night air blowing through the truck stop. At the pumps, Julian asked several truckers for a ride east and was turned down. One trucker explained that it was against company policy and another told him that liability and the possibility of lawsuits prevented him from picking up anyone, and he couldn't take that chance. Julian was perplexed by these answers but didn't argue.

This is getting me nowhere, he thought to himself, as he watched the big rigs pull in and out of the truck stop. He got up and walked out into the parking lot where a large number of rigs were parked close together with the diesel engines running. He noticed one woman walk around from one truck to another and knock on the cab doors. He walked up to her to see if she could help him get a ride.

"Ma'am, excuse me, ma'am," Julian asked.

The woman turned around. "Yeah?"

"Ma'am, I was wondering if you knew if any truckers

were going to be takin' on riders?"

"A ride? Good luck, kid. But if you keep tryin' you'll find some pervert to let you into his cab. You got folks around here?"

"Nope." Julian started to feel like this could be a bad idea.

"You a runaway?"

"No, I just travel on my own, that's all."

"You be real careful, kid!" She turned and walked toward another truck. Julian thought she sounded a lot like his mother, same accent in her voice. He watched her walk away, then he turned to look for another driver. Julian sat down on the step of one of the trucks and waited. Before long, a driver walked up to him.

"You're sittin' on my truck."

Julian glanced up. "Uh, sorry mister, I was just looking for a ride."

"Just get the hell off my truck!"

Julian jumped out of the way and decided to head back to town. He wasn't going to wait around for someone else to beat him senseless.

As he got farther down Campstool Road, he looked back, glad to see the lights of the truck stop in the distance. He wondered which was worse for him: going back into town where he was a wanted criminal, or being harassed at a truck stop. He felt safer taking his chances in town. Maybe he could find a warm spot to sleep for a while. He wondered about the old man at Catherine's house. *Why was he trying to stop me? Why was he saying that he knew me? I hope I didn't hurt the old guy.*

The driver of a large black pickup didn't see the

young man walking on the side of the road.

"Mercy ER, we have a hit and run, a young boy, approximately fourteen years old. Multiple injuries, broken leg, internal bleeding, head trauma." The ambulance raced toward the hospital, their critically injured patient barely clinging to life.

CHAPTER 17
Breakfast

Saturday morning, as she promised, Catherine quietly made her way through the small closet door in Sarah's room, and down to the kitchen fixing breakfast before anyone else was up. Sarah and Gracie's brief kitchen tour the previous evening was just a blur of surprises, so it took a little time to figure out which knobs and dials to use.

Once she figured out how to turn the lights on, she stood in awe at how beautiful the kitchen looked. Dark granite countertops, matching appliances, shiny polished metal, and nothing with open flames. Being alone to explore this amazing place excited her.

Just opening the refrigerator became a spectacular moment. It was incredible, so much food and it had different compartments for every kind of treat. She searched through every drawer and shelf. She was sure she could get used to this.

She had been poisoned—her poor old kitchen now seemed lifeless, boring, and even a dangerous place to fix supper. The single light bulb hanging precariously in the middle of the room was dim; lifting the pots and pans to the sink was comparable to any weight-lifting competition. Her 1927 modern refrigerator was noisy and threw off enough heat from the electric motor to heat the entire house—if it turned on—and then, opening the refrigerator took the arm of Goliath. Poisoned, she was.

After several attempts at making scrambled eggs in an electric skillet, she managed to get a full batch of fluffy eggs piled in a bowl, and into the oven to stay warm. While she cooked, Catherine's thoughts circled her changed life; she felt like it could be a dream, dazzled by so many bright, shiny moving parts.

The night before, when she was riding in the car with Mike, she thought it might be fun to tell her girlfriends about the wild new adventure she was living, but now—after spending a night at home—she wouldn't dream of it. Anyway, she knew they wouldn't believe this in a hundred years.

By the time Catherine had gotten home, it was too late to go over and see her mom, Anna. Catherine knew she would be worried. Catherine made a promise to herself to go back and visit sometime today. She might even tell her about this amazing event she'd been swept up into. Then again, as with her friends, how would she explain this?

Catherine's mind switched back to the task at hand, and she moved quickly to turn the bacon and pancakes. She found out the electric stove was much faster than her wood stove, hard to get used to and it didn't smell right either—no smoke. She wasn't sure if she liked it. With wood, she knew how to time her cooking, time to get organized and lay things out, and prepare other foods.

* * * *

A distant clank noise woke Mike. It took a moment for him to realize he heard a sound. His mind wove the sound back into his dream and he drifted back to sleep again. A clink. This time, he woke up. He had invited Catherine back for breakfast!

Mike flew out of bed, pulled on a pair of jeans, and stretched a T-shirt over his head while brushing his teeth, then tiptoed downstairs to see if it was his invited guest.

To his surprise, the dining room table had already been set; he could smell bacon and pancakes. He couldn't imagine a more wonderful smell, coupled with the feeling of anticipation he felt. Mike managed to be quiet enough to sneak up on Catherine and stand in the kitchen doorway, watching until she noticed. Catherine had elbows on the counter with her back to Mike, deep in thought, trying to figure out how the coffee machine worked. She was wearing a pair of jeans or something that looked like jeans, and a white cotton blouse. *Remarkable*, he thought to himself. After all her talk about how strict the dress code was for teachers. He was pleased to see she was engaging with this new technology and worked so hard to be a helpful guest. *She's a wonderful woman, indeed.*

Then, Catherine said something out loud to herself. "It says coffee on it, so then the darn thing should make coffee, right?" Mike couldn't help himself and spoke up.

"Good morning!"

"Whoa!" Catherine grabbed her heart and turned around. "You scared the devil out of me!" She breathed and smiled back. "Good morning."

"What's all this? Huh? I was going to fix *you* breakfast."

"Well, I'm an early riser and got hungry, so I thought I'll just get this breakfast started." She turned slightly and picked up a fork to flip the bacon.

"Are you having an issue with the coffee maker?" Mike gestured toward the coffee machine.

"I think I am. I'm talking to it, but it isn't working. I'm not sure which button to push." Catherine looked at the coffee machine and tapped a black button.

"Yeah, it can be intimidating. Would you like me to set it?"

"That might be a good idea; I certainly couldn't do it. If it doesn't percolate, I'm not sure how to run it."

Mike walked over and set up the coffee maker with water and ground coffee beans.

"You're pretty brave coming through that closet door all by yourself, you know," he complimented. Catherine smiled and flipped a pancake.

"Yes, I suppose." Catherine smiled. Then Mike posed a question.

"So, have you figured out what all this is about? I mean, here we are, two people from different times . . ." Catherine turned around and leaned against the counter. He could tell she must have been asking this question, too.

"I don't know. I might as well be from a different planet, so much has changed."

Mike opened the cabinet and pulled out his favorite coffee cup.

"Would you like some coffee, Catherine?"

"Yes, Michael, thank you." Mike poured a cup for both of them. He opened the fridge for his favorite creamer, nodding to Catherine to ask if she wanted some.

"Oh, no. Thank you."

He continued his answer to Catherine. "I know, I feel the same . . . It's just the strangest thing. I'm an engineer by profession, so I deal with practical, everyday provable things; there is no mystical middle ground. So, this has me baffled—I don't know how to explain it. I'm in the business of explaining stuff, and sometimes, very complex stuff, yet this is way beyond my skill set."

Catherine sipped her coffee, listening to Mike trying to understand their mystery. Mike poured more coffee.

"To me, it's a little scary that we both had this mysterious closet in our house and didn't know it. I mean, we don't know what could happen, and this thing with Julian, some bad things could have already happened. Until we know more about it, if it's all right with you, let's you and I try to manage this thing and keep it between us, if we can. I'm pretty sure we don't want the world to know about this."

"Sounds just fine to me. I know I certainly don't want anyone else to know. Just having this experience with Julian has scared me enough." Catherine set her coffee down to take the bacon out of the pan. "I'm glad you thought about that and I appreciate being asked my opinion."

"I couldn't imagine doing it any other way," Mike admitted. "You're just as much a part of this as I am."

"Thank you, Michael. In a way, though," said Catherine, "I do sort of feel sorry for Julian. He's been through so much, I'm sure he did it out of fear. I hope he didn't mean to do anything bad---he just didn't seem to be that kind of kid to me. Being a teacher, I think after a while, you get a sense for the good ones and the bad ones."

"I'll bet you are. Myself, I wouldn't have the patience to wrangle a bunch of kids in one room. I'd go nuts. You certainly have my respect." He grinned.

"It's something you commit yourself to. If you can't be committed to it, don't even try, because it will drive you crazy," Catherine said. She grabbed a spatula off the counter and walked across to the stovetop. "I'd better flip some more pancakes; I've already burned a few. This darn thing cooks so fast."

Mike took another sip from his coffee. "I know that the girls and I have met this wonderful, smart teacher and now we have a mystery to solve. A pretty interesting mystery. Strange, but interesting." The sound of running feet broke into Mike's words, and in seconds, Sarah and Gracie were in the kitchen, hugging their dad and then Catherine.

* * * *

After a full breakfast, showers, and fashion tips with Catherine, they got into Mike's SUV and drove to the hospital to see how Fred was doing. When they walked into Fred's room, he was sitting up in bed and eating a snack. Catherine and Mike were surprised at Fred's recovery. When the girls came in, they ran over to hug Fred.

"Hello, my girls!" Fred hollered. Catherine stood back at the doorway while Mike grabbed Fred's free hand. Catherine knew Fred hadn't seen her yet and wondered if he might not remember who she was. Catherine thought about how she would have to come to terms with this time change with her own life, especially seeing Freddy now, as an old man. For her, just a few days had passed since she last saw a younger Freddy, but for this man Fred, it had been over seventy years.

"Fred, you sure look better than you did last night," Mike said. As Mike and Fred continued to talk, Catherine watched Fred and tried to imagine the young man he used to be. Then, in that small moment, as he teased Sarah and Gracie, she saw him—she saw thirteen-year-old Freddy inside the old man. Inside, he was still there. Catherine felt a comforting warmth envelop her. She smiled. It was something she could feel, not say out loud.

"I feel so much better, too. This modern medicine, Mike, it's just amazing what they can do now." Then Fred looked up at Catherine and squinted. He opened his mouth as if he was going to say something, but he couldn't. Catherine noticed that look of excitement growing on his face; his eyes opened up and filled quickly with tears.

"Now, could this sweet woman be my favorite teacher, Miss Tanner?" Fred held his arms out; Catherine quickly rushed over to wrap her arms around Fred, tears welling up in her eyes as she kissed Fred's whiskered face. Gracie and Sarah excitedly jumped up and down. Catherine pulled back, wiping tears, and took a corner of the bed sheet to wipe Freddy's eyes.

"It's been quite a few years for you, hasn't it Freddy?" Catherine asked as she held on to one of his thick, wrinkled hands.

"Yes, Miss Tanner, I guess I'd better be able to count how many since you taught me my first arithmetic problems." Freddy grinned at Catherine.

"Sweetheart, since you're not my student anymore, you can call me Catherine."

"Miss Tanner, uh, Catherine . . ." Fred cleared his throat. "There's something that I've been wanting to tell you."

"Freddy, you've been waiting all this time? Of course, yes, Fred, what is it?"

"You know that little job you gave me to do, well . . ." He cleared his throat again. "I have to tell you that, over the years, that little job was a Godsend. It kept me going when times were tough for me. But I didn't want to let you down. Thank you for watching out for me and being the best teacher a guy could have, and . . ." Fred stopped and wiped his eyes. "And for coming back to finish the school year with us." Fred gave Catherine a big grin and a wink. "You have no idea how much that meant to all of us kids."

Catherine realized what Fred was saying, but knew it wasn't time to talk more; her mind wasn't ready.

"Thank you, sweetheart." She looked him in the eyes. "That's what makes being a teacher worthwhile." Mike walked over and put his hand on Fred's.

"Are they feeding you okay, Fred?"

"Too much of that green squiggly stuff, I know that for sure." Fred looked up at Mike and Catherine. "It looks like you two are getting along okay." Mike laughed a little. Catherine gave Fred a dismissive glance.

"Well, considering the strange circumstances we met under, I guess yes, things are going well, Fred," Mike admitted. "By the way, has the doctor told you what the verdict is?"

"Oh, they're going to run a few more tests later today

and he says they'll let me out of this place soon. I think the doc said tomorrow afternoon." Sarah and Gracie huddled closer next to Fred so they could hear how he was doing.

"That's great!" said Catherine.

"You do know that we're going to come and pick you up as soon as the doctor releases you," Mike offered. Fred grinned at Mike.

"That's pretty nice of you, considering I messed up your flower bed and all."

"We'll settle on that later." Mike patted Fred on his shoulder.

"What about that boy, Julian? Have you heard anything about him?" asked Fred.

"Nothing at all. I thought we'd resume our search for him today. That's why I asked Catherine to come back. Unless he hitched a ride out of the area, we should be able to find him."

"You know," said Fred, staring at Catherine, "Julian, he didn't do this."

"Are you sure, Fred? Didn't you try to stop him?" asked Catherine.

"Oh, I sure did," he continued. "You know, I've been watching your house closely ever since Mike and the girls moved in."

Sarah and Gracie both looked at each other, surprised. "Ah, ha!"

"What's the deal?" Mike butted in, asking the girls.

"We thought Fred was some kind of perv or something, always watching our house," Sarah said, smiling at Fred.

"I hope not," Fred answered. "Anyway, I was watching

the house, in a nice way; because of Catherine's little note—the one I was trying to get down out of a box the afternoon I fell—, I knew something was going to happen. So, I was prepared when I saw him come out around the side of the house. I had walked over to your house and managed to stop him on your lawn." Fred's voice was weak. He paused, caught his breath, and continued.

"I told him that we had met before, on the streets of Cheyenne. He asked me what I was talking about and started walking away—I grabbed him by the nape of the neck, and he pushed me back with his arms. I stumbled backward and my foot went into a soft spot in the yard, then I fell over and hit my head on something. I must have completely passed out. I don't remember anything after that. I know he was acting in self-defense; I wouldn't blame him for what he'd done. It was my dang balance that I don't have anymore, that's the problem!"

After a few more minutes, Mike, Catherine, and the girls headed out. As they walked down the hall to the elevator and down through the lobby, Catherine noticed an officer in the hospital lobby who was at Mike's house the previous night. She mentioned that to Mike, so they walked over to say thank you.

"Officer Koenig? Mike Roberts, we spoke yesterday. We've just been up to see Fred Perkins."

"Oh, sure," replied the officer. "How's he doing?"

"Quite well. He's sitting up and teasing the girls, so I'm pretty sure he's on the mend."

"That's good. Sometimes we never hear how the victim is doing after they're taken to the hospital. Say, you mentioned to keep an eye out for a young boy, right?"

"Yes, around thirteen or fourteen years old. We were just on our way out to look for him."

"Well, I don't know if this could be the same one or not, because we don't have a positive ID, but late last night, a young boy was brought into the emergency room. He'd been hit by a truck out on Campstool Road, east of town."

Catherine grabbed Mike's arm and said to him, "It could be Julian."

Mike turned back to Officer Koenig. "Do you have any idea where he would be right now?"

"I'm afraid he was hurt pretty bad, probably up in ICU. Is he related to you?"

"Well, no, he's just a . . ." Mike looked over to Catherine for support.

"He's a close friend from my hometown," she said.

"Oh, okay, you might check with the desk and see if they'll let you see him. I would sure like to know if this is the kid you're looking for. As I said, he didn't have any ID on him, so we'd like to resolve that."

Mike, Catherine, and the girls went back over to the elevators and the critical care unit desk. Mike asked the duty nurse if they could see the young man brought in last night.

"Are you related?"

"No, we're not, but we've been searching for a young boy, about fourteen years old, that ran away from our house yesterday. We need to know if this is that boy; we'd like to identify him. He was Ms. Tanner's student." Mike threw in the white lie for expedience, pointing to Catherine.

The nurse at the desk called for a supervisor to come over. After she was informed of the situation, she looked at the charts and waved to Mike and Catherine to follow her.

"Come this way." She escorted them down the hall and to a room with one bed, surrounded by computers, monitors, tubes, red blinking lights, and buzzing sounds.

"This is the boy's room, but let me tell you, he suffered severe injuries last night." She spoke quietly. "His left leg is broken in two places, a broken arm, a collapsed lung, a concussion, multiple cuts, scrapes and he's bruised up something terrible. They worked on him most of the night and just finished about two hours ago. I'm not sure if you'll be able to recognize him or not. His face is swollen and bruised so much it may be hard to tell."

"Do you have his clothes somewhere?" asked Catherine.

"Yes, in a bag, here in the corner of the room." The nurse walked over, picked it up, and brought it back to Catherine.

"Sarah," asked Catherine, "you may be able to help identify his clothes since you saw him yesterday morning." Catherine held the bag open. Sarah put one hand on the bag and looked, then stepped back.

"Oh, pee-you!" she exclaimed, waving her hands in front of her nose. "Yep, that's Julian's stuff. I remember that smell from when he was holding me down." Mike walked over to get a closer look at him. He motioned to have Sarah come over next to him.

"Sarah, honey, if you'd rather not, I understand, but if you can see if this is Julian, it would help us." Sarah nodded and leaned over closer to Julian's bedside. She studied his face for a few seconds and then turned around and moved over closer to her dad; tears filled her eyes.

"Dad, he looks so awful."

Mike hugged Sarah. "I know honey, but can you tell if that's him?"

"It's really hard, Dad, but I'm sure it's Julian." Sarah wiped tears out of her eyes.

Mike and Sarah walked back to the nurse's station, Catherine and Gracie following behind, to tell the duty nurse that they were sure it was Julian. Catherine confirmed his name as Julian Daniels, from Joplin, Missouri, and that he had no family.

Sarah and Gracie decided to stay in the waiting room to watch TV while Catherine and Mike sat in large chairs near the doorway to Julian's room. Mike noticed Catherine fidgeting with her hands; he could tell she was upset.

"This is so awful," Catherine said, turning toward him. "He is a good boy—he didn't deserve this to happen—it wasn't anything so bad," she said, playing down Julian's theft from her.

"I feel bad, too," Mike said. "I wished I would have taken more time to search for him last night. I feel this is partially my fault."

"No, Michael, how could you have known? It's just a terrible accident." Catherine squeezed Mike's arm, reassuring him. She got up from the hospital chair and walked over to Julian, put her hands on his forehead, and began quietly talking to him. Sarah and Gracie walked back into the room, apparently bored with the few channels available.

"Julian, it's Catherine, Catherine Tanner. You're going to be okay. Just get better and we'll be in to see you every day." Julian lay motionless as Catherine took his hand to hold it. In a few moments, Catherine felt a sensation. She looked back at Mike with a surprised face.

"He squeezed my hand," Catherine whispered. "I think he can hear us . . . right, Julian?" She felt Julian's fingers move slightly. "Yes, he squeezed my hand again! Sarah, go ahead, you say something," Catherine urged. Hesitatingly, she walked around the other side of the bed, reached over to Julian's hand, and took it in hers.

"Julian, this is Sarah, you know, from Catherine's house, the girl you tied up?" Julian squeezed her hand.

"He squeezed mine, too," she said. "We want you to get better, Julian, so I can beat the crap out of you."

"Sarah!" Mike and Gracie yelled over to Sarah. Catherine, standing on the other side of the bed, put her hand over her mouth, but didn't say a word. Her grinning eyes told Sarah how she felt.

"Okay, Julian, I'm just kidding, kind of, but really, we want you to get better." Julian squeezed Sarah's hand again. She smiled at Catherine.

Catherine moved forward and took Julian's hand once more. "Julian, we're going to let you rest now. You've been in a bad accident and you need to get better. The doctors and nurses will take good care of you. We'll be back to see you real soon, okay?" Julian squeezed Catherine's hand again and then she thought about something. She looked over at Mike and smiled.

"Julian, one more thing. We just talked to Fred, the old man outside the house. He is here too, but Julian, he's all right, so don't worry about that, you just get better."

Julian squeezed Catherine's hand one more time.

* * * *

In a few minutes, back in the car and headed home, Sarah and Gracie had fun telling Catherine about malls, shopping trips, shoe stores, and day spas. Catherine couldn't believe the changes to her simple and quiet little town of Cheyenne.

Once they arrived home, Sarah and Gracie ran to their rooms. Catherine seized the opportunity to pull Mike aside; it was time to talk about a few things. She led him to the couch and motioned for Mike to sit down. She could see a slight hint of concern on his face. She smiled and took a breath.

"Michael, all of this has been so fantastic to me. I'm sure you can imagine how, ah, awkward this has been, for both of us. But I need to tell you that I have to go back and get my homework done for school on Monday and I promised myself that I would go back and check on my mom. I hope you understand."

"Sure I understand, Catherine. I didn't expect we could take all of your time. But, you know, I love— well . . ." Mike corrected, "I have to count the girls, too: *We* love having you with us."

"Thanks, Michael." She hesitated, and her small hands began to fidget. "There's something else you should know. My father died just a few years ago."

"Oh, Catherine, I'm sorry." Catherine could see the concern in Mike's eyes.

"Thank you, Michael. My mother lives just a few blocks away from where I live, from where this house is, so we visit nearly every evening—you know, just to stay in touch. It's just Mom and me, so she counts on me, and I count on her."

"I understand," Mike said. "My folks live in Denver, but we don't see them very often, probably once a month, if that. It's nice that you have your mom so close. I'd sure like to meet her, sometime."

"Yeah, well, we'll have to think about that for a while. She would probably have a heart attack if she knew about this. If you think I'm old-fashioned . . ." Catherine's voice trailed off. "It's been good for her to have me to talk with. My grandmother died this last year, too, so with all of this happening, we've drawn so much closer, I'm sure you can imagine. Anyway, I'm glad you understand why I need to get back."

"Will you be able to come back tomorrow, when we bring Fred home?" asked Mike.

Catherine sighed. She was torn between this exciting experience, feelings for Mike and his daughters, and that deep need to spend a little time at home alone with her feelings, to ponder on all these confusing emotions. Everything seemed to be moving so fast. Part of that check on her feelings had to do with speaking with her mom. Anna, despite being old-fashioned, was Catherine's emotional home base.

"I can't promise, but I'll try." Catherine managed a weak smile and got up from the couch to walk upstairs, then stopped. She could see the disappointment in Mike's eyes. Catherine didn't want to hurt him. She turned around and took his hands.

"Michael, there's another issue I'm struggling with."

She studied his face to see if she could read him. For the entire time Catherine had been around Mike, she sensed a sincere, caring person; she was hoping those qualities would help now.

"Michael, this . . . this is just not *real*. You're not real, this whole experience is not real. It can't be. I feel like I'm in a dream. For me to meet you and the girls, like this, in such a bizarre way . . . How is this possible?"

Mike's face revealed a pained expression, something she thought meant he didn't comprehend. Catherine wanted to see an expression that told her he had it taken care of. Why risk her future as a teacher, something she had been working on all her life, for this unbelievable situation? Catherine wanted to know if her life meant something to him. She took a deep breath and sighed. She was pleased that Mike remained patient.

"I'm a real person; I live in real-time and take care of my mom. I have students; I dress the way I dress. To have my world just flip like this and these weird illogical things happen . . . well, it just doesn't happen, not in my world. So, maybe you can see why I'm a bit hesitant to make too many plans here. I have so much there, things I need to attend to. Am I making any sense?" Tears slowly formed in her eyes as she waited for his response.

"Catherine, I'm not very good at hiding my feelings. I'm sure you have a pretty good idea that I like you, so I'll just skate past that for now. We don't have to rush or do anything that is going to make you feel uncomfortable, nauseous, or pressured."

Catherine gave Mike a comforting smile. "You know how I feel."

Mike looked up at the stairs. "I know you're going to go back—and you should; you have to meet your obligations and certainly see your mom and friends." Mike took Catherine's hands. "Catherine, you just do what you need to do and if it works out to come back and visit, please know without a doubt, that we want you here with us any time you can. I worry that the little closet door is unpredictable. It could be gone tomorrow. We just don't know how much time we have, I don't want to lose you."

Catherine smiled and pulled on Mike's hands to bring him in close for their first hug. She wanted to kiss Mike but hesitated and turned to go up the stairs, Mike following closely behind.

After she left Mike's house, she had dinner with her mom and tried to explain the crazy experiences she had been through. After a couple of days, despite her mom's warnings and concerns for her safety—and quite possibly her sanity—Catherine decided to go back.

By nine o'clock Sunday morning, Catherine's mom, Anna, was at church praying while Catherine was making her way cautiously through the small closet doorway and into Sarah's room.

CHAPTER 18
Apologies

Sunday afternoon, Mike, Catherine, and the girls were at the hospital to pick up Fred. Mike had received a call from the hospital that Fred had been released to go home.

Mike asked Fred if he wanted to go over and see Julian up in the critical care unit. Fred agreed; he wanted to visit Julian before going home.

When they walked into Julian's room, nurses had just made sure his IVs had been set correctly before they walked out. Mike pushed Fred's wheelchair up to the bed, and Julian weakly looked over in his direction. Catherine went to Julian's bedside as Mike took Sarah and Gracie out of the room to talk with Julian's doctor, who was standing outside studying charts.

Freddy put his hand on Julian's bed as Catherine leaned over to speak in Julian's ear.

"Julian, good morning, son." Julian slowly opened his eyes and turned to the sound of Catherine's voice.

"Good morning, Miss Catherine," he answered in a weak, raspy voice.

"Julian, Fred is here, the gentleman outside the house. He's getting released today. He wanted to come in and visit you before he left. Is that okay?"

"Sure, where is he?" Julian painfully shifted to see

Fred. Freddy touched Julian's bandaged hand.

"Hey, buddy, that's all right, don't try to move. You need to lie still."

"I guess so . . ." Julian started to say, his voice weak and body sore. "Guess I'll be laid up for a while . . . Are you okay? How did you get hurt?" Julian asked Fred.

Catherine wasn't surprised that Julian didn't recall what happened when Freddy tried to stop Julian. She wanted to see how these two would get along, now.

"Yeah, I'm okay," Fred answered. "Oh, I just fell, that's all. I really can't remember." Fred waved his hand and shrugged off his injury as nothing. "I'm sorry I scared you back at the house. Didn't mean to, you know, I was just trying to let you know who I was and . . . well, I wanted to stop you from hurting yourself, or anyone else."

"I wish I had more sense; seems I'm shy about that. How did you know?" Julian asked slowly.

"Because, son, Miss Tanner here had asked me to keep an eye out for you. I know this is hard for you to understand, as it is for each of us." Fred looked around the room to make sure just the family was listening. He whispered, "That closet thing—you know, that closet that lets you travel through time and all—well, um . . . it's the darnedest thing. You see, back in 1928, I was a student of Miss Tanner's and I was with that group of boys who she stopped from slugging on you, remember that?" Julian's eyes opened wide as he remembered.

"You were . . . ?"

"Yeah, that was me, sorry to say. Anyway, Julian, I'm sorry about that. I figured I owed you something, so when Miss Tanner asked me to help, I couldn't refuse. It took me seventy-two years to make good on that promise, but I did." Julian moved a little under the sheets and pulled out his one arm that wasn't in a cast and offered it to Fred.

"Julian Daniels, sir. Nice to meet you."

Catherine teared up.

"Fred Perkins, sir, my honor to meet you. And I hope all is forgiven between us."

"Thank you, Fred, it is," Julian said. He turned to Catherine. "Now, I need to apologize to Miss Tanner." Catherine looked up hesitantly; she wasn't expecting this.

"Miss Tanner, I'm so sorry for taking your wooden box. I hid it in that house, at this time, but when I came back to return it, it was gone. I was going to bring it back to you, I was."

Catherine knew Julian was doing his best to apologize and she loved how sincere he was. "Thank you, Julian, I'm glad you confessed. We'll find it, someday."

Mike and the girls walked back into the room and up to Julian's bedside.

"Julian," Catherine interrupted herself, "this is Mike Roberts; he now owns the house, the one that used to be mine. And these are his daughters, Sarah, whom you've already met, and her younger sister, Gracie." Julian slowly turned to look at Sarah and held his hand up to her. He apologized to her too, for hurting her wrists and ankles.

"The worst part, Julian," Sarah joked, "was that you told me you hoped I didn't have to go to the bathroom. Well, I did. By the time Dad found me, I had almost peed my pants."

Julian grinned and squeezed her hand again.

"I'm sorry, Sarah. I hope you get a chance to get even

with me." Catherine came up behind the girls and hugged them.

"Well," Mike said, "I'm just glad that everyone is all right or at least on the mend. We'd better get Fred home and tucked in for the night, and Julian, we'll be back to visit you tomorrow sometime, okay?" Catherine and the girls walked over to Julian to say goodbye, then Fred came over. As Mike and the girls quietly left the room, Fred and Catherine lingered behind.

"Listen, Julian, get yourself all better, then you can decide what you want to do. I'll be coming in to visit you, too—if they still let me drive, that is."

"That'd be great, Fred." Julian hesitated. "Fred, Catherine?"

"Yes, son."

"What is going on? I mean, the closet door, the time change and all . . . What in the heck is that all about? This whole thing has me so confused."

"I know, son, it's just too much to think about, you know, that it could be real. But it could be a dangerous thing too; we have to be careful," Fred warned.

"Maybe after you get better and out of here, we can figure it out," said Catherine. "You just rest for now and we'll see you in the morning."

"Okay, thanks." Catherine helped Fred turn his wheelchair around to leave the room. Julian looked up at the ceiling and closed his eyes. Catherine wondered what he was thinking.

* * * *

Later that day, Mike and Catherine got Fred settled in his house and then walked back across the street. As they walked, Catherine sensed that Mike wanted to say something. Before he got a chance, she broke the silence.

"I hope I haven't been dreaming all of this."

"I hope not either; it would spoil my dinner."

"Somehow, I think you would still manage to fit dinner in, even if it was a dream," Catherine teased.

"Oh, man, where did that come from?"

"Teachers have a sense of humor, you know."

"I guess I'm finding that out. I'll have to talk to Fred about how funny you were in class."

Catherine laughed as they walked up on the porch and sat down on the bench. Mike leaned forward, putting his elbows on his knees, rubbing his hands, as if preparing to pray in earnest. "I heard Fred tell you that he was happy you came back to finish the school year, so I've been preparing myself, knowing you've got to go back."

"Yes, I know, that's why this is so hard. I'm a teacher, and it was quite difficult to get that job, especially for a woman my age. I've dedicated myself to my work and my students. I've got a contract with the school, but more than that, I can't let the kids down. I have to complete the school year with them."

"I'm just being selfish," Mike admitted. "I've found someone that I'm sure I have extremely deep feelings for and I want her to stay. These are such bizarre circumstances . . . I mean"—Mike hesitated and stared down at the ground—"who would have imagined a time warp inside our closet?" He looked back into Catherine's eyes. "Catherine, I want you to know that this is your decision to make and I'll accept whatever you decide. I also want you to know that I care for you very much and whenever you decide to come back and spend more time with us, it would make me, and the girls, extremely happy."

"I know, Michael. I care about you and the girls so much. You're a great guy and it's obvious you're a great dad . . . and you picked a nice home." Catherine grinned. "I'm just not ready. Do I give up the only life I've known for something so unpredictable and unknown? Not to mention this huge difference in time. I've always considered myself a forward-thinking, modern woman. But in this world, I feel totally out of place and instantly I'm old-fashioned. And, little sweetheart Sarah wants to give me a closet makeover, whatever that is."

Mike laughed. "Sarah is too funny, and that's a good example. The girls and I would have so much fun introducing you to so many new things. Yes, it's a bizarre thing, but it brought us together. And look, just look how well you have adapted to all these new things—you truly are a modern woman. You could have the best of both worlds. If you do decide to go back and stay, I couldn't fault you. At least, I've still had this much with you."

"Thank you for saying that. I just have to go back. I have my mother to look after, my classroom, the kids waiting for me, and so many other projects to finish," she said, trying to keep her emotions under control.

"How am I going to manage with Fred? And then, when Julian gets out, I won't have you there and it just seems to me that you're the one that makes this all worthwhile. I'm sure Fred and Julian will see it that way, too," Mike said.

"Mike, you'll do just fine. I promise I'll think about my decision and let you know as soon as I can."

"Well, you know where I'll be and I'm just a closet door away from you. If you do want to talk to me, I guess we could just leave notes inside the little door and visit with each other that way."

* * * *

Over dinner, Mike explained to the kids that Catherine needed to go back home. The girls were disappointed, and both ran around the table to hug Catherine.

After dinner, Catherine made her way up the stairs, followed by her entourage of admirers. Sarah and Gracie held on to Catherine's hands. On the way up, Sarah stopped and looked up at Catherine.

"Can't we just come through the closet and visit you, whenever we want?"

Catherine gave him a look that said, *Do you want to help with this?*

"Sweetheart," Mike said, "I just don't know how stable this thing is—what if it disappears and you're lost? I'm not sure if I want to take that chance. I don't want either one of you to try this unless I know about it. For now, we've decided to leave a note for each other once a week and you girls can leave one, too. Otherwise, I don't think we'd better mess with it too often."

Mike pulled open the closet doors and pried open the small door for Catherine to slide into.

The girls received one last hug then Catherine turned

and crouched to crawl into the wood-framed opening. Mike leaned over and pushed the door shut. Mike stood, holding both of his daughters close to him. There was a long period of silence.

"I'm sure going to miss her."

"You like her a lot, don't you Dad?" Gracie asked.

"Yes, sweetheart, I do."

CHAPTER 19

Healing

Monday morning came and Mike felt like he had a hangover. Before moving a muscle to get up, he stayed in bed to let his mind run through all that had happened. It all came down to Catherine—he missed her so much. It was easy for him to imagine her lying beside him in his bed and talking to her about what was on the schedule today or what happened yesterday. With her around, he even felt better about the girls' safety. The girls trusted Catherine and so did he. Today, he was the only one for them to rely on, as it was before.

There's an old saying: *What you don't know won't hurt you*. Today, Mike *knew*—and it hurt, it hurt bad. He remembered feeling this way after Elizabeth was gone. He loathed this feeling and he wanted it gone. As before, he was going to have to fight hard not to let it ruin or tear him apart. It made him cry to remember his pain of losing Elizabeth. He felt like an addict; he needed to put something in the space of loss.

Mike told Sarah and Gracie to check in on Fred every afternoon after they got home from school and then he would go over and see him when he got home from work. After that, they could go see Julian at the hospital and if Fred felt well enough, he could come along, too. Over the next several weeks, both Fred and Julian continued to improve. After a month, Fred was well enough to begin his neighborhood walks again. Sometimes, Sarah and Gracie would walk with him.

After five days, the doctors got Julian up out of the wheelchair and let him stand for just a minute, and increased his time each day after that, so that by the end of the next week, he was taking steps. At the end of the third week, his young body had healed enough that he was able to go home. Mike and Fred were there to get him. On the way home, Mike asked Julian a question.

"Julian, son, it sounds like you've had a pretty rough life so far. Any ideas about what you'd like to do now? Do you have any family waiting for you somewhere?"

"Well, sir, I don't have any family, here anyway . . ." Julian's voice trailed off; he seemed in deep thought. "I thought about going back to Missouri. I don't know if I will or not. There might be some people back there that would like to hang me by a rope, I'm sure," Julian said.

Mike was surprised at his answer but didn't want to influence him. Mike silently wondered what thoughts troubled Julian.

"Well Julian, it's certainly up to you. We have this unique gift given to us, this door to the past, or the future, to use however we want—for a little bit of time, anyway."

"If I go back, you know, to the other time, I'd want to go see some friends. I know my mom probably doesn't want to have anything to do with me, so I wouldn't be going back for her—at least not for a while, anyway." They pulled up to the house and Mike came around to help Julian out of the car. Mike opened Julian's car door when

Fred spoke up.

"Julian," Fred started, "I'd like you to come to live with me for a while. You and I go way back, heck, clean into 1928, eh? Anyway, uh, would you consider staying at my house? You know, at my age, I could use a young helper around and I could show you some of the new-fangled things we do nowadays. Besides, Julian, we're right across the street from Mike and the girls. Would that work for you?" Mike helped Julian swing around in the car seat to slide out and handed Julian his crutches. Julian leaned forward to hold on to his crutches.

"Yeah Fred, that would be great." A smiling Fred patted Julian on the shoulder.

"Well, good enough. Let's get you moved in that direction." Fred pointed to his home across the street.

CHAPTER 20

Surprise

Six Months Later

In the late spring, Mike, Sarah, Gracie, Fred, and Julian spent time shopping for garden supplies. Sarah and Gracie kept trying to get Mike to swing by the mall to help Julian pick out some decent clothes. Julian had no trouble picking up the latest music and often tried to mimic rap singers on TV, sending Sarah and Gracie into giggling fits.

Mike had been growingly concerned about Fred's health; he seemed slower and looked unusually pale the last few days. When he mentioned something to Fred, he always got the same answer.

"Oh, I'm all right. You know, at my age, feeling tired is good, that way for sure I know I'm alive." Mike had insisted several times for Fred to call if he isn't feeling well; no one wanted anything to happen to him.

After visiting the store, Mike invited Julian and Fred over for ice cream at the house. When they arrived home, the girls raced into the house to try on their new clothes as Fred and Julian walked home to drop packages off before coming right back.

Inside, Sarah was the first to notice the smell. Her eyes lit up and she ran to the kitchen. As Mike and Gracie walked in, they also noticed the sweet smell of spice, like apple cobbler.

"Mmm," Mike said. "That smells nice. Did we have something cooking when we left?"

Gracie ran into the kitchen ahead of Sarah and squealed in delight. Curious, Mike followed to see what was going on. As he entered the kitchen, he saw Catherine hugging each of the girls. She looked up at him and smiled.

"Catherine!" Mike hurried over and threw his arms around her. It had been six months since they'd seen each other, and far too long.

Catherine greeted Mike with a hug and a kiss. "Funny thing, I missed you and the girls so much, I couldn't get you off my mind." Mike gave Catherine another kiss, and Gracie and Sarah joined in the hug.

"I'm so glad to hear that," he admitted. "I've been the same way. Did you get to finish the school year, though?"

"Yes," replied Catherine. "And it was so wonderful—the kids were great. Fred was right, I'm glad I stayed for them. Now, do you want some of my special apple cobbler?"

"Can I hold you and eat it at the same time?" asked Mike. Following their noses, Fred and Julian walked into the kitchen.

"Oh!" cried Catherine. "Look at you guys!" Fred came up to Catherine first and gave her a loving hug and kiss on the cheek.

"Catherine, it is so nice to have you back with us. Not a soul here has been doing very well with you gone."

"Oh, Fred, cut that out, you're going to make me feel needed."

"It's true, Catherine. Fred is confessing how we all feel," Mike told her. Catherine blushed and grabbed a tissue for her nose.

"And Julian!" She grabbed Julian for a hug. "Julian, look at you, you've gotten taller and you're so handsome! Are you feeling better, all healed up?" she asked.

"Yes, ma'am, doing a lot better." He reacted shyly and tried to hide his voice from Catherine.

"Julian!" she yelled. "Your voice has changed, oh my God, Mike, our baby has grown up!" Catherine teased.

"Have I gotten taller too, Catherine?" asked Gracie.

"Oh, I'm sorry, yes dear, you sure have, I hardly have to lean over to hug you anymore," Catherine said. "Pretty soon you'll be taller than me."

Mike leaned against the kitchen counter, grinned, and took it all in. His heart and soul were filled up again. *Go ahead*, he thought to himself, *soak it all up, every last ounce, and let it go on for a thousand years, then we'll do it again.*

* * * *

Early the next morning, in Mike's guest bedroom, Catherine's first sensation was the smell of clean sheets on her bed, then the unmistakable smell of bacon. *At least that hasn't changed*, she thought. She rolled over on her back, surveying the room she was in and thinking about the last six months since she met Mike coming through the small closet door.

She wondered to herself, *I wish Mom would come with*

me sometime and see what I'm seeing. A few months ago, her life was predictable and organized. She had a peaceful life teaching a great class of students and earned enough to buy materials to make a new dress, now and then. She even put a little away for retirement. Today, who knew what could happen? Her life had become a whirlwind.

Before today, the only thing missing was someone special in her life—not that she had any shortage of suitors trying to win her heart. It was just that to her, no one offered anything better than the life she already had. She was happy with her single life—she had friends and had accomplished something, a teaching position. It might have been out in the middle of nowhere, but it was a position. Why change for a guy that wants you to be his maid service, mommy, and cook? What was she going to get out of it?

Now, today, or so it seemed, she had Mike. This guy came along, entering her house—uniquely, no less—and stirred up dangerous and exciting thoughts and feelings. Catherine grabbed her pillow and buried her face in it.

Then, a soft knock at the door; she knew who it was. "Catherine? Mademoiselle?"

"Yes," she answered playfully as she yawned and stretched. "Who is it?" In Mike's best fake French accent, he tried to entice her to open the door.

"It ees zee 'otel chef; I 'ave made nice breakfass for you, no?"

"Just put it by the door, chef, and I'll get it later," she teased.

"Zee chef ees growing anxious to esserve you in

person. May zee chef enter?"

Hmm, this is getting serious, I'll have to cover up. Catherine neatly spread out her bed's duvet, puffed up her pillows, and pulled the sheet up to her neck. She had heard once that modesty was the strongest aphrodisiac.

"Zee chef may enter!" she commanded elegantly. The door opened and in walked Mike with a huge smile and an apron that read: *Kiss me, I'm not allergic anymore.*

"Ha!" She pointed. "How do I know for sure?"

Mike looked down at the words on his apron, forgetting he had it on. He chuckled to himself as he read it, then looked up.

"Trust me," he replied, as he plopped alongside her, on the bed. "Did you sleep okay?"

"Yes, very well, thank you," Catherine answered, looking to make sure the blankets properly covered her up. Her face turned to concern. "I have been thinking about Fred," she told Mike. "His color didn't look good last night. Have you heard from him today?"

"No, not yet this morning, but we can go check on him and Julian after breakfast."

"That would be nice, I'm so anxious for Fred. It may not seem much to you—I've only known him as a young boy, so to see him as such an older gentleman . . . well, it has affected me, a lot."

"I can only imagine how you would feel, especially with all of the traumatic events you've been through."

"You know, not to get off the subject, but it's something I've appreciated about you."

"What's that?"

"I think it's great how the girls have grown so fond of Fred. Have you noticed?"

"I sure have, and I love it. It's also nice for Fred; he loves being treated like a grandpa. His daughters and grandkids, in Denver, don't get up here to visit him very often, and my folks don't get up very often either, so Sarah and Gracie still have Grandpa Fred to tease and love. People around here love Fred; he's everyone's buddy."

"And what about you?" Catherine asked Mike. "Do people around here like you?"

"Oh, well, that's a different story altogether." He added, "And, please, don't be going around the neighborhood asking anyone, either. Let me give you the number of my parole officer; he'll give you a good recommendation, I hope."

Catherine smiled and patted his hand. "No, seriously, what kind of person are you?" she asked, in her most sincere voice.

"You're going to trust me to tell you?" Mike kidded.

"You told me to trust you, right?"

"But I'm not good at describing myself; I mean, could you?"

"I'm asking the questions, so now you have to answer and remember, I am a trained professional teacher. I'm good at asking questions."

"Hmm, let's see. Well, what part do you want to know about?"

"What do you think I need to know?"

"Well, now, the list is pretty long to answer that question," Mike answered truthfully.

"Do you think we like each other?"

Mike smiled and nodded yes.

"We haven't known each other that long. How do you know you like me?" she asked.

"Chemistry, my sweet. It was there when we first met."

Catherine didn't disagree. "Okay, I'll give you that one, but tell me what kind of a person you are. If there's going to be more than just a physical attraction, then I want to hear your version of what you're like inside."

"Oh, gosh, that all makes too much sense. You are very good." Mike continued, "I'm an honest person. I'm a Christian—not the best, mind you, but I do take the girls to church most Sundays. I'm not a playboy, not a big spender, but I'm not a cheapskate either. I think I'm a considerate, loving person and try to spend a lot of time with my family . . . well, with my girls." Mike looked down, away from Catherine.

"What is it?" she asked carefully. "Would it be fair to ask about the girls' mother?"

"Elizabeth," he said. "Yes, it's okay to ask. It's been four years." He gave her a half smile. "She was your age when we married. Sweet, wonderful woman; the girls are proof of that. I suppose what they get from me is their temperament. Anyway, she got cancer and battled it for a year and a half before it took her. She was so strong, I still can't believe the pain and sickness she put up with. I couldn't do it; I couldn't be as strong as she was."

"She sounds like an incredible woman and mother. Seeing how your girls are, she must have been quite a lady to have had such a strong influence on them."

"I hope you take this as a compliment," said Mike. "I'm attracted to you because I see that same kind of strong character in you. You're so confident. And, I think you would have to be. To have accomplished everything you've done, being a teacher and all. The girls recognized it right away, so much faster than I did. For so long, I was just mesmerized by how beautiful you are."

"That's very nice of you to say." Catherine appreciated the comparison to a woman he deeply loved. "Confidence must come from my teaching experience, huh?"

"No doubt, I'm sure that has a lot to do with it." Mike continued, "So, anyway, after so much time has passed, friends and family—even the girls—have told me in so many ways that I need to move on. And I have—I mean, I haven't dated yet, but maybe like you, I just haven't met anyone who I felt good enough about, to take that plunge and go on a date, until . . ." Suddenly, Mike leaned over and pulled Catherine close, wrapping his arms around her. She didn't fight him, and to his joy and surprise, she came in closer. It felt like she fit inside his whole body—it was perfect—the warmth between them became his Heaven. He could feel her relax in a way that spoke all the words he ever wanted to hear.

He knew that no matter how wonderful he felt, she still needed to hear something from him. He took a shallow breath, released Catherine, and leaned back so he could see her face. He propped himself up and held one of her hands on her fingertips, looking down at them, then he glanced up into her eyes. He spoke slowly, deliberately.

"Catherine, sweetheart. I can't explain why this has

happened, it just has. I would like to believe . . . that God had a lot to do with this." Mike paused and swallowed. "I do know that I've met a fabulous girl and I'm sure glad it's happened . . . and I know for sure that I want it to keep happening."

Catherine didn't say a word.

"I, I . . ."

"Yes?" Catherine smiled, a quizzical expression on her face.

Suddenly, Catherine's bedroom door burst open and Sarah and Gracie ran into the room, yelling for Catherine, piled on her bed, and crawled under the covers with her.

Mike knew his moment was gone, so he got up and told everyone that breakfast was ready and to please come into the kitchen: "So zee chef can esserve!"

* * * *

A couple of weeks later, Mike and Catherine planned to host a birthday barbecue for Sarah's birthday. Catherine had been going back and forth to her place every couple of days to check in on her mom, Anna. She invited Anna to come to the picnic—and to the future—but she resisted. The whole idea sounded preposterous to her. She was sure this could be the work of the devil. Catherine gave up and told her that she'd be gone for a few days with Mike and the girls. She reassured her mom that sleeping quarters were separate from Mike's and there was no hanky-panky going on.

It was a pleasant early summer afternoon. Catherine and the girls were in and out of the house preparing salads, putting more chips in a bowl, and getting condiments for the table. As Catherine was stirring the instant lemonade, she heard a noise. She quickly turned her head and there stood her mom, Anna, in the kitchen doorway.

"My God, Mother, you scared the heck out of me!" Catherine ran over to hug her mom. "Mom, did you come through the closet all by yourself or did the devil come with you?"

"Oh, just stop it! You told me enough times how you did it. Well, I'm a smart woman, too. I figured I could get the hang of it, and . . . I did!" Anna kissed her on the cheek. "I guess I just got tired of being alone, honey. You're so excited when you talk about how things are here and Michael and the girls and the boys, I thought maybe I should go ahead and see this new place."

"Oh, Mom, I'm so glad you did. Come on, let's go meet everybody." In a few minutes, she was introduced to Michael, Sarah, Gracie, Julian, and Fred. Catherine found her a comfortable chair in the shade.

Within the hour, Sarah finished opening her presents and Mike was getting ready to serve homemade ice cream when a lull in the conversation gave Fred a chance to speak to everyone. He cleared his throat and sat up in his chair.

"Mike, ladies. Julian and I have been talking quite a bit, and it looks like he's decided to go ahead and go back, to his time." The conversation quieted down as Mike looked over to Julian.

"Is that right, Julian?"

"Yeah, I think I should go back. All this new stuff, you know, it's a lot to take in. It's a lot of fun and all, and I would like to see home again. It's been quite a long time now since we first bumped into each other, huh?" Julian said, patting Fred on the shoulder.

Julian, now fifteen years old, had grown taller and a few muscles had appeared; he wasn't as thin as that thirteen-year-old street punk back in Joplin. Now, his scruffy brown hair was more frequently combed, his voice had changed and he seemed wiser and calmer.

To Fred, Julian had begun to mature into a strong young man. Fred told Mike recently that in many ways, Julian had become like a son to him. After losing his only son, Mike was sure Julian had filled, to some degree, that empty spot in Fred's heart.

"I understand, Julian, although you know we've all grown quite fond of you and if you wanted to stay, it's just fine with us," Mike said, hoping Julian would reconsider.

"I appreciate that, Mike. I don't know, my head is spinning . . . maybe I'll miss you guys too, and want to come back here. It's just that I promised myself I'd do this. I've saved up a little money—, more than I could have saved back in 1928, and with that, maybe I can live a proper life."

"I think it's a sign of how much you've matured, Julian. When you keep your promises, honor your commitments, that's a good thing," Mike said.

"Thanks, Mike." Julian reached over and shook Mike's hand; Catherine came over and hugged him.

"When do you want to go, Julian?"

"Maybe in the next day or two, probably on Saturday, leave early—you know, get a good start on the day."

"Come over Saturday morning. We'll all have some breakfast, fatten you up a little more, and then we'll open up the door for you."

"That will work, Mike, thanks."

After Fred and Julian left to go back home, Mike, Catherine, and Anna were visiting when Gracie came up and interrupted.

"Can I still have some ice cream?"

CHAPTER 21
Going Home

As planned, early Saturday morning, Mike was up to help Julian make his way through the closet door to go back home. Sarah kept a lookout for them at the front window. In a few minutes, she yelled, "Here they come, Dad!"

Julian's walk was hesitant, allowing Fred, who walked with a cane, to keep up. Sarah could see Fred's hands stirring last-minute advice to Julian like a father giving his son instructions on how to live his life.

In the middle of the street, they stopped. Fred handed Julian an envelope. As they stood together, he patted Julian on the back, then reached around and hugged him. It seemed to Sarah that Julian was nervous. Fred took his handkerchief from his back pocket and wiped his eyes. As they continued their walk toward the house, Julian kept looking over at Fred. Sarah opened the door before they had a chance to knock.

"Good morning, little miss." Fred reached over to Sarah and grabbed her up for a hug. "And where's my little squealer, Gracie?"

"Oh, she's in the back with Catherine and Dad, watching them cook breakfast. Come on in." She turned to Julian. "Hi, Julian, you okay?"

"Yeah," he said. Fred walked past Julian toward the

kitchen. "I'm okay, I guess. Just have a long way to go and a lot of stuff to go through in the next few days, I'm still not too sure how it's all gonna happen, but I gotta do it." Sarah could tell that Julian's thoughts were somewhere else.

"Ah, Julian, my man, come here!" Mike called as Julian and Sarah walked into the kitchen. "Are you ready for this?"

"As ready as I can be."

Catherine pointed to the food, indicating that everyone should load their plates. "Come on everyone, go ahead and fill your plates, it's all ready." She took Julian to the side to tell him something. "Julian, Mike, and I got to thinking, you'll need to have money—I mean money that is from that time. If you go back with today's currency with these later dates, you're going to raise some eyebrows and there's a chance they might not take it."

"Yeah," Mike added. "We think we've found a way to solve that problem. Fill your plate up and come on in the dining room."

A few minutes later, Catherine said, "After we talked about the money issue, I went back and took some of the money out of my account at the bank in Cheyenne. So, here it is." Catherine slid a zippered money bag over to Julian.

"But, you . . . you can't . . ."

"Now, don't you be telling me I can't young man, or I'll be sending you to the corner!" Julian got up and walked around the table to Catherine to give her a long hug.

"Ah, Catherine," he said, his voice breaking. "You didn't need to do this. I have some money."

"Well, it only makes sense. You know it's going to be a tough trip, especially given the times you'll be going back to. Mike and I also thought that the best way for you to travel from Cheyenne back to Missouri would be by train. You'll have to check departure times as soon as you can."

"Catherine, this is . . . I, I can't think of words to say." He opened the bag and just stared at the money and shook his head.

"Eight hundred dollars should be enough to get you out to where you want to go and help get you started on whatever you want to do. But, Julian, I can't warn you enough—and you remember, don't you?—about people who will try to get your money. Be careful wherever you go, okay?" Catherine waved a warning finger at Julian.

"Yeah, I sure learned about that on the way out, didn't I?"

Catherine smiled and turned to Mike. "Okay, now, Mike, would you say a prayer before we begin?"

"Sure, Catherine. All right everyone, let's pray for a safe trip for Julian." Mike looked around as everyone lowered their heads. "Lord, please be with our dear friend Julian as he steps out on his journey. Please, Lord, be with his every step and every action; guide his way, Lord, guide his way. Lord, we also ask that you bless this food that Catherine so wonderfully prepared, bless Sarah and Gracie for their hard work cleaning up after breakfast"—Sarah peeked over to Gracie and they both made a face because they knew that they were just assigned to the kitchen clean-up crew— "and bless our dear friend Fred for being the best neighbor anyone could ever have. In all this, we ask in the name of our savior, Lord Jesus Christ. Amen."

* * * *

After a filling breakfast and more conversation about what Julian should do and what he was going to encounter, Julian pushed his chair away from the table. It was time to leave. At the closet, everyone said their goodbyes and Fred gave Julian a farewell hug.

"Remember me, pal. I'll be with you the whole way. I mean it," Fred emphasized to Julian, looking him directly in the eye.

"I know, Fred. Thanks for watching out for me."

"Yep, just take it easy, don't force nothing. Just let God be your guide; you know we're all praying for the best for you, but if something does happen, keep your cool, okay?"

"I know, Fred."

"And I wouldn't go telling anyone about this whole door in the closet deal, you know what I mean?" asked Fred. "First of all, they ain't gonna believe you, and second, if they do, you'll have all of creation over here trying to shove their fat butts into that hole. So, it's best to keep it quiet."

Julian laughed at Fred's description. Even Fred chuckled at himself.

"Yeah, okay, Fred. You too! You're the old codger, you take care of yourself. You'd better be here, too!" Julian leaned down and shoved his duffel bag into the closet doorway. He gave Fred one last nod and pulled the small door shut.

CHAPTER 22
The Trip

1929

The first thing he noticed, cramped up in the tiny space, was the heat. After a few seconds, he pushed open the small door, threw his canvas duffel bag of clothes out onto the floor, and crawled out into the musty-smelling bedroom. *I miss air-conditioning*, he thought. Julian laughed at himself as he looked around the small room, sat down, and opened his bag, to make sure he was ready.

The toughest part of the journey so far was removing the fancy running shoes Fred had bought for him. Fred had instructed Julian to leave them inside the closet and if he ever decided to come after them, they would be there. It was a sad moment. He pulled a pair of plain brown work boots out of the bag. Julian and Fred had bought new boots, roughed them up, and covered them in the dirt just to put a little age on them.

Julian knew he couldn't talk about his experience or show off something modern. All those new electronic gadgets had to be left behind. He sat for a minute and thought to himself about what he had been through, and what he knew was to come. Julian felt like he had lived several lifetimes over the last couple of years.

He leaned forward to get himself up, grabbed his

duffel bag, and made his way through Catherine's quiet house, to the front door. As he opened the door, a short, dark-haired kid jumped in front of him hollering, what he thought was a wild Indian war whoop. Julian remembered this young hooligan as the kid that jumped him with several others when he first got to Cheyenne.

"Woohoo!" Freddy screamed up close in Julian's face.

"What the—!" Julian jumped back, dropping his duffel bag, ready to hit someone if he had to. "Freddy?"

"Yeah!" Fred grinned, his bushy brown hair hanging down across his face.

"God, you gave me a start! Scared the living hell out of me, man. What the hell are you doing?" Julian gasped.

"Miss Tanner left me a note at Mom and Dad's a couple of days ago. Miss Tanner asked me to show up and be here at her house, at precisely this time, and asked me to hang out with you, at least until you leave Cheyenne. She thought you might be a little confused or, ah, you know, need someone to help you." Fred laughed again and Julian came over with a right jab and nailed him on his shoulder.

"Oww!"

"Shut up! She did not!" Julian knew she did but couldn't tell Freddy. "I owe you that one, at least."

"I guess so," replied Freddy. "She said you would need help, I'm pretty sure that's what she meant."

"Well, thanks for being here, man, I appreciate it," Julian said.

Freddy stared at Julian for a few seconds before asking, "So, how come you look so different? I mean, I know it's been a while, but where have you been? I know you just haven't been sitting in Miss Tanner's house all this time."

Julian cringed at Freddy's question.

"I've been traveling, to other places. Miss Tanner let me stay at her house." Julian had to lie to Freddy, so he wouldn't have to explain the secret of the door. "For now, I've got to go down to the train station to get my ticket."

"Good enough for me. Can I tag along?"

"Sure, let's go." Julian picked up his bag and threw it over his shoulder. Julian made sure the front door of the Tanner house was shut tight then turned around and jumped off the front steps to catch up with Freddy, already out on the street.

The clean smell of the wind blowing through the pine trees and the warm summer afternoon quiet felt familiar to Julian. Life here was less complicated. The traffic and background freeway noises were gone. He could hear birds, the continuous whisper of the wind, dogs barking in the distance and, best of all, he and Freddy were walking down the middle of the street, not concerned about getting run over. As they walked, Julian remembered something Freddy said earlier.

"Freddy, you said Miss Tanner left a note?"

"Yeah."

"I'm sure she meant that she wanted you to help me get stuff together for my trip back to Missouri," Julian said. "And she knew you didn't have anything else to do, being the middle of summer and all." As Julian spoke, a passing Model T honked at the boys; they waved.

"Yeah, it's pretty boring around here. I'm always seeing so many automobiles and trains moving west—people searching for jobs, I suppose. I'm about ready to take off myself. Just like you did."

"A lot of automobiles? You should see Kansas City, Freddy, you have no idea!"

"Yeah? Kansas City? Probably a lot more autos, huh?" Freddy asked.

"Yeah, that's where I'm headed, down that direction. I'm going farther south, down to Joplin, Missouri. It's probably pretty quiet down there, though, just like here."

"I don't know, never been there." Freddy looked over to Julian. "So, how come you left there?"

"My mom. She left me high and dry. Took off with some strays. I don't know what the deal was. She thought she had to have someone. After he came along, it was just a matter of days and they were off. So, I picked up and took off, too!"

"Wow, to have the guts to just leave, that's crazy. Maybe that's what I should do, just take off."

Julian stopped walking and turned to Fred. "Why would you want to leave? I mean, you have a nice family, a mom and dad, a home. That's the kind of life I would have died for. I can't understand why you would want to give that up."

"Yeah, I guess I've been lucky so far. I haven't had to look for a new home or anything. I want some excitement; I'm so bored."

Julian shook his head. "I guess it's just human nature to be restless," he wondered out loud.

"So, what are you going to do when you get down there?"

"I have some business to take care of down there and I want to find my mom. I'm not sure where she ended up, and maybe I can find out." Julian sighed. He remembered someone else. "Then, there was this girl, Jean."

"I knew there had to be a girl—that's what you were after, right?"

"She was just a great friend to me, Freddy. I could talk to her about stuff. I want to know what she's doing. Plus, if I can find my mom, I'd like to get that resolved," Julian said, looking over at Freddy. Julian felt unsure about how much to tell Fred because, for all he knew, it was all gone, anyway.

"Once I take care of things, then I can move on with the rest of my life. Right now, I need to check the timetables and get my tickets."

"If you want, we can run over to my place—I gotta couple ah bikes, so we won't have to walk down there."

"Sure, I suppose, but I'm also going over to Dixie's when I get done. I haven't seen her and Monte forever, and I need to say hi. You got time for that?"

"Brother, I have all summer long!" Freddy emphasized with his outstretched arms.

"Let's go then, come on!" yelled a grinning Julian, happy to be moving again, running ahead of Freddy.

Before long, the boys were at the station—the magnificent Union Pacific train station with a church-like bell tower and great hall that looked more like a French cathedral rather than a busy train depot in the middle of nowhere. It was designed to show power and strength as it stood tall among the long line of one-story, drab buildings that faced the main line of the railroad tracks.

As Julian and Freddy walked into the great hall, the sound of their footsteps on marble was quickly drowned out by other passengers' conversations, echoes of yelling children, and the sounds of wheeled luggage carts rolling through the terminal. Julian and Freddy walked up to the Union Pacific route map and train timetables, standing mouths agape, eyes fixed on the lists of information. Finally, Julian found the timetable for his destination: Kansas City, Missouri.

Route Timetable

Cheyenne, WY – Kansas City, MO

St. Louis – Colorado Limited No. 128

Features: Observation car, parlor car, Pullman sleeping cars, coach class, and a dining car.

Departs Cheyenne: 7:30 a.m. (day one)

First Stop: Denver, CO

Departs Denver: 11:30 a.m.

Also stops at Oakley, Ellis, Ellsworth, Salina, Junction City, and Topeka, Kansas.

Arrive Kansas City, MO: 7:55 a.m. (day two)

Kansas City Express No. 104

Features: Observation car, parlor car, Pullman sleeping cars, coach class, dining car, and club car

Departs Cheyenne: 1:15 p.m. (day one)

First stop: Denver, CO

Departs Denver: 9:30 p.m.

Also stops at Oakley, Ellis, Ellsworth, Salina, Junction City, and Topeka, Kansas.

Arrive Kansas City, MO: 4:10 p.m. (day two)

At the fare window, Julian asked about the fare to Kansas City for the Kansas City Express number 104.

"That would be \$10.25," the clerk replied.

Freddy turned at looked at Julian, surprised. "Jeez, that's a lot of money, eh?"

"I'm okay, Freddy, I've got it." Julian pulled out his zippered money bag.

"I wish I could go, but it's just too much money," said Fred, looking down at the ground.

Julian turned around, wondering. He excused himself to the ticket master and pulled Freddy back from the counter.

"Your parents wouldn't let you go anyway, Freddy, even if you had the money. They'd pitch a fit if you told them you were going to Missouri."

"No, they wouldn't. Especially my mom, hell, she'd pay you to take me."

"Are you sure you want to go? Because I don't know how it's going to go down there."

"Sounds exciting to me . . . besides, what would I do here?" Freddy asked. "You're the only excitement going on around here. Besides, watching those stupid jalopies and trains move west just ain't my idea of a thrill."

"I guess so, but if you're serious, I'll pay your way, but you'd better be sure this is okay with your folks. We'll have to go up and tell them what's going on."

"Wow, Julian, that would be neat. It'll be okay with them."

Julian turned back to the ticket counter. "Sir, I guess we've decided to get two tickets."

"Did you want the 1:15, today?" asked the clerk.

"Better make it 1:15 tomorrow, please. I need time to

visit some friends here in town."

"Do you want to pay the extra $8.40 for a sleeper berth?" inquired the clerk.

"How long does the trip take?"

"It's an overnight trip. You'd arrive after four tomorrow if you left today."

"No, just give us two regular tickets, no sleeper car, please." With the transaction completed, the boys walked out of the hall and grabbed their bikes.

"Julian, buddy, thanks again, this is gonna be so damn fun!"

"Are you going with me over to Dixie's?"

"Certainly, I wouldn't miss it. Besides, they have the best food, right?"

"Monty does put out a good plate of slop. Then we'll have to get up to your house and make sure you can go on this trip with me."

The warm summer afternoon felt good to Julian, even if he didn't know how it was going to turn out. He was moving and doing the very thing he had been planning in his mind for so long. He was filled with excitement to see Dixie and Monte, and taking Freddy along made this trip seem like more of an adventure rather than putting himself out there all alone and a victim to whatever bad luck would come along.

Dust stirred up as four bicycle tires raced from the station toward Dixie's Diner. When they arrived, the bikes were thrown against worn-out tires, painted white and half buried in the dirt and gravel, on the parking side of the building.

As they entered the diner, Dixie looked up to see a

whirlwind of commotion coming through the doors. "Oh my God, Monte! Monte! It's Julian. Monte, get out here right now! Julian, I can't believe it, where have you been, darlin'?"

The boys threw their stuff into a booth and walked over to see Dixie. In a few seconds, Monte came out from behind the swinging kitchen doors, tying his apron. By now, Dixie had grabbed Julian and was hugging him. When he pulled free, he introduced Freddy.

"Dixie, this here's Freddy, Freddy Perkins, he lives here in town."

"Freddy, nice to meet you," Dixie replied.

"And this is Monte, our cook."

"Nice to meet you, kid," replied Monte. "And what about you, you little turd, where you been hanging out? We've missed you." Monte grabbed Julian and gave him a quick shake on his shoulders with his large hands.

"Oh, I've been out of town, doing some traveling," Julian said, stalling. "I took off for Denver one night and I got a job down there for a while, but I missed you guys and decided to come back—for a short visit, anyway." Dixie stood with her hands on her hips listening to Julian's story.

"Well, I don't know if that's a good enough story or not, but we're sure glad you came back." She pinched Julian's cheek and turned around toward the counter. Not willing to let it go, Monte piped up.

"You couldn't have at least stopped by and told us you were going?"

"Kind of a last-minute deal, and it was after you were closed, so I just took off. I didn't think I'd be gone that long, anyway, right Freddy?"

"I don't know, Julian, I didn't take no trip. I'm not sure

where you went either."

Monte laughed at Freddy's honesty as Dixie motioned for them to come over to the counter and sit down.

"You boys want a milkshake or something to eat?" Always a sure bet, the two teenagers readily agreed to burgers and a shake and sat down at the counter before Dixie was finished talking. The boys stuffed their faces, much to the delight of Dixie, and then Julian cleared his throat.

"Miss Dixie, Freddy, and me, we're gonna go on another trip, tomorrow." He looked up from the remnants of his burger with a grin.

"What? What are you two going to do now?" Dixie asked.

"I had always planned to go back to Missouri and try to find my mom, so that's what I'm gonna do. I've saved up a little money and I just figured it was time to go."

"Freddy, you're on board with this?" asked Dixie, now acting like more of a mother. Freddy nodded yes and kept chewing on his mouthful of burger and shake. His eyes darted away from Dixie's glare.

"We even bought our train tickets, earlier today. We're leaving on the 1:15 tomorrow."

"You hear that, Monte? These two hon-yockers are gonna leave again!"

Julian could see Monte's white hat jump up and in a couple of seconds, he was out front standing next to Dixie again.

"How long you gonna be gone this time?" asked Monte.

"Probably about a week, not much more than that—if I can help it, anyway."

"You saved enough for the train ticket?"

"Yep, already bought them."

Dixie shook her head and walked away to take care of customers on the other side of the restaurant. She told them loud enough for Julian and Freddy to hear her, "You'd think these two were world travelers, the way they come and go. I tell ya." Julian and Freddy laughed at Dixie's teasing.

"Darn, well, I guess you're set to go then, huh?" asked Monte.

"All we gotta do is get on the train tomorrow. We'll come down for breakfast before we take off, though." After more ribbing from Dixie and Monte, the boys left to go up to Freddy's to get permission for him to go.

It wasn't difficult to convince Freddy's parents to let Freddy go with Julian, but they made it clear they didn't have any money to give the boys for the trip. Freddy could go, but he had to pay his way.

The boys bunked in Freddy's room and fell fast asleep in a matter of minutes, each having their dream of high adventure—so close now, they could almost touch it.

* * * *

Just before noon, Fred and Julian were at the train station, bags packed, bellies full. People were starting to gather for the arrival of the Kansas City Express steam train, from the west.

The train crew always changed out in Cheyenne because of the long hours coming in from the overnight trip out of Salt Lake City. The trip between Cheyenne and

Salt Lake City took a larger-than-normal locomotive steam engine because of the three mountain passes they had to cross on the way. The rest of the way to Kansas City was relatively flat, so a smaller engine could do the pulling.

In another hour, they were sitting in a seat on board the passenger observation car and ready to go. Soon, "All aboard!" was yelled, followed by two loud whistles, and the train began to move. The passenger cars jerked into motion and every passenger felt the pull as the train quickly gained speed, the sound of steel on steel roaring louder, and they were off. Before long, it seemed, they were moving at incredible speeds through the barren hills of eastern Wyoming, on their way to Kansas City, Missouri.

"Juli, look at this!" Freddy was pointing to the field alongside the tracks. "The rows of the field look like the long legs of someone running alongside us. Cool, huh?"

"Yep, pretty neat." Julian was uninterested in Freddy's excitement—he'd experienced travel before. Now that they were underway, he was thinking about what was coming up. "Fred, I think once we get to Kansas City, I'll try to find a car, so we can drive down to Joplin. I'm not sure if there's any passenger train service, otherwise, we'd have to walk."

"I'm okay with that, but do you have any money?"

"Yeah." Julian had to be careful. He didn't want to give away where some of his money came from. "I've been working a lot and saved my money and sold a few things, so I got some money, probably enough to buy a car."

"Neat, let's get an auto with a rumble seat, we can pick up girls, huh?"

"Freddy, this ain't exactly a party trip to Daytona Beach!"

"Daytona Beach? Where's that?" Freddy asked, eyes wide open.

"Oh, just a place in Florida." Julian dismissed it with a brush of his hand.

"Julian, you know everything. You're like a world traveler, huh?"

"Not exactly, Fred, I just saw it in pictures." Julian turned around and stared directly ahead, and Freddy turned back to look at Mr. Longlegs in the cornfields of Nebraska.

* * * *

Once in Kansas City, Julian and Freddy walked several miles south of the train terminal before they found a good selection of car dealers. On one side of the street, the car dealer's sign read BUDDY'S AUTOMOBILE SALES AND SERVICE – "TO GET THE MOST FOR YOUR MONEY, SEE BUDDY!" On the opposite side of the street, down a block, was another dealer: FANCY JIM'S. Tired from walking, they strolled into Buddy's lot and sat down on the nearest running board to rest.

"She's a beauty, huh, boys?" The car salesman startled the boys as he walked up to Julian and Fred. A big puff of cigarette smoke billowed out of his mouth and nostrils. "Yep, she's a beaut!" He propped his foot up on the running board and took another long drag, blowing it off over the car. *This must be Buddy,* Julian thought.

"Well, yeah, mister, it's a fine-looking car, for sure. So, what's the price?" asked Julian. Not trusting anyone, Julian put a hand over the folding money in his pocket.

"This car is almost brand new, son. This is a 1927 Dodge Brothers Touring automobile, and this ain't no regular car, boys, *this* is a piece of art and it's going to cost your daddy a pretty penny—this is a Model 126." He got up close to Julian's face; the smell of his breath was noxious. "Nine hundred bucks, kiddo, your daddy got that in his pocket?" He laughed. Without waiting for an answer, he said, "I didn't think so. Is your daddy gonna be coming down to look at cars or are you just wastin' my time? Because I need to keep this area clear of riff-raff and open for buying customers, you know what I mean, boys?"

"Well, my daddy didn't send me down here to buy no automobile, sir."

"Ah . . . your daddy didn't send ya, huh. Your uncle or your mama?"

"Nope, just me and Freddy, here. We're looking for a car," Julian said without flinching.

Buddy pulled the wet plug that once was a cigarette out of his mouth and glared at the boys with disbelief. He lit up another cigarette.

"Ah, yeah, right, and I was just about to give my ex-wife more money. Listen, kid, that ain't gonna happen, so beat it!" He blew smoke in Julian's face and turned around to go back to his small shack at the rear of the lot.

"I don't see any other customers waiting to buy anything!" Julian yelled after him.

Buddy spun around and pointed his cigarette at him with an incredulous face. "Are you serious, kid, you want to buy a car?"

Julian pulled a wad of folded bills out of his pocket and waved it in the air. "It's okay, I'll just walk over to Fancy

Jim's and see if he wants to deal with me!"

"Now, hold on boys, let's not get carried away." Buddy rushed back toward Julian, eyes focused on the cash, which was quickly dropped into Julian's pants pocket. "Okay, gents, let's say you're going to buy a car." Buddy regained his cocky stance, his boney fingers tapping on the hood of the car. "How much you got, huh? You flashed some greenbacks, but do you have enough?"

Julian hesitated. "Well, I'm not gonna just pull my money out and tell you to take whatever you want, but I have enough to buy a car, so I'm gonna look at cars."

Buddy got up close to Julian's face. "Do you have a driver's license?"

Julian turned his head and put his hands back in his pockets. "Do you want to sell cars, or do you want to be a policeman?" Julian smarted back. "I'll get one. Not your problem, so don't worry about it."

"All right, all right." Buddy waved off. "I'll just trust that you'll take care of those minor details." He moved back to the car. "Okay, son, let's have a look at one of these cars. You were looking at this beautiful Dodge Brothers, Are you still interested?"

"Tell me about it, what do I get?"

Buddy went through the details of the car and explained how it operated.

"So, like I said, this car is nine hundred bucks. Is that in your price range or are you wanting something a little fancier?" Buddy propped his foot back up on the running board and drew a puff. The smoke blew away slowly in the humid air.

"Nope, it's the kind of car I'm looking for, but it's way

too much money."

"Yeah, son, that's why I asked. Maybe you want to see something over in the older used cars part of the lot, huh?"

Julian didn't budge and offered something else. "No, maybe you'll just sell this car to me for less money."

"I don't think so. This car is worth every penny on the price tag. Let's just go over here and look at some of these other fine cars." Buddy took his foot down and turned to walk away.

"You take six hundred for it?"

"What? Say that again?" He leaned his ear toward Julian.

"Six hundred bucks, flat out, that's what I'm offering for this car."

"Yeah, right, get out of here, kid!" Buddy turned around again.

"How many offers have you had on it today?" Julian challenged him. Buddy stopped and turned again.

"Kid, so many, I can't even count them. It's early yet; the good buyers don't come out till later after they get out of work." He chuckled through another puff of smoke.

"Yeah? Well, time's marching on, brother, it's already late afternoon," Julian scoffed. "Maybe you should call your lot *Buddy's Midnight Auto Sales*, eh?" Standing beside Julian, Freddy laughed.

"Listen, chump, don't get smart with me." Buddy came up close to Julian again. Freddy stepped back a little, halfway expecting a scuffle.

"Then take it or leave it," Julian said sternly back to Buddy. Julian's years of living on the street and having to make it on his own had suddenly started to pay off. This felt good to him, he was having fun. Buddy seemed to relax; his shoulders slumped, and he rubbed his chin.

"I like your spunk. I'll tell you what, my young friend, I'll do you a favor, the price will be nine hundred bucks, but I'll throw in, at no charge, mind you"—he pointed his finger at Julian—"I'll throw in a spare tire and a clean rag for when you need to change the oil. Now, that's a pretty good deal." Buddy acted proud of his generous offer. Julian knew better.

"Now, that," replied Julian, "is pretty lame." Freddy laughed. "In fact, it's *damn* lame. I'll repeat, just in case you didn't hear the first time . . . Six hundred bucks, and you'll still throw in the towel and spare tire, to boot. Got anything else you want to include?" Julian pointed right back at him.

This annoyed Buddy; he gave Julian another look like he was going to steamroll over him. Then he flinched. "Eight hundred bucks and that's my bottom, can't go any lower." He waved his hands and nodded like he was done. At this point, Julian knew he had him.

"Six hundred bucks, but I'll add another fifty to it because I feel bad for you," replied Julian. Freddy shook his head in disbelief.

"Why do you feel bad for *me*?" asked Buddy, his cigarette drooping from his mouth.

"'Cause your ex-wife will probably end up with most of this money!"

Buddy smiled and waved his agreement with that statement.

"Okay, okay. You know, kid, you're killing me, but you're probably right. I'll tell you what. I like you, so I'll cut you a break. I'll let this beautiful car go for seven-fifty, tops!"

"Well, Buddy, that's getting better. And as much as I'd like to buy this car from you today, I'll probably have to go on down to that Fancy Jim's lot. I'm sure he'll make us a hell of a good deal. Especially"—Julian pointed his finger at Buddy—"when I tell him what a good deal you were going to make us."

"That thief? Hell, he'd sooner rob you blind than give you a good deal."

"And you're not?" said Julian over his shoulder as they turned to walk away. Before Julian and Freddy made it to the next car, Buddy came running up quickly behind them.

"Listen, kid, what's your name?"

"Julian, sir."

"All right, Julian, what's it gonna take to put you in that car? I mean, I can't go six hundred, but maybe I can do seven and a quarter . . ."

"Seven even."

Buddy took his handkerchief out of his shirt pocket and wiped his brow, shook his head, a worried look on his face. "Done!" replied an exhausted Buddy, and just as quickly he said, "Damn, I'm giving this car away. This doesn't include the spare, you know."

"That's fine, I'll go over to Fancy Jim's and buy a spare for fifty cents."

"Oh, crap kid, okay, for another fifty cents, I'll throw in the spare, just don't go over there and give him any money."

"Why not, why are you so worried about Fancy Jim getting any business?"

"'Cause it'll just end up with my ex-wife—he's married to her now, that slimy good-for-nothin' . . ."

Julian and Freddy laughed. It turned out that Julian was

right after all. Julian couldn't help himself; he had to rub the salt in the wound a little deeper.

"Buddy, you mean to tell me your wife got a better deal from Fancy Jim?"

"Don't test me, boy!" Buddy pointed his finger and Julian and then smiled. "Yeah, I suppose she did, but in the end, I'm better off. I don't have to sell as many cars as Fancy Jim does, that poor bastard. Come on over here, Julian, let's go do the paperwork."

Freddy glanced over to Julian, his eyes as wide as the Mississippi River. In thirty minutes, the paperwork was complete, and the deal was done.

Two excited young men driving out of a car lot, papers in hand and a new adventure before them. Behind them, the forlorn used car salesman couldn't find a match for his nervous cigarette habit.

"Gonna be a heck of a trip!" yelled Fred over the sound of the chugging engine.

"Yep, gonna be a heck of a trip." Julian honked the horn.

* * * *

After a fine dinner and gas, the pair headed out again into the warm evening. They decided to bunk down in the car for the night since it had wide front and back seats, plenty of room for the slim teenagers to sleep on. They stopped at a Ben Franklin store on the way and bought a couple of blankets and pillows. About forty miles south of Kansas City, in some open farm country, they found a haystack just off the dirt road and pulled in behind it.

Once the pillows and blankets were sorted out, it didn't take them long to relax and settle down. Since the car didn't have windows, the slight warm summer breeze provided a full aroma of the surrounding countryside as it wafted through the open car. Julian had something on his mind, and this was a good time to bring it up.

"Freddy?"

"Yeah, Juli."

"Sure is quiet out here, huh?"

"Got that right. Almost too quiet. If it weren't for those cows mooing and the sound of cow crap hitting the ground, it'd be downright unbearable." The thought of that sound made them both start laughing.

"Freddy, when we get to Fannie's brothel, it's probably gonna be pretty ugly."

"Well, then, why don't they get them some better-looking girls?"

"Naw, Freddy! I don't mean that way, I mean Fannie. She probably ain't gonna be in a real good mood when she sees me, that's the only thing I'm worried about. She may try to smack me over the head with a frying pan, or at the very least, pull one of my ears off. That was one of her favorite things to do to me."

"Man, that sounds awful, why on earth would you even want to try?"

"I just have to know, Fred, I just have to know. I have been thinking about it so much, I just want an answer, you know?"

"Yeah, I guess. I'd probably want to know, too."

"And the Dean boys. If they catch up with me, that

could be bad."

"Those are the guys you have been telling me about, with the bad reputation?"

"Yep, them's the ones. Anyway, if it does get bad—I mean if something happens to me, especially if the Dean boys are involved—I probably won't make it out alive, so you got to get a message to Miss Tanner for me, okay?"

"And just how am I gonna do that?"

"You'll have to take the automobile back to Cheyenne, for me."

"Oh, jeez Julian, I can't do that."

"Yes, you can. I did it without an automobile. I walked most of the way, rode in horse carts, hitchhiked, and any other way I could."

"Yeah and look how well you did. I don't want to get beat up that much." Fred laughed.

"It won't be so bad. You'll have the car! If you want, I can leave some money under the seat here, and you can just take the car up through Kansas City and north to Lincoln. From there, head west on Highway 30. I have a map in the car, you'll see it," Julian said.

"That sounds a little easier."

"I hope so. Better yet, how about we just don't have any trouble, just have a fun trip and go home," Freddy said.

"Sounds okay to me."

Both boys lay on their backs looking out the open windows to the stars. The breeze got cooler, so Freddy pulled up his blanket.

"You know Julian, nothing's gonna happen, I just know it. You can get out of anything."

"I hope so, Freddy, I hope so."

"Julian?"

"Yeah?"

"Gonna be a heck of a trip, huh?"

"Yep, it's already been a good one."

CHAPTER 23
Secrets of the Chest

2001

During the days after Julian left, Catherine settled into her new surroundings, learning how appliances, phones, washing machines, and microwaves worked, and how to find channels on the television set. Catherine had a feeling that Fred was feeling lonely since Julian left, so she would occasionally walk over and ask Fred to go along with her, talking about all the modern changes to their old city and neighborhood. A few times, Catherine was able to convince her mother, Anna, to come and stay for several days. In the evenings, Mike and Catherine made several trips back and forth through the closet to bring her stuff over.

A few days later, in the evening, Catherine mentioned the wooden box that Julian had taken. Mike remembered that he had put it on a shelf and covered it up in the garage. Without saying anything about it, the next night after dinner, Mike went out to the garage and sneaked it back into the house, then put it on the dining room table. When Catherine walked in, Mike was sitting at the table, offering it to her. She stopped cold in her tracks. Her eyes opened wide.

"Where did you find this?" she asked.

"When I first looked at the house, before I bought it, it was stuffed in one of the upstairs closets. The real estate lady said I might as well have it; no one knew where it came from. So, after I bought the house, I put it in the garage, covered it up, and forgot about it."

"Oh, my God, this means so much to me, I can't tell you." She leaned over and gave Mike a big hug.

"Let's open it up and see what I have. The key, where did I put the key?" She ran into the guest bedroom and was back in a couple of minutes, holding up a small key. When she put it into the lock, it clicked and opened.

"You see," she said, "nothing valuable, except to me. A few pictures, some old jewelry my mom had, some real estate papers, and . . ."

"Wait a minute," Mike said, "who's in this picture? This looks like you."

Sarah and Gracie came into the kitchen.

"Yes, it is me, my parents, and little brother James. This was when I was eight or nine. Little Jimmy, he's my guardian angel." Catherine's eyes misted up.

"What happened to him?" Sarah asked.

"A long time ago—for you anyway—this was my parents' house, I was raised here." Catherine looked at Sarah and Gracie. "And I loved it here. One day, my little brother Jimmy, who was only four at the time, came up missing. We thought he had wandered off, maybe walked to a neighbor's house or someone took off with him. We never found him, we never knew what happened. Everyone in town helped us search, too."

"Oh, how awful," Sarah said.

"It broke my parents' hearts, they just weren't the

same after that. Eventually, my folks left to go back to India as missionaries. They rented the house for a while to an older couple, and when they left, I purchased the house from my parents after I graduated from college in Denver. We didn't want the house to leave our family. We always believed that Jimmy might one day walk through the front door and we would be a complete family again."

"That is a terrible thing to happen to a family, I'm sorry," Mike said sympathetically.

"Well, it's been so long ago and I was only seven at the time. Now it's just a distant memory."

"Do you remember him?" Gracie asked.

"Sweetheart, he was just the cutest little boy, but full of mischief, always teasing his older sister. I loved it. I still miss him."

Mike did some quick math on a piece of paper and thought. "If this happened when you were eight and he was four, that's eighteen years ago, he would be twenty-two years old now."

"I suppose so," Catherine guessed. "What are you saying, that he could be still alive?"

"I don't mean to get your hopes up, but what if? I mean, since we have this strange time gateway upstairs, what if James was the first one to find out what happened when you go into that space?"

"That would be too cool," Sarah said.

"But, after eighteen years, do you think he would still be around here?" Catherine asked.

"Why not?" said Mike. "All I'm saying, for your family's peace of mind, is that it might be a possibility and we should start looking. We have computers now, we can trace names."

"James was a smart little boy, but I'm sure he wouldn't have known enough to tell someone what happened," Catherine said, shaking her head. "It's just too fantastic, but sweetheart, I love that you're trying. Thank you anyway." For that, Mike got another kiss and hug. Sarah and Gracie rolled their eyes.

CHAPTER 24
Welcome Home

In the morning, in a car with no side windows, it was easy for Freddy to smell the heavy, dense scent of cow manure. With his next curious whiff, urine, and salt, followed by a warm breath brushing across his face.

With eyes still closed, he was enjoying the warmth when a strong, ugly breath blew down on his face. *Nope, too long, too large*, he thought. *Couldn't be Julian's.* Quickly followed by a snort and slippery, wet . . .

When Freddy dared open his eyes it took a split second to realize he was lying beneath a milk cow's hairy jaw—and something clear and slimy was streaming down from it, incredibly fast.

"Yeehoo!" Freddy's scream made Julian jump and bounce his head on the steering wheel. The cow roared back, throwing drool and dirt clods in every direction, and alerting her sisters to bellow and run away from the danger, creating more barnyard dust to blow into the one night, mobile bedroom of two young men.

"Oww! Criminy, what's wrong?" screamed Julian.

"That goll-derned cow, jeez! He was trying to eat my head."

"Oh, right, I'm sure that cow was hungry for your sour-puss." Freddy wiped his face off with Julian's new oil towel.

"I could have drowned in that slobber, damn cow!" Freddy yelled.

"Least you could've done was get some milk from that cow while you two were kissin' each other," Julian teased.

Freddy took the towel and snapped it on Julian's backside. Julian scrambled out of the open-sided touring automobile and flipped the handle on the passenger door to grab Freddy. Freddy managed to escape out the other side, running around the dusty black automobile for revenge. It wasn't long before both of them ran into piles of fresh manure.

"Fred, you big rat turd! Look, now you've slopped cow crap on my pants!"

"Here's some more, you pickle-faced monkey!" Fred took a handful of cow manure and lobbed it over at Julian. Julian dodged most of it, running headlong, ending up in a nearby canal. Freddy, covered in dust, manure, and spit, jumped in to wash off, too. The next few hours were spent laying clothes and shoes on the side of a haystack to dry out.

"I sure hope the traffic is light this morning." Freddy looked around for any spectators on the country road.

"Gonna be an awful sight if they see us, that's for sure, huh Freddy?"

"Not me. If they see my body, they'll want pictures!"

"Yeah, for *Ripley's Believe it or Not.*"

They both laughed until their stomachs ached. No more manure throwing; it was time to clean up and move down the road. After a few miles, Julian noticed a small sign ahead.

"*Early to bed.* Well, that was interesting, huh?" Julian said. Soon, another sign appeared. "*Early to rise,*" Julian read. "It's getting better."

Freddy read the next one, "*Was meant for those old-fashioned guys.*"

"Oh, I know what these are," Julian said. "I saw them on the way up, after I left Missouri. Here's one more: *Who didn't use . . .*" Just over a little crest in the road, they saw the last sign: "*Burma shave.*"

"Doesn't make me want to shave," Freddy said.

"Me, either," Julian replied.

* * * *

Julian and Freddy arrived in Joplin around suppertime. Julian was hoping he would get to the Sunset early enough before any customers arrived. Julian turned into the alley behind the Sunset and pulled into the dirt parking area, close to the back door. Julian looked around suspiciously.

"Something seems wrong. It just seems too quiet to me. I remember so much activity around this town. This is just spooky."

"What are we going to do?" Freddy asked.

"We're just going to walk into the brothel and ask Fannie if she knows where my mom went."

"Just like that?" asked Freddy.

"Yeah, pretty much like that."

"Julian, think she'll ask where you have been?"

"I'll just tell her I decided to take off, she don't need to know more than that. I'm just going to play it by ear."

"Brother, you got more gumption than I do, that's for sure."

"It'll be okay, let's go."

They stepped out of the car and walked around the large house to the front steps. Julian flinched when several backyard dogs barked suddenly, and a couple of kitchen lights flicked on as the boys made their way up the steps of the large house. Julian hesitated just as he started up the steps, and Freddy bumped into the back of him.

"What are you doing, come on," Freddy urged Julian.

"It just ain't right," Julian said, whispering.

"You're telling *me*, this whole thing is crazy." Freddy shrugged and started to turn around.

"No, I'm not talking about that, I mean, look. This place looks closed, it looks dead, no lights, no people walking in."

"Well, I'm not sure I know what a brothel is *supposed* to look like," Freddy replied in a matter-of-fact voice.

"It doesn't normally look like this, got to be lights on or something." Julian approached the large wooden door. Julian thought about knocking, but then just pushed to see if it would open.

The door easily swung in, and Julian walked into the dark foyer. The familiar smell he expected seemed muted—not alive and brilliant, not full of pipe tobacco and perfume. Only stagnant and stale, like no one had moved the dust for a while.

As he walked farther in, Freddy closed the door behind him, and the room darkened. Julian noticed the familiar layer of blue cigar smoke wasn't drifting over the room, he didn't hear Joey playing the piano; in fact, no one was there to greet him—Fannie always greeted customers at the sound of the big door opening.

The boys stood for a few minutes in silence. Then, from the back of the room, Julian could see a light coming from a partially opened door leading to the kitchen.

"Let's go back," Julian said softly. Freddy stayed behind him, cautious of what would come next. They stepped down into the front parlor area, toward the back of the house and the kitchen. Julian stopped when he reached the grand staircase leading upstairs. So many of the exotic decorations and paintings Fannie had collected over the years were missing from the walls, leaving odd shapes of faded colors on the wall coverings. Several of Fannie's beautiful velvet furniture pieces were gone, too.

"Wow, I can't believe this!"

"What?" asked Freddy.

"The furniture, a lot of it's gone! Where has all the stuff gone?"

They continued back through the hallway to the kitchen. Julian peered through the opening, then pushed it wide to enter. There, at the table, smoking a cigarette, was Bernice, the Indian lady, sipping a drink. At the sound of the door opening, she turned to look. She grinned, showing several front teeth missing, tried to get up, and stumbled against the table to steady herself.

"Hello, Bernice."

"Julian, oh, my Julian, baby! Come here, my little man!" She hugged Julian. A tall woman, she once scared Julian because of her size. Now, he was just as tall. She appeared to be somewhat hunched over as if defeated. The smell of smoke and booze threw Julian back when she grabbed him and squeezed tightly. "Julian"—Bernice took another drag from her cigarette—"what happened to you, honey, where did you go? We've missed you so much."

"Bernice, this is my good friend, Fred, Freddy Perkins."

Bernice put her hand out to Freddy. "Fred, good to meet you." Julian noticed that Bernice didn't hug Freddy. *Lucky.*

"Bernice, where's everybody at, where's Fanny?" In this big quiet house, Julian tried not to be too loud but was anxious to know. Bernice turned back toward the table to pour another drink.

"Julian, over the last year or so, with business being so slow, most of the ladies have gone, what with the terrible economy, you know, and Fannie, she's been pretty down, not feeling herself. Just heartbreaking, just heartbreaking."

"You mean, all the gals that were here are all gone?"

"Yep, pretty well gone, only me and Cee Cee are here, and she only comes in once a week, if that. The rest, all gone. Lupe and Jean left a couple of years back, not sure where they went to. Maybe Fannie would know." Bernice waved her hand up in the air, holding tight to the drink with the other.

"Too bad, I wanted to talk to both of them," Julian said.

"Dang, I was looking forward to meeting Jean, too." Freddy shot a glance at Julian and smiled.

"Miss Fannie, she in her room, but she don't come out much. Things are really serious with money. I don't know if Miss Fannie will keep the house or not." Blue smoke puffed up as Bernice took one last pull on her cigarette and rubbed the remaining bit out between two fingers and a broken ashtray.

"Aw, it's just so hard to believe." Julian shook his head in disbelief.

"Yes, ever since she lost her money to that bastard Shorty. Things got real sour for her, now she's plumb broke." Bernice looked over to Julian, pointing upstairs. "You'd better go say hi to her." Julian slowly got up. He motioned to Freddy to stay sitting.

"Freddy, I'll be back in a few minutes, Bernice will keep you company."

Freddy waved off Julian, as he walked out of the kitchen. Julian chuckled when he heard Bernice ask Freddy if he wanted a drink.

Down the dark hallway and past the bar, he turned left to go up the grand staircase. Each step was calculated; he wasn't looking forward to this. Julian talked himself into knocking on Fannie's door.

"Hello?" Julian could barely hear the voice coming from inside.

"Hello, come in," came the voice again. Julian turned the glass knob and pushed the door open. He stepped inside and could see Fannie sitting in an upholstered chair staring out the window. She had turned to look—Julian figured she was probably expecting to see Bernice. Her eyes brightened up when he walked closer.

"Julian? Julian, my sweetheart, son. Come here, boy!" Waving Julian to come closer, she stiffly got up out of the well-worn chair. Julian walked over to her and they embraced. Fannie started to cry.

"Oh, my sweet boy, why did you leave me? Why didn't you say goodbye, Julian?"

"Fannie, I'm sorry, I just had to leave." Julian hadn't prepared for a warm reception and wasn't sure what to say to this, especially coming from Fannie. In his mind, he was sure she was happy he'd left.

"Son, you didn't have to leave. Things would have been better, surely you could have seen that?" Fannie stared into Julian's eyes, tears flowing down her face. "And look at how much you've grown, and your voice!" She stood back. "Just look at you, you're such a handsome man, now!" Julian was shocked. Fannie seemed truly proud of him.

"Fannie . . ." Julian gave a little chuckle. "I expected that I'd get my ear yanked off the side of my head. I didn't think you cared enough for me to even worry where I was!"

Fannie seemed shocked to hear Julian say this.

"Julian, sweetheart, I took care of you, don't you remember? Yes, I certainly had to discipline you—and often—but look at you, you're a strong, good man. Your mother certainly didn't do you any good, I had to do it."

"Have you heard where she is?" Julian asked, carefully.

"No." Fannie almost spit out the words. "Not since she left. Are you gonna look for her?"

"I'm not sure. I guess I thought I'd start here and see if you knew where she went to. She said that she and Mack were going to Detroit, but I'm not sure. Once she left, I knew I had to leave, too." Fannie seemed tired. "Your mother was the first to leave the Sunset. After that, things slowed down and each of the girls left, one by one. I just didn't have enough walk-in traffic to make it worth their time."

"Bernice told me you were getting ready to close up, is that right?"

Fannie turned and sat back down in her chair. "Yes, it looks like I'm going to close," she answered, staring at the floor. "I owe so much to the bank. They can take my home whenever they please. I had planned to close anyway—it's a nasty business—but now I can't even afford to buy groceries. I've even sold some of the furniture downstairs, a few dollars here and there. You don't want to hear an old black woman carrying on like this. Let's go downstairs and I'll cook you up something really good to eat. Good Lord, you must be starving."

"No, no, no, Miss Fannie, please, you don't have to do that. Besides, I brought a friend with me and it would take *too* much food to feed him. I'll tell you what, I'll run down to Barney's Café and bring some dinner back to you, how would that be?"

"Oh, no, Julian, I can't have you be bringing no restaurant food in here, I'll just get up and do some cooking, Bernice can help me." She started to get up, but Julian came over and put his hands on her shoulders to hold her down.

"No, Miss Fannie, I'm already on my way, it's my treat. You just take your time coming down the stairs and I'll be back in a little bit." With that, Julian was out the door and gone. He ran down the vacant stairway and into the kitchen. He could hear Freddy and Bernice laughing. When Julian opened the kitchen door, he could see that

Bernice had succeeded in tempting Freddy with shots of bourbon.

"Freddy put that down! Come on, we're gonna go pick up dinner for Bernice and Miss Fannie! Bernice, you go ahead and set the table, Freddy and I will be right back, Miss Fannie is on her way down." The back door slammed shut before Bernice could summon up an argument.

"What's goin' on?" asked Freddy as he tried to keep up with Julian.

"Freddy, Fannie is completely broke, the bank's gonna repossess the house."

"Ah, jeez," Freddy said.

"On top of that, she wanted to fix *us* something to eat! I said no way, we'll go get dinner. I wanted to get out of there before she could talk me out of it." As they walked down the alley behind the large homes, thoughts of Julian's past troubles rushed back into his mind.

"Boy, this brings back a few memories. I can't tell you how many times I've run up and down this old alley, Freddy. This was my main street, morning or night, it was my street."

Julian and Freddy walked into Barney's Café and sat at the counter. Julian noticed a dark-haired waitress facing away from them; she seemed to be counting her tickets. When she turned around, her face lit up.

"Juli!" She rushed up to the counter and reached for Julian's hands. A smile of remembrance trickled into Julian's mind and it hit him.

"Maria? Maria Lopez from school?"

"Yes, you didn't forget about me, did you?" Julian, embarrassed that he forgot a classmate—especially a classmate who looked this good—blushed, trying to come up with something clever to say back to her.

"Well, ah, been traveling, out west. Maria, this is my friend Freddy, Freddy Perkins; he's from Cheyenne, Wyoming."

"Wow, that's a long way from here. Nice to meet you, Freddy." Maria and Fred shook hands, then she turned back to Julian. "Are you going to stay in town for a while?" Julian ignored her question and asked another one.

"You've changed, Maria. Didn't we used to throw dirt clods at each other?" Julian smiled and soaked in her face. She came up close and touched his nose with her finger.

"Yes, and I always let you hit me," Maria teased.

"Aww, that's not true, I was just a good aim," Julian said. "Really, you let me?"

Freddy slapped Julian on the back and laughed.

"Yep, but you didn't hurt me, you threw nice," Maria said.

"Please, Maria, don't say that kind of stuff here, in front of Freddy. I'll never live it down. Anyway, we promised Fannie we'd get some food and get right back."

* * * *

In twenty minutes, the last sack of sandwiches was handed over to Julian and Maria made him promise to come back and see her. Freddy was over grabbing a few more napkins when Julian gripped his arm *hard*, startling him.

"What the . . ." Freddy could sense that Julian had frozen in place.

"Freddy," Julian said coldly, "don't look up, just turn around and we'll walk out through the side door to your left." Both boys turned together and had moved a couple of steps when they were spotted.

"You're not gettin' away that easy!" a loud voice boomed from across the room.

"Run, Freddy, run!" Julian yelled. Before dodging out the back door, Julian yelled back, "Maria, tell Fannie!" The boys took off out the side door of Barney's Café. Julian could hear Maria screaming his name.

"This way!" The boys raced through doors with grocery sacks flailing in the air. They rounded the corner of the restaurant and came to a dead stop. Pug and Lenny Dean, along with a couple of Shorty's drinking buddies from the mine, Lil' Ricky and Junior, blocked their path.

"Now ain't this a great day, boys. Looks like we're gonna have some lunch."

Julian and Freddy tried to back up but were stopped by Junior. Surrounded, they were pushed back into the alley along the side of the café. Pug grabbed a bag of sandwiches from Julian's hands and threw them up against the wall of the building across the alley. Julian knew this altercation was going to be painful. Freddy froze in place, his eyes darting around for a way to escape, but Julian hadn't thought about escaping, only surviving.

"Pug, you let Freddy here go, he ain't no part of this!" Julian growled to Pug.

"If he's with you, he's gonna be dead with you. You owe us big time, and I mean a lot of gold, big time." Lenny stepped up past Pug, spit on the ground at Julian's feet.

"I think you been out of town, so I'll give you a news

flash. Our daddy, Shorty, was killed in a mine accident six months ago. So, do you know what that means? It means that what belonged to our daddy now belongs to us. That box of gold you stole from our daddy is ours."

"It never was Shorty's. He stole it from Miss Fannie, I was just gettin' it back for her."

Lenny swung his fist hard across Julian's face, throwing spit and blood on the gravel. Junior lifted Julian back upright. Lenny got up close to Julian.

"Listen, asshole, unless you want your little buddy here to have a bad day just like you are, tell us where that box of gold is, and tell me now, before me and the boys break every bone in your body."

Julian wasn't going to tell. *I've been beat up before,* he thought, *maybe I'm used to it.* Freddy looked over at Julian, his eyes wide open.

"What's he talkin' about, Julian?"

"They stole gold from Fannie, I got it back!" *Bam!* Immediate pain seared through the middle of his face. He felt his nose being broken; blood splattered from his face and he fell to the ground. The arms and hands of Pug and Lenny, like Lil Ricky and Junior's, had become hard and calloused from heavy mine work. Before he could react, Freddy too, was hit and fell, bleeding from his mouth. Both were kicked repeatedly with steel-toed boots.

"So, now do you remember? Because we're only getting warmed up!" Pug yelled, leaning down close over Julian's bloody face.

Julian couldn't open his mouth to answer, he just shook his head. The pain was unbearable. A few feet away, Freddy moaned. Before Julian could do anything else, he felt large hands under his armpits lifting him. He was hit again hard in the stomach and chest repeatedly. He could hear Freddy getting the same treatment. His soul ached for Freddy; he wanted to say he was sorry. He couldn't tell if he cried tears or blood.

"Put 'em in the back of my truck!" yelled Lenny. "We'll take them over to the mine, put them in the kiln room, for now. We'll hang them over there."

Julian's mind couldn't comprehend what he was hearing; his thoughts seemed to glide through dreamlike streams of pain, in and out of consciousness.

CHAPTER 25
Send Help

Sitting at his kitchen table the morning after Julian left, Fred let his coffee cool just enough to take a sip. He felt the trickle of morning light stream through the curtained windows warm his aching bones. It felt nice. Fred thought back to when Margaret put up those curtains; she was so proud of herself. He could have cared less, but if she was happy, he was happy, and that was what drove the happiness in their sixty-year love affair.

That's what he appreciated about these small moments of peace. They allowed him to remember his life with Margaret, his two daughters, and his son, Dennis. *Precious life, goes so fast and so hard.*

Another sip of coffee. He knew his memory failed at times, he chuckled to himself; getting older was no picnic. Maybe it was his way of being lazy, just go on with life. It didn't work that way, and he knew it; he knew things had to get done, and besides, there was no one else to do it.

As the sunlight silently warmed his pant leg, he tried to remember exactly what chores he had planned this morning. The notes he left on the calendar were helpful, but it was easy to confuse which chores he had or hadn't done. He pulled down an older-looking note; maybe it was something he should just throw away. Then he saw it. A note he had written long ago—something he had spent so many years reminding himself to remember, a note to look inside the last page of his diary. The small notebook was neatly crammed between a hundred other old books on his dining room bookshelf.

Fred rose slowly from the kitchen table, holding on to the side of the counter, and walked over to the shelf. His large fingers pinched clumsily, slowly pulling out the diary. On the last page, a simple handwritten note in pencil: *Send Mike and Catherine to Joplin to rescue us, fast!*

Just a few words, but those words caused a flood of memories to wash over Fred.

He had to think hard. Fred needed to make sure what he was supposed to do. At one time, he knew all the details, so surely, he could remember them *now*. He moved slowly back into the kitchen and sat down at the table. Fred kept staring at the note, trying to think of details.

It took several tries at scribbling notes to himself, but soon, long-forgotten memories came back. Fred hit the table hard with his closed fist. He could almost feel the pain of that day.

It was Saturday morning, so Mike would most likely be home. Fred made several more notes to himself and then walked into his shop for some tools.

Within the hour, he was sitting next to Mike with a cup of coffee at the kitchen table. Catherine, Sarah, and Gracie had left earlier to have a girls' day at the mall. Fred had a serious look on his face.

"Mike, I need you to save my life."

"Fred?" Mike hesitated. "What?"

"I need you to save Julian and me," Fred spoke firmly,

his voice gruff.

"Fred, you know I would do anything for you, or Julian."

"Mike, this is hard for me." Fred stared down at the table. "Mike, a long time ago, I had left a note for myself. This was after I came back from Joplin and settled here. The note I wrote was to remind me to send someone back to help rescue me and Julian. Mike," Fred insisted, "the boys are in serious trouble and need your help. They need to be rescued."

* * * *

Fred's facial expressions told Mike that something dangerous was happening; he had never seen Fred this agitated.

"I don't know how this door thing all works, it's just too unbelievable for me," Fred was saying, "but I do know that if we don't get them some help, I fear that all I've ever done will get wiped out and maybe not ever happen!"

"I've been worried about Julian," Mike said, nodding. "Now, with what you're saying, there must be something going on. What do we need to do? Do you have any ideas?"

"Thanks, Mike. You know if there was any other way, I'd do that, but this needs to happen right away. I know if we can get this done quickly, it'll turn out okay, because I went through it. It took me a while, but I remember most of what happened."

"Can you tell me what's going on? Where is Julian?" asked Mike.

"I don't know if Julian ever mentioned the Dean

boys, but he had several run-ins with them back in the day. When we arrived back in Joplin, we had gone down to the local restaurant to get some dinner for Miss Fannie, the lady who ran the brothel, where Julian lived with his mother. Those boys spotted us at the restaurant and beat us up with something awful then took us down to the mine. We are being held hostage, down in the zinc mine, there in Joplin. It's an awful situation, Mike," Fred admitted. "I hate to think about it. Even today it's hard to think we were that close to getting killed."

"Wow!" Mike said. "It's amazing you two could find that much trouble in such a small town!"

"Well, that being said, there's something you might not be all right with." Fred cleared his throat.

"What is that, Fred?"

"Catherine and the girls have to go with you."

"No, no, no, Fred, I don't think so. I mean, is it really necessary? It sounds like this could be a pretty dicey situation. You're saying there would be explosives?"

"Yes, Mike, because Catherine knows the country you'll be going through and she's also familiar with the time." Freddy tried to reassure him, "It'll be all right; she and the girls won't be in any danger. I know how this turns out, I promise. Look here, Mike, I've got some notes, let me tell you what needs to happen."

Fred opened a piece of paper and showed Mike a list of events that would happen. He went on to explain what he was going to need to rescue the boys and how it would take place.

"If I've done this correctly, you will need to leave tomorrow. You should arrive in Joplin within a day or so of when we have been taken, hostage. I'm not exactly sure of the timing, you know, it's been a while. I've kept notes in this diary since 1929."

"Okay," said Mike. "You laid it out for us, huh?"

"Yep, just have to go do it." When Fred finished going through his list with Mike, Fred asked Mike to walk back over to his place to see something.

"I didn't want you to see this until now—I've been holding on to it for many years. Now you need to see it because it will be in your future." Fred opened the large doors to his garage and pulled the cover off a beautiful, mint-condition Chrysler Imperial.

"Mike, this is the car you'll be buying in Kansas City."

Mike was stunned. "Fred, she's beautiful!"

"Yep, she's a wonderful car, huh? A 1929 Chrysler Imperial. So, when you get back to Kansas City, find the Chrysler dealer, this will be the best car for you." Fred winked at Mike. "And, as soon as you get back," Fred said, looking Mike in the eye, "get this old buggy out of here and over to your garage, because I've been wanting to clean this space out for a long time."

"What? You're giving this to me?"

"Heck no! I'm not giving this car to you. It's yours, you bought it, remember? Or you will be anyway when you get back to Kansas City." Fred chuckled. "You only paid $863! The rest you'll figure out when it happens. I don't want to spoil the fun you'll be having. Now, you need to get going and get those ladies packed up!"

Fred grinned as Mike gave him a hug and together, they covered the car back up.

* * * *

In a couple of hours, Mike was explaining to Catherine and the girls what Fred had told him and that they would need to leave as soon as possible. Mike expected a flat no from Catherine, but instead, he found her and the girls jumping with excitement, especially at the news that they would have to shop for new clothes in a 1929 Cheyenne clothing store before they left on the train.

"We get to buy new clothes *and* ride on the train!" yelled Sarah. "Gracie, you get to wear some really neat old-style clothes, like Catherine had, remember? And, we'll get those boots that tie up to your knees!"

"Catherine, do I have to wear those kinds of shoes?" Gracie whined.

"I'm not too sure what we'll find, honey, but we'll find something you'll like. Won't it be fun?"

"Yeah, I guess, but can I still take my own blanket?" Gracie said, looking up at Catherine.

* * * *

In the morning, Mike got everyone up to start gathering what supplies they could take with them. Catherine had already helped Sarah and Gracie through the closet door and they were looking in her spare closets for extra clothes. Catherine remembered that she had some dresses from when she was a little girl, so the girls had something to wear on their way into town to shop for the rest of the trip.

When Catherine finished, she was elegant in one of her best school outfits, normally kept in a chest at the end of her bed. By nine-thirty in the morning, they were through the closet door and on their way down to the Cheyenne city center.

At the station, a few hours later, Mike, Catherine, and the two girls appeared to be the typical family of 1929, all cleaned up and somewhere to go. They had already walked around the station several times admiring the history lesson unfolding before them. Catherine had the most wonderful time explaining how things worked and what modern conveniences people had or didn't have, back in 1929. Mike could tell that Catherine was ecstatic as she described the layout of the station and the workmanship put into the train depot.

Mike was excited to tell them that they were taking the same train that Julian and Freddy were on at 1:15 p.m., number 104, Kansas City Express. After a while, Mike began fidgeting as badly as the girls, nervous that he wouldn't be able to pull off the rescue as planned. He had to keep reminding himself that Fred was alive and didn't seem to have any serious scars from his adventure, but he was still concerned about it. Catherine could tell he was worried about something else and tried to comfort him.

"Michael, what's up? Are you worried about the train trip?" she probed, scooting up next to him.

"No, I'm just trying to organize everything in my head that Fred told me. I hope I can pull it off okay." Mike knew, despite Fred's promise, that he was putting Catherine and the girls in danger by taking them on this trip. Fred had tried to reassure him that all would be okay, yet he felt uneasy inside about it.

"Well, he must have a tremendous amount of faith in you, or else he wouldn't bother asking you," she reassured with a smile.

"Yeah, you're probably right, I just needed something to worry about, I guess. What did you tell your mom about where we'd be?" Anne had called last night and wanted to come over the next day, and Catherine had to come up with a quick story to ward her off the trail.

"I told her you had a surprise trip come up and were taking me and the girls along. Although she was a bit put off, I told her nicely there was just no way around it." She grinned like a sly fox.

"Good job, I knew you'd come up with something."

In the background, Mike could hear the rumble of something approaching and the growing sound of a train whistle approaching the station. "Come on girls, let's go see this big train pull in!" Soon, they were out to the passenger loading area in front of the station. Sarah and Gracie were so excited they could hardly contain themselves. Their new long dresses blew wildly in the wind and Catherine yelled over the screaming brakes and hissing steam to hold on to their fancy spring hats so they wouldn't blow down the tracks.

When they got ready to board the train, the girls lined up in front of Catherine and held their hats with one hand and a small satchel in the other. Mike had purchased sleeper berths for them along with the regular passenger fares. Sarah wanted to go right away to the berths and climb into their spaces. Gracie would have tagged along quickly, but Mike held her back and tactfully convinced both girls to come up with him and Catherine to the observation car and have some snacks and a juice drink. Soon, they were underway.

In Kansas City, Mike followed Fred's instructions and purchased, with the excitement of a teenager buying his first car, a new 1929 Chrysler, paying a grand total of $863, cash, with the spare tire thrown in for free. While he was doing that, Catherine and the girls walked down the street to a couple of clothing stores to look around for more accessories and bargains.

It wasn't long before Catherine heard a honk. She peered out through the front picture window to see Mike dressed up with a hat, scarf, and driving goggles; he was donning the biggest grin she had ever seen. She gathered up the girls and went out to see Mr. New Car Guy.

"Well, now aren't we fancy in our new auto, huh?" asked Catherine. "Did they throw in the new scarf with that?" Sarah and Gracie laughed at their dad in his new car which looked a lot like something Bonnie and Clyde would drive.

"Hey Dad, can we call you Clyde?" Sarah yelled over the clutter of the engine noise.

"You sweet ladies are in quite the mood today, huh?" Mike retorted with a smile. "Why don't you jump in, I'll take you for a ride."

The car puttered off, scarves and hats fluttering as they drove, windows down, from the busy city and into the peaceful Missouri countryside and the dusty, bumpy dirt roads. Mike felt great. It took several Missouri roads for the grin to relax from his face, but every time he turned to look at Catherine or his daughters, it returned, wide as a country mile.

After some time, he sighed to let some of the excitement ease off a little. He daydreamed and hoped that this would be a fun adventure—*Or maybe,* he thought, *a challenge, a manageable one.* Not something that got hurt anyone or, God forbid, killed—just an exciting little challenge that he could successfully take care of. At least, that was his desire.

The tools Fred listed to bring along forebode something else and deep in the pit of his stomach, he wondered if these challenges would be as easy as Fred let on. He didn't trust this time-change thing they were experiencing; how did he know it would turn out the way Fred expected? Then again, *What could go wrong?* Mike thought to himself. After all, Fred told him that things worked out okay.

Mike had been a Boy Scout and he still lived by their motto, so he always tried to be prepared. But, how do you prepare for these circumstances—how could he know what to prepare *for?* His intuition told him to relax and enjoy what came, let instincts guide and maybe find out how smart he was, or not.

In the background, the happy chatter of Catherine and the girls pulled him out of his uneasiness. Catherine seemed to be having fun pointing out to the girls how people lived back in the 1920s as they passed by little towns, horse-drawn hay wagons, and other automobiles.

An hour outside of Kansas City, the bumpy ride started to take a toll. The hot afternoon sun and humidity started to wear on the girls and though they were only traveling at thirty-five miles an hour, Mike was concerned that the car might overheat. It was Gracie who spoke up first.

A request for a bathroom break and a change of clothing from fancy dresses to blouses and shorts was brought up, voted on and the measure passed, unanimously.

Mike took the opportunity to cool down the car with some anti-freeze that Fred suggested they should bring along—which answered one of the nagging questions about how some of the supplies were going to be used. After they got back on the road, dust from frequent patches of dirt road and passing farm trucks made Sarah roll up her windows and keep a scarf up against her face to keep the dust out. Gracie stuck her head out the window, on her side like a little puppy until they passed a large dairy farm and the smell helped her decide to roll her window up, too.

Late in the afternoon and about halfway to their destination, Mike found a roadside motel. Once they had everything out of the car, the girls took a bath and Catherine found a spot on one of the double beds to stretch out. Mike pulled out the papers Fred had given him and started to read. Catherine got up and powered on the RCA radio, turning the large dim yellow dial until she came to a station playing classical music. The signal moved in and out, but still, it provided a gentle sound in the background.

Catherine laid back down on the bed and propped her head up so she could watch Mike study. She found herself scrutinizing him, trying with emotions in check to see if he was the guy she hoped he was. She felt comfortable with him; he wasn't overbearing, and his sense of humor lightened up somber moments.

The papers Fred had given to Mike had a drawing showing a layout of Joplin with a mark for Shorty's house, the mine location, and the downtown area approximate to Fannie's brothel. Though Mike knew that the boys would be chained up somewhere at the mine, Fred had been unclear on exactly what area—and the mine could be a maze of tunnels.

This was the part that gave Mike the most worry. Fred's memory had faded, and details of their fantastic trip had become small bits of thrill and regrets that became clouded up into something that didn't make complete sense. Mike was concerned about how accurate this information was. Nevertheless, at the end of the day, he had a mission and it would be carried out.

The girls finished their baths and came out wrapped in towels, crawled up onto the bed with Catherine, and snuggled close to her. Catherine knew she loved these little girls; it was obvious to Mike that they adored her.

"Look at your poor dad over there, trying to figure out what we're going to do when we get to Joplin."

Mike looked over with a grin. "You'd better hope I figure this out because if I don't, I could damage the time warp machine and we may never get back to modern time," he said.

"Oh, well, that wouldn't be the worst thing in the world, would it?" Catherine asked.

Sarah perked up. "I don't think so."

"So, you think you could live without a *mall?*" Mike asked, with a devilish look on his face. Sarah immediately recanted.

"Uh, never mind."

Mike knew Sarah clearly couldn't live without a shopping mall; it was part of her DNA. "Just as I thought,"

Mike said. He looked back at Catherine, eyebrows raised, giving her one of those *I told you so* looks. Mike rolled up the papers and picked up one of the small news pamphlets on the desk.

It was getting dark outside and the quiet of the small town seemed eerie to them. Catherine had warned them that the only thing electronic would be the lights and they would be dim and hard to find compared to the usual thousands of bright lights they were used to in the cities.

Sarah and Gracie slipped on their nightgowns and opened the door to the motel room. Once they stepped outside, except for the sound of a few million crickets and a farm truck that had just passed, it was silent.

"Wow!" Sarah said. "There's only one light outside on a pole. And you can hardly see it for all the bugs flying around it. Look at all the stars!"

"Where? I can't see, where?" Gracie scurried around Mike to see.

"Duh, just look up there!" Sarah pointed to the sky and Gracie's eyes grew big.

"Wow! Come here Catherine, come here, look!"

Catherine got up from the bed and stood behind the girls staring at the star-filled sky. Mike got up, and walked to the door behind Catherine and the girls. Catherine leaned back against him, he put his hands on her shoulders. Back in the room, with Chopin's "Nocturne #2 in E Flat Major" fading in and out on the radio, the moment was quiet and peaceful.

* * * *

The next morning, they packed the car, paid $5.50 for the room and they were down the road stopping at the first whiff of hot breakfast and coffee they could find.

Later, in the afternoon, an overcast sky rumbled from distant thunderstorms; lightning pierced downward from the ever-growing dark clouds along the horizon, and the air felt muggy and still. A dusty black sedan pulled up in front of Fey's hardware store and two adults and two small girls—dressed in dark clothing, heads bowed low—rushed inside. Several old men sitting on benches across the street could have mistaken the group for the Dalton Gang or Bonnie and Clyde. They'd been known to frequent the area. *Keep an eye on them.* The town remained calm and quiet.

They moved quickly. Each had a list of supplies to get. Mike hurried to the tools and grabbed a large pack of batteries and the largest chain cutter he could find. Catherine found matches, and Sarah located a couple of wooden fruit boxes and a wagon. Gracie went directly for the small toys. Her mission was critical. She was to find the noise-makers.

Suddenly, they magically appeared at the gloves and picked out the right size for each hand before the clerk could intervene and ask if he could help; he couldn't. To Mike's chagrin, the wooden floor creaked incessantly, forcing him to walk like he had sore feet, hoping to make less noise. They moved as silently as possible, except for Gracie, to the cash register. Then it got interesting.

"So," Mr. Orville Fey said in a long Southern drawl, "how are you fine young folks doing today, huh?" He slowly looked up, and only saw blank stares. Finally, Mike said something.

"Well, I guess we're just fine, now, aren't we honey?"

"Yep, sweetie, just fine," Catherine agreed.

"Very good, very good." Orville looked over the assorted tools, gloves, wire, toys, and one gingham-dress stuffed doll. Mike looked over at Gracie with a look that said, *It's not on the list.* She knew she had him, he couldn't say no. It also wasn't in the plan to argue about it.

"Let me see here," he said, as he rummaged through the pile. "You know, ma'am, we have a sale on right now on our fabric, two yards of the cotton blend for fifty cents, just in case you're interested, that is." He glanced up at Catherine, his spectacles magnifying his eyes.

"Oh, no thanks, I have plenty of fabric. We'll just take what we have here." Catherine motioned with her hands to go ahead.

"Okay, okay," Orville answered slowly, "it's my job, just thought I'd mention it. No problem." Mike began fidgeting.

"You know, honey . . ." Mike turned to Catherine. "I just plumb forgot that we'd better get over to the church as soon as we can, too, to pick up those chairs for the meeting tonight." He thought he could hurry Orville up with a sense of urgency, but only brought on another round of questions.

"Oh, what church are you going to get chairs from?"

"The Christian church over here south of town," Mike answered, realizing he'd just opened up Pandora's box. Orville glanced up with a puzzled look. Catherine jumped in and tried to save him.

"Girls, why don't you just go on out to the car, we'll wrap up here real quick."

"Okay, Mom." Sarah and Gracie shrugged and lumbered off toward the front of the building.

"Well, which church is it, 'cause I can't think of one in that direction?" asked the curious clerk.

"Sir," Catherine said as she looked Orville in the eye, "we're on kind of a tight schedule here, so can we go ahead and ring up?"

"Oh, why yes, ma'am, I didn't mean to intrude, just trying to be helpful, you know. And please, just call me Orville." Orville reached for the first few items and started to punch the numbers, one by one, into the old register.

"That's okay, Orville, we're just trying to get down the road and we have two hungry little girls and so much yet to get done today. I'm sure you and the missus are familiar with that."

Mike had left money with Catherine and was wandering around the store. The creaking of the old wooden floors told Catherine exactly where he was at all times. As soon as Orville finished, she paid him cash and rounded up the supplies into the wagon.

"Mike, honey, come here and help me get this, will you?"

"Coming, dear!"

"You folks have a nice day, ya hear? And come back in soon!"

"Thank you, Orville, we will." They both lugged out their supplies and loaded up the car. Once they were back on the road, the rush of air moving through the car felt wonderful to them, and the mood changed for the better.

CHAPTER 26
Cold, Dark, and Lonely

The last few miles into Joplin were somber and quiet. The sun poked out for a little while in the morning, but as they moved farther south, the skies turned overcast and occasionally rained. Sarah wrapped herself up in a light blanket on the small back seat to read a book, Mike contemplated how Fred's plan would play out, and Catherine had pulled Gracie up front with her and Mike to read one of her school books.

Rolling into Joplin was anticlimactic; the girls expected more of a city. As they drove along the main Route 66, large trees blocked most of the homes from view. Being from the high plains, they weren't used to the heavy overgrowth of trees and shrubs. Even though Mike had the address, he still managed to miss a couple of turns before ending up on the right street. As he turned the corner, just a few blocks off the main drag, he spotted the correct house address.

A gray mist from the heavy rains seemed to distort the graceful appearance of the once-grand home. As they pulled up and parked, everything seemed silent, except for the patter of rain falling on the car's roof. At this point, according to Fred's directions, he was clear: *Go to Miss Fannie's, she'll help you. Here's the address . . .*

Catherine looked at Mike, who pondered his next move. After all, Mike did promise that they would find Miss Fannie Jo Blakely, the infamous madam Fred spoke of. Freddy's descriptions left the reader to wonder: Was she truly wonderful or wicked? Both personalities seemed equally possible.

"What are you going to do, Dad?" Gracie asked.

"I'm just wondering how to do this, honey."

Catherine giggled. Mike looked over at her and smiled. This once-magnificent house was a brothel, and Mike was reticent about exposing his two impressionable daughters to what could be inside. Not that he knew a lot; Fred did not describe the interior of the establishment.

"Why don't I just go on up there and see if Miss Fannie is in, then I'll explain why we're here, okay?" He turned to look at Catherine and the girls for their approval.

"I think that's a good plan, Mr. Roberts," replied Catherine. She jokingly nudged his shoulders to get him to move out of the car. Gracie and Sarah joined in poking him.

As the door slammed shut behind him, he held his hand over his brow to keep the rain out of his vision. He turned back to see three pairs of eyes curiously watching his every move. Moving up the steps, he admired the large, wide veranda around the front part of the house. The front door was larger than he had imagined. He knocked, then waited. Nothing, no sound. Not even a vibration of footsteps coming down steps or walking near the door. More knocks, louder. He looked around and tried to peer into the windows. Nothing—until he heard the slight squeak of a window being rolled down.

"Try the back door!" yelled Catherine. Mike looked at her for a second, then waved okay. He cautiously moved around to the back and up onto the wooden porch Julian had been so familiar with. The door was unlocked. He opened the screen door, pushed the kitchen door, and stepped inside. Within a few seconds, he smelled a pungent aroma of spices. Walking into the kitchen area, he spoke.

"Hello? Hello?" Finally, a sound. Mike heard a chair move from inside.

"Yes, in here," a muffled voice replied. Mike continued into the kitchen and found who he assumed to be Fannie, sitting at a table.

"Hello? Are you Miss Fannie?"

The black lady dressed in a housecoat looked to have been laying her head down on the table. Maybe she had been crying.

"I'm so sorry to bother you, ma'am. My name is Mike Roberts. I'm a close friend of Julian's." Mike hesitated. "And Freddy's."

Before he could finish, Fannie's eyes lit up; she lifted herself from her chair and clapped her hands in praise.

"Oh, thank you, Lord! You're here to help me find the boys!" Her voice shouted out excitement. Mike was surprised by her sudden burst of energy.

"Yes, I am. And I have my family here, too. Freddy suggested I contact you if anything should happen to him or Julian."

Fannie moved closer as he was talking and before he had finished, she had grabbed him and hugged him tightly.

"You have your family here?" Fannie asked. "Where are they? Let's get them in here; it's so nasty outside."

Fannie leaned over to look out the back windows and couldn't see anything. She stared back at Mike, with a puzzled expression. "Well, son, where are they? Let's go get them!" She started walking out toward the front foyer.

"Yes, yes, ma'am. I just parked out front," Mike hurried behind Fannie as she rushed to the front of the house to greet Mike's family. "I just wasn't sure where to park."

"Don't worry about that, now, son. Oh, there they are!" Fannie glanced out one of the front windows and spotted the car. She immediately walked over to the large front door, opened it up, and started waving to Catherine and the girls to come inside.

"Honey, you go out and get your luggage and make sure those young ladies get in here right now!" Fannie ordered Mike along, pushing his backside with a shove.

Fannie was so excited, she stood wringing her hands, anticipating this unknown family into her house. As Catherine and the girls ran up to the porch, Miss Fannie greeted them each with a hug and a kiss on the cheek.

"Welcome ladies, I'm so glad to have you here. Sweet Lord, I have been praying for this to happen, I just knew he would answer my prayers, yes, please. Y'all come in, please."

Fannie chatted nonstop, escorting the girls inside the house, leaving Mike out in the rain to gather up luggage, pillows, and blankets. Inside, Catherine and the girls walked through the foyer and into the front receiving room, astonished at the lack of furnishings—just a few small chairs were left here and there, against the wall. It seemed like a moving company had come in and taken all the furniture.

"Catherine, is that right? And your daughters, they are just the most beautiful ladies I have ever seen, I swear!" Sarah smiled politely and Gracie giggled, embarrassed. She moved to get behind Catherine's long skirt.

"Honey," said Catherine, "this is Miss Fannie, Julian's dear friend." Gracie peered from behind Catherine's dress. "I'm sorry about this shy one, she'll warm up in time. Her name is Gracie."

"Hello, Gracie," Fannie said, "I'm so pleased to meet you. I just love your name, it's very popular for young girls, nowadays."

"Daddy named me after my grandmother, she died," Gracie said.

"Gracious, I'm so sorry to hear that," answered Fannie. Catherine quickly intervened.

"And this young lady is Sarah," Catherine said.

"You are so pretty, little lady, I'll bet you just drive those young boys wild!"

"Well, we hope not yet." Catherine blushed at her remark and wondered if she was now deciding when Sarah would be able to see boys. Sarah looked up at Catherine and grinned a look that said, *What you don't know won't hurt you.*

"Ladies, I am so sorry about the furniture. You know, times have been so very tough. Of course, the business I used to have here is gone, which is really for the better—it wasn't a good business anyway, but we won't speak any more of that, shall we."

Catherine nodded in agreement. Behind her, she could hear Mike coming in the door struggling with several large pieces of luggage.

After everyone got settled in, Mike excused himself and drove down to the market to purchase groceries to make dinner. When he returned, he and Catherine sat across from Fannie and told her about Fred's instructions to rescue them, which confused Fannie how Mike knew so much about what was going on. To her, the boys had just gone out for dinner yesterday and never came back.

"But, how did you know, Michael, if this just happened yesterday?"

"Fannie, it's really hard to explain, but the safest way to say it is that Freddy left us a note." Mike hoped his explanation would leave her satisfied. "If he didn't come back by a certain time, we were to come looking for him, so here we are."

Fannie looked back at Mike with a quizzical stare.

"Well, okay, but it's just amazing that you're here. Truly, the Lord does work in mysterious ways, I just don't know how, but he does."

"So, Fannie," Mike began, "when did you realize something was wrong? Did you hear about any trouble or maybe they just left town or something?"

"After the boys left, it was quite some time. I have another lady that lives with me, Bernice—she's an Indian woman who's been with me for many years—she started to worry and decided to go looking for them." Fannie continued, "After a while, she ran back to the house and told me that her friend, Maria, down at the restaurant, had told her that the Dean boys had beat them up and taken them away. Maria was just beside herself. She wanted to tell me herself but had to stay at work." Fannie wiped tears from her eyes.

"Bernice explained that Maria heard one of them say they were taking them to the zinc mine. Maria feared they wouldn't be found—and certainly, not alive; there are a lot of abandoned mine shafts all over Jasper County, they could be anywhere. Considering the reputation of the Deans, no one doubted the worst could happen."

Bernice arrived at the house after being out most of the afternoon trying to find more information about where the boys were taken. Mike sat down with Bernice while Fannie and Catherine finished preparing dinner.

After dinner, Mike said, "It's worth all the traveling over dirt roads, just to sit here and eat this wonderful food." Catherine suggested to Fannie that she should open a restaurant; she would probably do quite well. The rest of the evening, Fannie, Bernice, Mike, and Catherine planned what they would do.

They knew the Nasty Dog zinc mine ran twenty-four hours a day; sixty-two men worked per shift—twenty-eight above ground, thirty-four below in the shafts. Mike thanked Bernice for the great detective work she did. She told Mike that she still had several close friends on the inside. Her best contact told her exactly where the boys were and that they were still alive but in bad shape. The Dean boys had been telling some close friends that they didn't want to kill Julian or Freddy, just hurt them bad enough that they would never come back to this town again.

The problem was, as her scout explained, the Dean boys weren't exactly men of their word and certainly didn't understand what the word *enough* meant. He was sure by the time the Deans finished with Julian and Freddy, someone would have to help identify the bones. He didn't want that to happen and told Bernice the best times to hit the mine—that's why they were planning to do it in the morning.

Fannie called in a few IOUs of her own. The Joplin police chief, Billy Hawkins, was a friend of sorts. She had helped him catch several wanted felons while visiting her establishment and had arranged for a private meeting with one of her young girls to satisfy an ongoing investigation he was handling by himself. He would arrange for the actual police escort into the mine and his men would spread out from there.

The problem at hand: Julian and Freddy were down in an abandoned shaft area. They couldn't just waltz in and go right to the site; someone at the mine would have to take them to that area. The Dean boys were mine foremen; they had their hands on the keys. Everyone knew that as soon as they caught wind of what was going on, they would hightail it to the shaft and destroy any evidence, quickly. They had to move fast.

Mike told Catherine that he didn't want her or the girls to go inside the mine, but he wanted them there, inside the car and outside the mine gates. Catherine and Gracie were fine with that plan, although Sarah wanted to go in. Catherine asked Fannie if she and Bernice wanted to stay with her, in the car. Fannie readily agreed, but Bernice, like Sarah, preferred to get in the middle of the action. Though Mike couldn't tell Bernice what to do, Sarah was told in no uncertain terms that she was not going past the mine gates.

* * * *

Breakfast plates were being cleaned up and the last few cups of coffee were being poured when a loud knock at the back screen door made everyone jump. Bernice walked back to see who it was. Police Chief Hawkins walked in behind Bernice and greeted everyone.

"Good morning, Miss Fannie," he said politely, tipping his hat with a grin.

"Good morning to you, Billy! How's the missus doing?"

"Ah, she's just fine, just fine. Had a little bit of the 'fluenza lately, but it seems to be cutting back now. She'll be fine." The chief sat down at the table and Bernice put a full cup of hot coffee in front of him. "Thank you, Bernie."

"Chief, this here's Michael Robert and his beautiful bride Catherine and their lovely daughters, Sarah and Gracie." Mike didn't bother to correct Fannie, and Catherine got another chance to blush.

"Pleased to meet you, Mr. Roberts, Mrs. Roberts. Hello, little ladies. I hope you're staying out of trouble while you're in our fair city." He pointed teasingly to Sarah and Gracie. They both laughed.

"I'm going to rob a candy store as soon as I find one," Sarah quipped.

His eyes opened wide up. "Now, that sounds like a good idea. You give me a call, I'll help you!" Chief Hawkins replied.

"Chief," interrupted Mike, "sorry to get back to

business here, but I have a couple of questions."

"Sure, Michael. I guess we'd better get on with it. Fannie, I don't suppose you've heard anything else, you know, about where the boys are being kept?"

"No Chief, not a thing."

"Chief," asked Mike, "how many men will you be taking along this morning?"

"Got six. Couldn't get any more. Four of my own guys and two extra from the Webb City force. I think we'll be okay. I'll be having our dispatch girl call down to the mine about ten thirty this morning, to tell them we'll be in to pick up a felon. That's a fairly common occurrence. So, they won't be immediately alerted seeing us pull in. Of course, with so many men coming in at once, that may trigger an alarm with them Dean boys, I don't know. Michael, do you plan on going in with us?" asked Chief Hawkins.

"Yes, I do. I know what Julian and Freddy look like and I'm fit enough to be of some help."

The chief smiled; he knew Julian all too well from his hoodlum days in Joplin, but it had been a couple of years since he'd seen him, so his looks might have changed despite that he had no reservations that Julian was still a hoodlum.

"That'll be okay, Michael. You probably know what this young Freddy fellow looks like, too, right?"

"Yes, I sure do," Mike said.

"I'm going in, too, Chief," piped up Bernice. She was standing in the background leaning in the pantry doorway, her arms crossed. Chief Hawkins looked over at Bernice, and Mike could tell he wasn't too keen on the idea.

"Now, Bernice, why do you want to do that? This is an extremely dangerous place, and you probably already know, some of those shafts run several hundred feet deep."

"Chief, my dad came down here and started in the mines; that's where he died. It's just something I need to do." Chief Hawkins put down his coffee cup, sighed, and looked up at Bernice.

"I really can't let you go in there, Bernice. You'll just get in the way. And if it gets too dangerous, then I'll have to worry about you. It just ain't gonna work, sweetheart, I wish I could, but it's just too dangerous."

Bernice took a deep breath. She turned around and left the room without saying anything. Everyone knew she was disappointed, and Mike was sure this wasn't the end of her involvement. Chief Hawkins looked over to Fannie and shrugged. Catherine got up to go see if Bernice was okay.

The chief, glancing at his coffee, took a firm grip on the mug and took one last drink. He stood and told them he would wait for them at the police department. From there, they would drive over to the mine.

* * * *

The first part of the plan worked great—they got inside the gate. Two patrol cars and Mike in his car with Catherine, Sarah, Gracie, Fannie, and Bernice parked in front of the Nasty Dog mine office. Catherine, the girls, Bernice, and Fannie remained in the parked car while Mike grabbed his duffel bag of equipment and went inside with the officers.

For everyone left outside, nerves set in. Catherine knew the plan, but she started tapping her fingers right away; she knew she couldn't just sit tight waiting for the plan to unfold.

A mine superintendent, Bill Conklin, expecting a warrant to be served, was surprised when Chief Hawkins told him that the Dean brothers were holding two boys hostage deep in the mine. After introductions, he explained to Mike his concern was that they were down in one of the shafts, in an area not currently being mined. Bill also told Mike they weren't alone—one of the other shift bosses had told him earlier that the Dean boys had several other friends helping them.

Mike grew more nervous. He knew where that area was, from Fred's descriptions, yet it still gave him a sinking feeling in the pit of his stomach. It had been two full days since Julian and Freddy had been taken, hostage.

"You know, Chief, I have no idea why they're down in that area," Bill said. "But apparently, they told Edith, our scheduling clerk, that they'd be down there for a while. Maybe we'll be reopening that area again. Shoot! I don't know."

"Well, Bill, that's just the place we want to go. Can you take us down there?" Chief Hawkins asked.

"Follow me. We'll have to go down through the kiln area to the number three shaft and ride down from there. I'll be asking a couple of other supervisors and lead foremen to come along to help us." He threw some papers on a desk behind him and walked over to a key cabinet to retrieve the keys to operate the cage that would take them down into the shaft. He waved them all to follow him down the hallway and out the back of the building.

Mike walked fast to catch up to Bill and Chief Hawkins, but some of the other police officers lagged behind; Mike thought that as fast as they were moving, those three officers might be left in the dust. Mike's frustration grew with each second. From what Fred had told him, he knew that despite ending up okay, Freddy and Julian still endured considerable pain waiting for the rescue. They didn't know the rescue was coming.

The entire mining operation was a blizzard of zinc dust. The floors, every piece of equipment, and even the men's faces and clothes were covered with a combination of light- and dark-colored dust. Mike's first thought: *How would you be able to recognize anyone?*

To Mike's amazement, no one wore protective masks or eye protection. He had to remind himself this was 1929. Mine safety wasn't a big deal then. Except for the hard hats with small lights, the only other safety equipment was one's desire for self-preservation and quick thinking. When he caught up with the chief and Bill, they were in the large noisy kiln room, talking with mine foreman Bob and his lead guys Kelly and Stan about how many men the cage would hold.

"This is one of our older shafts—this cage can only hold six men going down! We'll be going to the two-hundred-foot level, not too deep!" Bill yelled out to anyone that could hear. Bill waved to his foreman, Bob, and two mine lead guys to join up with them.

Mike was frustrated and anxious to get moving; he thought the Dean brothers could be down there beating the boys again or trying to move them to another location.

Chief Hawkins picked Mike and his three officers—Vernal, Eldon, and Buster—to go with him on the first trip down. Mine Supervisor Bob would also be going down to run the lift and show them where the Dean boys might be.

"I'll take you guys down, show you a few things down there, then I'll go right back up for my mine foreman," Bob said. Everyone agreed.

Bob put his key in and then pulled down on the large switch and the cage jerked downward at a terrific pace.

Mike had seen his share of elevator shafts and rigging from his experience with the power company, but this was a new world. Jagged, falling rocks, questionable cables, and a patched-up power supply made him squirm. Within a few seconds, the cage jerked to a stop. Powdered dust swarmed up everywhere around them. The three police officers, each in their twenties, had looks on their faces like they were running from a freight train. Mike felt like laughing, except he knew he probably bore the same look.

"You see over there!" Bob pointed to a dimly lit row of twenty-five-watt light bulbs hanging precariously from a line along the top of the shaft. "Down there is where I think they've gone to, can't be sure, but that's what I think. If you want to start making your way down that way, I'll be back shortly with the other guys and we'll join up with you!"

With that, the cage jerked back and was gone. Silence enveloped them. It wasn't so much silence, just the lack of any other sound except breathing. Heavy, hard breathing.

Walking behind the officers through the tunnel—Mike noticed that each of the officers had holstered pistols—he was defenseless. As they cautiously made their way along the tunnel wall, everyone's eyes slowly adjusted to the light.

"Stop," Chief Hawkins whispered. "Let's listen for a minute. We don't know how far down this tunnel goes. For all we know, those buggers could be just around one of these corners."

Mike remembered Fred telling him he could hear them, so they must be in the right area. What he didn't know was what to expect when they found them. Mike spotted a miner's pick leaning against the tunnel wall and picked it up. *Something is better than nothing*, he thought.

"Hear that?" asked the chief. Everyone froze. As they listened, they could hear a small sound coming from a distance down the tunnel. They began to move again, and rocks and sand crunched under their boots. The tunnel ceilings seemed to draw closer and the lights flickered, giving Mike's heart pause. He didn't want to get stuck two hundred feet below the surface of earth, without lights.

Mike followed behind the chief and his three guys. Even with the small bulbs on their hard hats and the weak light from the bulbs overhead, it was extremely hard to see very far down the shaft. Every hard hat beam of light barely filtered through a misty layer of dust, jerking around without focusing on any object.

They were holding onto the backs of each other's belts and following one behind the other. Mike stayed farther behind, still carrying his duffel bag of tricks. Then, Mike's worst fear: The overhead lights flickered again, then went out completely. Someone yelled, "They know we're here!"

The chief and the officer behind him only heard a

second's worth of rushing air. The large flat metal shovels hit the chief and Officer Vernal dead on, laying them out cold and knocking Officers Eldon and Buster, behind them, down like dominoes—except for Mike. With small streams of lights flailing around the tunnel, they were like sitting ducks, being slammed with each swing of the shovel.

Large dark figures moved effortlessly, swinging and hitting. Mike turned his hardhat light off and crouched to avoid getting hit. He thought *They don't know I'm here.* He maneuvered himself closer to one of the dark shapes and with every ounce of muscle in his body, swung the pick around to the legs of one of the men.

"AHH God!" The man screamed in pain as the sharp end of the pick drove deep into the muscle of his thigh. He rolled down on the ground screaming for help.

"Pug!" the other one called. "You okay?"

Mike managed to pick up Pug's shovel and pummeled the guy yelling for Pug hard in his face, dropping him cold. Pug ran off. Mike yelled for Officers Eldon and Buster and told them to put cuffs on Pug's friend and get him back up the elevator and hold him.

The chief and Vernal were getting up. Shaken, they were still able to help tie up the man Mike hit before looking for Pug's whereabouts. Chief yelled back to Mike that the guy he hit was Pug's brother, Lenny. That made Mike happy—he figured one bad guy down, one to go.

Mike knew he didn't have long. Pug would pull that pick out of his leg and come looking for him. Mike had just a few minutes. It was time to bring out his secret weapon.

The duffel bag he had been unceremoniously

carrying around now became his best weapon, full of tools Freddy told him to bring. He untied the drawstring and pulled out the most important one—this one, Fred made him promise, that no one else could see it. He thought it might jeopardize the future. Out came a high-intensity LED flashlight with a wide lens. Once he flipped it on, he was able to see the entire width of the tunnel. He grabbed his bag and ran straight ahead thirty yards and found the drilled-out area in the tunnel the Dean boys had used to chain up Freddy. From Fred's description a few days ago, Mike knew Julian was just a few more feet down from where Fred was.

As he came up to Freddy, he could see that his hands were chained, and his mouth gagged; an oil-stained rag protruded from his mouth. The chain was connected to a mine support post. Freddy weakly looked up, his hair hanging down over his face. The bright light was too much for his eyes, it hurt him. Freddy flinched away from the light and pulled his legs in, sure he was going to get another beating.

"I'm here to help," Mike whispered as he undid the gag.

Once the gag came down, Freddy tried to speak. At first, just a gravelly sound came out. "Am I dead yet?" he strained to ask in a raspy voice.

Mike hurried so he could turn off the light. He didn't want to make it any easier for Pug to find them. "No Freddy, you're still alive. I'm Mike, Julian's friend. We're here to get you out of here. So, let's get you undone here, so I can go over and help Julian, okay?" In the blue light of the flashlight, he could make out some bruises and cuts on Freddy's face and arms.

Then he saw it—a wire. Mike froze as his mind immediately raced with terrible thoughts. *He's got a damn bomb connected to these boys!* Mike knew just enough about explosives to know he didn't want anything to do with them. He had seen some of the construction crews using dynamite to remove large boulders from construction sites where his company built transmission lines, yet he never felt the need to get very close. Now he was too damn close.

"Are you the angel?" Freddy kept looking up at Mike. Mike knew Freddy was probably delirious.

"Just relax, buddy, I'm working on things here." Mike started to sweat; he needed information. "Freddy, do you know anything about the explosives they've got set up here?"

"Are you the angel?" Freddy mumbled.

Mike realized he was no help. Then, another terrible thought occurred to Mike: *If this stuff is on a timer, then it could go at any second.* Mike studied the wiring; it ran from Freddy across the tunnel floor and up to the area where he thought Julian might be. *It can't be too elaborate; these guys are only a couple of redneck miners. How much could they know about rigging up explosives?*

The wires weren't in any way connected to Freddy's chains, so he opened up his duffel bag and pulled out chain cutters. Mike put a link in the vice. It took two tries but finally, it snapped, and one chain around Freddy could be taken off. Mike then cut the other one.

Mike turned off the flashlight when he heard noises coming from down the hall, but he couldn't be sure what it was. Mike tried to recall Fred's instructions, but in all the excitement, his memory was fading. *"Just hurry,"* he remembered Fred saying. *"Just hurry."*

"Freddy, just stay put, don't move, okay?"

Fred didn't respond, he didn't move. Then Mike saw something else that made him shiver: Underneath Fred's side, a pile of dynamite—Fred was lying on it. Mike hadn't seen it until now. It was a good thing Freddy didn't move; he could be lying on a trigger mechanism. If Freddy did move, there was enough dynamite under him to turn this whole mine into one big pile of dust.

Mike moved to get up, duffel bag in hand, and turned his flashlight back on for just a few seconds, so he could see down the tunnel, as he stumbled his way toward Julian. He heard the sound of rocks being walked on, but before he could react *bam!* Something solid hit Mike hard on the side of the head and he went down, slamming against a rock wall. He reeled in pain, and an overwhelming sick feeling in the pit of his stomach made him want to roll over and cry from the agony. Instead, he rolled back up on his side and got up.

Mike didn't remember this part of the rescue in Fred's warnings—*Something I'll have to speak to Fred about.* He hoped a little humor would improve his mood. In that second, Pug had already lifted his shovel in the air and came down with another swing. Mike reacted faster and swung around, slamming a two-by-four hard into Pug's ribs, then pushed him down into the jagged rocks on the tunnel floor. Pug screamed as his bleeding leg wound scraped into the rocks.

Mike was hurt badly. Letting his instincts kick in, he shook it off, his head wound throbbing with pain. He stumbled as he jumped on top of Pug to hold him down. In the flying dust and dim light, he could barely make out dark images of two people fighting and screaming. *It's probably the chief.* Mike jammed his knees into Pug's wounded thigh to help hold him down.

"Ahh!" Pug screamed. He tried to twist himself over to get out from underneath Mike, but he was unable to move.

Mike noticed that one of the two people who had been fighting was getting up, and one person lying on the mine floor still wasn't moving. It must have been one of the mine workers helping Pug and Lenny. Whoever was up was now walking toward Mike. They weren't wearing a uniform, so it wasn't the chief. Mike froze for a second, then yelled out.

"Criminy, Bernice! What are you doing down here?"

"Kinda looks like I'm savin' your ass right now, doesn't it!" Bernice helped Mike lean down on Pug. "Anyway, I got more experience wrestling with these kinds ah critters than you do!"

"You did save my butt, that's for sure. Let me grab my bag; I have some handcuffs and tape. Hold on!" Mike strained to get up and slowly opened his duffel bag, pulling out a pair of handcuffs and a roll of duct tape. He turned around and took Pug's hands, snapping on the cuffs and wrapping his legs in duct tape several times, so he couldn't kick.

"Get off me, you're hurting me!" yelled Pug. "I'm bleeding, get me out of here, *now!*"

"I don't know how you did it, Bernice, but thanks."

"I just followed some of the other guys down, acted like I was part of the crew—no one seemed to mind. Just so you know, they got Pug's brother Lenny up above the ground and shackled up pretty well. And your wife already has a small hospital set up in the main office area, she's great. From the looks of you, you're gonna need her help, too!"

Now that Bernice mentioned it, he could feel something running down the side of his face, but he couldn't tell if it was sweat or blood; it didn't matter now.

"Thanks, she is pretty amazing. Bernice, I think Julian's just over there. I'm going to go up and check on him. You okay with this guy?"

"Yeah, I'll be fine," Bernice said. "Once he got a look at me, he got weak knees."

Mike smiled and spun around to go check on Julian. As he struggled up to get to him, Mike was stunned at what he saw: Besides being chained up to the rock wall, Julian had a maze of wires running around his body. Mike shined his light into the wires; he knew he would never in a million years figure out where everything led to, let alone figure out how to turn this mess off so it wouldn't explode. He took out his chain cutters and knelt next to Julian. He moved his flashlight so it didn't shine directly into Julian's face.

"Julian, Julian buddy, can you hear me?" Through the dim light, Mike could see that Julian's face was bloody and bruised. Julian moved slightly. "You don't have to move, pal, just lay still. It's me, Mike. We're here to help you."

Julian started coughing and weakly tried to turn to face Mike. "Mike." Julian tried to talk but barely whispered.

"Hey, buddy. We're gonna get you out of here. It'll be just a few minutes."

Despite his raspy voice, Julian was able to get a few words out. "Mike, good to see you."

"Just lay still until we figure out how to free you from this mess of wires and chains. I'll be right back, okay?" Julian opened his eyes slightly and nodded to Mike. A small, grateful grin appeared on his face.

He had to move fast. Mike grabbed the chain cutters and carefully chunked off one of the links, freeing Julian's hands. Then he grabbed his light to start looking for the lead wires for the explosives. In the background, twenty yards away in the darkness, he heard Pug spitting out the greasy rag.

"Get me out of here, I'm injured, I'm bleeding!" Pug screamed lying face down on the rocks, struggling to get free.

"Shut up, ya big horse turd! Or I'll beat you like a stubborn mule!" yelled Bernice. Mike could hear more yelling and commotion in the distance and could only hope it was the other policemen coming to assist. In a few seconds, a disheveled Chief Hawkins and two more men came up. They all looked like they'd been beaten up pretty well themselves.

"Bernice!" yelled the chief. "What in God's great name are you doing? I told you not to come down here!"

"I've always had a hard time minding authority, Chief. Anyhow, it's a good thing I did. Mike, there was about to get his head mashed in when I showed up."

"I'd let it go if I were you, Chief," Mike told Chief Hawkins as he walked back to where Pug was lying on the ground. Chief laughed and patted Bernice on the back.

"Get off me, get me out of here!" yelled Pug.

"Chief, he wants out of here because he's got these boys rigged up with explosives. They're on triggers, so if they move, this place will blow into next year!"

"Is that right? You numb-skulled bastard!" The chief yelled in Pug's ear. "Well, if your contraption goes off, be sure to wave at us on your way down to Hell, huh?" he goaded Pug. "You'd better hope it doesn't go off because you'll be the last one we're taking out of here." He jabbed his finger into Pug's side; Pug struggled to get loose. Bernice finally got up; she knew Pug couldn't go anywhere, hog-tied the way he was.

"Chief, we gotta get these boys out of here as fast as we can. I'm going to follow these lead wires to see if I can find the source of power and turn it off. If nothing else, you need to find a way to hold those triggers down long enough to get Freddy and Julian out of here, fast."

"I understand, Michael. I'll get over and get Freddy ready to go up. I think Bernice and Buster are over with Julian."

"Thanks, Chief."

"You're never going to find it!" Pug sneered. "If one of those boys moves, this whole place will blow!"

"You talking to me?" hollered Mike.

"You're the only person trying to figure this out."

"Tell me then, why won't I find it?" Mike shouted back to Pug.

"Because one of those boys is gonna move before you have a chance to stop it!" Pug said.

"It has to have power from somewhere," Mike yelled back. "Without power, it won't work!" He knew that two thicker wires came off from the back side of Julian and ran along one wall and then up to the roof of the tunnel. He followed it back over toward Pug, who was lying face down in the middle of the tunnel floor. Twenty yards away, Chief Hawkins was attending to Freddy.

"Doesn't matter, you'll never get to it in time. It's on a clock, so when it hits a certain time, BOOM!" Pug laughed. "And it's just about time!"

Mike looked down at Pug. "Well, I can't believe you'd put it on such a tight schedule, putting yourself in harm's way, so, where's the clock?"

Pug struggled to look up at Mike. In the faint shadows, Mike could see his face was bloody. "Sure, I'm gonna tell you where it's at," Pug sneered. "Kiss my ass!"

"Oops!" Mike kicked rocks in Pug's face and moved on, following the wires. He walked on farther until the wires disappeared up a small vent shaft, just as the small tunnel lights flickered back on.

"This is unbelievable!" Mike said as he stared up into the small shaft. Mike reached up and yanked on the wire, but it didn't budge.

"Told you so!" hollered Pug. Mike could hear more people coming up the tunnel. In a moment, Officer Eldon made his way through the tunnel to Mike. The chief was still sitting about thirty yards away next to Freddy, who was now awake and talking. Eldon told Mike that one of the mine electricians had come down to get the lights working again.

"Listen guys, we have to find where these wires go. The two boys are lying on piles of dynamite with triggers; if they move, this place will blow. I've got to get back up top and find out where these wires lead to. You guys need to help the chief find a way to hold those triggers down and get Julian and Freddy out of here. I'm going to find the power source and unplug it, hopefully before it explodes." Mike took off down the tunnel. At the cage, mine foreman Kelly was just getting ready to go back up.

"Kelly, I need to get back up top as soon as possible!"

Kelly waved to Mike. "Come on, let's go!"

On the way up, Mike told Kelly about the dynamite under the boys. He tried to think which shaft Mike was talking about and where it would be located on the mine property. "We have quite a few of those, can you give me a better clue?"

"It was about halfway down that tunnel from where the boys were."

"I've got a pretty good idea where that is, just keep up with me."

As soon as the cage door opened, the two men ran across the plant floor. Kelly spotted another supervisor and told him to get everyone out of the plant.

* * * *

Down below, Chief Hawkins realized how bad the situation was and began cracking the whip with his men to get them to hurry up and move.

"Guys, get over here and help me with Freddy. Bob, take Eldon and Vernal over to Julian. And remember, that trigger switch has to have pressure on it at all times!"

"Hey, what about me?" yelled Pug, still shackled, lying face down on the rocky tunnel floor. "I'm still bleeding, I need to get out of here!"

Chief Hawkins glared at Pug in the dusty din and grunted. "You can just lay there and rot, for all I care!"

"Get me out of here! Before that damn trigger goes off!" Pug screamed.

Bob and his crew managed to see under Julian, without disturbing the switch. They could see that it was just a simple toggle switch. Bob, the plant supervisor, stuck his hand under Julian to hold it down, while Eldon and Vernal lifted Julian and carried him out of the mine. Bob placed a heavy, flat rock over the switch and carefully stepped away. Bob immediately ran back to where Freddy was so he could help the chief do the same thing on the trigger, under Freddy.

"Hey, Chief!" yelled Pug. "Where's my brother, Lenny? Chief?"

Chief Hawkins was assisting two other mine workers to delicately lift Freddy as Bob lay on the mine floor to hold the trigger. The chief knew they were still dealing with a crude, homemade trigger that could either not work at all or be so sensitive that any slight movement could set it off—and trying to do all of this in the dusty darkness of a mine tunnel two hundred feet underground. All he needed right now was one more interruption.

"Don't make me come over there, you lame-brained idiot! Shut up, before I come over there and put a hole in your other leg! Okay, let's lift him, are you ready, Fred?"

"I don't think so, oww! My ribs hurt! What about Julian, is he okay?"

"Son, don't worry about Julian, he's going to be okay, they've already taken him up. You're next—here, grab my shoulder." With a man under each arm, Freddy was picked up and lifted down the tunnel to the waiting cage. Vernal, who had already taken Julian topside, had come back in to see if the chief needed any more help. Instead, he only found a fuming Pug Dean.

"Hey, Vernal, get me out of here, I'm hurting bad."

"You might as well shut up for now, dumbass. The chief is gone and so are those two boys. You're just wasting your breath," Vernal drawled.

"Listen, creep, get me out of here. This place is gonna blow, trigger or no trigger, it's on a timer! Don't you get it?"

"Well, maybe you're right. I probably ought to go up and ask Chief what he wants to do with you." Vernal turned and walked down the tunnel toward the cage.

"What? What are you talking about? Where's my gurney? Isn't someone going to help me get up and help me out of this hole? Hey! Get back here! Vernal! Hey! Come back!"

* * * *

Kelly and Mike located the air shaft in a small metal shed at the back of a storage building, across the main yard from the plant. The wires Mike was searching for led from the opening of the inlet to a hardwood box just a few feet away. Inside, Mike found a simple switch unit attached to a small motorcycle battery. As Mike reached down to pull the wires out, the ground began shaking. When Kelly and Mike looked back to the mine yard, dust was rising from the center.

"Let's get out of here!" yelled Kelly. The two men leaped out of the metal shed and ran as fast as possible away from the yard as it began to sink in. Dust and smoke rose into the air—a deep rumble shook everything around the mine—then all went quiet. Both Mike and Kelly were half-buried by the churning dust. Mike looked at Kelly.

"You okay?"

"Yeah." They both crawled up to a level spot on the ground and dusted themselves off. When they turned around, they could see a depression in the mine yard fifty feet across and ten feet deep.

"We'd better get around to the main office and find out if everyone's okay over there," Kelly said.

Mike kept thinking to himself that Catherine and the girls were all right—they were still in the car, out front of the mine. Then he remembered Bernice saying Catherine had set up a place for the injured, in the front office. Mike overtook Kelly in a dead-heat race to the main office. His three-time-a-week jogging finally paid off. Vernal was the last person to come up and get out of the mine shaft before it exploded.

Chapter 27
Impatience and Boredom

Catherine knew the plan: She was to wait for the first group of injured police to come back out of the building before going in, and the more she thought about it, she knew that wasn't going to happen. Since she knew more of the plan than she let on, as soon as the police chief had disappeared down into the mine, she brought her troops into the mine offices to set up a triage.

By the time Julian and Freddy were brought up, two ambulances had arrived, and the medics had brought most of their modest medical supplies inside the building ready to treat their patients. Two injured mine foremen and Lenny Dean, knocked cold when Mike introduced him to the flat side of his own shovel, were the first to be treated.

Then Julian was brought up. Fifteen minutes later, Freddy was brought in. He was able to walk, with the help of two officers, but Julian had to be carried on a stretcher. He was extremely weak and bruised up so badly that he was hardly recognizable. When they were loaded in the ambulances, Fannie insisted on going along. She was going to take charge and be there to take care of her boy.

With all of the emotional distress and calamity around them, Catherine and the girls grew more nervous as time closed in—where was *their* loved one? No one could say where Mike was. Bernice told Catherine that she had seen him leave with Kelly to go up in the cage—he was chasing wires—but hadn't seen him after that. Chief Hawkins had already been patched up and was looking after his men and making sure Lenny was taken away.

By the time Bernice had come up, they had all made it out. All except for Pug—someone was sure he was still down in the mine. Vernal, who had gone down the shaft one more time, was sure.

In the mine office, when the ground beneath them started to thunder and shake, Catherine grabbed the girls to hide under a large map table in the middle of the office, as everything fell from the shelves, glass broke, windows cracked, and lights flickered. A large wall in the mine's mill area collapsed, throwing plumes of dust into the office.

"Girls, you okay?" asked Catherine.

"Yeah, just got dust everywhere!" Sarah said, spitting dust out of her mouth. Gracie was shaking and rubbing her eyes.

"No, no, honey," said Catherine, "let's get some water, don't rub your eyes."

Everything stopped and became instantly still, unusual for a place where the constant rumble of rock being crushed ran twenty-four hours a day.

A mine supervisor rushed in to tell them an explosion underground had created a crater out in the yard between the main building and the storage house.

Catherine didn't want to think the worst—*Let's keep busy.* She got the girls out from under the table, grabbed someone's jacket, and started slapping the table with it to remove the dust. Catherine noticed the flow of patients stopped. Several mine foremen helped with the clean-up; even Bernice showed up to help.

It was Sarah who noticed the tall figure running past one of the broken office windows. Mike, followed closely by Kelly, rushed into the damaged offices.

"Daddy!" yelled Sarah. Gracie jumped up to run over and hug her dad. Catherine's smile returned, although she tried to act composed before walking over herself to welcome Mike, covered with dust and blood, looking like he had barely made it out alive. Mike grabbed her by the waist and pulled her to him, telling her with one dusty kiss how much he had worried about her.

Catherine knew what he had gone through to make this all happen. He had rescued the boys, as he promised.

* * * *

Mike lay on the hospital bed motionless while a doctor and two nurses leaned over him to put stitches near the top of his head. In a few minutes, Catherine walked into the room and stood quietly in the background as a nurse and a medical aid finished covering most of his head with white bandages and gauze. Mike was left propped up in bed, appearing like a Middle Eastern sheik, waiting for his concubine to approach. When he saw Catherine, she was standing, arms folded and giving him one of those looks that seemed to say, *How in the world did you manage to do this?* He gave her back a big sheepish grin as she walked up to his bed.

"So, I suppose you want the hero treatment, now?"

she asked. Mike sensed a tinge of sarcasm in her voice.

"Naw, shoot, ma'am, I do this sort of thing every day, no need to fuss."

Catherine laughed, grabbed his face, and planted a big juicy kiss right on his lips. When she let go, he froze in place, trying to write down in his memory every single morsel of her touch and smell.

"Well, good then, because I'm not going to treat you any different," she whispered up close in his ear.

Mike looked up into her eyes. "Not a problem, sweets, just keep treating me the same old way you just did, and I'll be good as gold." His efforts earned him one more kiss. "Where are the girls?"

"They won't let me bring them in—hospital rules, you know. No one under sixteen allowed in unless they are a patient or parent."

"Oh, yeah. I remember those old antique rules. So, where are they?"

"Fannie and Bernice are with them, out in the waiting area."

"What have you heard about the boys?"

Catherine's mood changed, her face grew serious. She started to tear up. "Michael, they took such a hard beating from those Dean guys." She paused. "Besides a couple of broken ribs, a battered cheekbone on one side, and all his bruises, Julian has a broken leg, so he'll be laid up here for quite a few days. Certainly, he's no stranger to that type of pain. Freddy didn't get any broken bones, but he's bruised all over and they're both emaciated from two days of no food or water. Fannie was with me while I was talking to the doctor; she said she would be glad to take care of the both of them while they're in here, and after they're released from the hospital, they can go over to her place until they're better and able to leave. That is if they want to." Catherine glanced at Mike.

"Well, this is his home, so I suppose Julian will have to decide what he wants to do; after all, this is where he was heading when he left us. We'll just let him know he'll always have a place to stay if he ever wants to come back."

"Yeah, that's true. You let them both know, okay?" she asked Mike. "It'll mean more if it comes from you."

"I will."

Catherine gave Mike another kiss and got up. "Now, you get some sleep and I'll be back first thing in the morning with the girls. The boys will be in better shape to visit tomorrow. They've been sedated tonight, so they're pretty well knocked out for the evening."

* * * *

The next afternoon, after visiting with Catherine and the girls, both Mike and Freddy were up and had been permitted to visit Julian. Catherine took Sarah and Gracie back to Fannie's. With wheelchairs provided, Fred and Mike rolled into Julian's room to visit about what happened to them. Though finding it difficult with bandages and stitches, Julian spoke first.

"Well, I guess Freddy and I owe you, big time. From where we were, it was starting to seem like the jig was up, for us." Julian looked at Mike with gratitude in his eyes.

Mike appreciated Julian's words.

"I'm just glad I got the message from that old guy in Cheyenne"—he winked at Julian—"to come down and rescue you two wild guys. You know who I'm talking about, right, Julian?"

Julian nodded, with a smile, knowing that Fred must have remembered to tell Mike to come and rescue them. Freddy stared at them both like they were talking in some foreign language.

"Yeah, about that deal," Freddy piped up, trying to understand their conversation. "So, how did you know we were in trouble, Mike?"

"Well, Fred," Mike began, "back in Cheyenne, in my time, which is the year 2001, I got a message from an old man who had been keeping a beautiful 1929 Chrysler Imperial for me, in his garage over the last seventy-two years. This wonderful gentleman was faithful enough to hold on to that message and remember it at exactly the right time, to make sure we saved two young men from being killed."

Freddy swallowed hard.

"Freddy," Mike continued, pointing a finger right at him, "that wonderful old gentleman is *you*." Freddy sat back hard, in his chair, a blank expression on his face.

"Good thing he's in the hospital—he may need a nurse," Julian quipped.

"You okay, Fred?" Mike asked.

"Yeah, that's just a lot to take in, I guess." Fred paused. "Thank you for saying those nice things, and thanks for coming to help us, Mike. I guess I do owe you my life." Fred wiped his eyes, still shaking his head in disbelief.

"Aww, don't worry about it, Fred," Mike said. "You

and Julian are the real heroes here. You two have endured a lot of stuff over the last few days; Catherine and I are just thrilled you both are, at least, on the mend."

Freddy looked up at Mike, to make sure he knew what was going on. "So, me, in the future, right?"

"Yes," answered Mike. "Freddy, I know this is so hard to believe. We've all had a hard time believing this. But, somehow, there is a 'time port,' a sort of hiding door, if you will, in Catherine's house. We've used that door to come back to this time and save you and Julian, and *how* we knew to come back is because you remembered to leave a note for yourself, once you get back to Cheyenne. That note reminds you to tell me and Catherine to come and rescue you and Julian."

Everyone in the plain white, sterile hospital room sat still for a moment, looking at Freddy, wondering about this possibility. Fred perked up in his chair.

"I think that's a pretty amazing thing," he said. "Hard to believe, but still, pretty amazing."

Mike sighed and patted Freddy on his shoulder. Julian took a sip of water.

"Fred?" asked Mike. "So, do you want to make yourself a note and stuff it in your pocket, now?"

"Yeah, I think that's a good idea." Freddy got up and walked out to the nurse's station. Julian looked over to Mike. Fred was out of earshot, so he asked Mike a question.

"Do you think he's going to be okay with everything?"

"Yeah, he'll be fine. Freddy's been through a lot, that's for sure." Fred walked back into the room, stuffing a folded piece of paper in his shirt pocket.

"All set, Mike." Fred patted his shirt pocket. Mike walked over next to Julian's bedside.

"The doctor told us it was going to be at least two weeks before they were going to let you out of here."

"Yeah, I know," Julian answered. "And, that's okay. I need some time to mend up this stupid leg, it's still pretty painful."

"I need to get the kids back to Cheyenne—you know, school and work," Mike said. "Someone has to keep working to pay for the extravagant lifestyle we live, so I was planning on picking up our train tickets here and leaving from Joplin." Mike turned to Fred. "I think I know the answer, Freddy, but are you planning on staying here with Julian or do you want to go back to Cheyenne right away?"

Fred, leaning against the windowsill, stood up straight to answer. "No sir, I need to stay here and make sure Julian mends okay. Besides, it's kind of fun over there, staying with Fannie and Bernice. Those two are a hoot!" Mike agreed.

"I thought you might. You're a good friend, Freddy. I'm sure Julian knows it, too."

"Thanks, Mike. Me and Julian, we've had quite an adventure together."

"Yes, you sure have. Freddy, if you're feeling up to it, how about in the morning, you take us over to the train station and drop us off."

"Yes sir, but, ah . . . the automobile, what about your Chrysler, Mr. Roberts?"

"Freddy, like I mentioned, why don't you just take care of that for me."

"You're serious, you're giving me the car?" asked Freddy.

"Well, let's say I'm loaning it to you for a very long time. Someday, I want you to give it back to me, okay?"

"Mr. Roberts, you got a deal!" He whooped. "Yes sir, you got a deal and I'll take really good care of it, Mike, I promise—really, I promise!"

"I know you will, Freddy," answered a confident Mike.

"Because your life depends on it."

"Yeah, I guess so. I'd better do this right, huh?"

Julian waved a pointed finger at Freddy. "I'll be reminding you quite a few times, as well, Freddy. Remember, I want to get rescued, too!" There was a knock on the partially opened hospital room door.

"Come in," said Julian. His face brightened when he recognized Maria walking through the door. "Hello!"

"Hi, Julian, okay if I come in?"

Mike offered Maria his place next to Julian.

"Of course. Maria, this gent next to you is Michael, one of my best friends from Cheyenne, Wyoming, and of course, you met Fred the other day."

"Hello, nice to meet you." Mike could see that from this point on, his presence would just be extra baggage, so he excused himself, promising to be back in the morning.

After visiting Julian at the hospital to say goodbye, Freddy took Mike, Catherine, and the girls over to the train station. Mike unloaded the bags and assorted souvenirs they had collected on their quick rescue mission. After giving Freddy hugs and free advice, they were gone.

Chapter 28

Goodbye Again

In the days after Mike and Catherine left for Cheyenne, Freddy brought Fannie every day so she could visit Julian in the hospital. And, every day since, she packed them a sack lunch and sat for long hours to reminisce about young Julian and make Freddy go into laughing fits, mostly from the way Fannie told a story. Another regular visitor at the hospital was Julian's school friend, Maria. Julian hadn't admitted it to Freddy yet, but he had fallen in love.

Lately, the nurses had been letting Maria and Freddy help Julian get out of bed to start using his leg. He'd healed up fast, so the doctors expected him to be going home soon.

After another week of progress, Freddy came in to visit Julian and dropped himself into one of the hospital's wooden chairs next to Julian's bedside. He folded his arms.

"Pretty boring up here, huh?" asked Julian.

"Compared to some of the stuff we've been through, yeah. Feels like the thrills should just keep coming. Not that I want to get beat up anymore, but . . ." Freddy's voice trailed off. He stood up and looked out the window, into the distance.

"No doubt," Julian said. You know, I've been thinking. You probably want to get home, huh?"

"Naw, I'm good, it's kind of interesting here. I mean, I wouldn't want to live here, but I'm okay with it. Hanging out with Fannie is fun."

"Yeah, can't fool me, Freddy, I can see it, you're bored to tears."

"Well, except for some of the nurses, it is pretty boring here, yeah," Freddy admitted. Julian was happy he finally said it; he figured Freddy was relieved to finally let it out, but also sad. He didn't want to see Freddy leave.

"I've been thinking about going on up to Michigan when I'm able to get out of here. I think that's where Mom was going—I'd like to go there and see if I can find her. She wasn't exactly the best mom in the world, but she's my mom and . . . I miss her, you know?" Julian offered, trying to move the conversation ahead.

"Yeah, I know. I just thought you'd like to have me around while you're mending."

"You're a good pal, Fred," Julian said. "I just need to do this, and then maybe later on sometime, go back out to Wyoming . . . I don't know, that's just what I'm thinking. What do you want to do?"

"I don't know either, I guess go back to Wyoming and get a job. I just need to do something. I'm sure my folks are probably wondering if I'm dead or not, I've been gone so long, eh?"

"Yeah, no kidding!" Julian laughed. "Anyway, I'll be heading north. See what I can find," he said, his tone resolute.

"Yeah, that makes sense."

"I guess what I'm telling you is, whenever you think the time is right, you can take off, Fred. Don't worry about me."

"Yeah, okay." Fred sighed. "I'll go by and say goodbye to Fannie and Bernice and then just take off. Do you need anything before I go?" Freddy had his hands on the end of Julian's white wrought iron bed, scuffed at the linoleum floor, then let go.

"No, Freddy, I'm good, thank you."

"Okay, so, you'll be all right?"

"Yeah, I'll be okay if you remember that note some-place you can find it."

"I've got it, right here," Freddy said, patting his pocket. "You know, Julian, you've been better than a brother to me. Thanks."

They both smiled and gave one last shake.

"Been a heck of a trip, huh?" asked Julian.

"Yep, it's been a *hell* of a trip!" Freddy shouted. He walked out of the room, turning around one last time, smiled, and waved.

* * * *

A few days later, Julian was released and went back to Fannie's, where it was peaceful and quiet. Over the next couple of weeks, Julian spent his time carefully making his way around the floor, then the stairs, and eventually up to his old loft, a place he thought he would never see again. Just opening the door was a challenge—he felt old ghosts escape past him as he opened the door. *It's so bare.*

It looked like no one had touched it since he'd sneaked away that early morning over two years ago. His leg had some soreness, but it felt like it was mending—maybe stronger. A slow, calculated turn and he left that lonely loft behind. Julian felt in charge of his world: He decided what happened; he planned his future, his own path.

* * * *

"What are you doing, Julian?" Fannie yelled out to him from the front porch.

"I'm washing the car!"

"Why?"

"It's dirty, Miss Fannie!" Julian dropped the hose in the grass and walked up to where she was standing. "And, because . . ." Julian hesitated, looking her directly in her eyes. He knew Fannie expected this. "Because it's time for me to go."

"Oh, Julian, you don't need to go. We like having you here with us. We feel so much safer." Fannie grabbed Julian's hands and began to wring them. "Juli, please, please stay with us."

"Now, Miss Fannie, I've been telling you that I wanted to go look for my mom, right?" Julian asked.

"Well, now, maybe what if she comes back here and you've left? What good is that gonna do, huh?"

"Well, then too bad for her, I'll miss her. Or, you could just tell her to stay put, I'll be right back." Julian laughed. "Now, I'm going to go finish washing the car, I'm going to take off tomorrow morning and I want it clean."

"Supper is in thirty minutes. You'll come in soon, all right?"

"I wouldn't miss it!"

At dinner, it was just Julian and Miss Fannie. Bernice had left to visit relatives in Tulsa. When Julian walked in through the back door, he heard Fannie talking to herself at the stove. "Lord, Lord, why me? When am I going to—?" Her voice halted when she heard Julian coming through the back hallway. "Supper's ready, son, come and get it." Julian walked into the kitchen and up to the sink to wash his hands. "Son, you sure do wash your hands an awful lot, are you okay?"

"Yes, Fannie, I'm just a clean freak, I guess." Fannie glanced back at him with a funny expression.

After dinner, Fannie finished the dishes and put the tablecloth back on the table when Julian walked into the kitchen with something in his hands. Fannie threw up her hands over her mouth and gasped. It was the tin box she'd lost so many years before.

"Julian! Where in God's good name did you find that box?"

"Here Fannie, this is yours." Julian beamed as he handed it over to her. His heart finally felt warm and good inside; he hoped this would make the rest of Fannie's life better, too.

"Oh, my Lord! Julian! How did you get this?"

"Well, Fannie. All I can say is I wouldn't want to face those dogs at the Dean's house again, so *please*, don't let anyone take it from you again." Fannie stared up at Julian and gave him a big hug. She set the tin box down on the table and opened it up, revealing her entire collection of gold coins. Her tears dropped inside the tin box, making her laugh as she wiped it out with her dishtowel.

"Lord, Lord, Lord! Thank you, Lord! I will be able to

keep this house and my stuff! And, thank you, my sweet, sweet son!"

"I'm just glad I was able to get it back to you, Fannie."

* * * *

In the morning, Julian had his car loaded with the small number of possessions he owned and was ready to leave. Fannie walked him out to the car, holding his hand as she would never see him again. She carried a small basket with sandwiches, pickles, and cookies for his trip up to Michigan.

"Julian, son. Now, you promise to let me know where you end up, okay?"

"I will, Fannie. As I said, right now, I'm planning on heading north to Michigan to see if I can find Mom."

"What about Maria? You two have become so close," she said.

"I thought about asking her if she wanted to go, but she's got her job and I don't know what I'd run into up there."

"Never mind about that, silly boy, if you've got someone you know loves you and you feel the same way, then go get her. You'll regret it for the rest of your life if you don't. Now, here's your lunch for down the road. I want you to eat well, and stay healthy."

"Thank you, Mom." Julian loved Fannie as much as he loved his mom. As he said this and reached over to give Fannie a final hug goodbye, she started crying.

"Please come back and see me, soon?" Fannie asked, through tears.

"I promise." Julian looked Fannie in the eye. "You have a new start now, so I want you to live your dream this time, okay?" Julian got in his car and started it up.

"I will honey, please, be safe!"

The car drove away, creating a stir of leaves in the roadway. Fannie pulled her apron up to her eyes and watched. She felt that sadness from a heavy heart. Then, with a smile, she felt better.

At the end of the street, Julian's car turned left, into town. Fannie knew where he was going.

CHAPTER 29
Love Begins

The dusty 1929 Chrysler Imperial pulled up in front of Dixie's Diner. Even with steam roiling from the hot engine, no one turned to notice the stranger. Freddy honked his horn so they would. A few patrons inside turned their heads as Fred stepped out of the car and swaggered in. Dixie spotted him first.

"Freddy? Freddy, is that you?" yelled Dixie as he walked to the counter. She went over and hugged Freddy. "How you been, darlin'? Where's Julian, is he with you?"

"No, he's headed back home—he wanted to go see his mom—so I don't expect him around for quite a while," Freddy said.

"Aww, that's too bad, he's a good boy and a good worker. Monte! Monte! Come on out here and see Freddy, he's back! And what's that fancy car you're driving, huh? Pretty nice there, Fred! What have you been up to, to get this car, eh?"

"Just keeping it for a friend, Dixie; it ain't mine, I don't have any money. That's why I'm here—maybe you can use a hand?"

When Monte walked up, Dixie looked over to him for approval. "What do you think, Monte, can we find a job for this good-looking boy?"

"Hey Freddy, how are you?" Monte reached over and shook Fred's hand.

"I'm doing good Monte, good to see you!"

"What good-looking kid, Dixie, who are you talking about?" Monte laughed and started to cough. "Oh, you mean this little skinny runt? Can we find him something? Man, I don't know, Fred. Things have slowed down lately."

"Surely, we have something, huh?" Dixie asked, concern in her voice. "Come on back, let's look at the schedule." Dixie motioned for Freddy to follow her as she walked to the back of the restaurant. She flipped up the pages of the calendar to see where they could fit some time in for Freddy. "I could use one more person here in the kitchen to cover some of the shifts when Monte can't be here. You know, I don't want to work that poor guy to death . . . well, sometimes I do. So, let's see what we've got."

She made a few pencil marks on the schedule and turned to Fred. "I'll go ahead and put you down for a couple of days and then we'll see how it goes from there, all right?"

Fred let out an audible sigh of relief.

* * * *

Two weeks later, as Freddy was checking out at the end of his shift, a young lady walked in through the back door, past Dixie and Freddy, and clocked in.

"Oh, Freddy, I want you to meet our new waitress, Margaret. Margaret, this is Freddy. This is Margaret's first day."

"Hello, Freddy." Those simple words, without aim or cause, threw Freddy's mind into a whirl. It took him a couple of seconds to remember how to work his mouth and get an answer out.

"Uh, hello."

"Well, it was nice to meet you, too, Freddy." Margaret walked back out to the front to begin her shift. She gave him one last grin before she disappeared behind the swinging café doors.

"Freddy?" Dixie took his arm. "Freddy, remember your shift tomorrow."

"Oh, yeah, Dizzie, I mean, Dixie, I'll be here, no problem."

"Wear a white shirt!" she said.

"I will." On his way out, he tried to act Hollywood but stubbed his shoe on one of the barstools. Margaret saw it and giggled. Freddy had never experienced this type of embarrassment before, but soon, he would know what to call it. A love that would never die; was possible, in 1929.

CHAPTER 30

Broken Hearts

Cheyenne, Wyoming, 2003

"Sarah, would you hand me those pliers over on the counter?"

"Yeah." Sarah got up from her perch on the wooden fruit box near her dad's garage workbench and picked up the tool. "Here you go. So, is this bike gonna work okay when you're done?"

"Yes, and it will continue to work okay if you just keep it out of the goat heads along every road and sidewalk in town," Mike said, looking over to Sarah with a grin.

"I didn't ride in the weeds. I'll bet it was Gracie."

"Right. Whenever something breaks, it's neither one of you that had anything to do with it, it just happens by accident. Hmm."

"Next time, I'll try to fix it myself, then."

"I'd pay real money to watch that," Mike said, laughing out loud. Catherine walked into the garage and approached Mike.

"Honey, have you seen Fred today?"

"No, I haven't," replied Mike.

"I'm kind of worried about him. He's had that dumb cough for the last few days. Can we walk over and see how he's doing?"

"Sure, I'm done here; Miss Knievel here wants to get back on her bike."

"Very funny, Dad."

Mike picked up the bike and turned it over on its tires. Sarah jumped on and took off to her friend's house. Mike wiped his hands on a shop towel before he and Catherine walked across the street to see Fred.

* * * *

As was their custom, they walked around to the back door of Fred's house, usually finding him working on something out back. Not this time. Catherine knocked on the screen door a couple of times—no answer. She glanced up at Mike, concerned, then pushed the door open. They both rushed into the house, through the kitchen area, calling for Fred, with no answer.

They ran through the rest of the house and finally to Fred's bedroom where they found him lying on the bed. Catherine went quickly to Fred's side. Fred's breathing was shallow. When she touched him, he slowly opened his eyes.

"Catherine," he said in a weak voice. "I'm not doing too good."

"It's okay, Fred, we're going to get you to the hospital so we can get you taken care of. Just hold on, all right, sweetie?" She looked up at Mike; he knew what to do. Mike quickly ran into the other room and called an ambulance.

* * * *

Several hours later, Fred's two daughters Melissa and Linda, and their families had been notified and arrived at the hospital. While in the waiting room, Mike tried to call as many close friends and family as he could from Fred's home phone list. Because of hospital rules, they were taking shifts visiting Fred in his room. Mike and Catherine were trying to make sure that Fred's daughters and family were able to have as much time with him that they wanted.

As the night wore on, Fred's daughters decided to go to Fred's home, where they were staying. The grandkids were restless, and they hadn't been fed yet. They had been assured that Fred's condition was stable, and since he had been talking with visitors most of the evening between short naps, they didn't see much reason to hang around.

Another hour passed and the sounds in the hospital seemed to make the time stand still, almost as if everything was on one continuous loop of white noise: the constant beeping of heart monitors, assisted breathing machines, intercom calls, and the pixie-silent sounds of the nurses scurrying up and down the hallways to tend to the patients and families.

By eleven o'clock that night, Mike and Catherine, Sarah and Gracie were the only people left in Fred's room. The girls had curled up in one of the large chairs and were fast asleep. Both Mike and Catherine just couldn't leave; Freddy was *too* sick. The nurses moved in and out, quietly checking the numbers, and the IV connections, and leaving water for Catherine to apply to Fred's lips. She had been sitting by Fred's bedside for over an hour, holding his hand and, when he was awake, talking softly to him.

Mike was just a couple of steps away in another large

chair. Mike had noticed that Fred's breathing had become more labored. He reached over and tapped on Catherine's shoulder, and when she looked at him, he whispered "Breathing" to her. She nodded; she had also noticed the change.

Sarah woke up and walked over to be held by Catherine, next to Fred. Her heart was breaking, and it showed with her eyes full of tears as turned around to look at her dad and then at Catherine. She didn't want to lose her close buddy, who seemed to understand her every problem, would always listen to her, and always had great problem-solving ideas. He had become her real grandpa. Since Catherine treated him like he was her dad, it just seemed natural.

Sarah saw them first: An older man and a small woman walked through the open door from the hallway. She looked up at her dad and nudged his arm. The man silently moved his cane to steady himself, focusing straight ahead, searching for a certain old friend. The lady patiently held on to his arm and helped him along, smiling at Mike, Catherine, and the girls as they came in.

Mike whispered, "It's Julian." He was an old man.

Before he got to Fred's bedside, Julian stopped to greet Catherine, Mike, and the girls. Catherine patted Julian on the back, tears streaming from her face.

"Julian, I can't believe you're here. We know it must have been a hard trip for you," she said softly.

"It was fine—I travel pretty well, most of the time. I just have to get up and move every so often, or I'll stiffen up like an old man." Then Julian turned slowly to his wife. "Catherine, this is my wife, Maria."

"Hello, Maria," Catherine whispered. She helped Julian sit in the chair next to Fred's bed, then leaned over to speak to Fred. "Freddy, someone very special is here to see you."

Fred opened his eyes and turned his head slightly.

Julian got up to speak into Fred's ear. "Hello, my old brother, how come you're all laid up like this? Ain't you got work to do?"

Freddy managed a slight grin. In a weak raspy voice, he tried to answer. "Good to see you too, help me get up, so I can go work on . . ." Fred's voice gave out; he couldn't finish speaking.

"Well, at least have your sense of humor left."

Fred nodded.

"Fred, I brought my wife, Maria."

Maria stood up and reached over to take Fred's hand. "Hello, sweetheart. I'm sorry it's taken so many years to see you again. Do you remember when we met at the café in Joplin?"

Fred nodded slightly and looked back up at the ceiling. Maria sat down. Julian came back over and took Fred's hand. After a few seconds, Fred opened his eyes and turned to Julian. "Did you find . . . your mom?" he asked, his voice almost a whisper.

"Yes, yes, I did, Fred, thank you," Julian said. "After you left, I decided to ask Maria if she wanted to go with me, to find my mother. I convinced her to come. We went up to Michigan and found Mom." Julian paused. "Of course, Mack had left her a couple of months after they got there, so she was pretty happy to see us. We eventually moved back down to Missouri. Mom passed away a few years later, but at least we had her at home with us."

Fred made a face, knowing that it must have been hard for Julian to lose his mom a second time. As hard as it was to speak with his labored breathing, Fred wanted to talk.

"Julian, you had a good life?"

"Yes, Fred. Maria and I have three beautiful children and lots of grandkids, so I'd have to say, I've had a great life." Julian gently patted Fred's hand. Maria stood next to Julian, her arm around his shoulders. She leaned over and asked Julian if he wanted some water. He waved no.

Fred wanted to talk. He cleared his throat. "I'm glad for you and Maria." Fred coughed again; his throat and lips were dry. Catherine leaned from the other side and wetted Fred's lips with a small moistened sponge. Fred kept moving his lips and tried to point with the other hand—he seemed anxious to tell Julian something. When he coughed, Mike noticed that Fred's breathing became more labored. He stared at Catherine and held his hand to the side of his face as if he were making a phone call.

Mike whispered the words, "Fred's daughters." She nodded in agreement.

Mike quietly stepped out of the room to make two phone calls—one to Linda and one to Melissa. After a few minutes, he reported back to Catherine that Fred's daughters had fed the kids and left them at Fred's home with their fathers; they were both on their way back to the hospital.

Fred's eyes locked on Julian again. "Julian, I have to confess." Fred slowly motioned to Julian to move closer.

"What? Why, you old God-fearing coot, what on

God's green earth would *you* have to confess, especially to a heathen like me?"

"Margaret." Fred took another deep breath. "Margaret, Julian. Her name was Margaret Jean."

"Fred," Julian said. "Do you remember the day we stood in your bedroom and looked at your family pictures? I knew that's what your future was; I knew it was already in the plan." Julian squeezed Fred's hand.

"Then why?" Fred mumbled.

Julian thought he knew what the question would be, so he spoke for him. "Why did we go look for her at Fannie's?" Fred nodded yes. "Well, Freddy, I wanted you to meet Jean. Of course, my plan didn't work out; she wasn't there. So, I sent you home. I was sure surprised a few days after you left, I ran into her down at the grocery store, looking for a job. Remember how tough times were then? So, I told her that if she could, go to Cheyenne; she'd have a job, for sure, at Dixie's place—just mention my name. And, what do you know, buddy, she was there, wasn't she?"

Fred smiled weakly and coughed. A few monitors buzzed. The nurse walked in to check on the numbers, pushed a few buttons, and walked out without saying a word.

"But, Fred, you know the other reason I had to go there, even though I couldn't tell you at the time." Julian squeezed Fred's trembling hand. "Fred, my dear friend, when Pug and Lenny beat us up something awful?" Fred's eyes twinkled with a tear, and Julian knew he understood. "I had stolen some gold coins from Shorty's house. That's why they wanted to kill me—it's why so much of this happened. Originally, I wanted to keep the money for myself, but I couldn't do it—it belonged to Fannie—so after I sent you home, I gave it back to her. I knew I had to make my own way."

Fred's eyes turned toward Julian, he struggled to speak. "Thank you, Julian, for the best thing that's ever happened to me . . . been a hell of a trip, huh?"

"Yes, Freddy, it's been a *hell* of a trip."

"I miss her, Juli."

"Yes, I know," Julian said. He leaned in and whispered to Fred, "I'm sure she's waiting for you."

Fred gave a weak nod.

* * * *

For a long time, Fred lay still, eyes closed. Every once in a while, his lips would tremble, as if he were saying something, and Julian would pat his hand. Suddenly, Julian leaned forward to speak into Fred's ear.

"It's okay, Fred, my dear friend, you can go on home to be with Margaret, I know you want to be with her."

Fred opened his eyes slightly, just enough to see Julian one more time, then they gently closed. His breathing continued to worsen. Conversation stopped and the room became still.

After a long while of hard breathing, Fred's chest rose to take in one last, deep breath. As the air drifted out of his lungs, his spirit seemed to lift away, surely to a wonderful reunion with Margaret and their son, Dennis.

The room went silent, and tears fell.

"Oh, Freddy." Catherine wept as she rushed up to

Fred's bedside, opposite Julian and Maria. Julian buried his face into Fred's hands; Maria hugged him from behind. In the background, persistent beeping sounds fluttered and a nurse walked in to check Fred's pulse. In a few moments, she turned to everyone and announced, "He's passed on."

She reached up and turned off the monitors. The nurse walked to the back of the room, pulled the curtains around to hide the hall windows, then left the room. Only her shoes made a sound.

Chapter 31

Julian's Gift

Over the next few evenings, Mike and Catherine helped prepare dinners for Fred's family and friends coming in from out of town. In the evening, on the day of Fred's funeral, after most of the guests had gone, Julian and Maria came back over to Mike and Catherine's house to sit in the kitchen over coffee and cake. For over an hour, they talked about what had been happening to everyone: Freddy's two surviving kids, the grandkids, and the love of his life, Margaret.

Julian and Maria told stories about their children and grandchildren back in Missouri. Julian explained that after he and Maria moved back to the Joplin area with his mom, Millie, he got into the oil business and eventually became the manager of a large oil firm.

Then Julian paused, facing Mike and Catherine, and said something interesting.

"You know, I did explain to Fred what happened when I went through the door, but he told me he didn't ever want to do that; he was content right where he was. So, he never went through the closet door, as far as I know, did he?"

"I don't think he did—not that I know, anyway," Mike said. Catherine agreed.

"But, Catherine, didn't he take care of the house after you left?" asked Julian.

"Yes," Catherine answered. "You know, on our walks, Freddy told me lots of stories about when he and Margaret got married in 1933, and you know how bad things were then, right? So, it turned out to be quite a blessing for them to have this house to live in." Catherine sighed. "Unfortunately, his mom and dad hit hard times that same year, you know, like everyone else, so they moved into the house with Fred and Margaret, for a while. Eventually, they moved out to find work in Denver. Over the next several years, Fred's family outgrew the house, so he and Margaret purchased the larger home across the street so they could have room to raise the kids."

"He was a damn good man!" Julian grumbled, tapping his thick forefinger on the table.

"No doubt about that, Julian," Mike replied, "and so is his best friend, Julian."

"Thanks, Mike. It was my honor to know him." Julian stared at the tabletop, deep in thought. "I didn't come close to the man he was, though. We visited a couple of times over the phone, but I wish we could have been around here more." Julian looked up at Mike and Catherine. "We both stayed in that time, you know, so we could live our lives, somewhere we felt comfortable. Fred and I talked about it some, but couldn't imagine jumping ahead, like you did, Catherine. I guess we didn't dare to try it."

Catherine looked at Julian with surprise. "Julian, after what you two went through? I would say you both had courage. You have to remember that I had something to stay here for. You and Freddy didn't know what would happen on this side of the future, or have a reason, like I did." She glanced at Mike and put her hand on his. "I had my lover-boy here."

"You did good, Catherine. I am pleased with my life, too. I couldn't have gotten by without this little lady by my side," he said, smiling over at Maria.

"Thank you, sweetie," Maria reached over and rubbed the top of Julian's hands. Julian looked back to Mike and Catherine.

"Mike, I was glad that you and Catherine got to know Fannie. Eventually, Maria and I went back to Joplin. I got into the oil business and I did pretty well for a two-bit street kid. It didn't hurt that I had a little idea what our country's future was going to be like." Julian winked at Mike. Mike smiled. "We kept in touch with Fannie till the day she died. And, Catherine, I want you to know, she did take your advice," Julian said, pointing a crooked finger at her.

"What advice was that, Julian?"

"You told her that she was such a good cook, she ought to open a restaurant in that big old house, and so she did." Julian chuckled. And, she did pretty darn good, I might add."

"Oh, good grief!" Catherine said.

"She also did something for me that took me totally by surprise. After she passed away, we got a call from a lawyer guy up in St. Louis. It turned out Fannie signed the deed of that house over to me. You might remember, it was such a large house, almost a mansion, certainly compared to the house Maria and I lived in at the time. It was also in a really beautiful part of town, so we moved in, didn't we honey?"

"Yes, we sure did, darlin'," said Maria, shaking her head. "And I'm here to tell you, it took some major cleaning and renovation from being a restaurant. Julian learned how to do some carpentry work, to bring that big old house into livable condition for the kids. But once we had it done, it was a beautiful home. God bless Fannie," Maria said. "She continues to be a blessing to all of us. And I know Julian won't mention it, but a few years ago, he put a foundation together called Daniels-Blakely, to honor his mom and Fannie's names, to give scholarships to impoverished young women so they could go to college and make a decent living for themselves. Isn't that right, honey?" Julian blushed and waved off any admiration.

"Julian, that is so nice!" Catherine said. She reached over and hugged Julian. Mike, standing against the kitchen counter, came up behind Julian and patted him on the back.

"I'm glad we had the good fortune in our life to be able to do something like that," Julian said. "What a time we've had, huh? I think I've been able to experience the best of both times."

"You sure did. It's been an incredible journey for all of us," Mike said.

Maria nudged Julian and gave him a look.

"Oh, yeah, I almost forgot," Julian said. "My wife always tells me that there aren't that many shopping days till Christmas, so I'd better get something good done, pretty quick." Julian looked over to Mike and Catherine. "Michael, my dear friend, and Catherine, my sweetheart teacher who forgave me for the terrible wrong I did to her—for you both—Maria and I have a gift. So much has been given to us; we wanted to give back to you."

"Julian, you don't have to do anything for us, we're fine," Mike said.

"No, no, no," Julian continued. "Michael, when I started doing well in the oil business back in the late thirties, I started buying land—and of course, stock in my oil company. Today it's worth more money than I can count. Anyway, here is our little gift to you."

Maria handed Julian a large manila envelope and he dumped the papers out on the table.

"These are property deeds. There are several properties here in town and quite a few in Denver. The deed to your house is in here, too, Mike." Catherine threw up her hands in disbelief. "I have directed my legal counsel to make the necessary ownership name changes and even took care of the taxes, so Mike and Catherine, with *this*, we say thank you and God bless you."

Catherine nodded with a look of amazement. Mike smiled in disbelief and said, "Julian, I am completely speechless . . . this is the most generous thing anyone has ever done for us."

Julian stiffly reached over and slipped one of his calloused fingers through the coffee cup handle, leaned back in his chair, and grinned at Mike and Catherine. Julian's heart was pleased, too. He turned and smiled at Maria.

* * * *

In the morning, after Fred's funeral service, Julian and Maria Daniels were preparing to leave; Mike had asked his young friend, John, from the power company, if he wouldn't mind taking Julian and Maria down to the airport in Denver. John said he would be over in front of Mike's house within the hour.

Catherine and Mike both knew this might well be the last time they would ever speak to Julian and Maria. Sarah and Gracie had fun at the breakfast table remembering Julian as a young man and teasing him about being an awkward teenager in a strange new world.

When Julian got up from the table, he asked Sarah and Gracie to show him the palms of their hands. In each of the girl's hands, he placed a large gold coin—two of the coins that Fannie had given him, so many years ago. Both girls were amazed and excited with their shiny gold coins.

Chapter 32

Lost and Found

Late in September, several weeks after Fred's funeral, Catherine decided that she needed to get back to her house for a while. She'd been missing her mom and she wanted to spend some girl time together, tie up some loose ends, and maybe take her mom down to the Atlas Theater to watch movies for ten cents.

Catherine knew Mike wouldn't be thrilled with the idea, but she knew he would eventually be okay. She told him maybe a week, maybe more—she didn't want to be committed to a set time.

For Mike, his acceptance of Catherine's request was the only reasonable thing to do, so in place of romance, he got busy: cleaning the garage out, manicuring the lawn, downloading all the music off a website he'd been promising himself he would do, and even spending time tinkering with his pride and joy, the 1929 Chrysler.

One evening, Sarah walked into the kitchen where Mike was cleaning a spill in the refrigerator. "Hey, Dad."

"Hi sweetie, what are you doing?"

"Not much, except that when I got home from school, there were a couple of small boxes in my room, did you bring them up there?"

"What? Boxes? Let me go look." Sure enough, in

Sarah's room, stacked up by her closet were two cardboard boxes. "Well, maybe that's a sign Catherine's on her way back. Was there a note anywhere?"

"Nope, just the boxes. Smell them—they kind of stink, don't they?" Sarah asked. Mike leaned in closer, smelled, and was puzzled.

"Yeah, they sure do, I'm not sure what that smell is, though, maybe something burnt?"

Gracie walked into the room. "Are you going to open them up?" she asked.

"No, let's leave well enough alone," Mike said. "If she wanted us to open them, she would have left us a note. Besides, what if it's a gift for me?" He grinned. "I don't want to spoil the surprise."

Mike went back downstairs and knelt in front of the refrigerator to continue cleaning. In half an hour, he heard the girls coming down the stairs. To his surprise, they didn't run in to see what he was doing, but when he turned around, he looked up to see Anna, Catherine's mom.

"Now, that's what I call a good man, Catherine!" said Anna, standing behind her with Sarah and Gracie's arms wrapped around her waist.

"Well, hello Anna! Catherine, sweetheart, it sure is good to see you!" Mike got up off his knees and gave Catherine and Anna a hug.

"I'll bet you thought I wasn't coming back?" Catherine said.

"Almost, I was just about ready to come looking for you!" he lied. *Almost about ten million times*, he thought.

"We tried to come through over a week ago, but when we opened the small door, there was just plumbing, no open space. I was so upset, but I tried again the next day, and it was back."

Mike turned to Catherine, worried. "I guess that's a sign. It might close up and never come back. We certainly won't be able to trust it. Thank God you made it through this time." Mike, he turned to Anna. "Anna, can you stay with us for a while, this time?"

"How about longer?" Catherine asked.

"Sure, it's okay with me. What made you change your mind? I thought you were dead-set against coming this way."

"The house fire was the final straw for me," Anna said.

"What? House fire?" Mike's face showed his surprise.

"We woke up in the middle of the night to see the neighbor's house completely engulfed in flames. It was the scariest thing I'd ever seen. There was no way to put it out—no fire trucks, as you have here today, or medical services. It was so sad to see it burn completely down," Anna said.

"But, if it was the neighbor's house, how does that explain the smell from those boxes upstairs?" Mike asked.

"The winds blew smoke and ashes right toward Mom's house," Catherine replied.

"And, we were scared that it would catch my house on fire, too!" Anna added. She shook her head. "That poor family."

"Over the next few days, the more we talked about it, Mom decided that she would go ahead and come here with us and let that family use her home for as long as they needed it. Besides, Mike, I missed Sarah and Gracie."

"Ah! I was hoping you missed me." Mike laughed.

"Well, you picked a good time to come back. The refrigerator's all cleaned out and it's time to go shopping."

"Come on, ladies, let's go upstairs and see what's in those boxes," Anna said to the girls.

"I hope you know the real reason I came back, don't you?" Catherine stepped closer and looked up into Mike's eyes.

"I would like to think I know, but you might want to remind me, just so I have it embedded in my heart," Mike said coyly.

"If you only knew how deep, Michael Roberts, I just want to be with you, I don't care what time zone we're in."

"Sweetheart, that's the kind of message that will stay in my heart for all time. I guess there's only one more thing that would make my life complete. Catherine, sweetheart, would you be my wife?" Mike hoped he had completely surprised Catherine.

"Oh, Michael! Yes, sweetheart, I will! Oh, my God! I can't believe it! Can we go tell Mom and the girls?"

It only took a few minutes for the house to fill with excitement.

* * * *

Several weeks later, Catherine and Mike had gone into the kitchen to finish putting away the dishes and Anna and the girls were sitting in the living room getting ready to play a game when they heard a knock on the door.

"I'll get it!" Sarah yelled. "Dad, it's one of your guys from the power company!"

Mike came out from the kitchen to see John.

"Hey, Mike, I hope I'm on time?" he asked.

"You're fine, John, come on in. Glad you could make it tonight." He ushered John inside.

"Thanks, Mike."

"John, you know my girls, but I'd like to introduce you to Catherine's mother, Anna Tanner."

John took Anna's hand and held on to it, hesitating for a few seconds. Catherine walked in from the kitchen, wiping her hands on a dish towel.

"And, John, this beautiful lady is Catherine Tanner," Mike said.

John turned his attention to Catherine. "Catherine?" John asked. He quickly turned back to look at Anna, then back to Catherine.

"What's wrong, John?" Mike asked. John began to visibly tremble.

"Mike?" John asked. "This is pretty weird." Before Mike could answer, Catherine said something. She was staring at John as intensely as he looked at her.

"You look familiar, John," Catherine said, as she continued to rub her hands on her dishtowel. Mike watched intensely from the side, a satisfied grin on his face. The expressions he saw were exactly as he hoped.

"I'm . . . I'm sorry, it's just that . . . I think I had a sister named Cathy once, but it would be impossible . . . I must be off in dreamland." John scratched his head, his eyes darting between the floor and Catherine's eyes. Mike, just a few steps away from John, could tell that he was studying Anna's every feature, and, in an instant, Mike knew he was right.

"That's okay, John," Catherine said, folding her dishtowel. "I once had a brother named *Jimmy*," she said, making clear her brother's name. She glanced over at Mike to see if he knew what was going on. Mike smiled back and nodded to her.

"Tanner, huh?" John asked and gave Catherine an incredulous look. Then he turned to Anna and said, "So, you're Mrs. Tanner?"

"Yes," Anna said.

"John," Catherine began, "may I ask, how old are you?"

"Just turned twenty-four."

Mike watched as tears welled up in Catherine's eyes. Mike knew she had figured it out. Catherine's eyes jumped wide open.

"I once had a brother named James, but he disappeared . . ." Catherine said. She took a step, paused, and then walked toward John. Catherine dropped her dishtowel and threw herself into John's arms.

Mike could tell Anna was confused. How could she believe that one day she would ever see her son again? Impossible. What amount of grief had she suffered?

"Oh, my God, Jimmy!" Catherine cried. "It *is* you!" Catherine turned to Anna, "Mother, we have Jimmy back!"

Anna seemed stunned—she didn't move. Mike came up behind Anna. She started shaking as he put his arms around her shoulders, to help her move toward Jimmy. John turned to Anna, smiling, still holding on to Catherine and together they opened their arms to embrace Anna.

"You have your daddy's eyes," Anna said to Jimmy.

"I'm sorry . . . Mom. I didn't mean to do this, I tried

to get back home," John sobbed.

"It's all right, honey," Anna said, running her hands down her son's face. "We have you back with us now. Thank God for this miracle."

"What about Dad?"

Mike wondered if John would be curious about his father—after all, here was Anna, in the prime of her life. Asking for their father would be an obvious question to ask.

"Son, he was killed in a train accident in 1925. I'm sorry, honey, I wish he could be here with us now. He never fully recovered from losing you, sweetheart, but I'm sure he's always in your heart." Then Anna couldn't hold back her tears.

John turned to Mike. "Mike, Catherine, maybe you guys can help me with this. I'm really confused. How is this all possible? How did Catherine and my mom get here? It's been so many years."

"The same way you did, John," Mike answered. "Back in 1911, you must have gone through that closet door— and when you opened the door and came back out, it was the year 1983."

"Jimmy," said Catherine, "the first time, when I came through with Michael and Sarah, I went from 1928 to the year 2000, so now I am in this future time with you, too."

"Because of the little space in the closet?" John asked, furrowing his brows.

"Yes, and recently Mom decided she wanted to come to this time, too, so I brought her here." Catherine motioned to Mike. "Mike, come here, sweetheart. How did you know? When I looked over at you, you had that look in your eyes. How did you know?"

"I certainly didn't know at first," Mike began. "After we talked at dinner a couple of months ago, about your brother that went missing, I started thinking about different people around town. It just made sense that maybe your brother might still be in the area. The more I thought about it, boom! It hit me—here was this guy, right under our noses."

"Catherine," John said, "I had always suspected that this was the house I used to live in, but I wasn't sure. It was so long ago and the house had been remodeled. When Mike and the girls moved in, I wanted to help, mostly just so I could see the inside."

"I remembered that," replied Mike. "When we were moving in, John stayed behind a lot, looking in the different rooms, like he was trying to remember. Then, I also remembered that John had told me one time that he had been adopted. He was also the right age, so I eventually did the math, put two and two together."

"Oh, it's such a wonderful thing, I can't believe it!" Anna said, holding tight to John. "But John," Anna asked, "what happened to you, sweetheart? Where did you go?"

"I guess I was playing in the closet—I don't remember a whole lot, but probably just like Sarah and Gracie were doing, opened that little door. It was a simple thing—go in and come out, a little boy's curiosity, you know. When I came out, it didn't seem like things were different to me, at the time. I just went outside and started walking. I'm pretty sure I thought I was going to go to someone's house to visit, I don't remember. After a while, it all just seemed like a dream to me."

"Did someone find you or ask you what you were doing?" asked Catherine.

"Yeah, I probably got hungry, scared. My adoptive mom told me that a woman saw me crying and wandering around the neighborhood and asked me where my home was; she called the police and they asked where I lived. Of course, I didn't know; eventually, they took me somewhere. I told them I had a family, but they couldn't find anyone, so after a while, I was adopted out. I was raised just about a mile north of here, with the Kelley family," John explained.

"Do you remember if you had any dreams? Maybe about the house, or about me and Mom and Dad?" Catherine asked.

"I think I had reoccurring dreams about life from a different time. That's why when I got the chance to help Mike and the girls move in, I jumped at it." He looked around. "It just . . . seemed to me like this was the house. When I came inside the first time, I couldn't even describe the feelings I had, I got a chill all over my body. You know, like I'd been here before, I knew this place."

Catherine took John in her arms again and put her head against his chest. "Jimmy . . ." Catherine stopped herself. "I'm sorry, John. Please don't ever get too far away from me or Mom again. You'll never know how awful it was for us." A sob escaped her. "I felt responsible for what happened. I was your older sister and I was supposed to keep an eye on you, and then you were gone."

"I'm sorry, Catherine. I didn't know what I was doing, or what was happening to me. I wish I could remember more about the past." John glanced down at Catherine's tear-soaked eyes. "I do remember, though, I had a sister that I truly adored and looked up to . . . and the home, a home that seemed so cozy and warm. For me, too, it was all gone."

"This is so great!" Mike whispered to Catherine. "This alone was worth all we had to go through with the closet."

"Yes, it sure was," answered Catherine.

"I love you," Mike whispered to Catherine. She smiled.

"I love you too, sweetheart," Catherine whispered back.

The rest of the evening was spent talking about John's life with the Kelley family, Catherine's experience as a teacher, and Anna and Jim's ministry work in India. At the end of the night, no one wanted John to leave, but he promised to be over in the morning for a long-overdue breakfast his mother wanted to prepare for him.

After promises of frequent visits, phone numbers exchanged, and tears, their warm loving hands slowly let go. In a few minutes, John was driving off into the darkness, down one of the tree-lined avenues of Cheyenne. Mike held his arms close around Catherine to protect her from the coolness of the late evening. Anna reclaimed her comfy spot as grandmother between two happy little girls on the porch swing, a blanket draped warmly over them.

Catherine held a tissue to her eyes; the complex emotions of happy and sad made her heartache. Catherine sighed. Mike knew this was just the start. He kissed her on the neck.

About the Author

T.R. lives with his wife Janie in Caldwell, Idaho. After retiring from a business career, he was able to spend more time writing. He is also a musician (drums/keyboards), and songwriter, and plays with a local band. T.R. and Janie are grandparents to numerous grandkids, but if there's any spare time, he loves to tinker on woodworking projects and fix unbroken things.

T.R. has always dabbled with writing poems, short stories, and song lyrics, so when his children were young, he wrote an entertaining short story, about a small door in their closet. They loved the story, but kept asking, "Then what happened?" *The Hiding Door*, his first novel, is the result.

To learn more about this author,
please visit:

https://www.facebook.com/TRSchaap2020